P9-DEG-486

Books by Peter Abrahams

End of Story
Oblivion
Their Wildest Dreams
The Tutor
Last of the Dixie Heroes
Crying Wolf
A Perfect Crime
The Fan
Lights Out
Revolution #9
Pressure Drop
Hard Rain
Red Message
Tongues of Fire
The Fury of Rachel Monette

Coming Soon in Hardcover

Nerve Damage

And for Young Readers

Down the Rabbit Hole
Behind the Curtain

Peter
ABRAHAMS

END OF STORY

HARPER

An Imprint of HarperCollins*Publishers*

This is a work of fiction. Names, characters, places, and incidents are products of the author's imagination or are used fictitiously and are not to be construed as real. Any resemblance to actual events, locales, organizations, or persons, living or dead, is entirely coincidental.

HARPER

An Imprint of HarperCollins*Publishers*
10 East 53rd Street
New York, New York 10022-5299

Copyright © 2006 by Pas de Deux
Excerpt from *Nerve Damage* copyright © 2007 by Pas de Deux
ISBN: 978-0-06-113034-2
ISBN-10: 0-06-113034-6

First Harper paperback printing: February 2007
First William Morrow hardcover printing: April 2006

HarperCollins® and Harper® are trademarks of HarperCollins Publishers.

Printed in the United States of America

Visit Harper paperbacks on the World Wide Web at
www.harpercollins.com

10 9 8 7 6 5 4 3 2

To my nieces and nephews—
Lauren, Shane, Jake, Rachel, and Maddy

Curses? The dark? Struggling? Where's the source
Of these yarns now (except in nightmares, of course)?

—PHILIP LARKIN, "Whatever Happened"

Acknowledgments

Many thanks to Captain William McManamin of the Falmouth, Massachusetts, police and to James Cummings, Sheriff of Barnstable County.

One

"How is going the writing?" said Dragan Karodojic.

Closing time at Verlaine's Bar and Grille on Schermerhorn Street, no one left inside except Dragan, the dishwasher, mopping the floor, and Ivy Seidel, the bartender, cashing out.

"Not bad," Ivy said. The question—how her writing was going—was the biggest one in her life, with her all the time, and the true answer was she had no idea. What she had was a creative writing MFA from Brown, three summers spent at an upstate fiction workshop, the last on full scholarship, two abandoned novels, sixty-one completed short stories, ranging in length from one page to fifty-eight, and a drawerful of rejection letters.

"I myself have idea for novel," Dragan said.

"You never mentioned that," Ivy said, taking her tip money from under the cash tray in the register and stuffing it in her pocket.

"You are never asking," said Dragan, and the next thing

she knew he'd put down the mop and was sitting across the bar. Ivy liked Dragan. Hard not to—six months in the country, big smile full of crooked East European teeth, wide-eyed enthusiasm for things most New Yorkers didn't even notice—but it was after two and she wanted to go home.

"What is this thing," Dragan said, "for the cell-phone relays?" He made an expanding gesture with his hands, like a circle growing.

"Tower?" said Ivy.

"Tower, yes," said Dragan. "Cell tower." And he launched into a long and incomprehensible tale about a cell tower that picks up signals from a shadow world where the souls of all the extinct Neanderthals are plotting revenge.

"So," said Dragan, head tilted up at a puppy-dog angle, "I want truth: What is your verdict?"

Ivy walked home. A warm September night, as warm as summer, but somehow different. How, exactly? It was important to nail these things down, find the right words. But as Ivy reached her building and climbed the stairs to the front door, the right words still hadn't come.

She unlocked her mailbox, number five, found a single letter. *The New Yorker.* She tore open the envelope. Rejection. A form rejection, of which she'd already collected three from *The New Yorker*—they used thick paper, might have been sending out swanky invitations, if you were judging just by feel—but this time someone with an illegible signature had added a note at the bottom. Ivy angled it toward the streetlight.

The Utah part is really nice.

The Utah part? What Utah part? Hadn't she sent them

"Live Entertainment," an eight-page story that took place entirely at a truck stop in New Jersey? But then Ivy remembered a brief reference to a snowboarding accident in Alta. How brief? Three lines, if that.

Ivy unlocked the front door, walked up to her fifth-floor studio apartment. The staircase, the whole building, in fact, leaned slightly to the right, plus nothing worked properly and repairs never got done, but that didn't keep the rents low. Ivy's room, a converted attic, 485 lopsided square feet, cost $1,100 a month. She went in, slid the dead bolt closed, sat at the table, a café table she'd gotten for free from a failed Smith Street restaurant. Ivy switched on her laptop, found the Utah passage in "Live Entertainment."

> He fell but the direction must have been up because he landed in the top of a tree. The only sound was the kid he'd run over, crying up the trail. Far away the Great Salt Lake was somehow shining and brown at the same time.

That was really nice? Somehow much nicer than the rest of the story? Ivy read the whole thing over several times without seeing how. She decided to take *The New Yorker*'s word for it. She was capable of really nice and she interpreted really nice to mean publishable in *The New Yorker* and all that would come after.

Almost three in the morning, but Ivy no longer felt tired. She made herself tea, stood on the table, pulled down the trapdoor with the folding staircase and climbed up on the roof. The only good feature of apartment five, but so good she'd signed the lease even though it was more than she could afford.

Ivy stood on her roof, looking west. Over the rooftops,

across the river: Manhattan. She had no words for this view. Maybe the movies would always do that kind of thing better. But what the movies didn't capture, at least none of the movies Ivy knew, was the vulnerability. She saw it now, very clearly—the whole skyline could be gone, just like that, as everybody now understood but as no camera could ever show. A tragic magnificence, even futile, like . . . Ozymandias. Wait a minute. Shelley had been this way already. So maybe she was wrong, maybe a really good writer could still—

At that moment, with the lit-up Manhattan skyline before her, doubly in view, actually, the second image blurred on the water, and a soft September night breeze on her skin, soft and warm, but there was something impermanent about that warmth, even vulnerable, yes, that was it, the answer to the September night and skyline questions turning out to be one and the same—at that moment, Ivy got an idea for a brand-new story.

A story about an immigrant, a legal alien in New York, in Sting's words, but this one finds himself turning into a Neanderthal man. Was she stealing from Dragan? No. More like stealing Dragan, if anything. But this was how art worked. There was something brutal about it, a brutality, she suddenly realized, often evident in the faces of the greatest artists, like Picasso, Brando, Hemingway. She remembered the parting words of Professor Smallian at Brown, teacher of the advanced class and published author of three novels, one of which had been a *New York Times* notable book: *You don't have to be a good person to be a good writer—history shows it's better if you're not—but you have to understand your badness.*

Ivy went back down through the trapdoor, sat at the table, typed the first sentence that came to her mind. *Vladek felt strong.* She'd never written a story like this before, a story with magic in it. Maybe she should have, because this one—"Caveman"—took off and started zooming along under its own power. At times she could hardly keep up—like Lucille Ball when the chocolate conveyor belt got going too fast—hauling the words around, shoving them in place.

Ivy came to the last sentence, a sentence she'd known was in the wings many paragraphs ago—*The surgeon made some joke Vladek didn't understand*—and looked up to see it was morning, silvery light streaming in through her two little windows. She felt stirred up and wiped out at the same time; could smell herself. She read the story over, fixed a few things, started getting excited. This was pretty good.

Wasn't it?

That was the tricky part: you never knew. You needed someone else's opinion. Find a reader who is smart and honest, Professor Smallian had said, preferably a writer higher up the chain—*although a writer both smart and honest is unlikely to be found in such lofty precincts.* Ivy was lucky. She had Joel Cutler. He wasn't any higher up the chain, but he was smart and honest.

Ivy and Joel went all the way back to freshman year at Williams. They'd met on the Lady Ephs freshman soccer team, Ivy the goalie, Joel the manager, later wrote a poetry cycle together that earned them a trip to Oxford, and ended up co-editing the lit mag. They'd been reading their work to each other for years, now lived only a few blocks apart, were thinking of writing a screenplay together. Ivy printed a copy of "Caveman" and went out.

Joel lived in a big apartment in a beautiful prewar building right on the promenade, overlooking the river. Joel's father owned the building, owned lots of buildings in the Heights, Park Slope, Carroll Gardens. Andy, who'd been living with Joel for the past year, came out the front door carrying an old television.

"Hi, Ivy," he said. "Want a TV?"

He set it on the sidewalk, beside a lot of other stuff—a sagging armchair, two floor lamps, framed Mardi Gras posters.

"Redecorating?" Ivy said.

Andy glanced at her. "Not really," he said. He'd changed his hair, now had highlights. So did she, but his were better, more subtle. If she'd liked him more, she would have asked where he got them done.

"Joel home?" she said.

Andy wrote in the dust on the TV screen: FREE. "Yeah," he said.

Joel was in his living room, packing neatly folded shirts in a suitcase. He paused as Ivy came in, a creamy spread-collar shirt in hand. "Ivy," he said. "I was just about to call you."

Ivy glanced around, saw bare shelves, boxes of books and CDs, and through the kitchen doorway the fridge, open and empty.

"What's happening?" Ivy said. It almost looked like evictions she'd seen, but that didn't make sense.

"That's what I was going to call you about," Joel said. His face was pink, as though he was excited about something, or embarrassed. "It's all happening so fast."

"What is?"

Joel placed the creamy shirt carefully in the suitcase. "Cliché of clichés," he said, "but it really is like a dream."

Ivy waited.

"I—we're going to L.A.," Joel said. Then he laughed, a brief high-pitched laugh, quickly suppressed. A cuff link dropped off the edge of an end table. "L.A.," Joel said. "Los Angeles." He gave it an exaggerated Spanish pronunciation.

"For a vacation?" Ivy said. That didn't make sense either—he and Andy had just spent the last two weeks of August in a time-share on Long Island. And Joel hated L.A., had even written a story about its superficiality, one of his worst.

"The truth of the matter," said Joel, then raised his hands helplessly. "Maybe I should have told you before. No, delete that—I should have, period, full stop."

"Told me what?" Ivy said.

"But it was all so speculative."

"What was?"

"I mean by definition." Joel was pinker now, and it was excitement, beyond doubt.

Ivy waited.

He straightened up, met her gaze, at least for a moment. "I wrote a screenplay," he said.

Ivy didn't get it. "The one we were talking about?" she said. "The Moroccan story?"

"No, no, no, of course not," Joel said. "I'd never do a thing like that. That was ours—yours mostly, if the truth be known. This is completely different. Takes place at a fat farm, actually, in Scottsdale."

"When did you—"

"While we were away. It took four days, Ivy. And I was half-drunk most of the time. But the thing is—it sold!"

"You mean . . ."

"Adam Sandler wants to do it."

"Adam Sandler wants to make a movie of your screenplay?"

"Damon Wayans signed this morning. And it looks like Joel Schumacher's going to direct."

"About a fat farm in New Mexico?"

"Arizona. Scottsdale's in Arizona."

There was a pause. Joel picked up the creamy shirt and refolded it. A phone started ringing.

"How did all this . . .?" Ivy said.

Joel shook his head. "Andy met a guy from CAA on the beach. Actually didn't meet him at first, just kind of overheard him telling someone that Adam was looking for something new. I got the idea that night."

Adam already? "You've met him?"

"The guy from CAA? Of course. He's the one who read the—"

"I meant Adam Sandler."

"On the phone. But we're having lunch tomorrow." He glanced at his watch. A quick glance, easily missed, but that was when Ivy sensed a shift in their relationship. She didn't understand it, just knew it was fundamental.

"In L.A.?" she said.

He nodded. His mouth opened as though to say something—and Ivy knew what it was, the name of the restaurant; but he stopped himself. He put the shirt back in the suitcase and said, "I—uh—I'm not sure how you feel about this."

"I'm really happy for you."

"Yeah?"

"Yeah." Happy at least for the Joel she'd known for so long, although that Joel was interested in writing some huge brawling novel of America that the world would realize it had been waiting for and had never once even mentioned Adam Sandler.

"That's nice." He came over to give her a hug. They hugged. His skin felt hot. "What's that?" he said, nodding at the pages in her hand.

"Nothing," Ivy said.

Andy came in. "No one hears the phone?" he said, picking it up. "For you." He handed it to Joel.

"Hello?" said Joel. "Professor? . . . Rick? Sure, if you want, Rick it is . . . Thanks. DreamWorks. Thanks a lot. Yeah. That would be great." He hung up. "That was Professor Smallian."

"You've been in touch with him?" Ivy said.

"Not for three years," said Joel. "He read about it in the *Hollywood Reporter*."

Ivy tried to imagine Professor Smallian reading the *Hollywood Reporter* and failed completely. Things were happening fast, as Joel said. She actually wanted to sit down, but except for that one end table, the furniture was gone.

"Ten to one he tries to get you to hook him up with Justin," Andy said.

"Who's Justin?" said Ivy.

"CAA," Joel said.

He walked her down to the street.

"I was thinking of asking you something," he said.

"What?"

"I don't want you to take it the wrong way."

"What?"

"The Dannemora thing," he said. Joel taught a state-sponsored inmate writing course at a prison upstate. "I won't be able to do it anymore. I was going to just call and cancel, unless . . ."

"Unless what?"

"Unless you'd like to take it over."

Ivy gazed at Joel's face. It was a beautiful day, as beautiful as September gets in New York, the sky unclouded, the air somehow full of promise. For a moment, she thought she could see what he would look like a long way down the road.

"The drive up's a drag," he said, "but the gig's not completely uninteresting. And it pays a hundred bucks a shot. Plus gas."

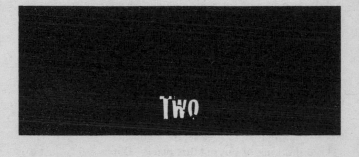

TWO

Cool," said Bruce Verlaine, owner of Verlaine's Bar and Grille.

"I haven't made up my mind," Ivy said, shaking up a Grey Goose martini for Danny Weinberg, an investment banker about her own age who came in a couple times a week after work.

"About what?" Danny said.

"Ivy got an offer to teach inmates upstate," said Bruce.

"Teach writing?" said Danny. Danny had asked to read her stuff, but she was shy about that, kind of a crazy stance for someone who wanted to be a published author.

Ivy nodded, slid his drink across the bar.

"Where upstate?"

"Dannemora."

Danny's hand paused on the stem of the glass. Ivy noticed for the first time that he bit his nails. "Horrible place," he said.

"Duh," said Bruce, his gray ponytail doing that little flip it did when he got sarcastic, which was often. Bruce was bad for business, but he didn't know it and no one told him. "It's a maximum-security prison, for Christ's sake."

"I know," Danny said. "I've been there."

"Inside?" Ivy said.

"Back in his former life of crime," Bruce said. "Danny the Ripper." Two suburban women with shopping bags came in and Bruce moved toward them, his chin, though a weak one, tilted at an aggressive angle.

"I'm thinking of buying this place," Danny said, "just to get rid of him."

Ivy laughed.

"I mean it." That was the kind of thing that kept her from really liking Danny. He sipped his drink. "I was up there last year, visiting a former client, Felix Balaban."

"What did he do?"

"Stole sixty million dollars," said Danny. "In effect."

"They send people like that to Dannemora?"

"At first he was in one of those country-club places, but he screwed up."

"How?"

"I don't know the details. Felix is a very aggressive guy, used to getting his own way. That didn't go over well."

"And now?" Ivy said.

"Now what?"

"What was he like when you saw him?"

"A changed man," Danny said. He looked at her across the bar. Nothing was quite symmetrical about his face, but all the parts added up to something pleasant. "Why are you doing this?"

"I said I haven't made up my mind."

"What are the factors?"

"Factors?"

"In your decision-making process."

Did Danny have an actual process for this, a little machine in his mind that took in factors and spat out decisions on command? Ivy didn't have a machine like that, nothing close. "I'm not sure," she said.

"On the plus side, for example," said Danny, "do they pay?"

"A little, but that's—"

"If you're a bit short, I could—"

"I don't need money."

Maybe she said that more forcefully than she'd intended. Danny looked down, swirled his drink. "It's a bad place, Ivy," he said, "with nothing but creepy people, prisoners, guards, everybody. *Evil*'s not too strong a word."

"You're talking me into it," Ivy said. Decision making, Ivy style. Later—brushing her teeth before bed—came rationale after the fact: Was evil missing from her work?

A long drive, as Joel had said, but not at all a drag. It got better and better as Ivy rode north in her little rental car, and by the time she entered the Adirondacks, autumn was laid out in full glory. How to describe it, to put it in words? Simply impossible, at least for her; it was as though God had fallen under the influence of Camille Pissarro. And when she left the Northway for smaller roads heading west, it got even better than that.

ENTERING DANNEMORA. First came a farm, with cows and a man in a plaid shirt tending a big smoky fire. Then an antiques place advertising original Adirondack furniture, some of it displayed in the front yard. After that, a few trailers, modest houses in need of paint jobs, and a four-way stop. Ivy had a MapQuest printout of the town on the seat beside her, was about to consult it when she saw the prison straight ahead.

The prison was hard to miss, so far out of scale to everything else that it could have been funny in another context, like a little kid's first stab at drawing a dog, say, where the ears might grow all the way down to the ground. The blank whitewashed walls were thirty feet high, maybe more, and ran on and on, right next to the sidewalk, guard towers jutting out over the street. Ivy drove under their shadows, a long, long block. Just before the end, the wall made a ninety-degree angle, then formed a recessed three-sided area with the gate in the middle. Ivy parked on the street and walked up to it. The gate itself was a black oblong, the paint so thick she couldn't tell if it was wood or metal, and so big it might have been a prop in a movie about trolls. No windows in it, and no signs, except for one little plaque from the state historical society. DANNEMORA PRISON, 1845.

Were you supposed to knock?

Ivy looked around. Across the street stood a bar called Lulu's by the Gate. Maybe if—

"Hey!"

Ivy glanced up. A guard in a blue uniform was leaning out of the tower, a rifle or maybe a shotgun—Ivy didn't know guns—in his hands, but not pointed at her.

"I'm here to teach the writing class," Ivy called up. "Joel Cutler's old class—I'm taking over. I've got my clearance from the bureau of prisons." She started to reach in her pocket for it, remembered a scene common to many movies, froze. "Okay if I reach into my pocket?"

"Huh?" said the guard.

"To show you the clearance paper."

The guard squinted down at her. "Administration," he said, and ducked out of sight.

"Where's that?" Ivy called up.

High above, a blue arm emerged, gestured around the corner.

Ivy walked to the corner of the prison, up the next street, a long gradual hill with the wall to her right, blocking out the sun. Sweat had broken out on her upper lip by the time she reached the back wall, although it wasn't hot and she was in pretty good shape. A stone building stood next to the rear wall of the prison. ADMINISTRATION. Ivy went in, introduced herself at reception. A guard with tight cornrows under her cap took Ivy down the hall and into an office with COMMUNITY PROGRAMS on the door.

"Here's the new writing person," the guard said.

The man behind the desk looked up. A man with a salt-and-pepper mustache, three stripes on his sleeve and a Styrofoam cup of coffee, almost lost in his hairy hand. The sign on his desk read SGT. TOCCO.

"Hi," Ivy said. "I'm Ivy Seidel."

"Got your clearance?"

She handed it to him. He looked it over.

"You're a pal of what's-his-name?"

"Joel?"

"Yeah," said Sergeant Tocco. "Joel." From the way he spoke the name, Ivy could tell he didn't like Joel. "True he got a movie deal?"

"Yes."

He glanced at the guard. "We knew him when, huh, Taneesha?"

"Was this the bald one with the stutter?" said Taneesha.

"Other guy," said Sergeant Tocco.

"The . . .?"

"Yeah."

"What kind of movie deal?" Taneesha said.

Sergeant Tocco shrugged. "Ask"—he checked the clearance form—"Ivy, here."

"It's for Adam Sandler," Ivy said. "I don't know the details."

"Adam Sandler," said Sergeant Tocco. "Funny in your book, Taneesha?"

"Uh-uh," said Taneesha. "But comedy's pretty personal."

"What the hell's that supposed to mean?" said Sergeant Tocco.

Taneesha bit her lip.

Sergeant Tocco turned to Ivy. "Ever been in a prison before?" he said.

"No."

He nodded as though he'd expected that answer. "Any questions?" he said.

"Maybe it would help if I knew something about the students," Ivy said.

"What students?" said Sergeant Tocco.

"She means the inmates," said Taneesha.

"Scum of the earth," said Sergeant Tocco. "You want to see their jackets?"

"Jackets?"

"Their records," said the sergeant, "what got them in here. Course they're all innocent, frame-job victims each and every one."

"Maybe later," Ivy said. "For now, just how many, their names, where they come from."

"Want to form your own impression, huh?" said the sergeant. "Must be a writer thing, Taneesha. None of 'em ever want to see the jackets. Not until after a month or two."

"Supposing they last that long," said Taneesha.

The sergeant nodded. He opened a drawer, rummaged around, pulled out a wrinkled sheet of paper. "You got Morales, Perkins, El-Hassam and Balaban. That's four."

"What about Dinsmore from C-block?" said Taneesha.

"In the hole," said the sergeant. "And Echeveria ain't going to be doing much mental work in future, if he lives. As for where they're from—all downstate, like ninety-nine-point-nine percent of our clientele."

His phone started ringing.

"Anything else?" he said.

"What happened to Echeveria?" Ivy said.

"Taneesha'll tell you on the way down." He picked up the phone. "And one little tip. That way you have, looking people in the eye? A no-no in here."

Ivy followed Taneesha along a brightly lit corridor and down some stairs. "What happened to Echeveria?" Ivy said.

Taneesha waved the question away. "You don't wanna hear none of that."

They came to a steel door. Taneesha knocked on it. "Writing teacher," she said.

The door opened. There were two guards on the other side, video cameras, a metal detector.

"License and car keys, teach," said one of the guards.

Ivy handed them over. The second guard stamped the back of her hand.

"You get 'em back on the way out," he said, "if this lights up." He shone an infrared torch at the back of her hand. The word *visitor* appeared in dark blue on her skin. "And if not—clang." The guard laughed at his own joke. The laugh spread to the others. Ivy laughed a little, too, didn't notice right away that the first guard had his hand out.

She gave him her bag. He dumped it out on a table: spiral notebook, two Bic ballpoints, cell phone, the *Collected Poems of Philip Larkin.* The guard swept the pens and the phone on the tray with her license and keys, put everything else back in the bag.

"No pens?" said Ivy.

"Had a pen sticking in B-block—when was that?" said Taneesha.

"Labor Day," said the first guard. "In the eye. I know 'cause I was on."

"What are we supposed to write with?" Ivy said.

"Plus Fourth of July weekend and Memorial Day," said the first guard.

There was a uncomfortable silence. Then Taneesha said, "Step on through and we'll get going."

Ivy stepped through the metal detector. She tried it again without earrings, then without earrings and belt, finally without earrings, belt and shoes.

"Enjoy your flight," said the second guard.

Three

A CO named Moffitt sat outside the library door. Ivy thought she smelled booze on his breath, but of course that was impossible.

"I just go in?" she said.

Moffitt looked up at her. He had a patchy little mustache. All the male guards she'd seen so far had mustaches. What was that all about?

"They don't bite," Moffitt said.

Ivy walked through the door.

" 'Cept when they do," he added in a low voice, probably to himself; but Ivy caught it.

"Be back in an hour," Taneesha called after her.

The library was small and very bright: fluorescent lights, cement-block walls, cement floor, metal shelves half-full of dilapidated books, mostly paperbacks. In the center of the room stood a rectangular steel table, bolted to the floor. On card-table chairs around it sat four men in tan jumpsuits, one at the far end, one on the left side, two on the right, spaced about as far from each other as they could be.

"Hi," Ivy said. "I'm Ivy, the new writing teacher."

They looked at her; but not in the eye. A no-no.

Ivy sat down in the empty chair at the near end of the table.

"Maybe it would help if you all introduce yourselves," she said.

Silence.

Then the man on the left—red-brown skin, tattooed arms, slicked-back oily hair—said, "Introduce? I know these guys already, way too much."

One of the men on the right—big, black, gap-toothed—laughed. The man next to him—slight, white, balding—glanced quickly around, then snickered. How could things go wrong so fast?

Then the man at the end, black, thin-faced, close-trimmed gray goatee, sitting up very straight, gaze directed at Ivy's forehead, said, "El-Hassam."

"Nice to meet you," Ivy said. "What's your first name?"

El-Hassam shook his head, a controlled, deliberate movement; there was even something regal about it. "No need for first names here," he said.

The tattooed man on the left leaned forward. His forearms were huge, bulging with cords of muscle. "You now entering a last-name zone."

"Seidel," said Ivy. "And yours?"

He blinked. "Morales," he said.

"Perkins," said the big man. He had a deep, rumbly voice.

"Balaban," said the little white guy. His voice was scratchy.

"But you can call him Felix," Morales said.

Balaban looked down, almost hanging his head.

"The exception," El-Hassam said, "that proves the rule."

"What the hell's that mean?" said Morales. "Makes no sense."

"Ask Ms. Seidel," said El-Hassam.

What the hell did it mean? Her very first chance to actually do something with this job—and at that moment she realized she really wanted to do something with it, in fact was tremendously excited on the inside—and she was about to blow it. Then, like a miracle, came a memory fragment from some long-gone pedant boyfriend, of whom there'd been too many.

"It's an old saying," Ivy said, "from back when *proves* meant 'tests.' So it means the exception that tests the rule, the hard case that tells whether the rule is right or not."

Silence. They were all looking at her, although none in the eye. Then Perkins laughed, deep and rumbling. "That's Felix," he said.

"The hard case," said Morales.

Then they were all laughing, Ivy, too; all laughing except for Felix, but even he had a smile on his face, if a little uncertain. The second group laughing jag that had enveloped her since she'd been inside. A big surprise.

Moffitt, the CO, leaned around the corner and glanced into the room. El-Hassam stopped laughing. The stoppage spread quickly, too.

Silence.

"*Proves* means 'tests,'" El-Hassam said.

"You knew that, Felix?" said Morales.

Felix shook his head.

"Shit, man," said Morales, "you should get yourself a refund."

"Refund?" said Felix.

"On your college degree," said Morales. He turned to Ivy. "Felix here went to Harvard U-ni-ver-si-ty."

"No," said Felix.

A vein throbbed in Morales's right arm, distorting the tattooed *L* in LATIN KINGS. "You calling me a liar, Felix?" His tone was light, almost friendly.

"Oh, no, no, no, no," said Felix. "Just that it was actually Cornell."

"'Cause I don't tell no lies," Morales said. "Ain't that right, Felix?"

Felix nodded.

"Felix here went to Harvard U-ni-ver-si-ty," Morales said.

A long silence. Then Felix nodded again, very slightly, but he did.

"Lots of great writers didn't go to college at all," Ivy said. A remark that didn't really follow, but she wanted to change the direction things were going and couldn't think of anything else.

"For instance?" said El-Hassam.

"Shakespeare," Ivy said.

"That true?" said Morales. "Shakespeare didn't go to no college?"

Ivy nodded.

"You know Shakespeare?" Perkins said.

"Some," said Ivy.

"Let's hear," Perkins said.

"You mean know by heart?" said Ivy.

"Yeah," said Perkins. "Know."

Shakespeare, by heart. She'd taken a Shakespeare course, but all the way back in sophomore year, and it had been an 8:30 A.M. class, so—

"'Tomorrow,'" she suddenly heard herself saying.

*". . . and tomorrow and tomorrow.
Creeps in this petty pace from day to day,"*

Oh God, could she have chosen worse?

*"To the last syllable of recorded time;
And all our yesterdays have lighted fools
The way to dusty death."*

It got quiet, so quiet Ivy could hear Moffitt burping outside the door.

Perkins leaned back in his chair. "Damn," he said.

"Dude must have spent time inside," Morales said.

"I don't think they know much about his life," Ivy said.

"Spent time inside, take my word for it," said Morales. "What about Hitler?"

"Hitler?" said Ivy.

"He was a writer," Morales said. "I read his book. He go to college?"

"I don't know," Ivy said.

"Knew a lot of shit, man," Morales said. "Hitler. It's all in the book."

"He started World War Two," said El-Hassam. "A hundred million people died."

"So?" said Morales. "Whose fault is that?"

Another silence. The vein in Morales's arm jumped again.

"What come after 'dusty death'?" said Perkins.

"The next line?" Ivy said. "I've forgotten." In truth, she hadn't. Next came the whole tale-told-by-an-idiot part, full of sound and fury, signifying nothing. Way too depressing. "Anyway, aren't we supposed to be writing?"

"You got the paper and the pencils?" said Morales.

"Paper and pencils?"

"You spose to bring them," said Morales. "How else we gonna write?"

No pens. Goddamn Joel. "My mistake," Ivy said. She started to get up.

"Hey," said Morales. "Where you goin'?"

"I'll see if Mr. Moffitt can help out."

Perkins laughed his rumbly laugh. "*Mister* Moffitt?"

El-Hassam reached into his pocket, pulled out a pen; a ballpoint, same make of Bic as the two confiscated from Ivy's purse. "We could take turns with this," he said.

Ivy sat down. El-Hassam had a pen. Pens were forbidden. Therefore? Should she call Moffitt in? Would there be any teaching after that? No. Gig over. Plus El-Hassam's pen was just a pen, unsharpened, unweaponized. And El-Hassam had such a calm air about him, almost like a spiritual leader. She was aware of their gazes on her. "What about paper?" she said.

Morales got up, picked a random book off the shelves, tore out one of the blank end pages.

"We'll try one of those chain poems," El-Hassam said.

"Chain poems?" said Ivy.

"Joel had us doing chain poems," said El-Hassam. "You know Joel?"

Ivy nodded.

"He's a fag, right?" said Morales.

This was a word Ivy would never use, except maybe coming from the mouth of some beyond-the-pale character in one of her stories. She had a lot of gay friends, had marched in the Gay Pride parade one year, believed in gay marriage.

"Right," she said. And immediately felt like a criminal herself. It wasn't all bad.

El-Hassam pushed the pen and paper in front of Perkins. "You start," he said.

Perkins hunched over the blank page, stuck his tongue between his lips. The pen—like a toothpick in his huge hand—hovered over the paper, then came down and began moving quickly. In a minute or two he was done, shoved the page across the table to Morales. Why not Felix, Ivy thought, who was beside him?

Morales didn't even read what Perkins had written. He closed his eyes tight, held on to the pen tight, just sat there, eyelids twitching a little. No one got impatient: El-Hassam closed his eyes, too, went completely still; Perkins's eyes glazed over; only Felix Balaban seemed wakeful, his eyes darting around. They met Ivy's, shifted quickly away, then came back. Should she say she knew who he was, mention the Danny Weinberg connection?

At that moment, Morales groaned, opened his eyes, started writing. He wrote more slowly than Perkins and in much bigger letters. The more he wrote, the more his body came alive, feet tapping, head bobbing, and that pulse, going wild in his forearm.

"A little time factor," Felix said.

Morales's pencil came to an abrupt halt. El-Hassam opened his eyes, and Perkins's unglazed.

Morales stared right at Felix. "What you say, amigo?"

Felix looked down, mumbled something about time that Ivy didn't catch.

"I don' hear you," Morales said.

"It's nothing," Felix said. "Nothing at all. Sorry."

"Sorry?" said Morales.

Felix nodded.

Morales glanced at El-Hassam and Perkins. "He sorry."

"Then that's settled," Ivy said. "Let's get back to work."

Perkins stifled a laugh. El-Hassam gave her a look, one elegant eyebrow raised. "Yes," he said.

Morales gazed down at the paper. "Lost my fuckin' concentration," he said, and passed it to El-Hassam. El-Hassam sent it on to Felix.

"I really don't have anything today," Felix said.

"Felix don' have nothin' today," Morales said.

The page went back to El-Hassam. He read what was already there, then started writing. There was a lot of pausing, a lot of scratching out.

"Gonna be real baaaaaaad if I'm blocked," Morales said.

"I'm sure that's not the case," Felix said.

El-Hassam kept writing. Ivy remembered a documentary she'd seen about the Tuareg, the blue men of the desert. El-Hassam's hands reminded her of those people. For a moment they could have been somewhere else, a mud village in the Sahara or a caravan stop. Then Moffitt was in the doorway.

"Time's up," he said.

Ivy glanced at El-Hassam. The pen was gone.

The men rose, filed out, Morales, Perkins, Felix, and El-Hassam last. He handed Ivy the paper. "Needs a title," he said.

"We'll do that next week," Ivy said. "See you then."

El-Hassam was about to say something, but Moffitt beat him to it. "Unless they all get pardoned," he said.

Taneesha led her out: down a wide corridor, across the open space to the gate, where new guards were on duty. They shone the infrared torch on the back of her hand. VISITOR showed up in blue and they returned her license, keys, pens, cell phone.

"Coming back?" Taneesha said.

"Of course," said Ivy, surprised.

"Lots don't," said Taneesha.

Ivy found her own way out of the administration building, out into the sunshine. All at once, she felt immensely powerful, completely free of worry and striving, at the tiptop of life. She crossed the street, walked up to a little park at the top of the hill. From there, she could look down, over the prison, across a broad golden flatland all the way to Lake Champlain, sparkling blue in the distance. That reminded her of the Great Salt Lake, which she had never actually seen, and those few lines liked by *The New Yorker*. She was going to get better than that, way better.

Ivy leaned against a tree, read the chain poem. None of them could spell at all, and El-Hassam was the worst. Many of Morales's letters were backwards and so were some of Perkins's. Also Perkins did a lot of capitalizing.

Corrected for spelling and those backwards letters, Perkins had written:

> *Tomorrow and tomorrow and Tomorrow*
> *Creeps in this Petty Pace from day to day*
> *To the Last syllable of recorded Time*
> *And All our yesterdays Have lighted Fools*
> *The way to Dusty Death.*

Somehow memorizing the whole thing just from hearing her say it once.

Morales:

> *I had wheels man! Bright orange Camaro! like a*
> *firebomb with a 427! and mag rims me and my*
> *homey stole off a jew in Trenton! Zoom! Took two*

hos on a cookout! Carmen and the one with the tits!
That one do what I want all the way home! Ooooo!
Not all the way, cause of we getting wrecked by this
eighteen-wheeler off of exit 79!

And he'd signed it, *Hector Luis Morales,* in big letters
with lots of flourishes, not unlike John Hancock except for
the backwards letters.
  And El-Hassam:

> *Last night a man dream of a knife in a drawer*
> *Very sharp knife ground sharp sharp on the stone*
> *With a twelve inch blade gently curve and a handle*
> *Made of mother pearl*
> *Sharp sharp for sticking in like nothings there*
> *No sound or friction nothing*
> *Last night a knife in the drawer*
> *The very very sharp sharp knife*
> *Dream of a man.*

Ivy drove home. She stopped shaking somewhere on the
Northway.

Four

Friday night at Verlaine's, and it was jumping.

"Who are all these cretins?" said Bruce Verlaine. "I've never even seen half of them."

"Paying customers," Ivy said.

Bruce snorted and sat some new arrivals at the very worst table, between the digital jukebox and the dank corridor to the bathrooms. They thanked him effusively, as if that would help their cause.

Danny Weinberg came in with a date, ordered Veuve Clicquot. "Aurore," he said, or at least that was what it sounded like, "this is Ivy."

"Hi," said Ivy, filling her glass.

Aurore gave a tiny nod. She was a knockout.

"*Salut,*" said Danny. They drank. "Ivy's a writer," Danny said.

"Rilly," said Aurore, setting her glass on the bar with distaste and looking around the room, in time to catch Bruce ripping the jukebox plug out of the wall. That meant someone had programmed a song Bruce had just decided he'd heard once too often.

"Right now she's teaching inmates at a prison upstate," Danny said.

"I have an excruciating headache," Aurore said.

Danny looked alarmed. "You do?" he said.

"Blinding," said Aurore.

Stroke, maybe? Ivy thought. "Would you like some Advil?" she said.

"Advil?" said Aurore, as though Ivy had suggested something lower class, and then she was on her way out, Danny following.

He came back alone about an hour later, wearing jeans and a T-shirt now instead of a suit, and ordered a beer. "She's been stressed lately," he said.

"What does she do?" said Ivy.

"They hit a coral head off Martinique," Danny said, "could have drowned."

"I meant for a living," said Ivy.

"Never stops," said Danny. "Charities, openings, appearances. She's in the Sunday Styles section practically every week."

Bruce came by, dropped Danny's tab in front of him.

"Mind settling this?"

Danny paid his bill at irregular times, maybe every few weeks, but he was a good customer, lived in the neighborhood and tipped well. He riffled through the pages, his eyes hooding slightly, then pulled out a platinum card.

"I wouldn't set foot in this dump," he said, "if it wasn't . . ." He finished his beer, ordered another. "How was the class?"

"Your friend came."

"Felix?"

Ivy nodded.

"We're not friends, exactly. He was a client. How's his writing?"

"He didn't actually do any that day."

"I'm not surprised," Danny said. "Felix is a numbers guy, strictly left-brained. But a brilliant numbers guy. He invented a kind of counterderivative that maybe three people in the world understand."

"Is that what got him in jail?"

"Not directly. Some temporary offshore options arrangement did the damage, the irony being that that little scheme was just a form of insurance to protect the investors. But the jury was too stupid to see it."

"Who were the investors?"

Danny shrugged. "Some pension fund," he said. "Nobody."

"What happened to the pension money?"

"The pension money?" said Danny. "Oh, that was the sixty mill. If you're interested, I could tell you the whole story over a late dinner." He shifted his hand on the bar, close to hers, but not touching.

Danny's hands were nice, except for the bitten fingernails. Danny was nice, too; threw his money around too much, but basically nice, and he liked her. Plus she was interested in Felix Balaban's crime. So, a late dinner with Danny: How bad could it be? At that moment a thought came in, kind of from a strange angle: Danny's hands weren't nearly as nice as El-Hassam's. And a follow-up: Danny had lean, muscular arms, but they were like a child's next to Hector Luis Morales's. Meaning? Ivy didn't know.

"When are you off?" Danny said.

Were they—El-Hassam and Morales—somehow more

manly than Danny? What a crazy idea! Crazy, and Danny
was basically nice, but Ivy replied, "Not until two," which
was a lie.

She left alone at 12:30, Dragan holding the door open for
you.

"I am soon ready for showing you my novel," he said.

"That was quick," said Ivy.

"Oh, yes," said Dragan. "So much easier than dishwash-
ing, this writing business, fifty, sixty pages from opening
kickoff to final whistle."

"You watch football while you write?"

"NFL on TiVo, every game," said Dragan. "Fantastic.
You, too, are a lover of football?"

"Not really."

Dragan looked surprised. "I am the true American," he
said.

"Congratulations," said Ivy.

He laughed an uncertain little laugh. Ivy started walking
away.

"I am labeling the title of my novel *All-American
Woman*," he called after her. "Or should this *Woman* be
Girl, in the normal speech?"

Ivy walked up to her fifth-floor room. T. S. Eliot wrote
standing up, Poe had laudanum, Dragan relied on the NFL.

Her message light was blinking in the dark.

"This is Sergeant Tocco up at Dannemora. Got another
inmate cleared to join the class. Name of Harrow. We always run it by the teacher first. If you can handle one more,
give me a call."

One more, why not? Ivy left a message in his voice mail:
"Yes."

Then she sat down at her laptop, had another look at "Caveman." *Vladek felt strong.* So she said, but as she read through, she found nothing that made him seem strong, or particularly Neanderthaly either. In fact, Vladek was more like a typical twenty-first-century boor, commonplace and, what was worse, kind of lifeless, too. Lifeless. Ivy force-marched herself through a slow reread. She saw nothing but the effort that had gone into it. The art, Horace had said, was in hiding the art, although many contemporary writers believed the opposite. "Caveman" was dead on the page. Dragan's novel, with cell-phone relays and the collective Neanderthal unconscious, was probably better. And if not, he could write another one on his day off.

"God damn it," she said. She pictured herself as she was, in this tiny box on top of four other slightly bigger boxes and all around way too many other boxes containing lone people just running through their thoughts. In what way, exactly, was this preferable to a late dinner with Danny Weinberg? An image flashed through her mind, fast, like a subliminal message: nice suburb, big house, ease. She slumped forward on her table.

Sometime later, Ivy found herself thinking of Hector Morales's arms. Huge, heavy, rippling, the tattoos never still. And then there was his slicked-back hair.

She sat up, switched on the laptop, opened a new file: *Caveman, Take 2.* She typed a new first sentence: *Vladek oiled his body.*

Ivy was still writing when the sun came up. This was pretty good. Wasn't it? She changed the last line from *The surgeon made some joke Vladek didn't understand* to *"This won't hurt a bit," the surgeon said.* Then, before any doubts could arise, she wrote a cover letter to *The New Yorker* thanking them for their kind words about "Live Entertainment"—craven, yes, but just look around—folded it in an envelope with the new "Caveman" and went downstairs to the nearest mailbox.

Ivy rented another subcompact—getting a slightly better deal this time, although the numbers still didn't make sense—and drove up to Dannemora for her second class. She parked at the top of the big hill, above the administration building. Cooler today, but the air was even clearer than before, details jumping out at her in high definition: red, white and blue bunting in a cemetery across the town; a glint of silver as a tower guard raised a mug to his lips; and all around an ocean of red, yellow and gold, calm but not still.

Ivy took her bag, walked down to the administration entrance. The doors opened and dozens of guards came out, some of them with lunch pails. Ivy stepped aside. They looked tired, and she could smell their sweat. Getting off now probably meant they'd been working most of the—

"Hey!" Taneesha, at the end of the line, stopped. "What's happenin'?"

"I told you I was coming back," Ivy said.

"Not today, you ain't."

Oh God. Had she gotten the day wrong? "Isn't it Tuesday? The class meets—"

"It's Tuesday," said Taneesha, "but didn't no one tell you?"

"Tell me what?"

"Aw, damn," said Taneesha. "You drove all the way?"

"What?"

"We're in lockdown. Been in lockdown since Sunday night."

"And that means?"

"Meaning no visitors, no programs, inmates in cells except for chow."

"How long does it last?"

"No telling."

"Any chance of it ending later today?"

"Maybe," said Taneesha. "But visitors and programs wouldn't start till tomorrow."

Ivy glanced up beyond the administration building to those walls, like some monument of the ancient world designed to say no in a big way.

"Tell you what," said Taneesha. "I'll buy you a beer."

Ivy never drank at this time of day, wasn't a big drinker in any case; at Verlaine's she'd had the chance to observe many big drinkers in action. "Sounds good," she said.

Five or six guards were already at the bar at Lulu's by the Gate. A hand-lettered sign on the mirror read NO OUT OF STATE CHECKS, NO IN STATE CHECKS, NO CREDIT CARDS. FOR CREDIT, SEE LULU. NO CREDIT. Ivy and Taneesha took a table near the dartboard. The view out the front window was prison wall, nothing but.

Taneesha clinked Ivy's glass. "Here's to retirement," she said. Taneesha looked about thirty. She lit a cigarette, took a long deep drag, blew it out, sipped her beer and said, "Ah."

"Hey, Taneesha," called one of the guards at the bar. "No smoking." But he was smoking, too; so were most of them, including the bartender. Everybody laughed.

"Just sucks you drivin' all this way for nothing," Taneesha said.

"I don't mind," Ivy said. "It's so beautiful up here."

"Huh?"

"The scenery," said Ivy.

"Scenery?"

"Maybe you get used to it."

"Had to move to Plattsburgh to take this job," Taneesha said. "Plattsburgh."

"Where are you from originally?"

"Queens. Sing Sing was my first choice. Whoever heard of not getting Sing Sing?" She drained her glass, held her hand up to the bartender.

"This one's on me," Ivy said.

"What does that tell you, when you can't even get Sing Sing?"

"I don't know," Ivy said.

Taneesha took another deep drag. "Don't listen to me. I'm in a bad mood, that's all. Enriquez does that to me."

"Who's Enriquez?"

"In A-block," said Taneesha. "Likes to jerk off in front of female COs. Catch you unawares, like it's some game."

"Is that why you're locked down?"

Taneesha laughed, spewing a few droplets of beer. "We locked down for little things like that, we'd be locked down till the end of time." Then she said, "Little things," and laughed again.

Ivy laughed, too. "So what was the cause of the lock-down?" she said.

"The usual," Taneesha said. "Inmate in B-block got his throat slit."

"He's dead?"

"Ear to ear," said Taneesha. "Bled out before anyone got there." She stubbed out her cigarette, paused. "In fact, he might have been in that class of yours."

"Oh my God," said Ivy. "Who?"

"Hey, Ernie," Taneesha called over to the bar. "Who was the guy in B-block?"

The guard who'd made the no-smoking joke said, "Wasn't it that little Felix dude?"

"Felix Balaban?" said Ivy.

The guards had a quick discussion, all agreed that the dead inmate was Felix Balaban.

"What happened?" Ivy said. "Who did it?"

Taneesha shrugged. "That's what the lockdown's about, trying to find out."

"But he was so harmless," Ivy said. "The crime was some kind of financial swindle."

"Yeah?" said Taneesha. "His writing any good?"

"Why would anyone hurt someone like him?" Ivy said.

"Maybe he sneezed the wrong way," said Taneesha.

"I don't understand."

"Or whistled a song somebody didn't like, or sat at the wrong table, or took his shower out of turn. Have to understand what you're dealing with, Ivy."

Scum of the earth, according to Sergeant Tocco. But Perkins had been moved by Shakespeare and could memorize it practically on first hearing, and Morales and El-Hassam had written poems with some real poetry in them.

"Smoke?" said Taneesha.

"No, thanks."

Taneesha poured more beer. "You coming back next week?"

Outside, the sun went over the wall even though it was only early afternoon, and it got dark in Lulu's by the Gate.

Five

Yes," said Ivy, rolling over to check the time. "I heard."

Danny was on the phone. Six A.M., but he was calling from work: Ivy could hear someone in the background talking about the Fed.

"It's so horrible," Danny said. "No one seems to know what happened."

"Someone killed him."

"Who?"

"They're trying to find out."

"Who's they?" said Danny. "Some goons upstate?"

"They're not all goons," Ivy said.

Danny's voice rose. "No? The judge was a goon, the jury were goons, the D.A. was a goon. They gave him five and a half years for moving paper around in ways that were perfectly legal and now—" She heard him pound his fist on a desk.

"But the sixty million dollars," Ivy said.

"What about it?"

"Did he steal it or not?"

"What kind of a question is that?" Danny said. "Not at your usual level, Ivy."

Ivy was silent. She got the feeling that this relationship of theirs, not even really begun, was about to hit its denouement without going through any of the intermediary stages, a record for her.

"The point is he's dead for no reason," Danny said. His voice got choked up.

"Sorry," Ivy said. "I guess you knew him pretty well."

"I told you I didn't." Danny took a deep breath. "He was a client, that's all. Of my boss, actually. But I was in meetings with him, and we went out a few times."

"Went out?"

"We took him to Bermuda for a weekend, things like that."

"And then you visited him upstate."

"I felt bad for him."

Ivy remembered the way Morales forced—maybe not forced, but somehow got—Felix to say he'd graduated from Harvard instead of Cornell. Then it occurred to her that Danny was a Harvard man, also had an MBA from the business school. She had a weird thought.

"This idea of Felix's," she said. "The one that got him in trouble—did you advise him on that?"

"My boss did," said Danny. "In general terms."

"The counterderivative thing."

"Right," Danny said.

A brilliant idea that maybe three people in the world understood.

"Tell me about it," Ivy said.

"The idea? Why?"

"I'm curious."

"You understand packaging debt?" Danny said. "This is similar in the sense that hedging—" And he went on for a minute or two, but Ivy, with no understanding of packaging debt or hedging, didn't follow.

"Who came up with the idea in the first place?" she said.

"Felix. I told you."

"But the germ of it," she said. "The seed."

Silence. Then, his voice colder than she would have thought possible, Danny said, "I've got to go."

"See you."

"Yeah."

On Monday, Ivy called Sergeant Tocco.

"Still in lockdown?" she said.

"Nope."

"Did you find out who did it?"

"Nope."

"But class is on?"

"Yup."

"Plan on doing this car-rental thing every week?" said Bruce Verlaine.

"There's supposed to be a bus from the Port Authority," Ivy said.

"Sure," said Bruce. "And when that gets old you can walk on broken glass." Bruce's eyes, narrow to begin with, narrowed more as a wine salesman he didn't like came in. "Tell you what, Ivy. I'll sell you the Saab."

Bruce had an old, maybe twenty years old, red Saab sedan. "How much?" Ivy said.

"Call it five hundred."

Ivy had $732 in her checking account, plus $200 or so in the drawer by her bathroom sink.

"Where would I keep it?" she said.

"I know a guy," Bruce said.

Bruce had never done anything like this before. Maybe he saw some reaction on her face, because he said, "Just mention me in the acknowledgments."

"Acknowledgments?"

"Of your first book," Bruce said. "This Dannemora thing is all about gathering material, right?"

The wine salesman approached, uncorking a magnum of rosé on the fly—Bruce despised rosé—an optimistic smile spreading across his face.

The red Saab was the second car Ivy had owned. The first was a Honda Civic her father had given her when she turned seventeen, a few months after the divorce. He'd left Cincinnati for Seattle and a new start later that year. Ivy's grades, verbal SAT and soccer had gotten her into Williams the year after that. By junior year, her mom had remarried, the new husband, a past president of the chamber of commerce, unbearable to Ivy after five minutes' exposure. Her mom, on the other hand, had never been happier. The Civic had gone up in flames Ivy's senior year, when she'd lent it to her boyfriend for a ski trip and he'd forgotten to check the oil despite her having told him about the leak maybe fifty times.

The red Saab was better in every way, paid for with her

own money, for one thing. And it didn't leak oil: Bruce was a stickler for maintenance, a stickler about everything. Ivy drove with the windows wide open, even though this Tuesday was much cooler, with a cloudy sky and the foliage past its peak, the brightness knob turned down on all the colors. She cranked up the radio and sang along.

Taneesha was one of the two guards working the underground gate between administration and the prison. "Good as her word," she said.

"Huh?" said the other guard.

"Ivy, here. The writing teacher. She's back."

"Published anything?" said the other guard, holding out the tray.

"No," Ivy said, depositing license and keys. She had no pens this time and had left her cell phone in the car.

"My cousin sold a cartoon," said the guard. "Paid him a hundred and fifty bucks."

"Who did?" said Ivy.

"Can't remember," said the guard. "One of those *Hustler* imitators."

Taneesha stamped the back of Ivy's hand with the invisible VISITOR and she stepped through the metal detector—beltless and in sneakers today—without a hitch. The great domed space beyond was empty except for an inmate pushing a laundry hamper. Ivy crossed it, followed the wide hall on the other side to the library. Moffitt was in his chair.

"Hi," Ivy said.

He nodded.

She went in.

Three men sat around the table, all in their previous

places: Morales on the left, El-Hassam at the far end, Perkins on the right.

"Hi, everybody," she said.

They looked up, faces impassive.

Ivy sat at the near end of the table, started to open her folder, paused.

"I was shocked to hear about Felix," she said, kind of crazy, as though she were expressing condolences to his family.

But maybe it was the right thing to do, because Perkins made a rumbling in his throat that might have been friendly and El-Hassam nodded in a way that might have been grave. Morales's face stayed the way it was.

"I can't think why anyone would want to . . . to do that to him," Ivy said. "He seemed so harmless."

"Maybe he did it to himself," Morales said.

Perkins laughed, a deep chuckle.

"That's not possible, is it?" said Ivy.

"Oh yes," said El-Hassam. "Very possible."

"But not in this case," Ivy said, "or they wouldn't have gone into lockdown."

No one said anything. The vein in Morales's arm gave a little spasm; for some reason reminding Ivy of a baby kicking in the womb.

She reached into her folder, her hands shaking a little, suddenly conscious of something that should have been obvious from the start, fact number one: how big they were—especially Perkins and Morales—and how small she was. But now came a paradox: maybe that disproportion helped make this teaching job right.

"Here are some pencils," she said. "And I typed up the poem you wrote." She passed out copies, her hands steady.

The men studied their work.

"Looks nice, all typed up," said Perkins. "Professional."

Morales smacked the table. " 'Bright orange Camaro!' " he said, his voice filled with delight, as though the line was brand-new to him. He read his poem to himself, face rapt, lips moving.

"This your title?" said El-Hassam.

"Just an idea," said Ivy. At the top she'd written: *Cause and Effect.*

" 'Cause and Effect'?" said Perkins.

Morales looked up. "What's that spose to mean?"

"I thought it connected to the poem," Ivy said.

"Cause?" said Morales. "Effect?"

"But I'm sure we can come up with something better," Ivy said. "Any suggestions?"

" 'Bright Orange Camaro,' " said Morales.

"What about the Shakespeare part?" said Perkins.

"Shit," said Morales. "That's not even original."

"It doesn't have to—" Ivy began, then heard footsteps behind her. She turned, saw an inmate coming through the door, Sergeant Tocco behind him.

"This here's Harrow," said Sergeant Tocco. "New student I mentioned."

"Ivy Seidel," said Ivy, rising and holding out her hand. "Welcome to the class."

Harrow shook her hand, quick, impersonal, exerting no force. He wasn't as tall as Perkins and Morales, nor was he bulked up; instead he looked fit in the manner of a rock climber or mountaineer.

"Sit anywhere," Ivy said.

Harrow glanced around the room. There was an empty seat beside Perkins—Felix's old seat—and another beside Morales, but Harrow took neither. Instead El-Hassam rose and moved over to Morales's side. Harrow sat where El-Hassam had been.

Sergeant Tocco hadn't left. He leaned over Morales and picked up his copy of the chain poem.

" 'Cause and Effect,' " he said. He looked slowly around the prison library. Then he read the poem to himself; everyone else just sat there.

"My brother-in-law had one of those 427 Camaros," Sergeant Tocco said, gaze rising from the page and settling on Morales. "Cool car."

"Yeah," said Morales.

"But how come you left out what happened to the two girls in that wreck? When you got hit by the eighteen-wheeler off of Exit 79?"

Morales didn't speak.

The sergeant glanced down at the page. " 'Carmen and the one with the tits.' What happened to them?"

Morales stared, a hard stare with real physical force that Ivy could feel, even though it was directed at nothing.

Sergeant Tocco let go of the poem. It glided down in front of Morales.

"Nice title," said Sergeant Tocco. "Write good, gentlemen." He left the room.

It was quiet. Ivy had a plan for today's class, but her belief in it was weakening. She passed out the pencils, plus blank sheets of paper for everyone. Morales crumpled his in a ball. Ivy almost flinched; maybe she did, a little.

"I thought," she said, "we'd pick something to write about, then each read our work aloud at the end. Any ideas?"

A long silence. Morales and El-Hassam were sitting very still, El-Hassam with his eyes closed, Morales with his hands balled into fists. Perkins was cleaning under his nails with the point of the pencil.

Harrow spoke. He had a quiet voice, quiet but not at all soft. "Car wrecks," he said.

Morales's head snapped around. "What you say?"

"She asked for ideas," Harrow said, his voice still quiet. "Car wrecks is an idea."

Ivy could hear Morales's feet shift under the table. For a moment, she imagined he was about to spring up.

"Unless someone's got a better one," Harrow said.

Silence.

"Time runs out," said El-Hassam. He leaned forward, wrote in capitals at the top of his page: *CAR REX*.

"Everyone agreed?" Ivy said.

No one said anything.

"Anyone disagree?"

Silence.

"Then car wrecks it is," she said. She took out a pencil and sheet of paper for herself.

"Hey," said Perkins. "You writing, too?"

"Sure," said Ivy. "Didn't Joel?"

"No," said El-Hassam.

"Oh."

"But we've forgotten all about him," said El-Hassam.

"A fag," said Morales, referring to Joel of course, but looking at Harrow.

Ivy thought about car wrecks. It really was a pretty good idea. Supposing, for example, you and someone you had to make a big decision about were driving somewhere, and just at the crucial moment you passed a horrible wreck and made up your mind. You could go either way. The wreck wrecks the relationship or else reveals its necessity. Ivy knew she'd have to compress everything to get it done in class, but maybe she could expand it later. She glanced around. Except for Morales, the men were bent over their papers, Perkins already writing.

The bridesmaids were all a little drunk, Ivy wrote. *The honeymooners were on the plane to Cancún and most of the guests*—Ivy raised her head. Morales was on his feet, moving toward the bookshelves behind Harrow. Everyone else was writing. Morales saw her and smiled.

"Check a word," he whispered, reaching up for a big dictionary. He moved very smoothly for such a heavily muscled man.

Ivy gave him an encouraging nod, went back to work.

—most of the guests had gone home. And it's one of the guests who dies in the wreck? How would that work? Sentence number two and already the story was shifting under her feet, in that maddening way stories had. Well, why not try it? *The mother of the bride was a little drunk, too. She sat in the car, shoes off, waiting for her husband. As he came across the parking lot, she saw that one of the bridesmaids, the pretty one with the—*

Something made her glance up. Not a sound, not a movement, something much less obvious, like a change in barometric pressure. And what Ivy saw, her mind had trouble taking in, first because it was so far outside anything she'd seen before, second because it happened so fast, and third because of the expression on Morales's face, an expression that brought a word to life: *murderous.*

Morales was no longer at the shelves, but standing right behind Harrow. He held the heavy dictionary—*Webster's Third New International,* unabridged, Ivy noticed—high over Harrow's head. Harrow, busy writing, the pencil wriggling fast, almost a full page already covered, was completely unaware. Then, just as Morales plunged the dictionary down with tremendous force, his chest muscles bulging with the effort, Harrow moved. He must have, because the dictionary struck the table with a heavy imploding sound like a hand clapping hard over a human ear, and Harrow was no longer in the chair. Instead, he and Morales were somehow on the floor, out of sight. Then came a crack that reminded Ivy of wishbones on Thanksgiving Day but routed through an amp turned up all the way, and Morales, in a voice that wasn't his at all, more like a woman's high-pitched shriek, screamed something in Spanish she didn't catch. The next moment, Harrow was back in his chair, fastening a button that had come undone. The moment after that, Moffitt was rushing into the room, reaching for things on his belt.

"What the hell's going on?" he said.

Except for Morales, they were all in their places, pencils in hand. Perkins was actually writing. Ivy closed her mouth.

Harrow looked down at Morales. "I think Morales hurt himself," he said.

Moffitt circled the table, eyed Morales. "How?" he said.

"He was checking a word in the dictionary," Harrow said. "Must have tripped."

El-Hassam got up, picked the dictionary off the floor, unwrinkled the pages, laid it on the table. "Heavy," he said.

"You telling me the dictionary tripped him?" said Moffitt.

El-Hassam shook his head. "Didn't see it happen, myself. The weight must have surprised him, coming off the shelf."

Morales was groaning on the floor.

"The weight of a book?" said Moffitt. "Morales? He bench-presses four hundred pounds."

Perkins looked up from his work. "Angle make a big difference. Should be on a lower shelf."

"Heavy book like that," said El-Hassam.

Morales rose, his face white, his right arm hanging out to the side a little. His left hand supported the elbow; gently, as though it were a baby's arm, easily damaged.

"What's with your arm?" Moffitt said.

"Twisted in the fall," said El-Hassam.

"Wasn't asking you," said Moffitt. "Did you twist it in the fall, Morales?"

Morales stood still for what seemed like a long time; and not quite still, but trembling slightly. Then he nodded.

Moffitt's gaze went from Morales around the room to all of them, then back to Morales.

"What were you looking up?" he said.

Morales said nothing. His skin glistened with sweat, the tattoos now colorless, gleaming like fish scales. His arm was out of the shoulder socket; Ivy could see the ball joint, pressing the fabric of his tan sleeve.

Harrow was writing. Eyes on his work, he said, *"Internal combustion."*

"He was looking up *internal combustion*?" said Moffitt.

Harrow nodded. "So he could write more about that Camaro."

"Fuck the Camaro," said Moffitt. He turned to Ivy. "What did you see?"

Somewhere in the prison a man started laughing, a shrill laugh that went on and on.

"It all happened so fast," Ivy said. "I really couldn't say." Her voice wavered at the end, a little unsteady.

"No problem," said Moffitt. "This shit goes down all the time."

Six

T'aneesha and another guard appeared, took Morales to the infirmary. By then the hour was just about up, no chance to read aloud. Ivy went over the car-wreck pieces when she got home.

Perkins had written:

> *The way to Dusty Death*
> *And All our yesterdays Have lighted Fools*
> *To the Last syllable of recorded Time*
> *Creeps in this Petty Pace from day to day*
> *Tomorrow and tomorrow and Tomorrow*

—exactly reversing the order of the lines he'd memorized before. Was he making some point about car wrecks? Ivy didn't know. Was *creeps* a verb or a noun in this version? She didn't know that either.

El-Hassam, corrected for spelling—except for the title, which Ivy liked the way it was—had written:

Car Rex

A car waits in the alley
Black car with wipers whap whap and lights
Off
Wait patient black car
All the time in the world
Wait wait rev rev day and year go by
So patient
Black car rev and rev
Motor howl
Wait for the white car to come in sight.

And Harrow:

There were two funny parts about the ice storm that killed my daughter. The first was how much she loved all kinds of weather. The second was that I always had a feeling she'd die young. A smart guy might have added up those two funny parts and figured some way to keep her safe. But that's not me. Just ask around.

Ever seen an ice storm? It's like the whole world got preserved under glass, and not any old glass but a special glass blown out of diamonds. Of course it turns out to be one of those beautiful shams. Some people might say that's life—a beautiful sham—but tell me: Where's the beauty part? But back to the ice storm, a sham because the sparkle melts away and it ends up being deadly instead of beautiful. As you shall see.

Except for what ended up happening, this ice storm was typical in every way. Probably boring to describe, so I'll skip it and pick up where I'm driving home. This was one of those places I didn't like living, down in a hollow at the bottom of Ransom Road. I liked being up high. That was back then—now I couldn't care less. Joke on me, you say. But it's on you.

Ransom Road was steep and ended in a long curve down at the bottom. My daughter used to watch from the front window, all set to run out when I came home. She had these tight blond curls that bounced in the sunlight.

One other boring thing, but this I can't leave out if the story's going to make any sense, was the state of my tires at the time. Retreads and old ones at that, practically smooth. They had that glazed look, like worn-out driveshaft belts. Glass on glass, if you see where I'm going. Never would have passed the inspection if I hadn't

Blank page after that. Out of time, or had Harrow stopped for some other reason? One more unknown.

Ivy read Harrow's piece again, and then once more. It got better and better. So many good things: alive on the page, for one thing, pictures you could see without effort, details that stuck in your mind; plus ideas popping up all over the place—and ideas popping up all over the place was right at the top of Professor Smallian's list of what makes the very best writing.

And what else? A kind of confidence, a confidence, Ivy

realized at that moment, that was missing in her own writing. She thought again of Professor Smallian's little aperçu about good and bad: *You don't have to be a good person to be a good writer—history shows it's better if you're not— but you have to understand your badness.* Ivy had read Professor Smallian's three novels, more than once. He wrote with confidence, too, lots of it. But—and now she was admitting it to herself for the first time—there were passages, and not a few, where she'd had to push herself to keep going, like reading uphill. There was nothing uphill about Harrow's writing. A short piece, yes, and not even finished, but: airborne.

"Plasma?" said Bruce Verlaine.

"Third generation," said the TV salesman, unaware that Bruce understood plasma in the context of blood only, also despised television in general and the idea of TV watching in Verlaine's in particular. The TV guy opened a glossy brochure with lots of pullout spreads and laid it across the bar. "This sixty-four-inch babe would look pretty stunning right up there."

"Where my Dalí is?" said Bruce.

"Dolly?" said the TV guy. He peered at the painting that hung behind the bar, a genuine Salvador Dalí Bruce had accepted years ago to close out a legendary tab. Lots to see in the painting—a bowl of fruit with a snake on top, metallic sunflowers, even one of those bent clocks—but no dolls or anything close. Bruce's left eyelid twitched, an unequivocal danger signal. Ivy moved to the other end of the bar.

A slow afternoon. That gave her time to flip open her laptop, do something that was only going to hurt. And what was the point? "Caveman," version two, the one that started with Vladek oiling his body and ended with the surgeon saying—oh, irony!—it wouldn't hurt a bit, was already at *The New Yorker;* unread, no doubt, but beyond recall. But maybe it really wouldn't hurt, maybe the story would take off from the first sentence, airborne after all.

Ivy, behind the bar at Verlaine's, a low autumn sun filling the place with silvery light, reread "Caveman." Airborne? Not from the first sentence or any other. Dead on the page, pictures it took effort to see, details that squirmed from your mind, refused to be nailed down. As for ideas: maybe a few, but not bubbling up all over the place. The whole thing was too laborious for that.

Was Harrow—this . . . prisoner—the better writer, despite all her writing, the MFA, the workshop scholarship? How could that be possible?

What did she know about him? Nothing. Maybe he'd stolen his little story—just a fragment, really—memorizing like Perkins a passage he'd seen somewhere. Would Dannemora inmates draw the line at plagiarism?

Ivy stopped herself. What a nasty, backbiting line of thought, not her at all, please God. And she had no doubt the work was Harrow's, knew it instinctively. Her best course was to—

"Something on your mind, Ivy?" Bruce said.

She turned, saw him watching from the other end of the bar. "No," she said, closing the laptop, reaching for a dirty glass.

Bruce held up his hand. "Lay off the busywork," he said. "No one in here anyway, God damn them." He glanced out the window, winced slightly, popped a few aspirin and washed them down with club soda right from the gun. "How much can you make off a novel, anyway?" he said.

"I'm not sure," Ivy said. "A lot, if it's a bestseller."

"How much is a lot?"

"Hundreds of thousands, maybe?"

"What's your percentage?"

"Mine?"

"The writer's," said Bruce. "On each copy sold."

"I don't know."

"Fifty percent? Forty? Twenty?"

"Probably toward the low end," Ivy said. "Anyway, I'm concentrating on short stories right now."

"What do they pay?"

"It depends on the magazine."

"For example?"

She had no examples.

"Your business plan needs work," Bruce said.

He looked out the window again. "Everybody picked this afternoon to join AA?" he said. "People have to drink, don't they? Stands to reason."

"Is that *your* business plan?" Ivy said.

Bruce looked annoyed. "What would most people rather do?" he said. "Read a book or get blotto?"

"I want a raise," Ivy said.

Bruce's face went through a number of changes. "Okay."

It got busy a little later, proving the rightness of Bruce's plan. Danny Weinberg came in after work. Ivy was a little surprised to see him, given the way their last conversation had gone. He'd brought someone with him, an unshaven guy with tiny glasses and a deathly complexion.

"Old friend from college," Danny said. "Whit, Ivy. Ivy, Whit."

"Hi," said Ivy. "What can I get you?"

"Single malt," said Whit. "What have you got?"

Ivy handed him the list; a long one—Bruce was serious about single malts.

Whit scanned it quickly, a very fast reader. "I don't see the Glenmorangie eighteen-year-old," he said.

Bruce was working the other end of the bar, but the vibes from his back going up carried a long way. "Sorry," Ivy said.

"A Bud, then," said Whit.

"Same," said Danny. "On my tab." Ivy served them. "Whit works at *The New Yorker*," Danny said.

"Oh?" said Ivy.

"Denial would be pointless," said Whit.

Had she ever disliked anyone so quickly? "What do you do there?" Ivy said, thinking, *Sells ads, answers the phone, makes cold calls*.

"Edit fiction," said Whit.

"Oh," said Ivy.

"Whit was editor of the *Crimson*," Danny said. "He's got a book coming out from—who is it again?"

"Knopf," said Whit.

"That's how you pronounce it?" said Danny.

"A novel?" said Ivy.

"I wish I had more hope for the novel," said Whit. "This is more of a refracted memoir."

Ivy and Danny were the same age; Whit had been at Harvard with Danny. So: a little young for memoir writing, no?

"Of?" she said.

Whit gave her a kindly smile. "Have to read the book," he said.

I'll hang myself first, Ivy thought. She said: "Looking forward to it."

"I was telling Whit you're a writer too," Danny said.

"I wouldn't—"

"And that you'd submitted a thing or two to *The New Yorker* in the past," Danny added.

"That's not really anything I'd—"

"Who's your agent?" said Whit.

"No agent," Ivy said. "I haven't published anything."

"Yet," said Danny.

One little word, but the most natural-sounding thing he'd said to her, and the nicest. Maybe it gave her the courage to say what came next: "But I've got something there right now."

"There?" said Whit.

"At your office."

"And I suppose you've been waiting to hear for geologic eons," said Whit.

"I don't expect anything soon," Ivy said. "I understand it takes a long—"

"What's it about?" said Whit.

"The story?" said Ivy.

"Yeah," said Whit.

"Tell him the story," said Danny.

Danny sounded a little like a Jewish grandmother impatient with an insufficiently self-promoting grandchild. And he was right: this was a wonderful chance, out of the blue. Then she had another optimistic thought: What if Whit was the editor who'd read the "Live Entertainment" story and scrawled that encouraging message at the bottom of the rejection form?

"Have you ever been to Utah?" she said.

"No," said Whit. "Is that where it takes place?"

"No," said Ivy.

"Then why—"

Off to a bad start. Should she explain that *Utah part is nice* thing? Instead she plunged off in another direction, talking too fast, brakes temporarily out of service.

"It takes place here—New York. 'Caveman'—that's the title. About an immigrant who comes with high hopes and nothing goes right—worse and worse, in fact—but he ends up hoping even higher."

"Hey!" said Danny. "That sounds great." He turned to Whit.

Whit took a sip of beer. "Horatio Alger in reverse," he said. "Nathanael West territory, with the immigrant angle grafted on."

"Well," said Ivy, "I wouldn't . . ." But he was right, completely. Or almost completely. "I left out that he turns into a Neanderthal man."

"Interesting idea," Whit said.

"Oh, thanks."

"Got a copy?"

"I already sent it to—"

"Another copy," said Whit.

"That you could give him personally," said Danny, enunciating with extra care, as though to an idiot. "Now, for example."

"I—I have my laptop right here," Ivy said. "Maybe I could use the office printer."

"I'll hook it up," said Bruce, suddenly appearing behind her.

She went into the back office with Bruce. He connected her laptop to the printer. She couldn't have done it alone, the way her hands were shaking.

"Prick just saved his life," said Bruce, handing her the pages.

"What do you mean?"

"None of my single malts good enough for him," Bruce said. "Orders Bud. That's how a guy ends up in an alley."

She went back into the bar, gave Whit the story. She expected him to fold it, put it in his pocket, something like that. But instead, without a word, he glanced at the first sentence—*Vladek oiled his body*—and started reading.

He was reading it? Right there in front of her? All those writers with stories submitted, past and present, waiting in their individual degrees of agony for an answer, never sure that a real human being would read their stuff: and here was this real human being reading hers practically on demand; as though Shakespeare had popped in with a grin on his face and fresh pages.

Had Ivy ever watched anyone as closely as she watched Whit now, trying to peer beyond the tiny lenses of his tiny glasses, through his eyes, kind of tiny, too, and into the part of his brain where judgments got made? It hit her that in Whit's case that might be just about the whole organ. But one thing was sure: he was absorbed. Wasn't he? Maybe "Caveman" was good after all, as good as she'd intended.

Whit didn't look up until he came to the bottom of page one; not a long time, but she'd already seen he was a fast reader. He met her gaze.

"Can't wait to sce how it plays out," he said, and now folded "Caveman" in two and stuck it in an inside jacket pocket. "I'll be in touch soon."

That had to be good, right? "Oh, thanks," said Ivy. "No rush." The most ridiculous thing she'd said in years.

Whit rose. Danny shot her a private thumbs-up as they went out the door. Of course: nothing out of the blue about this at all. How slow she was sometimes.

Ivy had a lot of trouble falling asleep that night. She just couldn't stop going over things, trying out various redos, reexamining every word that Whit had spoken, every look that had crossed his pasty face. It was only very late, exhausted at last, that her mind wandered over to Harrow, and the girl with the bouncing curls waiting at the bottom of the hill in the ice storm.

Seven

Next day: no call from Whit. Same the day after, and the day after that. Also no call from Danny. What did that mean? Good or bad? Ivy went back and forth on that question for a while—had to be bad. Although it might be good if, say, Whit had told Danny he loved the story but wanted to keep it a secret until he'd contacted Brad Pitt about playing Vladek. She finally gave in to weakness and phoned Danny at his office.

"Mr. Weinberg is in Hong Kong. I can put you in his voice mail."

Whit had said "soon." What did *soon* mean, exactly? She even looked it up.

And still nothing on Tuesday morning. Ivy gathered the Car Wreck pieces—all typed up and put in folders—and drove north, into the Adirondacks. Nothing good on the radio: she

played a game she sometimes played with herself, a game
that involved spotting little details here and there and finding some original way of describing them. Take how the
leaves had lost their full flush of color, as though some fever
had passed; and how fog hung low in the branches, like a
death shroud: Was there a fresh, original way of describing
that, making it add up to something new? Ivy tried and
tried, tried so hard, without success, that she took a wrong
turn off 22 and wound up on a dirt road that dead-ended by
a lake.

A few cabins stood by the shore. A sign on the door of
the first one read: WILDERNESS LAKE CABINS: RENTALS—
DAY, WEEK, LONGER. INQUIRE INSIDE.

Ivy pulled up next to a minivan, walked toward that first
cabin. An old pickup, painted a nonfactory shade of purple,
was parked beside it; from round back came thwacking
sounds. Ivy followed them. Behind the cabin she found a
lean gray-haired woman in a red-and-black-checked shirt
chopping wood. The woman saw her, paused with the ax
held high.

"I'm a little lost," Ivy said.

"Must be," said the woman. She had eyes the same color
as the lake behind her. "Where you trying to get?"

"Dannemora."

The woman brought the ax down in a short smooth
stroke, neatly splitting the log on the chopping block. "How
are you at shortcuts?"

"Not good."

"There's just one tricky part, but it'll save you an hour."

An hour? Had she gone that far wrong? Ivy checked her
watch. She didn't have an hour. "What's the shortcut?"

The woman came forward, drew a little map in the dirt
with the blade of the ax. "Two miles back—this old lane,

used to lead to a hunting lodge, long time ago. Hard to spot—go real slow after you start seeing a creek on your right. The lane's about a hundred yards past that on the left here—look for a big rock with a flat face. Straight up for half a mile and straight down for half a mile more, but you come out on blacktop. Take a right and you hit 374 in five minutes, be in Dannemora ten minutes after that."

"Thanks," Ivy said, taking one final look at those scratchings in the dirt.

"Best of luck," said the woman, turning back toward the woodpile.

Ivy set her trip counter to zero, drove back the way she'd come. After a mile and a half, a creek flowed out of the woods, narrow and bubbling, and ran along beside the road; she rolled down her window so she could hear it. Seconds later she spotted the big rock with the flat face—the kind of smooth writing surface where you'd expect graffiti, but not here. Just beyond the rock lay a small opening in the woods, half-overgrown with weeds and vines. This? Ivy turned into the opening at walking speed.

Ahead, with a little imagination, she could make out a two-rutted lane curving into the forest. She bumped her way along it, branches scratching at the Saab, a twilight gloom closing overhead even though it was still morning. More like a tunnel than a lane, really, boring through the woods. It began sloping steeply up, as the gray-haired woman had said. Then came two or three switchbacks—her tires spinning over mossy tree roots—and she reached the top. A small clearing lay on her right and on the edge of it something horrible and bloody was going on. At first she thought the huge guy bent over the ripped-open guy was actually eating him alive. Then the huge guy heard the car and looked up, eyes alert. A jolt of terror, the first real terror Ivy had ever felt, went through her. And then the scene straightened itself out and turned into what it was: a bear, not a man, and the victim, head now flopping over at an impossible angle, a deer. Somehow that—a bear, not a man—was less frightening. Ivy found that she'd stopped to watch.

Outside of a zoo, she'd never seen a bear before—or a deer. Now that the killing part was over, this bear was in no hurry. It reached into the deer and raised a purple glob to its long muzzle—almost delicately, like a connoisseur. At that moment, Ivy understood what was wrong with the "Caveman" story. Why would Vladek necessarily fail to grasp the essential brutality of—

Maybe the bear didn't like being watched. All of a sudden it seemed to have forgotten about the deer, in fact was on its feet and coming her way, first in a kind of rolling walk, a bit like a sailor, and then in a loping run that covered amazing amounts of ground. Ivy wasn't prepared for that, or for the intelligence apparent in its eyes. She stepped on the gas.

Stepped on the gas, but the car went nowhere. She stomped on the pedal. Nothing, except the shriek of the revving engine. Oh God. Why wouldn't—? Then she saw that the shift was in *P*. She jammed it into *D* and surged forward, just missing a tree. In her rearview mirror she caught a last glimpse of the bear up on its hind legs, head tilted slightly to the side. Twenty minutes after that she was walking into the library at Dannemora, right on time.

Three students at the long steel table: Perkins on the right, El-Hassam in Morales's old seat on the left, Harrow at the end.

"Hi, everybody," Ivy said.

"Yo," said Perkins.

El-Hassam gave her a little nod.

Harrow said, "How was the drive?"

That bear, head tilted to one side: Harrow's was like that right now. "Fine," she said, and passed out the folders, fresh sheets of paper, pencils.

"Drive from where?" said Perkins.

"The city."

"What's your ride?" Perkins said.

"My ride?" said Ivy.

"Your wheels," said El-Hassam. "Your car."

"A Saab," said Ivy.

"Sssaaaaab," said El-Hassam, like it was a strange foreign word, which of course it was.

"An old one," Ivy said.

"What year?" said Perkins.

"I'm not sure."

"You don't know what year your Sssaaaaab is?" said El-Hassam.

"It's very old," Ivy said, giving El-Hassam a quick look. Was he in a bad mood? "I just got it."

"How much you pay?" said Perkins.

"Five hundred dollars."

"How many miles on it?"

"I'm not sure of that either," Ivy said.

"Sssssaaaaab," said El-Hassam, a hiss this time, snake-like. His serene features, so difficult to reconcile with his poetry, were a little distorted today.

Silence. Then Harrow said, "Are cars the only topic of discussion in this class?"

"Somethin' wrong with cars?" said Perkins.

"Yeah," said Harrow. "They're boring."

"You sayin' cars is boring?" said Perkins.

"You got it," said Harrow.

The two men looked at each other, very quick, their gazes intersecting for a split second. The atmosphere changed, as though two live wires had touched.

"From a writing standpoint," Ivy said, "anything can be interesting. All depends how you handle it."

"You're saying cars can be interesting?" Harrow said.

"Sure," said Ivy.

Perkins smacked his huge hand on the table in triumph.

"The way you yourself wrote about those worn tires proves that," Ivy added quickly.

"What tires?" said Perkins.

"In Harrow's story," said Ivy.

"A story?" said Perkins. "I thought we was supposed to write poems."

"Or stories," said Ivy.

"You never said that," Perkins said.

"Sorry," said Ivy. "How about if Harrow reads his?"

"Out loud?" said Harrow.

"Or we could pass your copy around," Ivy said.

El-Hassam, sitting rigidly upright, eyes closed, said: "Take too long."

Another silence. Perkins cleared his throat, a deep tectonic rumble.

"Okay," said Harrow.

He opened his folder, took out Ivy's neat typescript. " 'Car Wreck,' " he began. " 'There were two funny parts about the ice storm that killed my daughter. The first was how much she loved all kinds of weather. The second was . . .' " Harrow read in a flat tone that grew flatter, if anything, but somehow increased the power of his prose, as though a mighty engine was being throttled way down.

From the very first sentence, everyone in the room was rapt; a unison Ivy could feel, like a moment in church. And they could have been in church, or anywhere else, the actual world fading away, replaced by the story world—Ransom Road, bouncing curls, ice storm. Ivy studied Harrow's face as he read, trying to see some physical link to what she was hearing. She saw intelligence, strength, self-possession, even a certain detachment, but nothing that suggested the link she sought.

Harrow came to the end: " 'Glass on glass, if you see where I'm going. Never would have passed the inspection if I hadn't . . .' "

Ivy, following along from her copy, wondered whether it would be a good idea to have each of them spend the rest of the class finishing the story in his own way. Or would it be better to let a discussion happen and just see where it led? And shouldn't Perkins and El-Hassam get to read their poems? She couldn't make up her mind.

But it didn't matter, because when Harrow came to that last unfinished sentence—*Never would have passed the inspection if I hadn't*—he just kept going, reading in that flat tone without even a pause after *hadn't;* although reading was surely the wrong word, the rest of the page being blank.

". . . slipped the mechanic a nickel bag. Always a safe bet with mechanics—the best ones are all stoners, helps them focus on little things."

Perkins, so softly Ivy almost didn't hear, said: "Shi'. Never knew that."

El-Hassam, eyes still closed but face serene again, nodded.

"One other funny connection," Harrow went on. "Now that connections are in the air. This one's about weed. Not the weed the mechanic got, but before that, when one day I came home to find my girlfriend passing a joint to my little daughter. You know the way sometimes your brain won't believe what your eyes are seeing? Got to fight that, of course, make it all line up, but I was just a kid myself back then.

" 'She likes it,' " my girlfriend said.

"She had real bad judgment, the girlfriend. That time it cost her a couple teeth. Then I opened the windows. The smoke made curling patterns on the way out, settled everything back down."

Perkins grunted. A little smile appeared on El-Hassam's face. Ivy had never seen him smile before. He looked like a sweet old man.

"But so much for connections, which is the whole point of this story," Harrow continued. "They say life is all about connecting, like that's a good thing. But when brain and eyes are lining up you know different. And what did my eyes see as I drove down Ransom Road in the ice storm, glass on glass?"

The rapt feeling in the room was growing and growing; and Harrow's eyes had a look of rapture in them, too, like he was just another listener. Ivy began to get an idea where this was coming from.

"A world turned to crystal, tiny rainbows everywhere, cold cold heaven. The door of the double-wide opens up and out comes my daughter wearing pink pajamas and boots with Goofy on them. Waving and waving, big grin. I toot the horn a couple times—she likes that. Then I touch the brake, just slowing down for that long curve into the driveway. But glass on glass, right? The car starts spinning like a helicopter with the blades shot off. My daughter—I can read her mind—thinks Daddy's playing one of his jokes, actually claps her little hands with delight. You know kids."

Harrow stopped speaking, looked up.

Silence. It built and built, became unbearable.

"And then what?" said Perkins.

"The end," said Harrow.

El-Hassam opened his eyes. "That's the end of the story?"

Harrow nodded.

"But what happened?" Perkins said.

"End of story," said Harrow, the rapt look draining from his eyes; and gone.

"Why did you choose to end it there?" Ivy said.

Harrow turned to her. "Is it a problem?"

What had Professor Smallian said about endings? *Always leave 'em wanting more.*

"No," Ivy said. "I was just asking how you made the decision."

Harrow shrugged.

"But what happened, man?" Perkins said.

Harrow closed his folder. "What happened after the end of the story?" he said.

"Yeah," said Perkins.

"Nothing happens after the end of a story," Harrow said.

"Come on, man," said Perkins. "What about the little girl?"

Harrow was silent. The skin on Perkins's face tightened.

"Maybe nothing happened to her," El-Hassam said.

"What you talkin' about?" said Perkins. "You even listenin'? Fuckin' car's spinnin' out, glass on glass."

El-Hassam sat back in his chair. "I'm listening, Perkins," he said, pronouncing the name with careful distaste.

Perkins rose, not quickly, but with enormous power, like something volcanic.

El-Hassam reached inside his shirt.

At that moment, Ivy amazed herself. She leaned forward, touched Perkins's hand and said, "I think El-Hassam is saying it could be a made-up story."

A long pause. Ivy felt a worm-size vein pulsing in the back of Perkins's hand.

"We're already down to three," she said. "If you kill each other off, I'll be out of a job."

They all turned to her. Harrow started laughing. El-Hassam took his hand out of his shirt. Perkins sat down.

"That it, man?" said Perkins. "A made-up story?"

Harrow stopped laughing. There were tears in his eyes. "What difference does it make?"

"Make a big difference," said Perkins. He turned to Ivy. "Don't it?"

"That's a big question," she said. "I—"

Moffitt poked his head in. "Time," he said.

The men got up. "Sorry we didn't get to the poems," Ivy said. "Next week."

They started filing out, El-Hassam first, then Perkins, and Harrow, coming from the end of the table, last. As he went by, Ivy said, "Have you done much writing?"

"No."

"Any?"

"No." He tilted his head slightly to one side, watching her. "Why?"

"Because your story's good," she said. "Really good."

"Yeah?" he said, and kept going.

On the way out, Ivy stopped by Sergeant Tocco's office. "Those records you talked about," she said. "The inmate histories."

"Jackets?" said Sergeant Tocco.

"I'd like to see Harrow's."

"Right on schedule," he said. He rubbed his jaw, fingers rasping on stubble. "You authors."

"Unless it's against the rules," Ivy said.

"What rules?"

"I don't know," Ivy said. "Violation of privacy?"

Sergeant Tocco laughed, a quick bark. "They're felons. They got no privacy." He tapped at his keyboard for a few moments. A nearby printer whirred to life. Sergeant Tocco pointed to the pages coming out. "Enjoy," he said.

Eight

Ivy drove out of Dannemora, Harrow's jacket in the writing folder beside her, still unread. In a cartoon, wiggly red lines would have been rising from it, like there was radioactive material inside. Was it crazy that she'd never asked what any of them—El-Hassam, Perkins, Morales, Harrow—had done? But why? How was it her business? She was the writing teacher, period.

While Ivy wrestled with all that, the car-driving part of her was having ideas of its own. It didn't seem to want to go home the normal way, was choosing the shortcut instead. Ten minutes on 374, five on narrow blacktop, and then the rutted lane, half a mile up—no sign of bear or deer at the top—and half a mile down. At the bottom, Ivy turned right onto the dirt road, passed the flat blank-faced rock, tried and failed to think of something good to write on it, and a few minutes later again dead-ended at the Wilderness Lake Cabins.

Ivy got out of the car, knocked on the door of the first

cabin. The gray-haired woman opened up. She had her hair in a ponytail now, must have been stunning when she was young. Ivy smelled gin; she worked in a bar, could smell distinctions between some of the tough ones like scotch and bourbon. Straight gin was easy.

For a moment the woman didn't recognize her. Then she did. "Couldn't find it?"

"Oh no," Ivy said. "I found it, thanks. Your directions were perfect. I'm back."

Behind the woman a fire burned in a stone fireplace. Music played: opera, about which Ivy knew nothing.

"And where do you want to go now?" the woman said.

Ivy laughed. "Nowhere. I want to rent a cabin for the night."

"This time of year?" said the woman.

"You're closed?" Ivy said.

"Not formally," the woman said. "I'll have to charge you."

Ivy had assumed that, of course. Was the woman drunk? Ivy also excelled at detecting grades of inebriation, but not this time. All she detected was that the woman's eyes were darker than they'd been in the morning. But, through the cabin window, so was the lake, meaning they were still the same color.

"How much?" Ivy said.

"Depends whether you want me to run the generator," the woman said.

A rifle—no, shotgun, with the double barrels—stood in one corner. "I don't know," she said.

"Can you get by without electricity for a night?"

Why not? Her laptop was charged and Bruce had left a flashlight in the glove box of the Saab. "Sure."

"Can you keep a fire going?"

"Yes."

"And remember to flush only once, before you go?"

"Okay."

"Then you don't need the generator," the woman said. "Ten bucks."

Ivy handed her the money. "Ivy Seidel," she said.

"Jean Savard," the woman said.

They shook hands. Jean's was cold and clammy.

"At the top of the shortcut," Ivy said, "I saw a bear."

"Uh-huh," said Jean. "Enjoy your stay." She handed Ivy a key with 4 on it.

Cabin four was the last one, farthest from the office. Ivy unlocked the door and went inside. Cold, but perfect: knotty-pine floors, brass bed with clean white pillowcases and a rose-colored duvet, a simple desk and chair by the window overlooking the lake. Plus a stone fireplace like the one in Jean's cabin, firewood and kindling in place. Ivy opened the flue, found matches by the poker stand, soon had a nice fire going. Way out on the lake something rippled.

Ivy sat at the desk, took Harrow's jacket from the writing folder. At the top of the first page, a full name from the last-name zone: *Evan Vance Harrow.*

Then came fingerprints, both hands, fingers and thumbs. Ivy found herself examining them closely, as though they could tell her something. There was a kind of beauty in all those black whorls, reminding her of a photography exhibit about shadows and sand dunes she'd seen at the Queens MoMA. Plus wasn't there something a bit moving in the knowledge that every single human being that had ever walked the planet shared these tiny markings? Whoa. Sometimes she was an idiot: the whole point of fingerprints was difference, not community. Was there anything different about Harrow's fingerprints? Not visible to the naked eye, of course, or at least not to hers.

Below the fingerprints were two black-and-white photos, full face and profile, cop-show style. There was even a number around his neck—RG17859. Harrow looked a lot different in the photos. Younger, for one thing, his face—now slightly grooved between the eyes—still completely unlined. Plus his hair had been much longer and straggly, and he'd worn an ugly goatee. He was a lot better-looking now, kind of counterintuitive, since he'd spent the last—her eye roamed down the page—seven years in prison. Who got better-looking locked up?

Evan Vance Harrow. Born: New York City, thirty-one years before. Arrested: at seventeen for assault, not prosecuted; at eighteen, car theft, six months probation; at twenty, possession of burglar tools, one year, sentence suspended; at twenty-three, second-degree murder and armed robbery, twenty-five years without parole.

She paged through a few sheets of onionskin paper with not much on them.

At Dannemora: written up for fighting, week one; fighting week two; fighting week three. Week four to present: clean.

Psychologist's report: No diagnosable malady. The prisoner has adjusted to prison life.

Not a word about a girlfriend with bad judgment, a daughter with bouncing curls, glass on glass. Ivy went through Harrow's jacket again, felt in some weird way she knew less than before. She tried to read something in his eyes, but he had shown the camera only absence: of fear, anxiety, anger, acceptance, defiance or any other emotion you might expect. What had he been thinking? The unexpected: that was already clear from his writing.

Outside, the wind was starting to rise, puckering the water. Kind of like goose bumps, as though the lake felt cold. Ivy took out her cell phone and called Sergeant Tocco.

"I've been going over Harrow's jacket."

"Uh-huh."

"Why is it called jacket, by the way?"

"Beats me."

"It says he's serving twenty-five years for second-degree murder and armed robbery."

"Correct."

"But it doesn't give any details."

"Details?"

"Exactly what happened, where, when, all that."

"What difference does it make?"

"It might help me understand his writing a little better."

"His writing's hard to understand?"

"In a way, yes."

"Like he uses big words?"

"It's not that," Ivy said. Out the window, Jean Savard, now wearing pajamas, walked down to the shore and tossed an empty bottle in the lake. "Did his crime have anything to do with a car accident, maybe running down a little girl?"

"Nope," said Sergeant Tocco. "But for every one where they get caught you can bet there's three or four others that stay unsolved."

"What was his crime?"

"Tell you what," said Sergeant Tocco. "I'll dig up something, have it for you next time."

A whole week. "I'm actually still in the area," Ivy said.

"Uh-huh."

Jean gazed out at the lake. Her pajama pants billowed in the wind. "If it's not too much trouble," Ivy said, "maybe I could swing over now."

"Swing over?"

"And collect whatever you dig up. I can be there in half an hour."

"No good," said Sergeant Tocco. "I'm off in twenty minutes."

"It would be a big help."

"Not to me."

"How about tomorrow?"

"My day off."

"Maybe you could leave it on your desk."

A pause. Then Sergeant Tocco laughed, a quick bark. "That a writer thing?" he said. "Not taking no for an answer?"

"Yes," said Ivy, recognizing the truth of it as she spoke.

"Writers are a pain in the ass," said Sergeant Tocco. "That's one thing I learned from this program. Might as well come on over to the house."

"The prison?" said Ivy, thinking *big house*.

"Hell no," said Sergeant Tocco. "Think I hang out here one second longer than I have to? I mean my place." He gave her directions. "See you in an hour."

Ivy looked out the window. Jean was no longer there. Ivy had a crazy thought: *She's in the lake*. Then she heard Jean's voice: "Rocky!" And a big dog went bounding by, like food was waiting in the bowl.

Sergeant Tocco lived on the north edge of town, about three miles from the prison. He had a little house, newly painted white with lima-bean-green trim, an actual picket fence, also white, and a lawn completely cleared of leaves, although they were all over his neighbors' lawns and the street. None of them had picket fences, or fences of any kind.

"Get you something to drink?" said Sergeant Tocco, out

of uniform now, almost like a different person in sweatshirt and jeans.

"I'm all right."

They sat in his front room, small, immaculate. A photo of a white-haired woman stood on the mantel, next to a basket of lacquered ears of Indian corn.

"I like your house," Ivy said.

"Bought it last year," said Sergeant Tocco. "Day I turned thirty."

That shocked her: not his pride of ownership, but the fact that he looked ten years older, maybe more.

"What's *your* place like?" he said.

Ivy told him.

"Own or rent?"

"Rent, of course. It's one of the most expensive parts of Brooklyn."

"You like living in the city?"

"Yes."

"Writers ever live in the country?"

"Sure."

"Never been there myself."

"Where?"

"New York."

"Never in your whole life?"

"Nope."

"Where are you from?"

"Originally?" said Sergeant Tocco. "Schenectady, but I grew up in Plattsburgh."

Plattsburgh—where Taneesha had been forced to move after she didn't get the Sing Sing job. "What's that like?" Ivy said.

"Right on the lake," said Sergeant Tocco. "Went fishing practically every day when I was a kid."

He gave her a quick sideways glance, a surprising glance that had nothing to do with inmate programs, jackets, their professional relationship. Ivy caught it and he looked away. She noticed he'd shaved off his end-of-day stubble.

"I got this off the net," he said, and handed her a print-out.

An article from the *Albany Citizen*, seven years old, almost to the day.

Guilty in Casino Murder
BY TONY BLASS

Evan Vance Harrow, 24, late of West Raquette, was found guilty today of second-degree murder and other charges resulting from last winter's robbery of the Gold Dust Casino on the Mohawk reservation in neighboring Raquette. Casino security guard Jeremy Redfeather died of gunshot wounds sustained in a shoot-out during the robbery. Also killed were two of Harrow's associates, Marvin Joseph Lusk and Simeon Carter. Ballistics tests confirmed that the bullet that killed Mr. Redfeather came from Carter's gun.

Harrow, who wore a ski mask during the robbery and fled after the shooting, was identified by a fourth gang member, Frank Mandrell. Mandrell was not present during the robbery and received a suspended sentence on conspiracy charges in an earlier trial. Harrow's wife, Betty Ann Price, is still being sought by police. A sum in the neighborhood of three to four hundred thousand dollars, believed to have been carried from the scene by Harrow, has not been re-covered. Harrow's lawyer, Mickey Dunn, Esq., de-nied that his client had any knowledge of the whereabouts of the money and maintained his inno-cence in a brief statement after the verdict.

   Harrow will be sentenced tomorrow. Under fed-eral guidelines, he faces a minimum sentence of twenty-five years without parole.

Ivy looked up. Sergeant Tocco was watching her, his pro-fessional gaze back in place.

"That what you needed?" he said.

"I don't know," Ivy said. "And it's not a question of need-ing . . ." Her eye was drawn back to the article, so strange to her, so complicated.

"That casino's only a couple hours from here," Sergeant Tocco said. "I remember the case."

"And?" Ivy said.

He shrugged. "Same old story. Some guys think they're smart, like Hollywood types in one of those heist movies. But they always turn out dumb." He met her gaze. "Which is what they are."

Ivy felt Sergeant Tocco's will, trying to get into her brain, form her opinions. "Was this wife of his"—she checked the copy—"Betty Ann Price, ever caught?"

"Not yet."

"And what about the money?"

"Ditto."

"So maybe someone wasn't dumb," Ivy said.

"A man died," said Sergeant Tocco.

Ivy felt herself blushing, and she wasn't a blusher. "Sorry," she said.

"Nothing to be sorry·about," said Sergeant Tocco. "*You* didn't do anything wrong." He spotted a fleck of something on the arm of his chair and brushed it off.

"It says here that he didn't actually fire the gun," Ivy said.

"Makes no difference under the law."

"That doesn't seem right."

"The hell it doesn't."

"And there's no mention of a daughter."

"Why would there be?"

Ivy took out Harrow's Car Wreck story, just the half he'd written down, and handed it to Sergeant Tocco. He read it.

"So? Maybe he has a daughter. Guys like that leave a trail of kids." He looked down his nose at Harrow's story. "You actually think this is any good?"

"I do."

He handed it back. "You're the writer."

The days were getting shorter. Outside, it was night already.

Nine

Ivy opened her eyes, sat up in the brass bed, looked out the window at Wilderness Lake. There was an island about halfway across. She'd taken no notice of it before—still so much work to do on her observational skills—but now she saw how strangely proportioned it was, like a weird detail in the background of some German medieval painting. The island had a small footprint, if that was the word, but rose steeply to a rocky peak, four or five hundred feet high, topped with a black cross.

Ivy got dressed and went outside. Jean was lifting a suitcase into the side door of the minivan; Rocky waited in the front seat.

"Morning," Jean said. "Sleep well?"

"Great," Ivy said. "I was thinking of staying another day." Thinking it right that moment, in fact, as she spoke.

"I'll be in Plattsburgh till the end of the week," Jean said. "After that, I'm closing for the season."

"Oh."

Rocky thumped his tail on the seat.

Jean gazed at her. "But you look like an honest person," she said.

"I'm good at impressions," Ivy said.

Jean laughed. "Tell you what. Can you remember to lock up the cabin when you go?"

"Of course."

"And leave the key under the mat?"

"I promise," said Ivy. "Plus I owe you for another day."

"Oh, don't—"

But Ivy did.

Fifteen minutes later, she had Wilderness Lake to herself. She walked along the shore, felt a cool breeze on her face, dipped her hand in the water: icy cold. There was a stretch of sandy beach in front of the cabins, and on it lay a rowboat, upside down. Ivy read the name on the stern: *CA-PRICE*. She flipped it over. The oars lay under the thwarts or whatever you called them; why was her terminology about so many things so sketchy? At that moment, Ivy resolved to learn the complete meaning of some technical thing every day; maybe even two. And while she was resolving, she was also dragging *Caprice* down to the water, stepping in, pushing off, fixing the oars in the locks, rowing.

The little boat skimmed across the lake. Rowing felt great. The sun rose over a tall stand of spruces on the eastern side and the day turned polychromatic. The Wilderness Lake cabins grew smaller and smaller, became a part of nature. The oar blades made cream-colored whirlpools that drilled down into the water and disappeared. Ivy took a satellite view of things: New York down there, Dannemora over there, her by herself right here. Clusters of people had magnetic power, the bigger the stronger. She felt close to the edge of both their reaches, that with one or two more strokes she'd break free of their pull and enter a brand-new world. Then the bow bumped up against the island, almost knocking her off her seat.

Ivy pulled *Caprice* onto a gravelly shore, tucked the oars safely inside. She stepped around some thorny bushes and into the woods. The ground, covered with crisp dry leaves, started sloping up right away. She found herself on a sort of path—rocky in places and crisscrossed with tree roots— that corkscrewed around the island, up and up. The trees got more stunted and the rocky core of the island came thrusting to the surface. Ivy had to go down on all fours a couple times, and was huffing and puffing by the time she reached a ledge just below the top.

She checked out the view. All wild nature except for three things: the cross, rising above her head from a crag that topped the peak; Jean Savard's cabins and a red fragment that had to be the Saab between the trees; and herself, Ivy Seidel, Queen of the Hill.

But she wasn't at the top yet, not the tip-top. She climbed over a boulder, got a foothold, wriggled up the crag, rose to her feet. Not much room at the tip-top, barely enough for the two of them, the cross and her. Maybe because of the lack of foot room and how high she was, the sun glaring off the lake way down below, Ivy got a little dizzy. She reached out for the cross.

"Ow."

A quick biting pain: she'd grasped a rusty jagged edge of the vertical iron bar and cut her palm. Ivy licked up the dribbling blood. Just a little gash, not deep, nothing really. She climbed back down to the ledge.

And that was when she noticed, almost hidden in a cleft in the crag, a hole in the rock. A hard-to-spot hole, but big enough for a crouching person to enter without difficulty. Ivy crouched and entered.

Inside lay a shadowy space, not too much smaller than some Brooklyn apartments she'd been in, including her own. It had a dusty smell, a bit like old books, but there were no books around, no objects of any kind. Except for this red-tipped thing, practically at her feet. Ivy reached for it, thinking, Lipstick. But no, not lipstick. It was ammunition, one of those shotgun shells, just the brass casing.

Ivy looked around, saw no more of them, and not even a footprint on the dirt floor, but it was easy to imagine a hunter holed up here during a storm or something like that. She stepped out into the sunlight. A cave: she'd discovered a cave, just like a character in one of those adventure stories she'd loved when she was a kid. Ivy crossed the ledge and flung the shell with all her might. It cleared the treetops, barely, and spun on down, glinting and glinting, then vanished in the water with a splash too tiny to see. But totally satisfying. Ivy lowered herself off the ledge and made her way down, sucking the blood off her palm once or twice. Maybe distracted, she forgot about the key to cabin four until she was miles away. Ivy stuffed it in the glove box.

She stopped in Albany on the way home—almost no detour at all—and went into the office of the *Citizen*.

"I'm looking for Tony Blass," she told the receptionist.

The receptionist cracked her gum. "Whom," she said, "shall I say is askin'?"

"It's about a story he wrote."

The receptionist spoke into her headphones. "Got a visitor here about a story you wrote." She listened for a moment, looked at Ivy. "He says what story?"

"The Gold Dust Casino robbery," Ivy said.

"She says Gold Dust Casino robbery," the receptionist said. She listened again. "He says go on through. Last cubicle at the back."

She buzzed Ivy through the glass doors of the newsroom. Ivy walked down a row of cubicles, past a man typing quickly at a keyboard, a woman on a phone saying, "Spell that," and at the end, a man in a short-sleeve yellow shirt and bright red tie, poking a fat finger into a can of Almond Roca. He looked up.

"Tony Blass?" Ivy said.

"Tony B, in person," he said. He handed her a card imprinted with a flattering caricature of himself and the words *The World According to Tony B—Monday, Wednesday, and Friday in your Citizen.*

"Ivy Seidel," Ivy said.

He wrote her name on a notepad. "Got something for me?"

"Got something for you?"

"On the Gold Dust story." Tony B plucked a piece of Almond Roca shaped like Great Britain from the can and popped it in his mouth; a tiny flake of brittle sticking unnoticed to his mustache. "News doesn't get much older than the Gold Dust saga—been six years at least since I filed anything on it. So it figures you've got something."

"Sorry," Ivy said. "I don't know any more than this." She held up the "Guilty in Casino Murder" printout Sergeant Tocco had given her. "I was hoping you could fill me in."

"On what?"

"The whole story."

"Why?" said Tony B.

"I thought you might have more details than made it into the article."

"Oh, I do," said Tony B. "Yes indeedy. And I suspect a hell of a lot more. But my question"—he glanced down at the notepad—"Ivy Seidel, is, what's it to you?"

"That's hard to explain," Ivy said.

Tony B licked his fingers, dipped them back in the can. "Take your best shot," he said.

"Well," Ivy began, "I've been teaching writing at—"

"Whoa," said Tony B. "You're a writer?"

That question again, still without a yes-or-no answer, unless it really was no. "Not exactly," Ivy said. "But I am teaching the—"

He held up his hand. "What's not exactly?"

"It's what I want to be," Ivy said, annoyed that he'd made her say it out loud. "But right now I'm teaching the inmate writing program at Dannemora, and—"

"That where they've got Harrow?"

"Yes."

"Ah."

"What does that mean?"

"I'm way ahead of you," said Tony B. "You thought you'd solve the Gold Dust case, put yourself on the map."

"Put myself on the map?"

"By writing a big bestseller," Tony B said. "True crime sells."

Ivy let a moment go by: she realized she didn't like anything about Tony B, most of all the way he kept interrupting her. "My interest is fiction, Mr. Blass. Harrow wrote a story that showed a lot of talent, in my opinion. I wanted to find out more about him."

Tony B had big watery eyes. They looked her up and down. "Harrow wrote a story?" he said.

Ivy nodded.

"Your interest is fiction?"

She nodded again.

He held out the Almond Roca can, rattled the contents sociably in her direction.

She shook her head.

Tony B helped himself, thought things over, said, "What do you want to know?"

"Something about his background, for starters," Ivy said.

"Harrow? He's a punk."

Ivy rejected that out of hand: no punk could write like that. "He must have had some education," she said.

"Attended West Raquette High." Tony B swiveled around to his screen, put on a pair of glasses, hit a few keys. There was a sweat stain on the back of his shirt, in the broad soft space between his shoulder blades. Strange, but something about that sweat stain told Ivy what she should have figured out already: he had dreams of writing the Gold Dust Casino bestseller himself. "Nothing in my notes about graduating," said Tony B.

"He grew up in West Raquette?"

"Yup."

"What's it like?"

"A dump."

"How about his parents, things like that?" Ivy said.

"Dead end," said Tony B. "Nothing in his background leads to the money. I checked it all out."

"The money that was stolen?"

"We're talking about something else?"

He wasn't getting it. "We are, actually," Ivy said. "Did Harrow have a daughter?"

"Not that I recall." Tony B scrolled down the screen, shook his head.

"But there was a wife," Ivy said.

"Yes indeedy," said Tony B. "Betty Ann Price. Want to see a picture, at least how she looked seven years ago?"

Ivy moved closer. She could smell Tony B's sweat and his deodorant at the same time. A photo popped up on the screen.

"Is she Indian?" Ivy said.

Tony B shook his head. "Casino rules—all the dealers dress in tribal regalia."

"She worked at the casino?"

"A relevant detail," said Tony B, "since it was an inside job, whether the D.A. admitted that or not."

Ivy was a little lost. She gazed at the picture of Harrow's wife, young and beautiful, with short straight blond hair and fine features. "I'd like to hear the whole story," she said. "From beginning to end, if you've got time."

Tony B checked his watch. "Buy me lunch?"

"Sure," said Ivy, thinking, *After all that Almond Roca, he won't be hungry.*

But he was. They went to an Irish pub around the corner—green awning, shamrocks, leprechauns, grease smells. Tony B ordered steamed mussels and the rib eye, medium, with a side of onion rings. "Ale or lager?" he said.

"I'm not really—"

He ordered a pitcher of ale.

Ivy had leek soup.

"Cheers," said Tony B.

"Cheers."

Tony B patted at his mouth with a napkin, getting most of the spillover, and sat back. "Beginning to end," he said. "Know the north country at all, along the St. Lawrence?"

"No."

"Indians have a chunk of land up there, both sides of the river, U.S. and Canada. Don't recognize the white man's border. Also they've got cheap gas and smokes, in case you're ever passing through." He poured himself more ale. "Plus the casinos. In this case, especially comparing with Vegas or even Atlantic City, the word's a . . ." He searched for the right one.

"Misnomer?" said Ivy.

"Yeah." He gulped down a big drink. "Gold Dust is the nicest and it's a pit. But guess how much money goes through there on a daily basis."

"No idea."

"A hundred and fifty grand. Every day. Maybe double on weekends. And that was seven years ago. How it was then, the cash just sat in a safe in the back office till the armored car pickup at eight A.M. Betty Ann Price dealt blackjack there until two months before the robbery, knew the whole setup. All too tempting for a gang of small-time local hoodlums, namely Marv Lusk, Simeon Carter, Frank Mandrell—the brains—and Harrow."

"You've got a good memory," Ivy said.

"I lived with those scumbags for six months," said Tony B.

"I don't understand."

"That's how long it took me to write a book about the case."

"So there is a book?"

"If that means a published book, no," Tony B said. "A great yarn—my agent kept hearing that—but no ending, not without finding Betty Ann Price and/or the money."

"Who's your agent?"

Tony B named an agent Ivy had heard of. "I fired the asshole," he said. "How am I supposed to find Betty Ann when the cops couldn't?"

"Is that what your agent wanted you to do?" Ivy said.

"Hard to believe," said Tony B. "Those New York publishing types live in a fucking dreamworld." He sliced off a big chunk of rib eye, shoved it in his mouth, then said something that began incomprehensibly because he was chewing at the same time. ". . . so dumb it almost worked—ski masks, smoke bombs, sawed-off shotguns. But this security guard, Jerry Redfeather, recognized Simeon Carter. Ski mask isn't much use when you're a local guy, six-six, three-fifty, so Redfeather yells through the smoke along the lines of 'Carter, you son of a bitch.' At which point Carter starts blazing away, Redfeather blazes back, Carter, Lusk, and Redfeather all bleed to death within a minute or two, and in the commotion Harrow gets away with maybe three hundred and fifty grand, the exact amount never established on account of how much skimming's going on. Meanwhile Mandrell's waiting in a boat down by the river—the plan being to get away to Canada, where Mandrell's got a cousin—but Harrow never shows up. The Border Patrol spots Mandrell and picks him up, thinking he's a smuggler. Mandrell cuts his deal about an hour later, fingering Harrow as the third man. Not long after that, they grab Harrow at his house—this is all the night of the robbery—but Betty Ann's gone and the money, too. Harrow got offered a deal of his own—lesser sentence in return for Betty Ann's whereabouts. He turned it down, meaning it must have been true love. Which is where we are, as of now. Any questions?"

Ivy tried to take it all in. Robbery going bad at warp speed: a wild story. Part comedy, part—not tragedy, exactly, except for what had happened to Jerry Redfeather—but whatever word fit all that brutality, greed, stupidity. "Do you think the deal's still in place?" she said.

"Harrow getting time off or something if he coughs her up now?" said Tony B.

"Yes."

"If it is," said Tony B, "he could have done it already. Why would he change his mind now?"

Ivy thought: *Because of this talent he has;* a confused thought, perhaps, that she kept to herself.

"And that's assuming he's still got anything relevant at this late date," Tony B added. "Help me with the onion rings."

But he didn't need help: they were almost gone.

"What was the relationship between Harrow and Frank Mandrell?" Ivy said.

"Relationship?" said Tony B. "Mandrell was maybe ten years older, the brains, like I said. He'd met Lusk in the joint and Lusk and Harrow were related somehow. Guess you could say they fell under his influence—Mandrell was a big, good-looking guy, drove a Beemer, I think it was."

"Did it bother him, trading in Harrow like that?"

Tony B laughed. "Bother him? We're talking about the jungle here."

"Is that how he put it?"

"Who?"

"Frank Mandrell," Ivy said. "When you interviewed him."

"I never actually interviewed him," said Tony B.

Had she gotten the story wrong? "But didn't he go free?"

"Sure did," Tony B said. "But part of the deal was an identity change. Witness protection. He dropped out of sight right after his trial."

The waiter appeared. "Dessert?"

"Talked me into it," said Tony B.

Ten

"You are so far liking this criminal job?" Dragan said.
Down in the cellar under Verlaine's, Ivy hooking up a keg of Stella, Dragan bagging trash. "Yes," Ivy said.

A bag split, and a wet glob slopped to the floor. Dragan stooped to clean it up without complaint. "What is in your mind the attraction?" he said.

"The attraction?"

"Attraction?" said Dragan. "This is an incorrect word?"

"It's a correct word," Ivy said. "I'm just not sure what you're getting at."

"Getting at," said Dragan. "What a primo American phrasing turn! I am getting at what is for you the good of teaching criminals?"

Ivy rose. "It pays," she said.

"You are making sense," said Dragan. "Money is talking and bullshit is walking—this I learn from day one. But how can criminals do good writing?"

"They can," said Ivy. "Even very good."

Dragan got all the bags lined up at the base of the stone steps leading to the steel door at sidewalk level. "I would ask big favor from you," he said.

"What's that?"

"To read my novel."

"It's finished?"

"Plus two revises and final polishing," said Dragan. "I will of course pay you."

"Don't be silly, Dragan," Ivy said.

"You refuse to read it?" said Dragan. "I perfectly understand."

"I refuse to charge you," Ivy said.

Dragan smiled one of his huge unsightly smiles. "So you will read it?"

"Yes. But just remember my opinion doesn't mean anything."

He wiped his hand on his apron, held it out. They shook. Dragan didn't let go right away. "You are American woman," he said.

"That's true," said Ivy.

"My school friends and I, we many times discussed American women."

"And what was the verdict?" Ivy said, withdrawing her hand.

Dragan took a deep breath, as though one of those all-or-nothing rolls of the dice was coming. At that moment, Bruce yelled down the stairs, "What the hell's going on? I'm dying up here."

Danny Weinberg was sitting at the end of the bar, in Ivy's territory, but first there were some college kids she had to take care of.

"I'll have to see some ID."

Out came driver's licenses from various distant states. They all looked good enough to be genuine. She handed them back.

"Never been to Alabama myself," she said to the boy with the Alabama license.

"Check it out sometime," he said in an accent a lot like Bruce's, Brooklyn born and bred.

"After you," Ivy said.

"Huh?" he said. One of the kids guffawed. 'Bama boy turned red. Ivy served them anyway: Bruce balked at any kind of close ID analysis. He was a businessman, as he frequently said, not a clerk at the CIA.

Ivy worked her way down to Danny. His suit jacket hung over the back of his chair; Ivy read the label—*Hugh Griffin, Gentlemen's Tailoring, London.*

"Hi."

"Hi, Ivy. How are you doing?"

"Good. What would you like?"

"I've got two bits of news," Danny said.

Her heart understood before the rest of her, started beating faster.

"Whit likes your story," Danny said.

Faster and faster. "No. He does?"

"He does," Danny said. He was smiling, not as big a smile as Dragan's, but his teeth were perfect.

"Really?"

"Really."

"You're sure?"

" 'She's got a sly screwball take on modern life,' " Danny said.

"That's what he said?"

"Quote unquote."

"A sly screwball take?"

"Verbatim."

"But is that good or bad?"

"Good."

"Maybe it's a put-down."

"It's not a put-down."

"How do you know?"

"I know him."

"Screwball," Ivy said. "That's like those thirties movies."

"Yeah?"

"Bringing Up Baby."

"Don't know that one," Danny said.

"So maybe . . ." Ivy began. So maybe since the screwball reference had probably been lost on Danny, he might have misunderstood Whit after all. She looked into Danny's eyes, tried to see whether she could trust his interpretation.

"What's with that look?" Danny said. "You're scaring me."

"Where did this conversation take place?" Ivy said.

"What conversation?"

"With Whit, for God's sake."

"On the squash court, actually. We—"

At that moment, the door burst open and the Boerum Hill Gay Bowlers came in, about a dozen of them, in their pink satin team jackets. All of a sudden, everything speeded up, the way it did sometimes at Verlaine's. 'Bama boy was holding an empty beer bottle on his head, an amusing frat-boy signal for another round. Bruce, shaking up two martinis with savage force, glanced over at her.

"Got to go," Ivy said.

"When are you off?" said Danny.

"In an hour."

"How about dinner?"

Ivy paused.

"Don't you want to finish your cross-examination?" Danny said.

Ivy laughed.

They met at the River Café, sat at a window table. A barge glided by, all dark silhouette except for the pilot's face, green in the glow of his instruments, and a crewman at the stern reading a book by flashlight.

"Been here before?" Danny said.

"Way out of my price range," said Ivy. "I didn't know you played squash."

Champagne arrived. The cork popped with a promising little explosion. Ivy ordered the duck special.

"Excellent choice," said the waiter.

"Thanks," said Ivy.

This was nice. Her mind, restless and greedy tonight, wanted to flash forward to vignettes in the life of Ivy, best-selling novelist. She tamped it down as best she could.

"I try to get on the court once a week or so," Danny said.

"With Whit?"

"That was our first time," Danny said. "He's not much of a player—no touch at all."

"How did 'Caveman' come up?"

" 'Caveman'?"

"The title of the story."

"Oh, right," Danny said, refilling her glass, empty already. "I asked if he'd read it yet."

"And?"

"And what I told you," Danny said. "The sly-screwball thing."

"What else did he say?" Ivy said.

"That was it."

"Nothing about when he'd get in touch?"

"I'm sure it'll be soon," Danny said. "Relax."

Ivy relaxed. Yes, why not? So good to just relax.

Danny told a funny story about a recent flight to Taipei, a stressed-out flight attendant and a pet tarantula on the loose in business class. The duck—yes, an excellent choice—came and went. So did another bottle of champagne.

"Do you ever think of writing novels?" Danny said.

"Sure."

"Got any ideas?"

"There was one," Ivy said.

"All ears," said Danny, pouring more.

"It's not developed."

"I'll keep that in mind."

Ivy had never told anyone about this, not even Joel. But . . . but if things were really going to happen for her, why not? Why the hell keep holding back? She licked her lips. "It's about a surveyor. You know, those guys who—"

"I know."

"Anyway—" She took a big drink, really good champagne, the kind that just tastes better and better no matter how much you have—"this surveyor starts to find that nothing measures right."

"I don't get it," Danny said.

"First it's just little things, like the lot on an architect's plans doesn't quite line up with the lot on the ground. But then it starts happening everywhere, and soon she's—"

"She?"

"Why not?" Ivy said.

"No reason," Danny said. "Sorry. Go on. This is fascinating."

"It is?"

"More," said Danny.

"There isn't much more," Ivy said. "She gets to the stage where she's measuring everything—skyscrapers, cathedrals, bridges—and it's all a little off."

"The whole world's out of whack?" Danny said.

"Exactly."

"Wow."

"Yeah?" Ivy said.

"Wow," said Danny.

Ivy felt his foot against hers, under the table. She did nothing about it.

"And then what happens?" Danny said.

The bill came. While Danny paid, Ivy gazed across the river at that lit-up Manhattan skyline that always transfixed her. But now something was different, personal for the first time: not like she owned the place, but at least she belonged.

Then they were out walking, the night air cool but still. "And then what happens?" Danny said again, taking her arm. Ivy let him.

"Well," she said, "all this would have to relate to other things going on in her life."

"Like what?"

"That's where the development comes in."

Silence, except for the soles of their shoes clicking on the sidewalk; Ivy's that staccato high-heeled female click, Danny's the more muffled male kind.

"I know you'll come up with something," he said. "The perfect screwball something."

Ivy laughed. Maybe she really would come up with the perfect something; maybe she had it in her. Danny squeezed her arm. She squeezed back. A fancy block or two glided by. Then they were outside his place.

"Care to come up for a minute?" Danny said. "I could make coffee."

Ivy hesitated, even rocking back and forth slightly. She felt strong, physical, hot. The whole city was urging her on. But how much did it have to do with Danny?

"Or tea," he said. "Even hot chocolate."

"Sounds good," Ivy said.

And it was good; great, in fact, the first time, when those metaphors of lava buildups and eruptions or longtime dams finally bursting rang true. Months and months of not doing this couldn't be good, had to pollute your personal ecology in some way.

"Wow," Danny said.

Which reminded her that he was there, too.

The second time: not so good.

Although maybe that wasn't true for Danny, who said, "Wow squared," and cuddled up. But he was a very smart guy, noticed a lot, so soon she had a little space to herself. They lay there on the most comfortable bed she'd ever lain on, the lights low in his beautifully decorated bedroom, real art on the walls. She could feel him thinking.

"Something on your mind?" he said.

"Not much," Ivy said. "Just . . . this is nice."

"Yeah," said Danny.

A boat hooted in the river, or out in the harbor.

"Some music?" Danny said.

"If you want."

"What do you like?"

"Lots of stuff. What have you got?"

"Everything," Danny said.

"Everything?"

"Well," said Danny, "two hundred and seventy thousand downloads at last count. And wait till you hear the sound."

"How about Elvis?" Ivy said.

"Presley or Costello?"

"There's only one Elvis," Ivy said.

Danny rolled over, flipped open a laptop, tapped a few keys. Then came "Are You Lonesome Tonight?"—and yes, the sound was great, like Elvis was one pillow over.

"I love how he does that talking part," Ivy said.

"You do?" said Danny. "Isn't it a little hokey?"

"I guess so."

"But hokey can be good, right?" said Danny. "Is that what you're saying?"

Ivy was silent. She didn't feel like this sort of discussion.

"Something wrong?" Danny said.

He was so nice: What was the matter with her? But she was suspecting something: how exhausting his conscientious attempts to understand her completely, A to Z, would get.

"No," she said, "nothing wrong at all."

He patted her hip. Then his hand slid under her, came up between her legs.

"What was the other thing?" Ivy said.

"The other thing?" said Danny.

"You said you had two pieces of news. What was the second one?"

His hand went still. "It's a little out of left field," he said.

"Go on."

"Felix Balaban's wife wants to talk to you."

Ivy sat up. "What?"

"One of her lawyers was in the office the other day.

There's lots to clear up, as you can imagine. I happened to mention I knew someone who'd seen him in prison."

"Meaning me."

"Did I do something wrong?" Danny said. "I had no idea it would lead anywhere."

"What does she want to talk to me about?"

"The lawyer says she's still very upset. She wants some closure."

"How can talking to me give her that?"

"Who knows?" Danny said. "But look at it from her point of view. Her husband fiddles with some numbers—at the very worst—then gets whisked away behind walls and ends up with his head practically cut off by person or persons probably forever unknown. I think she just wants contact with a normal person who saw him in there."

"I only saw him once," Ivy said. "There really isn't anything to say."

"She's not a bad person," Danny said. "And of course she's left with the kids."

"He had kids?"

"Two girls—eight and ten, I think it is."

"You know it is," Ivy said. "And you've got their names in reserve."

Danny laughed. "Casey and Tamara."

His hand started moving again.

Ivy left before dawn. Danny didn't wake up. She walked home, let herself in, climbed the five flights. Her message light was blinking.

Whit?

You have one new message:

"Hello. I had a technical question for you. Maybe some other time." *Click.*

Ivy listened to it three times, just to make sure, but she'd known from the first syllable: Harrow.

She played it again. And once more.

Eleven

I'm Natasha Balaban. Thanks for coming."

Ivy shook hands with Natasha Balaban. She knew places like the Balabans' existed but had never been inside one; a Park Avenue place with the kind of furniture and rugs you saw in quiet museum side rooms. Maybe from being in constant touch with all that luxury, the air itself was different: still, thick, even weighty.

"Please sit," Natasha said.

Ivy took the nearest chair, small, gilded, delicate. It made an alarming little creak. Natasha sat opposite her on a velvet footstool. She wore black silk; Ivy had on jeans and her short leather jacket.

"Coffee?" said Natasha.

"I'm all right."

"It's no trouble."

A door opened and a uniformed maid appeared. She served coffee in beautiful translucent china cups. Natasha added cream and two spoonfuls of sugar from a heavy silver serving set; Ivy had hers black. The coffee itself tasted like what you'd get in any bodega.

Natasha took a little sip, lowered her cup, and didn't touch it again. "Danny Weinberg tells me you're a writer," she said.

"Trying to be," said Ivy. But she thought: *The New Yorker!* Maybe they'd put one of those cute little drawings—a flowerpot on a stoop, say—somewhere in her story.

"He says you're very talented," Natasha said.

"I don't know about that."

Natasha gazed at her: something a little askew about that gaze, didn't have to be a surveyor to see that.

"Oh, I'm sure Danny's right," Natasha said. "He's very clever. Felix always said so, and he had excellent judgment." She took a cigarette from a silver box, or perhaps platinum, from how solid it looked. The maid entered with a lighter. Natasha inhaled deeply, blew out smoke, and added, "About that sort of thing. In other ways, his judgment must have been not so good. To state the obvious."

Ivy nodded.

Natasha took another deep drag. "What was he like?"

"Who?" Ivy said.

The maid refilled Ivy's cup and withdrew.

"Felix, of course," said Natasha.

Natasha was asking what her own husband was like?

"In that writing class of yours," Natasha said, her voice sharpening with impatience.

"Oh," said Ivy. "The thing is, I only saw him once. I'd just taken over the class when he—when . . ."

One of Natasha's eyelids trembled. "Yes," she said. "I'm aware of the sequence." A cylinder of ash fell in her lap, unnoticed. Then came a silence, broken at last by Natasha. "*Felix* means 'happy' in Latin. Did you know that?"

"Yes," Ivy said.

"Not me," Natasha said. "We'd been married for years before I found out—first marriage for both of us, if that matters."

"Yes."

Natasha gave her a sharp look. "Meaning you think it does matter?"

"Yes."

Natasha took another drag, then dropped the cigarette into that lovely cup; kind of shocking, like an act of violence, and the sizzle it made seemed to fill the room. "*Felix* means 'happy,' " she said. "But I didn't know. You're a word person. Tell me—are there lots of words like that, with secret meanings?"

"I don't know about secret," Ivy said.

"Hidden, then," said Natasha.

"Yes," said Ivy. "At least partly hidden."

"I thought so," Natasha said. She rose, looked out an enormous window. The top of the Chrysler Building seemed very near. "So what was your impression of Felix?"

A timid little wreck: the true answer, but why say it? "As I mentioned, there wasn't really time to form an impression," Ivy said. "Plus I'd never been in a prison before—it's kind of overwhelming."

"But writers notice things," Natasha said.

Ivy said nothing.

"Well?" said Natasha. "Isn't that true?"

"He seemed . . . quiet," said Ivy.

"Felix was not a quiet man," Natasha said. "He must have said something."

Ivy thought back.

You calling me a liar, Felix?

Oh, no, no, no, no. Just that it was actually Cornell.

And:

What you say, amigo? I don' hear you.

It's nothing. Nothing at all. Sorry.

Sorry? He sorry.

"Nothing I can remember," Ivy said.

Natasha made a dissatisfied sucking sound, tip of her tongue against her teeth. "What about his writing? Did you save it?"

I really don't have anything today.

Felix don' have nothin' today.

"He didn't actually write anything," Ivy said.

Natasha turned, surprised. "Why not?"

"I don't know," Ivy said.

"Did the others write?" Natasha said. "The other prisoners?"

Gonna be real baaaaaaad if I'm blocked.

I'm sure that's not the case.

"They did," Ivy said.

A door opened again, but this time it wasn't the maid but a silver-haired man in a three-piece suit. "Traffic," he said.

"You're just in time," said Natasha. "Ivy here has been explaining that Felix didn't write anything in their one class together."

"Oh?" said the man.

"Ivy Seidel," Natasha said, "Herman Landau, my attorney."

"A real pleasure," Landau said, shaking hands. He had a rich, warm voice, a gentle grip, and—big surprise considering all that menschness—an unfriendly gaze. "I hear nothing but good things."

"From whom?" said Ivy.

"Danny Weinberg, of course," said Landau. "A young man on his way." He pulled up a chair like Ivy's. On a tapestry behind him, a knight with too-close-together eyes held his sword high. "Any idea why Felix didn't write anything, Ivy?"

"No."

"He was an organized man," Landau said. "Absolutely abhorred wasted time. So why would he bother to attend a class and not participate?"

"I don't know," Ivy said.

Landau sat back, crossed his legs; his pants made an expensive swishing sound. "Did the other inmates write?"

"She says they did," Natasha said.

"And what did they write?" said Landau.

"Poetry."

"Poetry?" said Natasha.

"Poems," said Ivy.

"And what were these poems about?" Landau said.

"Different things," Ivy said.

"Was Felix one of those different things?" Landau said.

"I don't understand," said Ivy.

Natasha made that quick sucking sound.

"Was Felix the subject of any of the poems?" Landau said.

"No."

"Was he mentioned in them?"

"No."

"Perhaps indirectly?"

"No," Ivy said. But at the same time, the last lines of El-Hassam's poem floated up in her mind: *a knife in the drawer / The very very sharp sharp knife/ Dream of a man.*

Landau sat a little straighter. "You're sure?"

"Yes."

He smiled; his teeth looked much younger than the rest of him. "I wouldn't mind having a quick look at the poems if you've still got them."

Ivy said nothing.

"*Do* you still have them?" Natasha said.

"Yes."

Natasha came closer. "Then we'd like to see them," she said.

"But why?" Ivy said.

"Why?" said Natasha. "Because they killed him, that's why."

"You're saying someone in the writing group was responsible?" Ivy said.

Landau's eyes shifted quickly to Natasha. "Not at all," he said. "But I'm sure you can imagine how painful this lack of closure is to Natasha and the children—to everyone who knew and loved Felix, for that matter."

"Closure meaning finding out who did it?" Ivy said.

"And meting out the appropriate response," Landau said.

"But isn't the prison still investigating?" Ivy said.

"In their way," Landau said.

"Meaning they don't give a shit," said Natasha. "For which they will pay."

Landau shot Natasha another quick look.

"You're going to sue the prison?" Ivy said.

Landau held up his hands. "Let's not get ahead of ourselves. Right now we're just hoping you can help us make things right."

"I don't see how," Ivy said.

"By showing us the poems," said Natasha. "We just told you."

Ivy shook her head. "There's nothing helpful in the poems."

"Then why can't we see them?" said Natasha.

Ivy rose. "It would be violating a trust."

"What is she talking about?" said Natasha.

"I'm baffled myself," Landau said. He turned to Ivy. "I can't imagine you signed any nondisclosure contract with the inmates."

"No."

"Then?"

"I'm their writing teacher," Ivy said. "Period."

Landau gazed up at her.

"Tell her," Natasha said.

"Tell me what?" said Ivy.

"That we'll subpoena her fucking poems." Natasha said.

"I'm sure we're not headed to extremes," Landau said.

"Are you?" said Natasha. She got up and left the room.

Landau sighed. "I believe she's still in shock," he said. "The children are devastated. Felix adored them. They wanted to visit him in prison, if you can imagine, but he wouldn't allow it." He leaned forward, patted the arm of Ivy's chair. "Please sit."

She sat. "I don't see why you're so focused on the writing class."

"It's just one area we're looking into," Landau said.

"But why the writing class specifically?"

"Felix called me after that class," Landau said. "I was on his list, of course."

"List?" Ivy said.

"The inmates have short preapproved lists of people on the outside they can call—collect and recorded."

"Collect?" said Ivy. "You hear an operator first?"

"Yes." Landau looked a little puzzled. "But the mechanics are beside the point. Felix found your class very upsetting."

"He did?"

"He'd hoped it would be a brief refuge. Instead he felt threatened."

"By whom?"

"He didn't say. That's where your help comes in."

"I'm not denying he felt threatened," Ivy said. "But I didn't hear any threats."

"Please explain."

"Felix wasn't like the others."

"In what way?"

"Softer, you could say."

Landau nodded. "Although he was a very hard man in the financial world. But of course things are different in prison. Felix had a terrible time, right up to about a week or so before he died."

"It got better?"

"They transferred him to a different block. He was being tortured by his old cell mate. I mean that literally. An obvious suspect in the murder, one of those Latin Kings, but the investigation is stalled for some reason. The new cell mate was different, took pity on Felix evidently, even to the point of confronting his tormentors. Felix was planning to bring him to the next writing class."

"Did Felix mention his name?"

"The new cell mate?" Landau took out a leather-bound notebook, flipped the pages. "Harrow," he said.

Just about everything Ivy had seen in the Dannemora library changed angles in her mind, forcing her out of the confines of writing teacher, period. "The man you want to look at," she said, "is Hector Luis Morales."

Back home, no new messages. Ivy checked that last old one.

Hello. I had a technical question for you. Maybe some other time.

No operator, nothing about calling collect. Ivy listened a few more times. Harrow didn't have one of those rich warm voices like Herman Landau. Landau's voice was about music and manipulation. Harrow's had other properties, less governable, maybe, like magnetism.

Less governable? Magnetism? Surely she was reading too much into it. Ivy listened once more just to be sure.

Twelve

"Hi."

"Hi, Danny."

"How are you doing?"

"All right."

"I've been thinking about the other night."

"And?"

"Just thinking about it." Danny's voice thickened. "A lot."

Ivy said nothing.

"And you?" Danny said.

In the background, a woman said, "Three and a quarter? Are they nuts?"

Danny lowered his voice. "Well?"

"Well what?" said Ivy.

"Have you been thinking about it, too?" he said. "The other night?"

The woman in the background said, "Then run the fucking numbers again."

"This isn't a good time to talk about it," Ivy said.

She heard a faint crash, like something had fallen off Danny's desk. "Is something wrong?" he said.

"It's not a good time."

"Tell me."

"I saw Natasha Balaban."

"I heard."

"Did you also hear that Herman Landau was there?"

Pause. "I didn't know that was in the cards," Danny said.

"You told me she just wanted contact with a normal person who saw him in there," Ivy said.

"That's what they said."

"They?"

"She," said Danny. "That's what she told me."

"So you didn't know about all these machinations."

"Machinations?"

"Like their own investigation," Ivy said, "and this lawsuit, and whatever else they're up to."

A longer pause this time. "Natasha's a very angry woman these days," Danny said. "Very angry and very rich."

But wasn't that the kind of thing that the boyfriend, man in your life, husband, was supposed to protect you from— not set you up for? Ivy kept that thought to herself: maybe it wasn't very evolved, a thought from the last century or the one before, when women weren't expected to protect themselves. She just said, "I'm the writing teacher. Period." *But no longer true: she felt a twinge inside.*

Danny laughed, a high little laugh that reminded Ivy of her high school and the smartest boy in the class. "But that's crazy," he said. "You're way more than that."

"Way more than what?"

"For Christ's sake, Ivy. Look what's happening with Whit. You're going places. Forget about Dannemora."

"I like that job," Ivy said.

"You mean you're not done with it?"

Clusters of people had magnetic power, as Ivy had realized rowing across Wilderness Lake; but Dannemora's power was disproportional, still strongly tugging at her here in the biggest city in the land, where it should have been completely overwhelmed. Why was that?

"Don't tell me you're going back there," Danny said. "It doesn't make sense."

In fact, she hadn't thought about it. This *New Yorker* thing probably did mean a whole new world opening up, but what parts of the old world should be preserved? She stole a line from Herman Landau, the kind of advice Natasha Balaban was probably paying seven hundred dollars an hour for: "Let's not get ahead of ourselves."

"Are you gathering material?" Danny said. "Is that it? Hasn't prison stuff been done to death?"

Professor Smallian had put that kind of question to rest on day one: *Everything's up for grabs—it all depends on the angle of attack.*

Ivy was walking up the block, a bag of groceries in hand— three Pink Lady apples, a pint of nonfat milk, carrots, lettuce, tomatoes, four ounces of smoked salmon, a loaf of seven-grain bread and a five-dollar bar of French chocolate, half of which she'd eaten on the way home—when she saw the mailman coming the other way. The mailman on Schermerhorn Street had a long gray beard, wore shorts all year long, hated dogs. Their paths crossed in front of Ivy's building and they ended up climbing the steps together.

"Seidel, five?" he said.

"Right."

He handed her a little bundle of mail.

Ivy mounted the stairs, groceries in one hand, mail in the other. She flicked awkwardly through the bills and catalogs, took a quick scan, and—what was that? A *New Yorker* envelope? She thumbed her way back to it, lost control of the mail, which slipped from her grasp, and—trying to snatch it from the air—she lost control of the groceries, too, and all kinds of things—bills, catalogs, apples, carrots, chocolate—went gliding and tumbling toward the second-floor landing. Ivy scrambled down the lopsided staircase, scattering this and that, finally laying hands on the *New Yorker* envelope.

She tore it open.

A letter. One single page. No check? Maybe a contract came first.But no contract either? Her eyes ran down the lines of type, way too fast to take anything in. She backed up, forced herself to go slow, word by word; even then the sense at first eluded her, as though she'd memorized vocab lists but in fact knew nothing of the English language.

Who was it from? Robert W. Whitmore, editorial department? Who the hell was Robert W. . . . *Whit.*

The language began coming back to her.

Dear Ivy,

After some deliberation here at the magazine, we've reached the decision that your story "Caveman" is not quite right for us at this time. It's still a fine piece of short fiction, marrying traditional narrative techniques with considerable postmodern thematic invention. On that point, it may be a little bit too "busy." Have you given any thought to expanding it to novel length?

Meanwhile, please accept this in an encouraging way. Send any future submissions directly to me at the above address.

Cheers,

not quite right
a fine piece
"busy"

Seven key words that added up to rejection. Rejection meant something was wrong with the story, but what? Ivy reread the letter, still had no idea. To come so close! Or had she? Maybe this was all a favor to Danny, and Whit hated every goddamn word. Was that possible? Was the whole world just a network of endless string pulling?

Ivy's heart was beating too fast, too light; she felt a bit dizzy, even stumbled slightly. A Pink Lady rolled off the lip of the second-floor landing and bumped its way down the stairs.

Ivy handed over her license—by now she knew to leave everything but that and the writing folder in the car—had her hand stamped VISITOR and passed through security. Taneesha met her on the other side, walked her to the library. An inmate watched her over a laundry hamper.

"How are things in the big city?" Taneesha said.

"Good question," said Ivy.

"Can't be worse than here," Taneesha said.

They went by a bank of wall phones Ivy had somehow missed before, inmates talking on every one, more waiting their turn.

"Is it true all calls are collect?" Ivy said.

"Oh yeah," Taneesha said.

"What happens if they try to make it not collect?"

"Won't go through," Taneesha said. "They all get their own PIN number so we know who makes any call, plus they're only allowed a few preapproved numbers on the other end, close family plus their lawyer." Taneesha glanced at her. "Why?"

"So they're not allowed cell phones," Ivy said.

"That's a joke, right?" said Taneesha.

Two big officers she'd never seen before stood outside the library.

"You guys know Ivy, the writing teacher?" Taneesha said.

"Hi," Ivy said.

They gave her a look that seemed a little long; maybe they were new. She went inside.

Three students already in place: Harrow at the far end; Perkins on the right; and on the left, his arm in a sling, Hector Luis Morales.

"Hello, everybody," Ivy started to say, but her throat had closed up and she had to clear it and try again.

"Hi, teach," Morales said. "I'm back."

He gave her a look that Ivy read as friendly and nothing else. She started handing out the pencils and papers.

"All stoked up for more poem writin'," Morales said.

"What would you like to write about?" Ivy said.

"Dunno," he said, taking a pencil and sticking it behind his ear. "Just wanna write and write."

"Great," Ivy said. "Anyone else have a suggestion?"

Harrow shook his head.

"How 'bout dusty death?" Perkins said.

"We did dusty fuckin' death," said Morales.

"Could do it again," said Perkins.

"Let's wait for El-Hassam," Ivy said. "Maybe he'll have an idea."

Morales laughed.

"What's funny?" Ivy said.

"El-Hassam," said Morales.

"Psych ward," said Perkins.

"What do you mean?" Ivy said.

"'Cross from the infirmary on A-block," Perkins said.

"But what's wrong with him?" Ivy said.

"Freaked fuckin' out," said Morales. "Seein' giant bugs and shit."

"But—" But El-Hassam had seemed so calm inside—except, she remembered that last time. *Sssssaaaaab:* when something snakelike had emerged. Ivy looked to Harrow, a look for help, as though to the only other sensible person in the room. No help there: Harrow was bent forward in concentration, already writing.

"You found something to write about?" Ivy said.

No reply. Harrow's pencil raced across the page, scratching out a faint sound like skiing in soft snow. Something made Ivy glance at Morales: he was watching Harrow, too. That huge vein in his forearm throbbed.

"Hey, man," said Perkins in his deep rumble. "Teacher talkin' to you."

Harrow looked up. The pencil kept going on its own for a second or two, like a primitive life-form with its head cut off. "What?" he said, his eyes foggy.

"She aksed you a question," Perkins said.

Harrow turned to her, eyes unfogging. "Sorry," he said.

"Nothing to be sorry for," Ivy said. "Find a topic?"

Harrow glanced down at the page, half-covered already. "Yeah."

"Maybe we could all take a crack at it," Ivy said.

"Crack," said Morales, making a little snickering sound.

"We writin' 'bout crack?" said Perkins.

"Nope," said Harrow. "Cops."

"Cops?" said Ivy.

"We all know something about cops," said Harrow.

"Amen," Perkins said.

"Teacher here don' know," Morales said.

"Huh?" said Perkins.

"What she know about cops?" Morales said.

They all looked at her.

"I once got caught shoplifting," Ivy said.

They all perked up.

"Yeah?" said Morales. "Rings? Watches?"

"Twizzlers," Ivy said.

"What the hell's that?" Morales said.

"Licorice candy," said Perkins. "My wife eat it all day long."

"You got a wife?" Morales said.

"One time," said Perkins.

Silence.

"This was the green kind," Ivy said. "I'd never seen the green kind before."

Harrow was smiling. Had she seen him smile before? Surely not, because she would have noticed how white and even his teeth were, all except the left—what was the word for those front ones? incisor?—all except the left incisor, made of gold. "How old were you?" he said.

"Fifth grade," said Ivy. "I must have been ten."

"What did the cop do?" Harrow said.

"Maybe it was a security guard, now that I think of it," Ivy said. "He told me if I ever did anything bad again he'd tell my parents."

"That it?" said Morales.

"And he said to stop crying."

Silence. Then Harrow started laughing. Perkins joined in, then Ivy, finally Morales, too. They were still laughing when Sergeant Tocco walked in. The laughing stopped.

"This must be where the fun happens," he said. He crooked a finger at Morales. "Got a minute?"

"Class ain't over," Morales said.

"For you it is," said Sergeant Tocco.

"Over for me?" said Morales. "I like this class."

"Maybe Balaban liked it, too," said Sergeant Tocco.

"Little Felix?" Morales said. His chair scraped on the floor. "What the fuck you talkin' about?"

"Play it that way if you want," Sergeant Tocco said. "But let's go."

Morales shook his head. "Not goin' nowhere," he said. "Class ain't done."

Three COs in riot gear pressed into the room, a hard wedge of clubs, shields, helmets. Morales jumped up, slipped his arm out of the sling. Sergeant Tocco took Ivy by the shoulder, pulled her out of the way. The COs crept forward with short precise steps like a six-legged organism. They bellowed at Morales: "Turn around. Hands on the wall."

But instead Morales lashed out with one of his legs, a tremendous kick that sent a shield flying across the room. Then he dove straight into the wedge, his huge fist pounding deep in the gut of the shieldless CO. The others struck back with their clubs, whacking Morales in the chest, the head, his bad shoulder. Ivy felt pain in her own shoulder, but it was only Sergeant Tocco's hand, squeezing hard. Morales cried out, went down. They fell on top of him, whacking and whacking.

From the other side of the table came a roar unlike any

Ivy had ever heard, deeply human but savage at the same time. Perkins vaulted right over the table, grabbed one of the card-table chairs, swung it at the backs of the COs struggling with Morales on the floor, swung it so hard it blurred in the air. Now a CO cried out, a cry even more agonized than Morales's.

Morales yelled, "Rip his head off."

Then Sergeant Tocco was on the other side of the library. He brought his club down on the back of Perkins's head, not especially hard but the placement must have been perfect because Perkins slumped to the floor without a sound.

A few minutes later, they were all gone—Morales and Perkins on stretchers, followed by the COs and Sergeant Tocco.

Taneesha entered. "You all right?" she said.

Ivy nodded. She realized she was squeezed up against the wall and came forward a little, legs not quite steady. Harrow sat in his chair with his hands folded on the table, hadn't moved the whole time.

"I'll walk you back," Taneesha said.

Ivy checked the clock on the wall. "Class isn't over," she said, feeling—somewhat crazily—very alive.

Thirteen

In the Dannemora library: Ivy at one end of the table, Harrow at the other; plus the wall clock. A very old wall clock, Ivy noticed for the first time. The red second hand paused with a click sixty times a minute, audible to her now with just the two of them in the room.

"You don't have to finish the hour on my account," he said.

"How about showing me what you've written?" Ivy said.

"I understand if it shook you up," Harrow said. He looked her in the eye, then away, then back again. Their gazes met; as they weren't supposed to in prison. "Scary shit like that," he added.

"You didn't seem scared," Ivy said.

"I'm used to it," said Harrow. "But there's a big gap between what just went down and your Twizzlers caper."

"What did just go down?" Ivy said.

Harrow shrugged. "Guess they want to talk to Morales about what happened."

"To Felix Balaban."

"Yeah."

"Meaning they think Morales was involved?"

"Oh, Morales did Felix, all right," Harrow said. He started folding his sheet of writing paper, making an airplane. "The only question is why it took them so long to figure it out."

Ivy felt her face getting hot, as though she were guilty of something bad.

"You okay?" Harrow said.

Ivy nodded. "Felix was so harmless," she said.

"What did he steal?" Harrow said. "Fifty mil?"

"I meant in here," Ivy said. "He was so harmless in here. Just a little guy, and all the others are so . . . physical. Why would anyone bother to hurt him?"

Harrow laughed. "You're funny."

"What do you mean?"

"People bother easily in this place," Harrow said. "The Kings especially."

"The Latin Kings?"

"They have a thing about respect," Harrow said. "Their only thing, really, and Felix had a way of talking that didn't go over well."

"They killed him for that?"

"Beats getting killed for nothing at all."

The clock ticked a few more times. Harrow finished his paper plane, sleek and tapered, making a tiny adjustment on one of the swept-back wings: a beautiful plane, actually.

"I hear you looked out for him," Ivy said.

Harrow glanced up "Who told you that?"

"His wife. I saw her a few days ago."

"Oh, yeah?" said Harrow. "Natasha, right?"

"Yes."

"How did that go?"

"She's very upset."

"Maybe she'll feel better soon," Harrow said. He paused, held Ivy's gaze. "When she finds out about Morales."

"You think so?" Ivy said.

"Wouldn't you?" said Harrow.

"I don't know."

"Sure you do," Harrow said. "Revenge feels good."

"Not to everybody," Ivy said.

"Call it justice, then," said Harrow. "Same feeling."

"What will happen to him?" Ivy said.

"Morales? He's a lifer already."

Ivy looked away. Nothing further was going to happen to Morales plus he'd done a horrible thing, so why did she feel ashamed of herself? "And Perkins?" she said.

"Perkins they'll throw in the hole for a while," Harrow said. "He just got caught up in the excitement. Lots of the guys in here are like that." He flicked the plane across the table. It flew in a long curve and glided down in front of her, landing smoothly.

Ivy unfolded it and read:

The Cop Who Busted Me

Let's call him Ferdie, maybe not as good a name as any, but it fits. Ferdie knocked on my door and said, "Police. Open up or we break it down." Or some similar cop hello that I didn't hear over the sound of the vacuum. Housework time, and I was just finishing up in the family room. Do I need to describe the family room? The only thing that might interest you was one of the photos on the mantel. Ferdie and I are both in it—Ferdie in the front row, beside the coach, holding the football, me in the back row at the end, smiling like I'd thought of something funny. Long gone, whatever that was.

Ferdie was nothing to me back in football days and less than nothing now. I'm happily going after dust balls under the tray table and the next thing I feel is his hard muzzle at the back of my head. Am I expecting company? No. That explains my overreaction and I don't even recognize Ferdie till he's down. Course he has backup—procedure is how they get control of the wild boys—and they work me over for a bit, completely understandable, no problem. Then Ferdie's back in the picture, a little different with missing teeth. One of them's in my hand; I've been clinging to it during the working-me-over part for some reason. Ferdie asks the big question, the one about where the money is. I can only laugh.

Ivy looked up. Harrow was watching her.

"Where did you learn?" she said.

"Learn what?"

"To write like this."

"Is it any good?"

"Don't you know?"

He shook his head.

"Did you go to college?"

"Have to graduate from high school first," Harrow said.

"You didn't?"

"Came close," Harrow said.

Ivy read the story again. "What made you decide to change tenses?"

"How do you mean?" said Harrow.

"Paragraph one's in the past, two's in the present."

"Yeah?" said Harrow. He got up, came around the table, read over Ivy's shoulder. His leg pressed a bit against the back of her chair. "Hey, you're right," he said, and returned to his seat, simple, everyday movements that should have made no impression on Ivy, but because of their economy and ease, did.

"You must have read a lot, growing up," she said.

Harrow shook his head. "But now I do."

"What do you read?"

"Right now I'm going through a Louis L'Amour phase."

Ivy had heard the name, couldn't quite place it. Harrow went to the shelves, brought over a worn paperback with a hard-eyed gunslinger on the cover.

"Never read him," Ivy said.

Still standing behind her, Harrow said, "I like the wide-open spaces."

Ivy felt a funny feeling down her spine, as though someone had blown in her ear. She lowered her voice. "How did you get my number?" she said.

"Information," he said, lowering his voice, too; and now she actually felt his breath in her hair. "Is there a problem?"

Ivy rose and faced him. "In terms of the preapproved lists and calling collect there is," she said. "Not to mention cell phones."

"Yes," said Harrow. "Better left unmentioned." He smiled. "But in terms of being the writing teacher—any problems there?"

Ivy thought about that. She was still thinking when Harrow backed quickly away. Taneesha stuck her head in the room.

"Time," she said.

Harrow put Louis L'Amour back on the shelf, started for the door. He stopped, turned to her. "Any chance I could see something you've written?"

Ivy checked her folder. She had El-Hassam's poem about the knife, Harrow's jacket, Tony B's article on the Gold Dust verdict, Whit's rejection letter—and a copy of "Caveman." She handed it to Harrow.

"Cool title," he said on his way out.

Ivy walked up the hill to her car, the prison wall on her right, the long view toward Lake Champlain scrolling up on her left. The intense fall colors were long gone, and now the dull ones were gone, too. The red Saab was the brightest thing around, by far. Ivy was unlocking it when she noticed a business card stuck under one of the windshield wipers.

Sergeant Tocco's card, with his name, position, and phone number printed on the front. She turned it over and found a single handwritten word.

Thanks.

Ivy ripped it up, tossed the pieces away. Getting in the car, she saw a guard watching from a tower high above.

Ivy drove out of town, came to the highway, pulled over. Bruce had left an old road atlas in the glove box. Ivy opened it to upstate New York, found Raquette, a little dot on the south side of the St. Lawrence. She totaled up the miles from Dannemora: 67.

Ivy got out her cell phone, called Verlaine's. Dragan answered.

"Ivy? This is you?"

"Is Bruce there?"

"Thanks God, no," Dragan said.

"Is something wrong?"

"Big dusting up with Chen-Li."

Chen-Li was the cook. "Don't tell me he fired him."

"Oh, no," Dragan said. "Chen-Li is quitting first. I am just now finished mopping up the damages."

"God."

"Any messages?" Dragan said.

"Tell him—" Ivy paused; she'd never done this to Bruce, not once. "Tell him I can't make it tonight."

"Cannot work the shift?" Dragan said.

"No."

"You are sick, or—"

"No. Just tell him I can't make it."

"I? I am telling him?"

"Put Anya on," Ivy said. "Maybe she'll work a double."

"Anya?" said Dragan. "She is quitting with Chen-Li."

Ivy drove into Raquette. First came a sign saying she was now on tribal land, then ramshackle houses with rusted-out car shells in the yards and glimpses of the river in between, followed by a gas station advertising the cheapest gas east of the Mississippi, plus tax-free cigarettes; and after that the Gold Dust Casino. She pulled into a half-full parking lot.

Ivy had been in a casino once before—spring break junior year, Paradise Island. She'd walked in, dropped a quarter in the first slot machine she saw, pulled the arm, and presto: $425, a silver torrent that spilled all over her lap. After that, she'd moved onto blackjack, losing every penny of her winnings plus a hundred dollars more, which meant skipping a few meals to make her money last the rest of vacation. The whole episode took twenty minutes. She'd walked out feeling punchy.

The Paradise Island Casino was a kind of cartoon palazzo. What had Tony B called this one? A pit? Ivy didn't see it that way, not from the outside. The Gold Dust Casino was built of logs, like a frontier cabin, but gigantic. She went inside.

"Welcome," said a middle-aged blonde in a buckskin miniskirt. "Here's a coupon for a free drink excluding champagne."

"Thanks."

"Enjoy."

Ivy wandered past banks of slot machines, most of them in use, onto a raised floor with roulette and blackjack tables and a deserted bar at the back. She sat down. A bartender appeared. Ivy asked for orange juice, sliding over the coupon.

"Juice is free," said the bartender, sliding it back.

Ivy gazed around the room, tried to picture the crime: three men in ski masks, smoke bombs, shotguns. Hard to imagine exactly how it was supposed to work in such a vast space. "Where's the office?" she said.

"The office?" said the bartender.

"The business office," she said. "Where they keep the safe, and all that."

"The safe?" said the bartender. "I wouldn't know."

He filled a dish with mixed nuts, pushed it toward her, then went off down the bar and made a phone call. Ivy sipped her juice, tried the nuts. Lots of Brazil nuts in there, her favorite. She realized how hungry she was, had a few more. A man in a business suit sat on the stool to her left. Another man, in a security-guard outfit, took the stool on her right. Kind of annoying, considering all the empty places, but Ivy had seen similar things at Verlaine's. When it came to single women, men could be—

"Got some questions, miss?" said the man in the suit. "I'm the manager."

Ivy turned to him: a copper-skinned man with glossy black hair. "Questions? I don't—" In the mirror she saw another security guard step up behind her. "Oh," she said. "You mean about the safe?"

"I do," said the manager.

The bartender watched from a safe distance. Ivy laughed. "For God's sake," she said, "you don't really think I'm—" What was the expression? She fished it up from her memory pool of bad movies. "Casing the joint?"

This was pretty funny, although no one else was laughing.

"Why else would you be asking?" said the manager.

"I—" What the hell was she doing, anyway? Ivy offered an answer that had some truth in it. "I'm interested in the robbery you had seven years ago," she told him. "I'm a writer."

"What paper?" said the manager. "You're supposed to go through our PR department."

"No paper," Ivy said. "I write fiction."

The manager was silent for a moment or two. "You want to write a fiction story about a robbery that really happened?"

"To use it as a base," Ivy said. "A taking-off point."

"Taking off to what?" said the manager.

"Good question," said Ivy. "I hope to find that out in the process."

The manager nodded, as though that made perfect sense. "What have you written?" he said.

The hateful question. "I haven't actually published anything yet."

"I'll need some proof," the manager said.

"Proof?"

"That you're a writer."

She had no proof—that was the whole goddamn point of her life right now. Ivy came close to saying: *Or what? What happens if I can't prove I'm a writer?* But then she remembered Whit's rejection letter. She reached inside her folder.

"Slow and easy," said the security guard behind her. A holster snapped open.

Ivy took out Whit's rejection letter slow and easy and gave it to the manager.

He put on reading glasses and read it. "I love their cartoons," he said, handing it back. "How can I help you?"

Fourteen

The manager held out his hand. "Leon Redfeather," he said.

"Ivy Seidel." *Redfeather:* a name like that was hard to forget; Ivy's hand wasn't quite steady when they shook. The security guards drifted away.

"Although I don't always get the jokes," Leon Redfeather said.

"Me neither," said Ivy. "I've been reading a little about the case, Mr. Redfeather."

"And you want to know if I was related to Jerry," Leon said.

"Yes."

"He was my dad," said Leon, rising. "I'll run you through the whole thing."

Somewhere nearby a woman said, "My lucky number's screwing up."

* * *

Ivy followed Leon back across the casino floor. "We were
smaller then," he said, "but the layout was just about the
same." He stopped near the entrance, heavy, brass-studded
wooden doors. "They came in at midnight, ski masks on, all
of them from West Raquette across the tribal line. The fourth
one—Frank Mandrell, supposedly the brains—was waiting
at the old boat ramp. I can take you down later. They had a
couple smoke bombs, handguns and a sawed-off twelve-
gauge, but how much of what happened was planned and
how much was improvised no one knows. First thing they
did was grab a waitress who was walking by right where you
are. Then they moved toward the counting room." Leon
pointed to a stretch of wall lined with slot machines. "The
old counting room," he added. "Two doors there back then,
counting room and staff room. My dad, just finishing his
break, came out of the staff room."

Ivy had an unhappy thought. "Were you here that
night?"

"Still in grad school," said Leon. "Hotel management."
The front doors swung open and mobs of people hurried in;
a bus was parked outside and more were driving up. "But
I've seen the robbery," Leon went on, "many times."

"It's on tape?" Ivy said.

"This is a casino," Leon said.

Ivy glanced up at the ceiling.

"Smile," Leon said.

They sat in Leon Redfeather's office, nothing grand or or-
nate about it, simple furniture, a view of the river—so wide
the northern bank was just a low smudge on the horizon—

and portraits of Indian chiefs on the walls. Ivy recognized Sitting Bull and Red Cloud. Leon slid a tape into the VCR.

Black-and-white: three men in ski masks flickered onto the screen. The smallest one had his arm around the throat of a woman in one of those buckskin miniskirts and held a gun to her head, the muzzle actually in her ear. Her mouth was open wide, a huge black hole. Leon stopped the tape. "That's Marv Lusk," he said. "A month or so out of jail, where he'd met Mandrell. Lusk was a cousin, distant, if I remember, of the guy in the back—Vance Harrow. The big one with the shotgun is Simeon Carter."

Leon pressed play. They all moved toward the counting-room door, a heavy steel door that didn't match the frontier-style decor. The door next to it—knotty pine with a wagon wheel on the front—opened and out came a security guard buttoning his jacket. His face reminded Ivy of the portraits on the wall. He took everything in right away, faced the big man with the shotgun.

The tape froze. "Dad was a big football fan," Leon said, "and Simeon Carter had come out of West Raquette High a few years before. Best lineman they ever had, twice the size of every other kid, or anyone else in the county, for that matter."

Leon rose, went to the TV. "This woman here?" An old woman with enormous glasses, umbrella drink in hand. "She heard the whole thing. My dad said, 'Hey, Simeon, you big dummy, what the hell do you think you're doing? Go on home before you land yourself in a heap of trouble.'" Leon paused, standing close to the image of his father. "A generation-gap kind of comment," Leon said. "Could have been funny under other circumstances."

"I'm sorry," Ivy said.

"He didn't need the job," Leon said. "Even the way revenues were then when we were starting out, he could have

lived off his share. But my dad . . . well, you had to know
him." He went silent.

Ivy stared at the frozen images: the terrified waitress, Leon's stern father, and three hidden faces, although Marv
Lusk's gritted teeth showed through the mouth opening in
his mask. Carter was looking down at Jerry Redfeather. Harrow was reaching inside his jacket; his posture seemed a little
awkward.

Leon went back to his chair, reached for the remote. Action. Simeon Carter swung the shotgun at Jerry Redfeather,
cracking him on the side of the head. Jerry toppled over,
but as he fell, he drew his gun. The muzzle flashed and
suddenly there was a big rip across the top of Lusk's mask
and he was falling backward. The waitress ran away. Jerry,
on the floor now, looked stunned, as though he'd had the
breath knocked out of him. Carter stepped back, the shotgun in one hand now, pointing down at Jerry. Jerry started
bringing his gun up. The shotgun went off, a big white
blast on the tape, and Jerry got jolted a few feet across the
floor; but Ivy also saw a smaller, simultaneous glare sprout
from Jerry's gun.

Carter peered down at his own chest, as though in surprise. He took two steps backward, then slumped to the
floor in a twisted heap. Harrow stepped over Carter's body,
stumbling a little, and tossed a canister to his right. He bent
over Jerry, ripped a key chain off his belt. Smoke came
curling into the picture. Harrow unlocked the counting-
room door and went in, gun raised.

The smoke grew thicker. Harrow came out in seconds, a
duffel bag over his shoulder. He ran to the left, out of the
frame.

Another man appeared, slow and cautious, a handker-
chief over his mouth. He knelt over Jerry, felt for a pulse in

his neck, moved on to Carter, finally to Marv Lusk. Lusk raised his head an inch or two. His lips moved.

"A doctor who happened to be there," Leon said. "Lusk tells him that it's all Frank Mandrell's fault."

Blood came seeping out of Lusk's mouth; then it poured. The smoke thickened. Leon switched off the machine.

His gaze met Ivy's.

"That must be hard to watch," Ivy said.

"At first," Leon said. But his eyes weren't quite dry.

"Your father was so brave," Ivy said.

"He wouldn't have seen it that way," said Leon. "Any of this helpful to you?"

Ivy didn't know. How hateful the tape was, in so many ways; the very worst, maybe, being how Harrow ripped the keys off Jerry's belt.

"Could I just see the very end part again," Ivy said, "where he runs out?"

Leon replayed the end. Harrow had one of those duck-footed runs, with a short, choppy stride, almost clumsy.

Leon drove Ivy along a bumpy dirt road that ran by the river and dead-ended at a huge willow tree, branches trailing in the water. They got out of the car, walked down a boat ramp, the cement all cracked, the sides eroding. A cold wind blew from the Canadian side. The river made a sound like *shhh*.

"Frank Mandrell was waiting for Harrow right here," Leon said. "He had a little runabout tied to the tree. The Border Patrol launch was out that night and they spotted him—his name had already gone out over the air. Whether Harrow double-crossed him wasn't clear, but Mandrell made a deal on the spot, giving up Harrow as the third robber. They grabbed Harrow over in West Raquette, where he was living with Betty Ann Price. Betty Ann was already gone and so was the money." Leon watched a Styrofoam cup float quickly by. "Two hundred ninety-seven thousand five hundred and twenty dollars was the exact amount, no matter what you've read. And there was no skimming. They must think we're stupid."

"Who?" said Ivy.

"White people," Leon said. "The counting-room jobs are all tribal. Why would we skim from ourselves?"

They got in the car. Leon turned the key but they didn't go anywhere; he watched the wind ruffling up the water in spiky little bumps. "What kind of story are you planning?" he said.

"I'm not sure yet," Ivy said. "I need to know more."

"Such as?"

"What Betty Ann Price was like, for example."

Leon turned up the heat. "Can't we start with an easier one?"

"I figured you knew her," Ivy said. "Didn't she work at the casino?"

"Dealt blackjack for a few months," Leon said. "She quit five weeks before the robbery. But as for knowing her, I guess I really didn't."

"How do you mean?"

"Ever thought how hard it would be to just vanish with three hundred grand, actually get away with a crime like that?" Leon said.

"No." She hadn't done much thinking about crime at all. "It would be like a job all its own."

"Exactly," Leon said. "The kind of intelligence, planning

and self-discipline required would guarantee success in practically anything legitimate."

"Are you saying Betty Ann wasn't smart?" Ivy said.

"Average," Leon said. "Except for her looks—especially her body, if you want the truth—she seemed like an average small-town girl in every way, the last person you'd pick to get away with something like this. Close to her sister, for example—who's still here, but of course any contact means game over. Ferdie keeps a pretty close eye on the sister."

"Ferdie?"

"Ferdie Gagnon, detective in West Raquette," Leon said. "A rookie cop, back then—he brought Harrow in." A big bird—hawk, maybe, Ivy wasn't too good at identifying birds—glided low over the river. "Want to meet him?" Leon said.

"You're the second writer's been in here asking about this," said Detective Ferdie Gagnon. Lots to see on Detective Gagnon's face: big nose, heavy jaw, ridged brow, and almost lost in all that two confident little eyes. "The first one had an angle."

"Tony Blass?" Ivy said.

"Yeah," said Gagnon. "Know him?"

"We've met," Ivy said.

"That book of his come out yet?"

"No."

"The way you say that's like it's not gonna."

He'd read all that in one word? "I don't think he's actively pursuing it right now," Ivy said.

"'Cause he can't sell it," said Gagnon. "Who wants to read an unsolved mystery?"

"That's what his agent told him," Ivy said. "What was it about Tony's angle you didn't like?"

"I don't remember saying I didn't like it," Gagnon said. He gazed at Ivy. Something shifted, just beneath the surface of his eyes. "Crimes can be complicated enough," he said. "No need to mix in a lot of conspiracy theories."

"Like?" Ivy said.

Another quick shift, just below the surface. "Like there was some kind of cover-up."

"Cover-up of what?" Ivy said.

"You got it," Gagnon said. "Carter and Lusk died on the spot, Harrow got twenty-five years, Mandrell pled out, and there's still a warrant for Betty Ann. Where's the cover-up?" He leaned across the table—they were in the Main Street Diner in West Raquette—and waited for an answer.

"Leon Redfeather doesn't think Betty Ann—" Ivy began.

"Had the brains to pull this off," Gagnon said. "I know what Leon thinks. But he's wrong on this one. Sometimes people turn out to be smarter than they let on." He pointed a finger at her; Ivy hated that. "So get one thing out of your mind—if she had help it didn't come from us."

"That was never in my mind," Ivy said. Although now it was.

Gagnon sat back. "Good," he said. "How's your coffee?"

"Good."

"Good." He poured another packet of sweetener into his. "So what's *your* angle?"

What was it? What the hell was she doing? Ivy poured sweetener into her coffee, too, even though she never used it, and stirred for maybe a little too long. The true answer—and this thought was barely under way before some minithought, quashed so fast it almost didn't register, popped up and told her she was lying to herself—the true answer had to do with Harrow's talent and her need to somehow find out where it had come from. But explaining all that, especially since Harrow and Gagnon had a history that couldn't be good, would only lead to a tangle right now; and wasn't it also possible that Danny was right about her motivation, and this whole thing was about gathering material?

"I don't have an angle, Detective," she said. "My intention is to use this story as the basis for a work of fiction."

"Like a murder mystery?" said Gagnon.

"Maybe," Ivy said.

"The only mystery guy worth reading is Ross Macdonald," Gagnon said.

Ivy didn't read mysteries, hadn't heard of him. "Can you recommend a title?"

"The Underground Man," Gagnon said.

"You read a lot?" Ivy said.

"Used to."

"And now?"

"Too busy." His cell phone rang, like the show part of show-and-tell. He opened it, said, "Yup," and flipped it shut. "So," he said to Ivy, "what next?"

"I'd like to see Harrow's house," Ivy said.

Fifteen

B een up this way before?" said Detective Gagnon.

"No," Ivy said.

They drove down Main Street in an unmarked car, went past a video place with dusty windows, a going-out-of-business furniture store, and some boarded-up shops. "Nothing too fancy," said Gagnon, watching her from the corner of his eye. "But a nice town."

"Is there much crime?" Ivy said.

"What you'd expect," said Gagnon. "Our main problem is lack of opportunities when the kids get out of high school."

"I'd like to see the high school," Ivy said.

"We can swing by," Gagnon said. "Our other problem is you throw a casino into a place like this, it's kind of . . ." He searched for a word.

"Destabilizing?" Ivy said.

He glanced at her. "Yeah. Exactly."

Gagnon turned off Main, away from the river, and climbed

a long hill. Fields opened up on the right, and then came goalposts and a low brick building with peeling trim. Gagnon slowed down. WELCOME TO WEST RAQUETTE HIGH, read one of those marquee-on-wheels signs out front. *Where the Future Happens* it added at the bottom, although the *e* had fallen off *future*. A school-bus driver in the parking lot lay slumped over his steering wheel.

"I understand you played on the team, too," Ivy said.

"Leon tell you that?"

Mistake: she'd actually inferred it from Harrow's "The Cop Who Busted Me" story, didn't even know it was true. Ivy was still thinking how to handle this, when Gagnon continued. "His dad was a big fan, came to all the games. Harrow and Carter were sophomores my senior year. We played together that one season."

"What position were you?" Ivy said.

"Know something about football?" said Gagnon.

"I was a cheerleader in high school."

"I don't believe it," Gagnon said.

"Give me a *B*," said Ivy.

"B?"

"For Brookfield," Ivy said. "The rampaging Rough Riders of Brookfield High."

"Any good?" said Gagnon.

"At science fair," Ivy said. And soccer: the truth was she'd dropped cheerleading to concentrate on playing goal after one year.

Gagnon smiled. "We went to the districts once or twice. I was the quarterback."

"Did Harrow and Carter get much playing time?" Ivy said.

Gagnon's eyebrows rose; she did know some football. His posture changed slightly, unstiffening. "Yeah, they got playing time. Carter was probably a potential D-one college player. And Harrow was fast—played wide receiver and ran back kicks."

"So you must have thrown passes to him."

"Sure. Hit him for a fifty-yard touchdown on Thanksgiving Day."

"What was he like?"

"As a high-school sophomore?" Gagnon thought for a moment or two. "Quiet."

He made another turn. The houses got farther apart and more run-down. A chicken flapped furiously in someone's yard, maybe still not convinced it couldn't take off. Then came a street sign: RANSOM ROAD. Ivy felt a strange little thrill, kind of like when in Paris her junior year she'd gone to the Louvre and seen the *Mona Lisa*—it was real. But Gagnon went right on by Ransom Road, kept going for two or three miles, then took a nameless dirt track into the woods. He rounded a bend, drove up a slope, and parked in front of a small house with trees closing in around it and a fading For Sale sign outside.

"This is it?" Ivy said. She'd expected a trailer, and at the bottom of a hill.

"Been empty for a year or so," said Gagnon. "Want a look inside?"

"Sure," Ivy said.

They got out of the car, walked up to the house. Gagnon unlocked the door.

"Is that some kind of master key?" Ivy said.

Gagnon pointed to the sign: GAGNON REALTY. "One of my mom's listings."

He led Ivy into an empty rectangular living room. It had a bare wooden floor, a mound of ashes in the fireplace, and yellow-and-red floral wallpaper that made you want to get out of there fast.

"It was all carpet at that time," Gagnon said. "Beige, I think. He was vacuuming, had his back to the door, didn't hear me come in."

"How long after the robbery was this?" Ivy said.

"Half an hour, forty-five minutes," said Gagnon. *Going bad at warp speed.* "As soon as Mandrell's tip went out, we headed here."

"Isn't it a little strange," Ivy said, "vacuuming at a time like that?"

"Probably getting rid of evidence before he took off," Gagnon said.

"And Betty Ann was already gone with the money?"

"Yup."

"He told you that?" Ivy said.

"Not in so many words," Gagnon said. "But it was obvious—no money, no Betty Ann."

Ferdie asks the big question, the one about where the money is. I can only laugh.

"Did he resist?" Ivy said.

"Not much," Gagnon said.

Then Ferdie's back in the picture, a little different with missing teeth. Gagnon looked strong, but nothing like Morales, and Ivy had seen what Harrow did to him.

Ivy walked through a low arch into the kitchen. She tried a tap at the sink; no water came out. "Why didn't they go together?"

"Smarter to travel separately," Gagnon said, "meet up at some prearranged spot."

Ivy opened a door, gazed down a flight of plywood stairs, covered in dust. One of those simple robberies gone wrong, a movie staple, but there was so much about it she didn't understand.

"What do you think the original plan was?" she said.

"Don't have to speculate," Gagnon said. "Mandrell gave it all up, part of his deal."

"And?"

"In Mandrell's version, the whole idea was Harrow's. We didn't give that much credence—Mandrell was smarter than the other three put together. After the robbery they were all supposed to meet at the boat ramp, Betty Ann included. The fact that she didn't show is how Mandrell knew Harrow was double-crossing him and not just improvising after Jerry Redfeather made his play."

"Meaning Harrow had it in mind the whole time?" Ivy said.

"You got it."

Ivy flicked the switch for the basement lights. Nothing happened. "If that's true," she said, "why was everyone so sure Mandrell was the smart one?"

Gagnon smiled. His front teeth: yes, a little too white and undifferentiated in shape to be real. "Good point," he said. Then he made a better one. "But Harrow's the one doing time."

"And Mandrell's in the witness protection program?" Ivy said.

"Part of his deal."

"What was he getting protected from?"

"Harrow, of course."

"But he's locked up."

"No reason you'd know this, being a civilian, but guys reach out from prison all the time," Gagnon said. "And Betty Ann's out there somewhere."

"Is she dangerous, too?" Ivy said.

"The kind of money she got away with?" Gagnon said. "Hires as much danger as you need."

"Leon says you keep an eye on her sister."

"Claudette," Gagnon said. "A year or two older. They were close."

"I'd like to talk to her."

"I can set that up."

Ivy bent down for a better angle on the basement. Faint light penetrated a high, dusty window, illuminating a low stack of cement blocks on the dirt floor. "I'd like to talk to Mandrell, too," she said.

Gagnon blinked. "He's in WP."

"But does that mean I couldn't talk to him?" Ivy said. "Even just on the phone?"

"I don't know," Gagnon said.

"Who would?" said Ivy.

Gagnon looked at her. "A mystery novel, based on the case?" he said. "That's what we're talking about here?"

"Something like that."

"I'll make a few calls," Gagnon said.

Gagnon arranged for her to meet Claudette Price at six. That left Ivy a couple hours to kill. She drove around West Raquette, finally understanding that most of what she saw was rural poverty, or something close. The football team was out practicing. On her third or fourth pass by the high school, Ivy stopped to watch.

The players wore orange game pants, white practice jerseys, orange helmets. Offense against the defense, with only a handful of reserves. They ran the same play over and over, one of those off-tackle plays that was just plain boring to watch. It started to drizzle. The boys got muddy, color fading all around, bright orange turning brown. After a while, the coach—a bent old guy—blew his whistle. The team headed back toward the school, which meant crossing the parking lot, cleats clacking on the pavement. The coach, mesh bag of footballs over his shoulder, came last. Ivy got out of the Saab.

"Coach?" she said. "A quick word?"

The coach squinted at her. He had wild white eyebrows and a nose that had been broken more than once.

"Do I know you?" he said.

"Ivy Seidel," Ivy said. "Have you been the coach here long?"

"Thirty-nine years," he said. "Does that count for long?"

Ivy ran through her story—book, research, robbery; it came out in a jumble that invited the answer no.

"You want to talk about Vance Harrow?" the coach said. "C'mon in out of the rain."

The coach had an office next to the locker room. Sounds of the boys shouting, laughing and crashing around came through the walls. The coach didn't seem to hear.

"Harrow was a pretty good player," he said. "But not in Simeon Carter's class. Carter was the best player ever come through here. Besides which he had a mean streak wide like so." The coach spread his hands. "Carter, I'm talking about. Could have actually ended up making some dough out of this dumb game."

"But?" said Ivy.

"He was a bad kid."

"And Harrow?" Ivy said. "Was he a bad kid, too?"

"Nope." The coach gave her a quick glare, then looked away. His voice, harsh and reedy, softened a little. "Growing up, town like this, you need some breaks."

"Did things go wrong after high school?" Ivy said.

"Went bad long before high school," said the coach. "Vance had the cards stacked up against him pretty good."

"Are you talking about his home life?"

The coach nodded. " 'Cept it wasn't even his home."

"What do you mean?"

"Kid lost his parents when he was eight or nine," the coach said. "Had to move in with some cousins or whatever they were. Pure trash."

"How did he lose his parents?"

"Killed in a wreck."

"On Ransom Road?" Ivy said.

"Ransom Road?" said the coach, voice back to normal. "Where'd you get that idea?"

"I must be mixed up."

"Must be," said the coach. "This wreck was up in Canada. They got caught in one of them ice storms."

Pieces of Harrow's story began rearranging themselves: *Ice storm, but not on Ransom Road; a house, not a trailer; at the top of a hill, not the bottom.* A quote from Picasso that Professor Smallian wrote on the board at the start of every semester popped up in Ivy's mind, a quote she'd memorized word for word:

Destroy the thing, do it over several times. In each destroying of a beautiful discovery, the artist does not really suppress it, but rather transforms it, condenses it, makes it more substantial. What comes out in the end is the result of discarded finds.

"Which," the coach went on, "was how Vance ended up living with the Lusks."

"The Lusks?" Ivy said. "Marv Lusk's family?"

"Trash," said the coach. "Pure and simple."

"Can you give me an example?"

"Trust me," said the coach. "A wonder he got out of there in one piece."

"Just a brief one," Ivy said.

"You're a writer—use your imagination," said the coach. "But what I can do is show you some tape."

"Tape?"

"Of Vance back then." The coach went to a shelf, plucked out a cassette tape, stuck it in a VCR. "We got a budget of nothin' up here, so excuse the quality." He fast-forwarded. "This is Thanksgiving, kind of a famous play hereabouts." He slowed the tape to normal speed: the ball at midfield, snowflakes blowing through the air. A team in purple and green waited at the line of scrimmage. West Raquette, orange top to bottom, trotted out of the huddle. The center—a huge kid—dug in over the ball.

"Carter," said the coach.

The quarterback came up under center. "Ferdie Gagnon, be chief of police here one day soon," the coach said, "but then he was just one more in a long line of mediocre quarterbacks come to curse me. And flanked out wide—that's Harrow."

"Number ninety-nine?"

"Yup," said the coach. "Thirty-one seconds left, down by five."

Carter snapped the ball to Gagnon, who backpedaled into the pocket. "Play's called goat forty-three slant," said the coach. His face got a little flushed: a dumb game but he still loved it.

Ninety-nine ran a diagonal pattern about ten yards downfield. Gagnon lofted a wobbly pass, much too high, but ninety-nine leaped up and grabbed it, came down already changing direction, darted past a tackler, dodged another, and took off down the sideline.

"Whee," said the coach, quiet, to himself.

Ninety-nine had a long, easy stride that looked effortless but chewed up the yardage. No one got near him. Touchdown. Ninety-nine wheeled in the end zone to greet his teammates, charging into the picture. The tape froze; a grainy tape, the focus not always right, but ninety-nine's grin was visible through his face mask.

"You're sure that's Harrow?" Ivy said.

"Huh?" said the coach.

"Ninety-nine."

"Course I'm sure," said the coach. "I look senile to you?"

"Sorry," Ivy said. "I just meant . . ." What did she mean?

"What?" said the coach.

"Did anything bad happen to him later on?" Ivy said.

"Hell, yes. He got himself caught up in that goddamn robbery and ruint his life."

"I meant did he get injured?"

The coach shook his head. "One of those shifty kids that's hard to lay a clean hit on. Played every down for me right through senior year."

"What about after high school? Did he ever get hurt then?"

"Not that I heard," said the coach. "What are you driving at?"

"I don't know," Ivy said, although by now she kind of did. Ski-mask Harrow was a duck-footed runner, slow and clumsy; this grinning Harrow frozen in the end zone was a beautiful athlete, born to run, his stride classic. And therefore?

The coach switched off the machine.

"Any of this help?" he said.

Sixteen

At six o'clock, the doors of the Wal-Mart near the bridge to Canada slid open. Some Wal-Mart workers came out, still wearing their smocks, and headed into the parking lot. One of them, a pretty woman with a wild cascade of blond hair, glanced around and saw the Saab. She came over, every step closer aging her a little more. The woman ended up looking about thirty-six or -seven, although Ivy knew she was a few years younger than that. The button on her smock read: *Hi! I'm Claudette. How May I Help You?*

Ivy rolled down the window.

"You who Ferdie Gagnon sent?" Claudette said. She had a husky, smoker's voice.

Ivy introduced herself.

"You're writing about Betty Ann?" Claudette said.

"Not directly," Ivy said. "But she's part of my research."

Claudette ran her eyes over the Saab. "This yours?"

"Yes."

"Nice ride," Claudette said.

"Is there somewhere we could talk?" Ivy said. "Maybe I could buy you dinner."

"You like Chinese?" Claudette said.

"I do." There was a Northern Szechuan restaurant around the corner from Verlaine's that she loved, and the Shanghai vegetarian place a few doors down from that was almost as good.

"Me, too," said Claudette. "Let's stop by the Tiki Boat."

"Should I follow you?"

"Nah," said Claudette. "I'm not in driving mode at present." She walked around the car, got in the passenger seat. "Hang a left out the lot." Claudette yanked off her smock and tossed it in the back. "Mind if I smoke?"

Ivy did mind, but that was no way to start. "Not if you don't," she said.

Claudette, pack of generics already out, paused. "Hey," she said, "that's pretty funny." She lit up, inhaled deeply, cracked open the window and tossed out her match. "Okay me stealing that?"

"Stealing what?" Ivy said.

"That not-if-you-don't line," Claudette said.

"Fine with me," Ivy said. She turned left, followed the highway along the river, back toward West Raquette. Nighttime now, the river blue black and oily, lights flickering on the far side. "It must be nice, living by the river," she said.

Claudette shrugged. "I don't fish or nothin'. Take the second right."

They sat at the back of the Tiki Boat, under a dusty red lantern with a few fly carcasses stuck inside. Claudette took off her jacket. She had a body that was crossing the line

from extreme voluptuousness to something else. The waitress came over.

"Share a firebowl?" Claudette said.

"Why not?" said Ivy, not sure what it was.

The waitress returned with a large earthenware bowl and
a male helper. He held a match to the mustard-colored liquid inside and intoned, "South Sea Firebowl." It blazed up.
Claudette tore the wrapper off her straw and, as the flames
died down, started slurping away.

"Gonna let me drink this all by myself?" Claudette said.
"You'll be sorry."

Ivy unwrapped her straw.

"Good, huh?" said Claudette a minute or two later.

"What's in it?" Ivy said. Despite her bartending experience, she really couldn't tell.

"You name it," Claudette said.

Ivy scanned the menu.

"Don't bother with that," Claudette said. "Piggy platter's
the specialty of the house." They ordered a piggy platter,
with a side of the Mongolian fries for Claudette.

"Mmm," Claudette said, licking her fingers. "So what do
you wanna know?"

Ivy, her head already buzzing a little from the South Sea
Firebowl, tried to organize all the information. The question that rose to the top was one she actually hadn't formu-
lated till that moment, although it had almost come up in
her talk with Tony B. "Do you think Harrow knows where
Betty Ann is," she said, "and is still protecting her?"

Claudette chewed thoughtfully. "If he is," she said, "it
just proves how dumb men can be."

"What do you mean?"

"Don't tell me you think men are smart?"

"Some of them, yes," Ivy said.

"Then maybe we're not going round in the same circles," Claudette said. She pointed a rib bone at Ivy. "What I've had fucking up my life is men that *think* they're smart. Catch the difference?"

"I do," Ivy said. She took another sip from the South Sea Firebowl; not as bad as she'd thought—maybe one of those drinks that got better as you went along. "Speaking of smart men," she said, "everyone keeps saying how brainy Frank Mandrell was." Claudette, reaching for another rib, paused. "Did you know him?"

"Everybody knows everybody in a place like this," Claudette said.

"But Frank Mandrell wasn't from here, was he?" Ivy said.

Claudette glanced at her over the firebowl. "True," she said. "He came from Montreal originally."

"Via the prison where he met Marv Lusk."

"We got to talk about that shithole while I'm eating?"

"Did you know him?"

"Course. Went to kindergarten together, for Christ sake."

"What was he like?"

"Marv? You know." Claudette sucked up a little more from the firebowl. "A loser."

"And he met Mandrell in prison."

"Something of that nature."

"What prison?"

"Over in Canada somewheres," Claudette said. "The joints are better up there. More humane, like."

Had Claudette done time? Ivy was wondering whether to go into that, and if so, how, when Claudette added, "So they say."

"How did Lusk end up in a Canadian prison?" Ivy said.

"Marv? Easy." Claudette lit a cigarette, had a little smoke break.

"Are there any Lusks still around?" Ivy said.

"Nah."

"What happened to them?"

"They got what they deserved, one way or t'other."

"Such as?"

"You name it."

Ivy, without really thinking, took another strawful from the firebowl. Possibly a mistake. Everything shifted a little bit. For example, all of a sudden she felt like she'd known Claudette for years and that Claudette wasn't so bad.

"I'm trying to organize all these events," she said, "put them in a time line."

Claudette exhaled a smoke plume. "Why bother?"

That struck Ivy as hilarious. She laughed and laughed. Claudette joined in. Ivy started crying a bit, and got a grip. She went to take another sip; so did Claudette, and their heads touched for a moment over the bowl. The next thing Ivy knew, Claudette was looking at her in a new way.

"I misjudged you," she said.

"How do you mean?"

"You must be one of those types that make a bad first impression."

"Like how?" Ivy said.

"Tight-ass bitch," said Claudette. "But you're not. Not a hundred percent, anyway."

Ivy laughed again, a normal laugh this time. At that moment, she understood deep down something she took to be fundamental about life; the first realization of that type she'd ever had. To get from people you had to give a piece of yourself, a real piece that mattered. Just being nice was not enough. She glimpsed a distant future where her writing had a theme, actually said something important.

"Thinkin' deep thoughts?" said Claudette.

"Not really," Ivy said. "Do you miss Betty Ann a lot?"

Claudette winced, a tiny movement, mostly in the eyes. She stubbed out her cigarette, more forcefully than she had to. "Where did that come from?"

"It just popped out."

"Well, pop it right back in," Claudette said, loud enough for the bartender to glance over. "Fuckin' right, I miss her. We were like twins." She corrected herself in a much quieter voice. "We are."

Ivy spoke quietly, too. "Does that mean she's been in touch?"

Claudette sat back in her chair. "Whoa," she said. "What the hell kind of question is that?"

"A natural one," Ivy said.

"Cop question, if you ask me," Claudette said. "Think I'd tell you if she would've?"

"Probably not," Ivy said.

"Fuckin' right," Claudette said. The bartender looked over again. "My lips are like this." She zipped them shut. But, a moment or two later, unzipped them enough to fit her straw in and down a little more from the firebowl. She saw Ivy watching her and talked around the straw. "But since you're so nosy, not a word from Betty Ann in seven years. No phone calls, no letters, nada."

"Where do you think she went?"

"No clue," said Claudette. Her straw made that reaching-the-bottom-of-the-well sound and she looked up. "But why do you care? It's just a story—you can put Betty Ann any-wheres you want."

"Not really," Ivy said. "Where she ends up has to fit with the character."

"Hey," Claudette said. "That's pretty interesting. How about another one of these?"

"Another firebowl?"

"I'm not on till four tomorrow," Claudette said. "This is practically my Saturday night."

"I'm driving," Ivy said.

"Don't priss out on me," said Claudette, raising her hand. The waitress came over. "Hit us again," she said, took another look at Ivy and added, "the little one."

The little one turned out to be a slightly smaller bowl that still required the male helper. "South Sea Junior Firebowl," he said, and lit it up.

"I'm havin' some fun for fuckin' once," Claudette said. "You?"

"Yes," Ivy said. "Where were we?"

"End has to fit the character?"

"Before that."

"Frank?"

"Yes," Ivy said. "Tell me about Frank."

"Like what?"

"How well you knew him for starters," Ivy said.

Claudette's eyes crossed slightly. "I knew him."

"And?"

"And so did lots of people," Claudette said. "Frank got around."

"How so?"

"If you knew him you wouldn't have to ask," Claudette said, trying the junior firebowl. "This one's even better."

"But I didn't," Ivy said.

"Huh?"

"Know him."

"Frank?"

Ivy nodded.

"Then we're on the same page," Claudette said.

"Same page?" Ivy said. "But you just said you knew him."

"I guess it's all relevant," Claudette said.

"I don't understand."

"Relative, maybe?"

Relative, relevant: the distinction started to elude Ivy. She was feeling a bit dizzy. "Meaning you thought you knew him but found out you were wrong?" she said.

"Something like that," Claudette said.

"Wrong in what way?" Ivy said.

"Want this one?" said Claudette.

"You have it," said Ivy.

"Merci." Claudette took the last pork ball, and with her mouth full said something like, "Ladies' men fool the hell out of me. Is that a sin?"

"Frank was a ladies' man?" Ivy said.

"Also ambitious," said Claudette.

"What was his ambition?" Ivy said.

"He wanted to open a chain of strip clubs, but I always thought he should shoot for the really big time."

"Meaning?"

"Hollywood," Claudette said. "Frank looked like that movie star, plus he'd been around, you know— spoke French, I kid you not. And don't leave out the Beamer."

"What movie star?" Ivy said.

"Oh, what's his name? Dark, a real looker, big smile, soulful eyes. Help me here."

"Denzel Washington?"

Claudette laughed, spewing firebowl spray across the table. "You're a hoot," she said. "I actually got a picture of Frank at home, case you wanna see."

"I'll drive you," Ivy said.

"Only way I'll get there," said Claudette.

Ivy followed Claudette's directions: into West Raquette, along Main, a right turn past the high school, soon another turn on a dark street, the houses growing farther apart.

"Hang another right," Claudette said.

Ivy turned right, the headlights glancing over a street sign: RANSOM ROAD.

"You live on Ransom Road?" Ivy said.

"Careful. It's steep."

Ivy drove down a steep hill. "This would be pretty tricky in an ice storm," she said.

"Ice storm?" said Claudette.

Ivy remembered that the ice storm, in the reality outside Harrow's story, had happened in Canada, not on Ransom Road.

"Pull in here," Claudette said.

Ivy parked in a driveway, her lights shining on a screened-in porch.

"It's not a trailer," she said.

"Huh?" said Claudette, her voice sharpening. "You thought I lived in a trailer?"

"No, I—"

"A fuckin' trailer? Like I'm some kinda—"

"No, no, Claudette. Please. I got mixed up. It's the firewater."

"Firewater? You mean the firebowl?"

"Yeah, sorry," Ivy said. "Firebowl, senior and junior, the whole wobbly family."

Claudette gazed at her for a moment, then laughed. "Are

all writers funny like you?" She gave Ivy's knee a squeeze, a little too hard.

They got out of the car, went into the house. Claudette flipped on the lights. Ivy was prepared for almost everything, except how tidy it was.

"Home sweet home," Claudette said.

"It's very nice."

"Thanks. The only place I ever lived. Me, my parents, and Betty Ann." She hung her Wal-Mart smock on a hook. "Now just me."

"Are your parents still . . .?"

"Lots of cancer in these parts," Claudette said.

"Sorry."

"What can you do?" Claudette said. She crossed the small living room, stood before the mantel. "Come see Frank Mandrell."

Ivy went over, looked at a framed black-and-white photo, about eight by ten. There were four people in the picture, sitting on a deck railing, drinks in hand, open water in the background. Ivy recognized three of them, although Harrow looked so happy she almost missed him. He was on the far left, his hair longer but without the goatee he'd worn in his arrest photo. He had one arm around Betty Ann. The two sisters sat together in the middle, the sun glinting on their blond heads. Claudette had been thinner then and much better looking, but she wasn't in the same class as her sister. Everything about Betty Ann was a little finer, as though Claudette was the preliminary sketch; and all those little refinements added up. Claudette had her arm around a man at the end.

"Frank Mandrell," she said.

Yes, a very good-looking man, especially if you liked the

type that knew he was good-looking. Mandrell was about ten years older than the others, deeply tanned, with nicely cut swept-back dark hair and a flashing smile. He was the only one looking directly at the camera: Claudette's eyes were on him; Harrow's on Betty Ann; and Betty Ann's eyes had an inward cast.

"Were you a couple?" Ivy said, getting the idea a little late.

"That summer was my turn," said Claudette.

"Meaning he had lots of girlfriends?"

"Anything that moved." Claudette caught some expression on Ivy's face. "Some men know how to drive women wild. Word gets around."

"That sounds like something from the back of a men's magazine," Ivy said.

Claudette gave her a quick glare. "That just means you never ran into one," she said.

That hit Ivy hard, a perfect and unforeseen bull's-eye.

"I like the funny you better," Claudette said.

"My liver wouldn't hold up," Ivy said, and Claudette laughed, her mood changing again almost instantly. Ivy picked up the photo, studied Harrow's face: it deconstructed itself into black dots and white dots. "Were your sister and Harrow married when this was taken?"

"Oh, yeah," Claudette said. "They'd been married almost a year by then. This was only a few months before the robbery."

"Did they have any children?"

"Uh-uh."

"No curly-haired little daughter?"

"Huh?" said Claudette. "Where's that coming from?"

"My mistake," said Ivy. "How was their marriage?"

"He loved her," Claudette said.

Ivy took another look at the picture. "I think I can see that."

"I mean really loved her," Claudette said. "Like adored, you know? Getting driven wild I got once or twice—and thank God for that—but adored, never." She took the photo from Ivy, gazed at Harrow. "The way he grew up, with the Lusks and all, there hadn't been much, you know . . ."

"Softness in his life?" Ivy said.

"Exactly," said Claudette. "He even wrote about it."

"Wrote about it?"

"I can show you," Claudette said. She went into another room, came back in less than a minute with a Valentine's Day card from Hallmark, slightly yellowed with age. "This came with the flowers he sent her." Claudette handed the card to Ivy.

On the front, a silhouette of a man and a woman watching a sunset. Inside, the printed script—*Love Is Ours*—was crossed out; instead, in ink:

Betty Ann,
The longest fall and the softest landing.
Forever, Vance

The handwriting hadn't changed at all, neat, a little on the small side, no hint of hesitation.

"Hard to believe he'd ever give her up," Ivy said.

Claudette went a little pale. "What are you saying?"

"Even if he knew where she was," Ivy said. "He'll never make a deal."

Claudette nodded. "You got that right." All of a sudden her face got twisted and she started to cry, big sobs coming from deep inside.

Ivy took a step toward her, touched her arm. "What is it?"

Claudette threw herself on Ivy, almost knocking her down. Her tears fell on Ivy's shoulder. She said something that got muffled in Ivy's sweater.

"I missed that," she said.

Claudette raised her face, now a complete mess. "I forgive her," she said.

"For the robbery?" Ivy said. An idea hit her. "Did you know they were planning it?"

Claudette let go, took a step back. "I don't know a thing."

"But you were close—did Betty Ann tell you?"

Claudette's voice rose, suddenly piercing. "The cops believed me. So who the fuck are you?" She lifted the hem of her T-shirt, exposing her flabby pale belly, and wiped her face.

"I think I should go," Ivy said.

Claudette nodded, her face still hidden behind the T-shirt. "Just write that I forgive her," she said, quieter now.

"Meaning maybe Betty Ann might see the book somewhere and know?" Ivy said.

"Maybe then she'll forgive me, too."

"For what?" said Ivy.

Claudette lowered the T-shirt. Her face was wet and blotchy, but she'd stopped crying. "I don't think your book's going to work," she said.

Seventeen

Tipsy. That was the word Ivy's late grandmother, back in Ohio, used to describe any degree of inebriation, including Grandpa's blackouts. Ivy, climbing into the Saab at the bottom of Ransom Road, felt tipsy. She drove to the top of the hill, made a turn, another, a bunch more, found herself passing through what seemed like miles of rolling farmland—the rolling effect bringing up a burp or two that strongly reminded her of the piggy platter and promised worse—and suddenly there she was on Main Street in West Raquette, only from the opposite direction of what she'd expected. That gave her the idea to check the speedometer. What she saw there lifted her foot right off the pedal.

Mileage back to the city? Lots. Time? Late. Condition of the driver? Could be better. Up ahead a sign missing some bulbs read: CAN-AM MOTEL—DAILY-WEEKLY-MONTHLY. What time did her shift start tomorrow? Four. Did the Can-Am look cheap? Very. How much cash did she have on her?

Not much—the bill at the Tiki Boat had been a bit of a surprise. Did she have her credit card, to be used only in emergencies? Yes. Did this qualify?

Ivy turned into the parking lot at the Can-Am Motel, hitting the turn signal a little late, like after she'd come to a stop. Then she noticed her shoulder felt damp. A moment or two later she remembered why, and the mania came to a stop, too.

Ivy awoke at seven, feeling much better than she deserved. And her mind had been working overnight, had her agenda waiting. Three quick stops on the way home: stop one—the Gold Dust Casino, where she picked up a dub of the robbery tape; stop two—West Raquette High, where the coach lent her the original of the Thanksgiving tape; stop three—the police station.

Ferdie Gagnon sat at his desk, checking boxes on a long form.

"Hey," he said. "I was hoping you'd swing by."

"Really?"

"Got something for you." He handed her a worn paperback novel with a coffee-stain ring on the cover: *The Underground Man,* by Ross Macdonald.

"I'll mail it back," Ivy said, taking a seat.

"Yours to keep," Gagnon said.

"Thanks," Ivy said. She tried to decide where to begin.

"Something on your mind?" said Gagnon.

"First of all, I appreciate how helpful you've been and—"

"I expect a signed copy," Gagnon said.

"Of?"

"Your book," Gagnon said. "The mystery novel based on the Gold Dust case."

"I'm a little slow today," Ivy said.

Gagnon checked another box on his form. "Those firebowls'll do it," he said.

Ivy went still. "Were you there?"

"Negative," Gagnon said. "But I told you—we keep an eye on Claudette."

Ivy didn't remember seeing anyone in uniform. "Was it another detective?"

"No need to get specific."

Ivy thought it over. "Or the bartender?" she said. "Is he on some sort of retainer?"

Gagnon smiled, exposing that cheap dental redo Harrow had caused. He nodded. "Your book's going to be great."

The first time he'd mentioned this supposed book, Ivy had felt a little bad. Now she didn't. "Do you also keep an eye on the football coach?"

He shook his head. "Just Claudette—and maybe one or two more from other cases," he said. "What did that old coot tell you?"

"He showed me some tape."

"Game tape?"

Ivy nodded. "I saw that Thanksgiving touchdown pass you threw to Harrow."

Gagnon's face reddened a little. "You were checking up on me?"

"Nothing like that," Ivy said.

"Then what?"

Ivy leaned forward. "This may sound pretty strange," she said.

"Try me."

"Was there ever any thought in your mind—or anyone's—that Harrow might have been innocent?"

Gagnon tilted back in his chair. "Are you going to end up being trouble?" He glanced at *The Underground Man,* lying in her lap, maybe wanting it back.

"Does that mean there *were* doubts?" Ivy said.

"None," said Gagnon. "On the part of nobody."

"But how come?" Ivy said. "Where's the physical evidence?"

"Physical evidence?" said Gagnon. "Didn't you see Leon's tape?"

"And the football tape," Ivy said. "That's my whole point. He doesn't have the same run."

"Lost me."

"The way Harrow runs on the football field is different from the way he—the way the man in the ski mask—runs in the casino."

The angle of Gagnon's head changed, heavy chin coming forward, little eyes withdrawing. "Different," he said.

"Completely," Ivy said. "The football runner is fluid and athletic. In the casino he's duck-footed and clumsy."

"And how about running with a football versus running with a duffel bag crammed with cash," Gagnon said. "Factor that in?"

"I did," Ivy said. "It's not enough to explain the difference."

He opened a drawer, found a stick of gum, put it in his mouth. "In your scientific opinion."

Ivy took out the two tapes. "If you just look at them, you'll—"

"Not going to do that," Gagnon said.

"Why?"

"Lots of reasons," Gagnon said. "But how's this for starters—Harrow pleaded guilty."

She was just finding this out now? All the patterns that

had been forming in her mind started to dissolve. Ivy had no response.

Gagnon chewed his gum, jaw muscles bulging. "For your story, of course, you can play it any way you want. But then you have to come up with some reason why an innocent man would plead guilty."

"Maybe to protect someone else," Ivy said.

"Such as?"

There was only one answer. "Betty Ann." New patterns began taking shape.

"Him not making a deal for a lesser charge was how he protected Betty Ann," Gagnon said. "He didn't have to plead guilty."

"Maybe it was his way of making a statement," Ivy said.

"Like what?"

Ivy had no idea. But her mind kept struggling, almost feverish; the feeling reminded her of taking tough exams, with lots of questions left and time running out. "Or maybe," she said, "he got bad legal advice."

"How about Carter and Lusk were faking death and now they're down in Cancún living it up?" Gagnon said.

Ivy felt her face going hot. "What are you saying?"

"Just brainstorming along with you," Gagnon said. "It must be fun to be a writer, scheming away. But in this business the truth is obvious, ninety-nine percent of the time."

His phone rang. He answered it. Did she have anything more? No. She waited for the call to end so she could say good-bye. Outside, rain was falling; it zigzagged down Gagnon's grimy window.

He hung up, looked at her, a new expression on his face, a little less self-assured, even puzzled. "That was the guy from witness protection," he said. "They had Mandrell set up down in Phoenix until about three years ago."

"And then?"

"He disappeared."

"I don't understand."

"Vanished," Gagnon said. "How they found out was the checks the feds were sending stopped getting cashed."

"Are they looking for him?" Ivy said.

"Did for a while. But it's not high priority."

"Why not?"

"Old news," said Gagnon. "Limited resources. And how are you supposed to protect a guy who won't protect himself?"

"Is he in danger?"

"Theoretically," Gagnon said. "Betty Ann's still out there." He thought for a few seconds. "But this probably means he's even smarter than we thought."

"How so?" Ivy was tired of hearing that. Harrow was the smart one: all you had to do was read his writing.

"Mandrell must've given himself a new identity, right?" Gagnon said. "Before only the feds knew who he really was. Now it's just him."

"So what does this mean?" Ivy said.

"Dunno," said Gagnon. "Maybe it could be—what's that little chapter sometimes at the end?"

"Epilogue?"

"Yeah," said Gagnon. "An epilogue to your book. But the Gold Dust case—the real case, if you get my meaning—is history."

A uniformed cop knocked on his open door. "All set at the courthouse," she said.

"On my way," Gagnon said.

Ivy rose, put the tapes in her bag.

"You could follow me," he said.

"To the courthouse?"

"Now that you mentioned Harrow's lawyer," Gagnon said, strapping on his shoulder holster. "He should be there, say you wanted to run some of your theories by him."

Ivy glanced at her watch. She had half an hour, tops, if she was going to make it back to the city on time. "I do," she said.

In the courthouse parking lot, a man with an umbrella in one hand and a loose and untidy sheaf of papers in the other was talking to two teenage boys in hooded sweatshirts who were getting drenched.

"Hey, Mickey," Gagnon called to him. "Got a sec?"

The man motioned for the boys to stay put and came over.

"Mickey Dunn," Gagnon said, "this here's Ivy. She's writing a mystery story based on the Gold Dust case."

"Yeah?" said Dunn. "Like for TV or something?"

"More in the nature of a book," Gagnon said. "She's got some questions about Vance Harrow."

"Yeah?" said Dunn.

"Maybe we could get in out of the rain," Ivy said.

Dunn's mouth opened a quarter of an inch or so; he looked a little confused.

"It'll just take a few minutes," Ivy said.

"Leave you to it," said Gagnon, and he headed up the courthouse stairs.

"Well," Dunn said, "I guess . . ." He turned to the teenagers. "You boys go on in and wait for me," he called.

"But, Mr. Dunn," one of them said. "What about that other thing, you know, at the golf . . ."

"What the hell are you talking about?" Dunn said.

"The trespassing," the other boy called over in what was meant to be a stage whisper.

"Just go on in, for Christ sake." Dunn waved them toward the courthouse. The rain came lashing down. A paper
or two got torn from his grip and blew away; he didn't seem
to notice. "How 'bout we sit in my car?" he said.

They sat in Dunn's car, an old sedan with an overflowing
ashtray, legal-paper-size documents wadded under both vi-
sors, and smells of stale coffee and wet dog. Dunn's hair,
going from red to gray, hung over his collar, a frayed collar
and not too clean. He fumbled for a paper bag wedged between the seats.

"Cruller?" he said.

"No, thanks," said Ivy.

He took a sugar-dusted pastry from the bag and bit into
it. "Vance Harrow, huh?" he said. "A blast from the past."

"You were his lawyer?"

"Uh-huh. Back when I was a PD. Now I'm out on my
own." He fished out a card and handed it to her.

"What was your strategy?" Ivy said.

"Strategy?"

"For Harrow's defense."

Dunn took another bite. "I told him to be polite in court
and wear a jacket and tie. Copping to it like he did, wasn't
much else to do."

"Did you ever ask why he wanted to plead guilty?"

"Must've been because he knew they had him cold,"
Dunn said.

"But did you ever discuss it with him?" Ivy was aware of
a sharpening in her tone; Dunn, slowly chewing, grains of
sugar sticking to his chin, didn't seem to notice.

"Not that I recall," Dunn said. "Lot of water under the
bridge since then."

"Not to mention spilled milk," Ivy said.

He nodded as though that made sense. "That, too."

Ivy watched his face in profile: untroubled, unstressed, unhurried. "Do you think Harrow was basically a good person?" she said.

"Oh, sure," said Dunn, gesturing at the courthouse with the remains of the cruller. The two boys hadn't gone inside, but waited under an overhang on the stairs, huddled in their sweatshirts, shuffling their feet. "Most of 'em are."

"Then how did he get mixed up in the robbery?"

"Simple greed," Dunn said. "That's the usual."

"Did you actually discuss motive with him?"

"With Vance Harrow?"

"Think," Ivy said, the edge in her tone now unmissable.

His eyes shifted quickly to her. "This book's important, huh?" he said. He thought; or at least sat still, for a few moments not even chewing. "Nope," he said. "No memory of a discussion like that."

"What about the casino surveillance tape?" Ivy said. "Do you have a memory of that?"

"Do I ever," said Dunn. "The tribe had just put that system in—I couldn't believe how sharp the picture was."

Ivy wanted to smack him. She took a deep breath instead. "And since it was so sharp, how would you describe the running style of the man in the mask?"

"The man in the mask?" said Dunn. "Meaning Harrow?"

"His running style."

Dunn pursed his lips. Rain drummed on the roof. "Urgent," he said.

"He had an urgent running style?"

"Wouldn't you, trying to get away with four hundred grand or whatever it was?"

"Two hundred ninety-seven thousand five hundred and twenty," Ivy said.

His eyebrows rose. "Thought it was more than that," he said.

"So did most casual observers," said Ivy. "Were you aware that Harrow was an excellent high-school athlete?"

"You don't say," said Dunn. "Silver lining—they got workout rooms in most of the state pens. Where'd he end up, again? Sing Sing?"

Ivy had to get out. "I won't take any more of your time." The door stuck. She banged it open, hard.

"That's it?" Dunn said, glancing at the dashboard clock. "I've still got a few minutes."

"Use them to find out about the goddamn trespassing case," Ivy said. The boys on the stairs were watching, the anxiety on their faces visible from across the parking lot.

Eighteen

Summarizing, then," said Herman Landau, motioning for this assistant to switch off the VCRs, "it's your contention that the man—or should I say person—in the ski mask is someone other than Vance Harrow."

"And therefore an innocent man is in jail," said Ivy.

She sat on a soft leather couch in Landau's office, the biggest office she'd ever seen, high above Battery Park, the Statue of Liberty half-lost in morning haze. The assistant ejected the tapes, laid them on Landau's desk and sat on the other end of the couch, pen in hand, legal pad in her lap.

"What would you have me do, Ms. Seidel?" Landau said.

"Get him out," Ivy said.

The assistant's pen scratched across her page.

"On the basis of these tapes," Landau said.

"Plus his lawyer was terrible," said Ivy.

"Drunk in court?" said Landau. "Taking payments from the district attorney? Habitually sleeping at the defense table?"

"Not to my knowledge," Ivy said.

"Then he was acting within permissible norms," said Landau. Behind him hung framed photos: Landau shaking hands with Ariel Sharon, Rudy Giuliani, Barbra Streisand.

"He didn't even have a grasp of the basic facts," Ivy said.

"Immaterial," said Landau. "What other grounds do you have?"

"I was hoping you'd come up with something."

"My time is expensive," Landau said, "although there will be no charge for this interview, as I mentioned, in gratitude for your earlier cooperation."

"Maybe Mrs. Balaban will help," Ivy said.

"Because of Harrow's purportedly kind treatment of Felix at Dannemora?" said Landau.

"Exactly."

"Was that your idea or his?" said Landau.

"Mine," said Ivy. "I haven't discussed any of this with him."

Landau's eyebrows—white, neatly trimmed and shaped—rose. "Harrow doesn't know of your attempt to reopen his case?"

"No.

"And never proposed a theory about who the masked robber might be—some old enemy, perhaps?"

"I told you—we never discussed this."

"Do you have any such theory of your own?"

"No."

Landau was silent. All the lights on his phone were blinking. A foghorn hooted in the distance.

"What is your interest in this?" he said.

"My interest in an innocent man rotting in jail?" Ivy said.

"They're not in short supply," Landau said. "Why this particular man?"

What the hell was she doing? That question again, struggling to be born, quickly smothered. "It's a series of accidents," Ivy said.

"How so?" said Landau. That soft, musical voice made going on, expanding your answers, very easy, must have trapped a lot of people. But then there was the disharmony of his surprising eyes: not antagonistic—nothing personal—just not friendly. He'd probably given Barbra Streisand the same look.

"Harrow came to the writing class," Ivy said, "encouraged, I guess, by Felix. A lot of the writing I've seen at Dannemora is pretty good, but Harrow is on another level."

"Do you mean a professional level?"

"I'm not really qualified to judge that, but yes," Ivy said. "He may have a huge talent." The assistant's pen made its quiet scratching sound, like some tiny digging creature. "In my opinion," Ivy added. "It got me wondering."

"Wondering what?"

About him. The true answer, but that might be open to misleading interpretation. "It's hard to put into words," she said.

"But wouldn't that be your strength?" said Landau.

That stung, despite his gentle voice.

"The *jury*, Mr. Landau, is still out on that," Ivy said. His eyes changed slightly; maybe not less unfriendly, but now more attentive, as though something interesting was going on at last. "But how's this?" Ivy said. "I wanted to see where that ability was coming from."

"To match the writing to the man?" said Landau.

"Yes."

"Perfectly understandable," Landau said. "How did you go about it?"

"First I looked at Harrow's jacket," Ivy said. "That's the—"

He held up his hand, familiar with the term.

"Then I poked around places upstate where he'd lived and where the crime took place. It never occurred to me that he might be innocent. That's the accidental part."

"What was the attitude of the people up there?"

"In what way?"

"Were they cooperative?"

"Yes."

"They responded to this scenario—matching the writing to the man?"

"Not exactly," Ivy said. "Somewhere along the way, this idea of maybe turning the whole story into a novel came up. I went with that."

Landau smiled; a smile of genuine amusement, although Ivy wasn't clear on what was funny. And—another surprise: the smile spread to his eyes, no longer quite so unfriendly.

"So your whole involvement with the writing program— how shall I put it—remained in the background?"

"It would have been confusing."

"Indeed," said Landau. He glanced at his phone. "I'll look into this, Ms. Seidel."

"You will? So you agree?"

"About what?"

"The tapes."

"I'll return them when we have copies," Landau said.

"But you agree about what they show?"

"You'll be hearing from me," he said.

"The discrepancy, I mean, between—"

"Soon," he said, and reached for his phone.

"Thanks, Mr. Landau," Ivy said, rising. "Thanks a lot. As for payment—"

He held up his hand again. The assistant came to the end of a sentence, made a period.

Ivy pulled a double shift. Highlights: One, the new cook lasted twenty minutes. Two, an inspector—tipped off by a vengeful Chen-Li, according to Bruce—discovered rat droppings under the Friolater, and demanded expensive changes. Three, Bruce decided it was a conspiracy and began an investigation in search of the traitor. Four, he settled on a suspect.

"I am not knowing this word *traitor,*" said Dragan.

"The rat fink who planted the rat shit," Bruce said. "Account for your whereabouts between four and six this morning."

"The accountant?" Dragan said. "Mr. Spiegel?" His English was failing him fast.

"Leave Spiegel out of this, buddy boy," Bruce said, backing Dragan against the jukebox. "He's a red herring."

"Herring?" said Dragan, who looked like he might start crying. "But is not even on the menu. How could these rats—"

Five, Ivy stepped in.

She went home after two, climbed the stairs to her apartment, flopped on her bed. The message light was blinking. She hit the button. Danny.

"Hi. How does weekend in Bermuda sound? Give me a call." Pause. "Anytime."

Weekend in Bermuda. Ivy closed her eyes. Pink sands,

mopeds, civility. Sounded good, although maybe not for a whole weekend. She fell asleep in a minute or two—fully clothed, teeth unbrushed, not like her at all—with gentle surf sounds rising in her mind.

The phone rang. Ivy fumbled around for it, a dream involving octopi breaking up in her mind and fading fast.

Danny? What was her answer going to be? The caller ID read: *unknown name unknown number.* Not Danny. Dragan? Had Bruce done something really horrible, like calling the INS? Ivy picked up.

"Hello?" she said.

"I liked your story."

Not Dragan, but Harrow. Ivy sat right up, awakening fast in her dark little room.

"Are you calling collect?" she said; an unmediated thought that came blurting out.

"That wouldn't be polite," he said.

"It's just that I thought . . ." *Better left unmentioned.*

He waited. Ivy heard no sounds on his end. He'd be in his cell now, another man sleeping right above or below, in Felix's old bed.

"I'd have accepted the charges," Ivy said.

"Very generous," Harrow said. "But we're off-peak right now. This is free." His voice was low and quiet, but not like he was trying to keep from being heard, more just the way you talk on the phone late at night.

"Which bunk are you on?" Ivy said.

"Bottom."

"Is that the preferred one?"

"I'll take a poll in the morning," Harrow said.

Ivy laughed.

"I assume you're not in a bunk-bed situation," Harrow said.

"That's right."

"What's your bed like?"

"Just a bed," Ivy said.

"What size?"

"Double."

"That's smaller than queen, right?"

"Yes," Ivy said. "It goes double, queen, king."

"Like the three bears," Harrow said.

Ivy laughed again. "I saw a bear—a real bear—the other day," she said. "Not far from you, in the woods."

"Were you scared?"

"Not for the right reason, not at first," Ivy said. "It was eating a deer. I thought it was two men."

"One cannibalizing the other?" Harrow said.

"Yes."

Silence: but of the kind that came with one of those very good phone connections; a silence that shrank the separating distance down to zero, and put the other person right there.

"'Caveman' could use something like that," Harrow said.

Sitting up, and now—despite her long day and how late it was—wide-awake, heart beating fast and light, like it was feeding on helium. "Maybe in the scene where Vladek winds up in the alley," Ivy said.

"Works for me," said Harrow.

Ivy had a pad and pencil on the bedside table. She switched on the lamp, scrawled: *bear deer—alley*.

"Writing it down?" Harrow said.

"I forget things that come to me in the night," Ivy said. "Thoughts," she added.

"Don't worry," Harrow said. "I'll remember. And after that he could call his mom."

A great idea: Ivy wrote that down, too. She turned off the light. "Can I ask you a question?" she said.

"That's your conversational style, far as I can make out."

"It is?" Ivy said. And then she was laughing again; both of them, actually, Harrow very softly.

"But I'm guessing writers have to be curious," he said. "So ask."

"Okay," Ivy said. "What went on in your mind just before you came up with that idea for the bear?"

"Nothing," Harrow said.

"No thoughts at all?" Ivy said. "No images or memories?"

"Nope."

"Not even a fragment?"

"Now you're badgering the witness," Harrow said.

When Ivy was really enjoying herself—this went way back—she liked to sit Indian-style, wriggling into a comfortable position. She was sitting like that now.

"It's just such a good idea," she said. "How it works with the whole Neanderthal theme."

"You're going to try it?"

"First thing in the morning," Ivy said.

"It's almost morning now," said Harrow.

"Oh no," Ivy said. "Morning's still a long way off."

"Let me know how it turns out," Harrow said.

"Sure," Ivy said. "Can . . . can I call you?"

Harrow laughed, that soft little laugh. Unlike so many other laughs that were out there, this one had no meanness in it; at least that was how Ivy heard it. "Next class will be fine," he said.

"You're giving me a deadline?" Ivy said.

"Why not?" Harrow said. "It must be nice."

"What?"

"Having deadlines."

Another silence. From somewhere in the background on his end came a faint metallic clang.

"You didn't finish telling me about your bed," Harrow said.

"A double," Ivy said. "Like I said."

"Describe it."

"It's a bit embarrassing."

"Yeah?"

"I've had this bed since I was little. The headboard's painted with toys—tricycle, dollhouse, red wagon, that kind of thing."

"You've got a headboard?" he said.

"Yes."

"How about your room?" he said.

"Describe it, too?"

"Yeah."

"Well," she said. "It's very small." She paused. At that moment, Ivy knew they were having the same thought: *Couldn't be smaller than his.*

"Go on," he said.

"I have a table that I use for a desk and for eating, plus there's a little counter with an icebox underneath and an oven beside it."

"What's on the walls?" Harrow said.

Ivy found herself on her feet, touring her own place. "Over here I framed a piece of stained glass from a garage sale. On this wall are some photos I took of commercial fishermen in New Bedford. And here's a charcoal sketch of me that a friend did."

"A boyfriend?"

"Yes."

"Is he there right now?"

"He's in the past," Ivy said.

Silence.

"Are you alone?"

"Of course."

Harrow took a deep breath, like he was relaxing. "What are you wearing in the picture?"

"It's from the neck up," Ivy said.

A little silence. "What's out the window?" he said.

"Not much," said Ivy. "But there's an incredible view from the roof."

"How do you get up there?" Harrow said.

She went through the whole thing—standing on the table, trapdoor, folding ladder.

"Feel like doing it now?" Harrow said.

Ivy climbed up to the roof.

"What do you see?" he said.

"Manhattan."

"Go on."

The truth was that the haze had been thickening the whole day and now things were foggy, those vertical light grids dim, all the towers vague shadows that might not even have been there. Almost nothing to see, plus the air felt raw and unpleasant. But Ivy didn't want to relay that, so she described the view as she'd last seen it from here, that warm September night before Joel left for L.A., the night she first thought of "Caveman."

"The skyline's all lit up," she said. "Huge and vulnerable at the same time, like it's not really solid, if that makes sense."

Silence.

"I hear a foghorn," Harrow said. "Is it foggy?"

"A little."

After that, neither of them spoke for a while. To her right, Ivy could see something happening on the Brooklyn Bridge, blue police lights flashing.

"Why did you plead guilty?" she said.

"How do you know a thing like that?" Harrow said.

"I read your jacket."

The phone connection changed: all at once Harrow sounded farther away. "Uh-uh," he said. "Wouldn't be in the jacket, not the plea."

"I also did a little poking around," Ivy said.

"Where?"

"Up north. The casino and West Raquette."

"Why?"

"Hard to explain," Ivy said. "That story of the ice storm got me thinking."

"How?"

"I wondered if Ferdie was a real character, for example," Ivy said. "Turns out he is."

Pause. "You talked to Ferdie Gagnon?"

"I did."

"Then you know it was all on tape," Harrow said, his voice fading a little more. "I had no choice."

"But I've seen other tape," Ivy said, "tape of you playing football."

"Football?"

"For West Raquette High on Thanksgiving Day."

"So?"

"Those aren't the same two people running."

Silence.

"They're not, are they?" Ivy said.

"Got to go," said Harrow, his voice now faint, no louder

than the siren sounds drifting all the way from the bridge.

"But you weren't even there," Ivy said. "I just don't understand."

More silence.

"Are you still protecting Betty Ann?"

Click.

Nineteen

Ivy awoke feeling refreshed, more refreshed than after any sleep she could remember in a long time. She stretched luxuriously—still in her clothes? uh-oh—and glanced at the bedside clock, expecting some number like eleven or even later.

Seven-nineteen. Seven-nineteen? She actually checked the little red P.M. light. Off. Seven-nineteen A.M. Ivy had read of hyperachievers who needed only three or four hours' sleep to go out there and throttle the competition; now, for one morning at least, she also knew how they felt: great.

Ivy got up, quick and eager like a kid, went into the bathroom, checked herself in the mirror. Hadn't looked this good in months. What was going on? She brushed her teeth; out of nowhere, her mind unspooled a vignette of Harrow washing himself in the shower behind her, whistling away.

Ivy got in the shower, alone, of course, although his imaginary presence lingered for a while. The water, hot for once and much more forceful than usual, drummed on her head, and aroused that tiny part of the brain—maybe really tiny in her case, which was her biggest fear—where inspiration happened, where the talent lay, the gift. In seconds, the whole Vladek encounter with the bear that might not be a bear and the deer that might not be a deer shaped itself, and what was more, bent the story in other unexpected places. Because, yes! The whole point of the story—at last she understood it!—was this Neanderthaly alien turning out to be the most civilized man of all.

The next thing Ivy knew, she was at the table, laptop open, damp hair wrapped in a towel, bare feet curled on the cold floor. She wrote up the changes. It was that easy, her mind in total control of the material, her fingers making small adjustments on the keyboard, the way a bricklayer *tap-taps* the last few bricks in place.

She called *The New Yorker* main number, asked for Whit, got put right through.

"Ivy?" He sounded wary.

"Don't worry," Ivy said. "I have no problem with the rejection."

"I like the story," Whit said. "But the demands on our space are—"

"It's all right," Ivy said. "The story wasn't good enough. The thing is—following someone's suggestion, actually—I've made some changes that really imp—that I'd like you to look at. I know this is kind of crazy, but—"

"It's a crazy business," Whit said. "Or should be. Send it over."

"Really?" Whit was turning out to be a surprise, maybe one of those people whose best side showed at work; and worst side came out in bars—like so many she'd seen.

"But you'll have to be patient," he said. "I'm swamped right now."

"Take all the time in the world," said Ivy, a crazy remark, but now she'd learned it was a crazy business—at least in ideal form—so maybe she belonged.

Ivy ran a brush through her hair, packed the new "Caveman" in an envelope, went downstairs. The fog had cleared: a cold day, cold as winter, with still air and a bright silver sky. All very energizing, and she was jazzed to begin with.

A bike messenger was running up the stoop as she went down. She turned, saw him pressing her buzzer.

"That's me," she said.

He handed her a padded envelope, hopped on his bike, and was gone.

Ivy checked the label: *Weiner, Landau and Pearl*. She sat on the stoop, opened it. Inside were the two tapes and a letter:

Dear Ms. Seidel:

I took the liberty of reviewing your tapes with an old and trusted colleague in the state attorney's office. While my colleague acknowledged the presence of a subtle distinction in body movement, he was unprepared to entertain the possibility of such distinction arising from the presence of two different people, as you suggest. Since the casino tape has already been introduced at trial, pressure for reopening the case would depend solely on the one new element, the high-school tape from years before. In his opinion, and my own, this is far too flimsy a basis for an un-

dertaking that rarely succeeds even in cases where injustice is both grievous and plain. In addition, the state regards the Gold Dust robbery as being particularly brutal and would fight with all its resources to prevent any new proceedings. In terms of the political background, the owners of the casino would strongly oppose any reopening, and smooth relations with the tribe are very much in the state's interests. Therefore, my advice is to let go of this matter. None of the above prevents you in any way from writing your "mystery novel" based on the case, and in this endeavor I wish you luck.

Ivy dropped "Caveman" in a mailbox, went back up to her apartment, and lay on the bed. She slept all day.

Writing folder in hand, Ivy walked through the administration building toward the security gate. Sergeant Tocco leaned out of his door as she went by.

"Got a sec?" he said.

She went into his office. He closed the door, waved her into a chair. A fluorescent tube buzzed overhead.

"Holdin' up all right?" he said. He stood by the window, watching an inmate slowly rake out a flower bed, a guard nearby.

"I actually enjoy the drive," Ivy said.

"Not the drive," said Sergeant Tocco. "The job."

"I like it very much," Ivy said.

"What about it, specifically?" said Sergeant Tocco.

"Just teaching itself," Ivy said. "I've never taught before."

"You could teach in lots of places. Why here?"

"I don't really know," Ivy said. "Maybe it has something to do with finding out how stubborn creativity is, hanging on in extreme positions." She realized the truth of that as she spoke, felt kind of proud of her answer.

Sergeant Tocco turned from the window. "We had a pedophile in here a few years back," he said. "Raped and strangled five little girls. He was amazing on the harmonica, played a couple times with Bruce Springsteen, I think it was."

He sat down at his desk, opened a folder. The name on the front: *Balaban.* "Ever had any dealings with the Latin Kings?" he said.

"Me?" said Ivy. "Of course not."

"Or negative back-and-forth with Hispanics in general?"

"No," Ivy said. "What's this about?"

"The Kings had it in for Felix, true enough," Sergeant Tocco said. "Come here with an attitude, you got to be able to back it up. They gave him a rough time." He paged through the folder.

"But?" Ivy said.

Sergeant Tocco slid a photo across the desk.

"What's this?" Ivy said.

"Surveillance from the showers in B-block."

The photo, grainy, black-and-white: a pale guy stood under a showerhead, washing his hair, one eye open, one closed. He was skinny, but had a slight paunch anyway, overhanging a defenseless-looking little penis. Felix.

"Check the time," said Sergeant Tocco.

White numbers in the top right-hand corner gave the date and time: 9:31:47 A.M.

"They found Felix at nine thirty-five," Sergeant Tocco said, "bled out to the right of those toilets where the cameras can't see, one of the defects of an old prison like this. A guard took a photo of the body, if you want to look."

Ivy nodded. He passed her another photo, this one in color: Felix, lying on bloody tiles, his neck a horror. Her gaze fled quickly, settled on the time code on the corner: 9:37:57.

"And here's another surveillance pic," Tocco said.

Two men were playing cards at a cafeteria-type table, bolted to the ground. One Ivy had never seen before. The other, playing cards almost lost in his huge hand, was Hector Luis Morales. She checked the top right corner: 9:33:12 A.M., same date.

Ivy looked up. Sergeant Tocco's eyes were waiting. "That's the cafeteria in A-block," he said.

Cafeteria in A-block? Showers in B-block? "I don't get it," Ivy said.

"Means there's no way Morales killed Felix," Sergeant Tocco said. "Have to pass through three gates from where he was, take ten minutes at least. Plus we'd have video of him en route, which we don't."

"But—" But it was impossible. *Oh, Morales did Felix, all right. The only question is why it took them so long to figure it out.*

"But what?" said Sergeant Tocco.

Ivy realized he was missing something. Maybe it wasn't Morales in the photo, just another inmate who resembled him; or had the Latin Kings figured out some way to doctor the time codes? It hit her that as in so many subgroups, there were two levels of knowledge in prison, insiders and outsiders. The inmates were the insiders and always knew more about what went on.

"I'm surprised, that's all," Ivy said.

"Lots of surprises in here," said Sergeant Tocco. "Which brings us back to where we started. Any problems between you and the Latin Kings?"

"I'd never even heard of them till I came here," Ivy said.

"What about Morales?"

"I had no problem with him either."

"Lots do," Sergeant Tocco said.

"Not me," said Ivy. "I liked his poem."

"So why did you give him up to Balaban's lawyer?"

"Oh," Ivy said, understanding dawning—so late—of where this was going. The answer had mostly to do with how Harrow had looked out for Felix: in a way, she'd been continuing his work. But that might not make sense to Sergeant Tocco. "The pain his wife was in," Ivy said. "And his kids. It wasn't right."

"True," said Sergeant Tocco. "But why Morales?"

Ivy thought back to that first class. "It was obvious in retrospect," she said. "There was a lot of tension between them."

"That's pretty much the rule in stir," said Sergeant Tocco.

"It was more than that," Ivy said. "Morales accused Felix of calling him a liar."

"About what?"

"Where Felix went to college," Ivy said. "It was actually Cornell but Morales insisted on Harvard."

"And Felix backed down."

"But not right away," Ivy said. "It was all so stupid. And even though Felix was terrified of Morales, he still made the mistake of trying to hurry his writing along."

"Hurry his writing along?"

"So he could get the pencil we were sharing," Ivy said. "I didn't realize how serious something like that could be in here."

"Right about that," Sergeant Tocco said.

"Morales gave him a murderous look," Ivy said. "Felix shrank away from it. Visibly."

"Any more?" said Sergeant Tocco.

"Any more what?"

"To why you named Morales."

"I'm not sure what you're suggesting," Ivy said.

"Nothing," Sergeant Tocco said. "Ninety-nine percent of the time you'd have been right. And maybe Morales would've slit Felix's throat eventually. It's just that someone else got to him first."

Was it Ivy's place to argue with him? No. Besides, she had no proof, just a moment of shared insider's knowledge.

Sergeant Tocco turned a page in the folder. "That leaves this little episode of Morales getting beat up by a dictionary." He scanned the page, the corners of his lips curling down, a facial expression Ivy had always disliked. "Which you realize no one believes."

Ivy nodded.

"So what's the real story?"

"It all happened so fast," Ivy said. "I didn't see."

Sergeant Tocco ran his thick finger down the page. "Word for word what you told Officer Moffitt," he said. He looked up. "Anything you'd like to add now?"

"Just that I'm sorry if I jumped to conclusions about Morales," Ivy said.

Tocco leaned forward. "Has one of these guys got you scared?"

"No."

"Like Morales, maybe? Did he threaten you? And then a couple of the others took care of him?"

"No one threatened me," Ivy said. "I was writing. My head was down. I don't know what happened."

Tocco gazed at her. "'Kay," he said at last, gathering up the papers and closing the folder. "Got a new writer for you today, if that's all right."

"Sure."

He reached for his nightstick. "And any objection to Morales coming back to the class?" he said.

"No," Ivy said, although the word came out a little unsteady.

"Wondering whether we told him about your tip?" Sergeant Tocco said.

"Yes."

"We don't work that way," Sergeant Tocco said.

"Okay, then," said Ivy.

Tocco rose. "Questions?"

Ivy got up, too. "Only who you think killed him," she said.

"Beats me," Tocco said. "I'd actually been planning a little talk with Felix. He was a smart guy, probably the smartest guy I've seen in here. Our shrink tested his IQ, just for fun. One seventy-eight."

"What were you going to talk to him about?" Ivy said.

"We got word from a snitch on B-block that Felix had put his brain to work on some sort of escape plan." He strapped on the nightstick. "I don't like escape plans."

"But it must be impossible," Ivy said.

"You'd think," said Sergeant Tocco. "Good luck with the class."

Twenty

Morales on the left, his arm no longer in a sling, hair long and oily; Harrow at the end, his tan shirt wrinkle-free and buttoned to the neck; El-Hassam, back on the right, a faint white film on his lips; and beside him, closest to Ivy, the new guy. The new guy was skinny, with butterscotch-colored skin—the smoothest skin Ivy had ever seen on a man—and looked about sixteen.

"Teach," said Morales, "meet the new author. This here's Babycake."

The boy, head down, stared at the steel tabletop.

"What's your real name?" Ivy said.

"Babycake his real name," said Morales.

Ivy turned to him. "We're in a last-name zone, remember?" she said. "Babycake isn't a last name."

"His last name is Pope," Harrow said.

The vein in Morales's forearm did its jumping thing.

"Great name for a writer," Ivy said. "Welcome to the class."

The boy nodded, kept his head down.

"The pope's a writer?" Morales said.

El-Hassam—giving off a bad smell today, hair matted and dirty, eyes red—said, "The pope is a murderer."

Morales's chair scraped on the floor.

"I wasn't talking about the pope in Rome," Ivy said. "Alexander Pope was a poet from long ago."

"What did he write?" said Harrow.

"Satire, I guess you'd say," said Ivy.

"What's satire, Babycake?" said Morales.

The boy made a little noise in his throat.

"It means making fun of things that need making fun of," Ivy said.

"Huh?" said Morales.

El-Hassam's eyes closed.

"Like Bugs Bunny," Ivy said. "He does it all the time."

One of El-Hassam's beautiful hands made an impatient little movement. "Recite this pope of yours," he said.

"Recite?"

"Like for Perkins."

"Where is Perkins, anyway?" said Ivy.

"Gone but not forgotten," said El-Hassam, eyes still closed.

"Dead?" said Ivy.

Morales started laughing.

"What's funny?" Ivy said.

"Perkins dead," said Morales. "Just the opposite—he got himself promoted."

Had Perkins somehow gone from solitary straight to freedom? "Where to?" Ivy said.

"Attica," Morales said.

"That's a promotion?"

"Better chow," Morales said. "What you like to eat, Babycake?"

The boy said nothing.

"Asked you a friendly question," Morales said.

The boy made that little noise in his throat, a kind of gurgle.

"Got no tongue?" said Morales. "Not what I hear."

"Recite," said El-Hassam. Drool appeared at the corner of his mouth.

Pope. Ivy had taken a full semester course of eighteenth-century English poetry but only one measly line came back to her. " 'Fools rush in where angels fear to tread,' " she said.

El-Hassam slumped forward, rested his head awkwardly on the table. No one seemed to notice.

"I thought that was a song," said Harrow.

Ivy looked at him. He was sitting up straight like an attentive student, hands folded on the table. She noticed something about him, how dark his eyes were, given his complexion. A striking effect, like from some specially compelling portrait: How had she missed it?

"That came later," she said.

El-Hassam groaned.

"Are you all right?" Ivy said.

El-Hassam didn't answer.

"Psych drugs," said Morales. "Mean shit."

"Do you want some water?" Ivy said. "El-Hassam?"

No answer.

"He ain't thirsty." said Morales. "What we gonna write about, teach?"

"Well," said Ivy, her eyes still on El-Hassam, "I'm not sure we should—"

"He's safe in dreamland," Harrow said.

Ivy rose and went around the table, handing out paper and pencils, laying El-Hassam's near his head. "I was thinking we could write about an important person in our lives."

"Huh?" said Morales.

"It could be anybody, from any time in your life," Ivy said. "A parent, teacher, coach, friend—you choose."

"Sergeant Tocco in my life," Morales said. "Big-time."

"Better to write about someone none of us know," Ivy said.

"How come?" said Morales.

"Or not," said Ivy. "Maybe it doesn't matter."

"Then how come you said it?" Morales said.

Harrow was already writing. The boy, head still down, had picked up his pencil. "Shh," Ivy said, and pointed to Morales's paper.

"Shh?" said Morales. There was a pause. Then he laughed again: in a good mood today, although Ivy had never heard laughter more aggressive. He slid his paper into place, reached for the pencil. "Does it have to be one of them poems?" he said.

"If you want," said Ivy. "Or a story."

Morales wrote *STORY* at the top of his page and underlined it three times.

Ivy grew aware of someone watching her. Harrow. "You writing, too?" he said.

"Of course," said Ivy.

The inmates, except for El-Hassam, were all writing. The library grew quiet, that same strange feeling that had crept into this room before, like the atmosphere from somewhere else.

Normally Ivy did some thinking—maybe even too much—before she felt ready to form word one. But right now, for some reason, she gave the matter no thought at all, the pencil taking off on its own.

> *Where was that photograph taken—you, Betty Ann, Claudette, Frank Mandrell? Claudette showed it to me. Did you know she lives on Ransom Road? Although not in a trailer—she got very offended when I said that. But of course you know that—it's their childhood home, where she grew up with Betty Ann. I understand about fueling your writing from bits of life here and there. The only bit from the ice-storm story that seems completely invented is the curly-headed little girl. You had no kids, so there's no curly-headed little girl, right?*
>
> *Anyway, it's a great photograph. The four of you are on a deck railing, with water in the background, a lake or maybe a river. Is it the St. Lawrence? The expressions on the faces are so interesting. I could tell from yours how attached you were to Betty Ann, how much you loved her. And still do, I'm sure, which explains a lot about what's happened to you. On the other hand, I once spent a whole class with this great teacher—Professor Smallian, maybe you'll meet him one day—discussing how pictures can lie.*
>
> *For example—Felix Balaban. I've just seen surveillance pictures that seem to show the impossibility of Mor—*

"All done, teach," said Morales, throwing down his pencil. "Want me to go first?"

Harrow, still writing, didn't look up. The boy put down his pencil at once.

Ivy checked the time. Ten minutes till noon? The hour was almost up. "Sure," she said.

Morales cleared his throat, hunched over his page. "'Story. An Important Dude in My Life,'" he said, then glanced around to see whether he had everyone's attention. Except for El-Hassam, head still on the table, eyes still closed, and Harrow, still writing, he did. His eyes locked on the top of Harrow's head. That vein in his forearm started up again, and then a huge fat one on the side of his neck.

"Nice title," Ivy said. "I'm all ears."

With enormous effort, as though fighting a gravitational pull, Morales broke off his stare, turned slowly to Ivy. "All ears?" he said. "What's that?"

"I mean I'm ready to hear your story," Ivy said. "Ready and eager."

Morales cleared his throat again, blew a little fleck of something off the page, restarted. "'Story. An Important Dude in My Life. An important dude in my life was Johnny DiGregorio.'" Morales wriggled in his chair, got more comfortable. "'Me and Johnny were friends. He was the first dude I ever beat the shit out of. In my whole life! What an asshole! All he had to do was give me that fucken scooter. The red one he got for Christmas. But he said no! Just like that. No! What he think I was gonna do with the fucken scooter? Eat it?'" Morales laughed at his own joke, looked up to see if anyone was joining in. The boy, who'd been watching him, made a sound that had the rhythm of laughter but sounded squeaky, and bent his head. Morales turned back to the paper. "'All he had to do was give me that fucken . . .' Shit, read that already." He muttered for a moment or two, eyes moving across the page. "Oh yeah, 'Eat it?' Ha. That's where I was. 'Eat it? So I popped him in the face!

Johnny D, that what we called him, Johnny D went down like that.'" He frowned, reached for his pencil, stroked out something, wrote in something else. "'Went down *like a ton of bricks,*'" he continued. "'Making it real easy to knee drop him in the nuts! So I did! That's when I found out for the first time. Hey! You really can beat the shit out of dudes! Real shit! Real shit comes out! Then the bell rang. The end.'"

Morales looked up, doubly triumphant, fighter and artist. Silence in the room.

"The bell rang?" Ivy said.

"Sure," said Morales. "For when recess was over. Time to go back in the school." Something like worry crossed his face. "You sayin' I should put that in, maybe explain a little?"

Harrow, not looking up, still writing, said, "He could call it 'Recess.'"

"Yes," Ivy said. "That would—"

"Don' wanna," said Morales.

Harrow raised his head. "Suit yourself," he said. "It couldn't matter less, anyway."

"Huh?" said Morales. "What's that spose to mean?"

"Figure it out," Harrow said.

El-Hassam opened his eyes, but otherwise didn't move, head on the table, a little pool of saliva forming under the corner of his mouth.

Morales started to say something. Ivy beat him to it.

"The title's fine as it is," she said, maybe louder than necessary. "Who's next?"

No volunteers.

"Pope," she said. "What have you got?"

"Um," the boy said. "Nothin'."

"Babycake got nothin'," said Morales. "Just like Felix, only pretty." He turned to Ivy. "Remember Felix, teach?"

"Of course."

"Big investigation about who cut his throat," Morales said. "Did my best to give them some help, even though they didn't ask nice." He leaned an inch or two across the table. "You seen how they didn't ask nice, right, teach?"

For a crazy moment, Ivy thought: *He knows.* But surely that was impossible. Her mouth went dry anyway. The noisy wall clock ticked away two seconds. Then Harrow spoke up. "We're wasting time here. Send over that sheet, Babycake. I'll read it."

The boy didn't move. El-Hassam suddenly sat up, wide-awake, and handed the sheet to Harrow. Harrow read it aloud.

" 'Bugs Bunny is my favorite influence. He thinks fast and don't take nothin' from nobody. When Elmer Fudd come after him with a shotgun Bugs bit off some carrot and shoved the rest down the barrel and the gun blew up and Elmer Fudd turned all black. This was when Elmer Fudd was hunting wabbits. He talks funny, I don't know why. I try to think what Bugs Bunny would do when I get in some situation but it always come to me too late or maybe never. Thanks for reminding me of Bugs Bunny, teacher. Sometimes I forget.' "

Harrow handed the sheet to El-Hassam. El-Hassam placed it on the table in front of the boy. The boy didn't notice. He was watching Harrow, a surprised look on his face, like he'd just stumbled on something new.

"That's good," Ivy said.

The boy turned to her. "Yeah?"

"Very," Ivy said.

"What the fuck?" said Morales. "Bugs Bunny ain't even real, for fuck sake."

"True," Ivy said. "But the thing is—"

Harrow rose. "That's no way to talk to the teacher," he said.

Morales pushed back his chair.

"Sit down, please," Ivy said. "We can express ourselves freely here and I have no problem with—"

Moffitt came through the doorway. "Time's up."

They all turned to him.

El-Hassam spoke. "We were just getting started," he said.

"Oh, then excuse me," said Moffitt. "I'll come back some other time."

But he didn't move. Everyone got up.

"It always goes so quickly," Ivy said. "Must be a good sign. Just give me what you wrote—I'll get it all typed up and we'll start with Harrow next time."

Ivy collected the pencils. Everyone filed out—Morales first, handing her his work, face blank, then two more blank faces, El-Hassam's and the boy's, and then came Harrow. He gave her his sheet.

"Sorry we didn't get to you," Ivy said.

"No problem," Harrow said. He looked down at her. Those dark eyes, but not like coal: instead, some harder rock and much more polished. "Wouldn't mind seeing yours," he said.

"Next time," Ivy said.

He smiled, went out. Ivy picked up a sheet of paper that had fallen under El-Hassam's chair and followed.

Something very strange was going on outside the door, something hard to take in all at once. It came to Ivy in pieces: first, an inmate who looked like Morales—same size, same enormous arms covered with the same tattoos, differentiated mostly by a burn scar covering half his face—talking to Moffitt, his tone aggrieved. Second, Moffitt turning to him, an irritated look on his face. Third, El-Hassam and the boy drifting across the polished floor of the great domed room. Fourth, Harrow, moving in another direction, toward some inmates in the distance. He didn't see: five, Morales, leaning tight to the wall, right by the door, behind Moffitt's back. And what was that thing in Morales's hand, held at waist level? Six, a toothbrush, lime green, nothing unusual except for the way Morales gripped it by the brush end and the fact of bringing a toothbrush to the writing class in the first place. And seven, how the brushless end had been sharpened to a point.

Morales lunged forward.

Ivy yelled, "No."

Morales drove the toothbrush into Harrow's back, between the shoulder blades. But not quite between the shoulder blades, because Harrow was already turning, and the toothbrush struck on the left side, more in the shoulder than the back.

For a moment, everything slowed down to no motion at all. Morales and Harrow, half-turned, were looking right into each other's eyes, as though participating in something intimate. The toothbrush stuck out of Harrow's back an inch or two. Morales reached out with the heel of his hand and pressed it all the way in, out of sight.

Morales smiled.

Harrow, face white but voice almost normal, said, "You can't write for shit."

Morales stopped smiling, but traces of it were still lingering when Harrow punched him with his right fist, very hard and from point-blank range, a punch that landed on Morales's left eye, the big middle-finger knuckle right on the eyeball. Morales staggered back, raising his hands to his face, and bumped into Ivy, knocking her down.

The back of her head hit the hard floor. Everything went white for a moment. A wave of noise roared in and the whole prison seemed to shake. Ivy rolled over, and through that white veil saw Morales down beside her, head turned sideways, the undamaged side up. A foot—sneaker, no laces—swung into the picture and stamped on that undamaged side of Morales's face, caving it in with a sound like a broomstick cracking.

Ivy rose to her knees. Harrow, swaying a little, blood pouring down his arm, stood over Morales. Moffitt came up behind him, nightstick raised, and swung it across the back of Harrow's head in a measured way. Harrow slumped down. The inmate with the burned face bent over Harrow and said, "Better hope you die now." Guards pulled him away.

Twenty-one

About twenty minutes later, Sergeant Tocco walked her out of the administration building. The wall cast its shadow over them and over the street, rising to the rooftops of the houses on the other side like a high-tide line from ancient times. The siren of the ambulance faded away.

"Where are they taking him?" Ivy said.

"Plattsburgh Regional, most likely," said Sergeant Tocco. "You all right?"

Ivy's hands were shaking, and for the first time in her life she actually needed a drink, but she said, "Yes."

"Glad to hear it," said Sergeant Tocco. "That would have been a nightmare."

"What would have?" said Ivy.

"You getting hurt," said Sergeant Tocco. "Would have meant my job."

"I'm sorry," Ivy said.

"Nothing to be sorry about," Sergeant Tocco said. "We dodged one, that's all. Have a safe drive back."

"Thanks."

"And best of luck."

"Best of luck?"

"With your future," said Sergeant Tocco, "down in the city. The writing program is suspended as of now. If we ever start up again, I'll let you know."

"But, Sergeant Tocco, I—"

He held up his hand. "Not your fault. These grudge matches end up playing themselves out, one way or another."

"I don't understand."

"Like between Harrow and the Latin Kings. After a while they get tired of killing each other and we get a little peace and quiet."

"But aren't you going to do something about it?" Ivy said.

Sergeant Tocco shrugged. "Probably transfer Morales somewheres else before Harrow gets out of the hospital."

"When will that be?"

"No telling," said Sergeant Tocco. "Sometimes never."

"Never?" Ivy said. "But he got onto the stretcher under his own power."

"I've seen some funny things," said Sergeant Tocco.

They climbed the hill, came to her car. "What about the other Latin Kings?" Ivy said. "Why not transfer Harrow instead?"

"Have to transfer him clear out of the country," Sergeant Tocco said. "The system's crawling with Latin Kings."

He opened the door for her. She got in.

"How old are you?" he said.

Ivy told him.

"If I were you," he said. "Forget all this. Go back to your normal life."

Ivy took out her keys. "Are hospital visits permitted?"

He gazed down at her, eyes invisible in the double shade of his cap brim and the high wall. "Why're you asking me that?"

"He's a very good writer," Ivy said. "Maybe even great, potentially."

"So what?" said Sergeant Tocco.

Plus he's innocent. But no point getting into all that with Sergeant Tocco. "So I'd like to have a discussion about his plans."

"Plans?" said Sergeant Tocco. "What plans?"

"Writing plans," said Ivy.

"A discussion in the hospital?"

"When he's up to it."

"A final discussion?" said Sergeant Tocco.

"I hope not," Ivy said. "My goal would be to get him published."

"A final face-to-face discussion, then," said Sergeant Tocco.

What about prison visits? Ivy thought, but she kept that to herself, too, and just nodded.

"You'll need approval from the warden," Sergeant Tocco said. Long pause. "Published?" he said. "Like in a real book?"

"Yes," said Ivy.

"I'll check with the warden."

"Thanks."

"But don't count on it."

The problem with thinking so much about the elements of stories, Ivy realized—elements like turning points, metaphor, theme—was that you could get swallowed up in see-

ing your own life that way and stop living normally. Maybe
Socrates was right about the unexamined life not being
worth living, but what about the overly examined life? What
was that? For example, the way she was paused like this
just outside the Dannemora town line at the junction of 374:
so easy to read it as a metaphorical crossroads or turning
point. Right led her back to the city, her shift tomorrow,
maybe even a weekend in Bermuda; left led to the two-
rutted turnoff that would take her to Wilderness Lake. No
reason at all to turn left, except for a vague desire to have
another look at the spot where she'd seen the bear. Why not
just simply live a little, stop examining? Ivy turned left.

Ten minutes later, she rounded the last switchback and
bumped up into the clearing. Nothing bloody and horrible
going on today. All the trees were bare now, their branches
black against a silvery sky. Ivy opened her folder, found
Harrow's page from the class.

An Important Person In My Life
*is you, the writing teacher. What do I know about
Ivy Seidel? Not much. I know about her "Caveman" story, and that she had a hard time writing
it. I know she likes coming here, and thinks she has
a feel for this place. I know what she looks like
when she's just about to get an idea. And then
there's her apartment—decorations, view, bed.
(For a little while she was my eyes, on the outside.
That really worked.)*

*What I don't know is how she'll look in eighteen
years.*

Ivy got out of the car, walked over to the edge of the
clearing where the bear had been. Leaves covered the

ground—brown from the oaks, red from the maples, yellow from some tree she didn't know. No remains, like antlers, hooves or a tail. No evidence. Ivy stood there, very still, waiting for some idea to arrive. She could feel it, struggling to be born, a new understanding, not a thought about her "Caveman" story, but of Harrow. Then she thought: *How do I look right now?* And the idea, whatever it was, sank back down, out of reach.

Her cell phone rang.

How was that possible in a place like this? She thought of Dragan, the cell-phone relays, the Neanderthal unconsciousness.

"Hi. It's Danny."

"Hi."

"I can hardly hear you."

She raised her voice. "Hi." And heard her own echo, the only sound in the woods.

"Where are you?" he said.

"On my way home."

"From the Dannemora thing?"

She heard a faint crack, somewhere behind her, turned and saw nothing, just the trees and that silver sky. "Yes," she said. "It's over, actually."

"The class? You mean forever?"

"Yes."

"How come?"

"It's complicated. I—"

"I missed that."

"Nothing. I'll explain later."

"I'm glad," Danny said.

"What?"

"Glad. And speaking of later, did you get my message about—" Static blotted out the rest.

"About what?" Ivy said, raising her voice.

The line suddenly cleared. "Bermuda," Danny said at the top of his lungs.

"Yes," Ivy said. She went silent.

Danny lowered his voice. "I've been thinking."

"About what?"

"Bermuda. It's stupid."

"I didn't—"

"Should have known," Danny said. "Not your kind of thing at all. I've got a better idea—Montreal."

"Montreal?"

"Yeah. They've got a cool music scene. I can get tickets to this warehouse thing on Saturday night. Word is the Edge is going to sit in."

"This is in Montreal?"

"Yeah. The Edge. How does that sound?"

Montreal. "Sounds good," Ivy said.

Sudden static. "Missed that."

"Sounds good."

"What did you—"

The line went dead.

Ivy heard another cracking sound in the woods, this one a little louder than before. A cracking sound but the woods were still. She got in the Saab, turned it around, drove home. *Montreal:* like something that was meant to be. At that moment Ivy got a bad feeling in her stomach, the kind of feeling that accompanied motives that were twisted and impure; but not bad enough to stop her.

"This is my dream," said Danny, his Boxster topping a rise on 91, "to own a place like that." He pointed to a picture-book Vermont farm on a distant slope: smoke curling up from the red farmhouse into a blue sky with puffy white clouds; sheep down below like fallen cloud scraps.

"When will you be able to make it come true?" Ivy said.

"Oh, I could do it now," said Danny. "It's just my dream."

Ivy gave him a long look. Danny had a nice profile: nice even lines, an intelligently shaped mouth, if that made any sense. He turned, caught her looking, smiled. "Whee," he said, and stepped on the gas. The car shot forward with amazing power.

"Danny!"

He slowed down. "Didn't meant to scare you." He patted her knee.

"Tell me what you do, Danny," Ivy said.

"You know what I do."

"I mean exactly," Ivy said. "So it sticks in my head."

"Why?" said Danny. "It's not that interesting, unless you're part of the action."

"Try me," Ivy said.

Danny nodded. "Okay," he said. "What do you know about finance?"

"Nothing."

"Sure you do. How did you finance the Saab, for example?"

"Bruce practically gave it to me."

"He did?"

"Yes."

Danny's brow furrowed. Ivy saw how he might look one day: actually better than he did now, stronger, more solid. What was there not to like about Danny?

"How long are you planning to stay at that job?" he said.

"Long as I have to," Ivy said.

"Won't be long."

"Why do you say that? Whit turned me down." She didn't mention the after-the-last-minute revision Whit had agreed to look at; a real long shot, she saw now.

"So I heard," said Danny. "But there'll be others."

"What makes you so sure?"

"It's obvious," Danny said. "And what about *The Surveyor*?"

"What about it?"

"That's what you should be doing."

Was it? Ivy didn't feel ready, not close. But at the same time—it suddenly hit her—wasn't this going back over the Gold Dust case a form of surveying, the way she couldn't make those tapes match up? What if she incorporated—

Water gleamed on the left, a long, wide lake. Lake Champlain? Of course: on the far side rose the Adirondacks, low and dark, Dannemora hidden behind them. Ivy grew aware that Danny was talking.

"Sorry," she said, "I missed that."

"No problem," Danny said. "That dreaminess, all part of where the writing comes from—I get it. I was saying I've thought of a cool way of teaching you about finance. So it'll stick in your head."

"What's that?" said Ivy. Harrow was somewhere over there, Plattsburgh Regional Hospital. She glanced at her cell phone for missed calls: none.

"I'll finance *The Surveyor*," Danny said.

"I'm sorry?" Ivy said.

"Meaning I'll pay you to write it," Danny said. "Say what you're making now at the bar, plus ten percent to cover expenses, throw in a new laptop."

"That's very nice, Danny, but I couldn't—"

"In return," Danny said, "I get the foreign rights."

"What foreign rights?"

"Europe, Asia, South America—there's surprising over-seas market strength," Danny said. "You retain U.S., of course, plus film and whatever subsidiary deal your agent works out with the publisher."

"But there are no foreign rights," Ivy said. "No agent, no subsidiaries, no book."

Danny waved all that away like a pesky fly. "Finance one-oh-one," he said.

"And how do you know all this lingo?"

"I've looked into publishing once or twice," Danny said. "A funny little business, not much to it, really." He turned to her. "Have we got a deal?"

"I just couldn't," Ivy said.

"Because you'd feel obligated?"

Ivy nodded.

"No obligation possible," Danny said. "It's an invest-ment. I just explained."

"What if I can't write the book?" Ivy said. "Or if no one wants it?"

"Then it's an investment that doesn't pan out," Danny said. "That happens. Finance one-oh-two."

"I'd feel bad," Ivy said.

"I wouldn't," said Danny. "That's why we hedge."

They drove up to Canada Customs.

"Well?" Danny said.

"I'll have to think about it," Ivy said, although she al-ready knew the answer was no.

Danny sighed. "I thought artists were supposed to be ruthless," he said. "Take what they needed, anything to get the work done."

That gave Ivy a sinking feeling. She thought again of those faces—Picasso, Brando, Hemingway. Andy Warhol, for God's sake. Even Joel turned out to be ruthless. Was that what she lacked? Did you have to be born with it, or live some desperate childhood? Could it be grafted on, say only for emergency use?

The window slid down. They handed over their passports. Danny's was full of stamps, even had extra pages inserted to fit them all in. Ivy's was blank.

"Purpose of your visit?" said the customs agent.

"Just visiting," said Danny.

Twenty-two

The Edge, who missed his flight or had visa problems or got busted by the Americans while changing planes at JFK—all stories circulated—never showed up, but the music was great anyway. First came Rabbit Lapin, a bilingual group with four drummers; then three singing guitarists who shared a guitar, passing it back and forth; and after that, the fastest-playing band Ivy had ever seen. They sang a song that might have been called "A Fuck to Build a Dream On" and sounded really good. By that time, just about everyone was dancing, including Ivy and Danny. He turned out to be a pretty good dancer, into the music, uninhibited, happy, a beer in his hand. Lots of heady beer around, all from Québecois microbreweries Ivy had never heard of; plus clouds of tobacco and pot smoke; and the steamed-up floor-to-ceiling windows of the old warehouse blurring the city lights.

"Fun, huh?" said Danny.

"What?"

He leaned in close, shouted: "Having fun?"

"Yeah."

A woman with frizzy hair went by, said something in French. Danny said something back in French that made her laugh.

"You speak French?" Ivy said.

"Junior year abroad," said Danny.

"What?"

He shouted, "Junior year abroad." They moved away from the music, stood by one of the windows.

"You came here?" Ivy said.

"Paris," Danny said. Ivy had spent her junior year there, too, but hadn't come close to fluency, or even a moderate level of understanding. "This is my first time in Montreal," he said, taking a swig and passing her the bottle.

"Mine, too," said Ivy.

"I'm glad."

"Glad?" She drank, handed the bottle back.

"That it's the first time for both of us," he said.

Danny looked into her eyes. His were very nice, gentle and lustful at the same time. All at once, the memory of Harrow's eyes overwhelmed them.

"What?" said Danny. "Is something wrong?"

"No," Ivy said. She touched the window, felt music vibrating in the glass. "Nothing's wrong. I'll be right back."

Ivy went to the bathroom, a huge unisex space with urinals, stalls, bar, couches, and a big party going on. She splashed her face with cold water and went to the bar. A phone book, spotted the moment she'd come in the room, lay at one end. Ivy leafed though it.

What did she know? That Frank Mandrell—the name now twice removed—had come from Montreal; that the getaway plan involved some cousin of his meeting the robbers on the

Canadian side of the St. Lawrence; that Mandrell had dreamed of owning strip clubs. Cousins didn't necessarily share surnames, of course, and Mandrell's cousin might have had no connection with Montreal, plus even if he had, there was no reason to think he'd still be here now, seven years later.

But.

There were three Mandrells listed in the Montreal phone book: James and Lise; P.; Victor and Gina. Ivy took out her cell phone and dialed James and Lise first, hunched over against the noise.

A woman answered, old and reedy-voiced. *"Oui?"* she said.

"Um," said Ivy. "Do you speak English?"

"Yes?"

"I'm looking for Frank Mandrell," Ivy said.

"Frank Mandrell?" said the woman. "You must have the wrong number."

"Sorry."

Ivy tried P. Mandrell.

"Yeah?" said a man.

"Frank Mandrell, please," said Ivy.

"Wrong number." *Click.*

And finally, Victor Mandrell.

"Hello?" Another woman.

"Is Frank there?" said Ivy.

Pause. "Frank?" This woman was much younger than the first, sounded a little slow and vague, maybe even high on something.

"Frank," said Ivy. "Frank Mandrell."

Another pause, this one very long. "There's no Frank here," she said.

"No?" said Ivy.

"No," said the woman. "There's no Frank, like . . ."

"Like what?"

"Like period."

Ivy knew.

"I must have made a mistake," she said.

"Must of," said the woman. "Because there's no Frank Mandrell, like I told you."

"What about Victor?" Ivy said.

"Victor?" said the woman.

"Yes," said Ivy. "Is he around?"

"Not now," said the woman.

"Where is he?" Ivy said. "I need to reach him."

"What about?"

"Business," Ivy said.

"Vic's at the club," the woman said immediately, as though Ivy had spoken a magic word.

"Which one?" Ivy said.

"Huh?"

"Which club. I thought there were a few."

"Uh-uh," said the woman. "Just Les Girls."

"That's on?"

"St. Catherine," said the woman. One more pause. "But, hey—how come if—"

Ivy clicked her phone shut, turned and found Danny beside her, watching.

"What's going on?" he said.

"Something to drink?" said the bartender.

"I couldn't help overhearing," Danny said "Who was on the phone?"

Ivy pulled him away. Was this another one of those turning points? They seemed to be coming quickly. Choice A: she could tell him about Harrow, his talent, her belief in his innocence. Choice B: she could just say, *Let's check out a strip club.*

"We need to talk," Ivy said.

"About what?"

"Let's go outside."

"Why?"

"It's complicated."

He gazed at her. His eyes changed. Ivy thought she saw something impatient there for the first time, maybe even hard.

"Whatever you say," he said.

They went outside, stood under an old-fashioned lamp-post. Danny shivered, buttoned his coat to the top button. "It's cold," he said.

Ivy knew it must be—she could see his breath—but she didn't feel cold at all. "I've stumbled into something kind of weird," she said.

"Where?" he said.

"In the writing program."

"At Dannemora?"

"Yes."

The look in his eyes: now she was certain. "One of the inmates—Vance Harrow—turned out to be very talented," she said.

"What did he do?"

"I don't understand."

"To get locked up," Danny said.

"That's what I'm getting at," Ivy said, and out came her story. A complete jumble: the worst hack, a third-rate Tony B, if that was imaginable, would have done a better job of organizing the material. But she hit the high points—the ski masks, the tapes, Harrow's shielding of Betty Ann, Herman Landau, this new amazing possibility that she'd actually tracked down Frank Mandrell, closing a circle in a way she failed utterly to explain. Her high points didn't include what she and Harrow had written in that last class, or those late-night calls.

Danny gazed down at her; a little strange, since she'd always thought they were about the same height. "Now you want to go to this strip club," he said. "Les Girls." He made the tawdry name even tawdrier.

"Yes," Ivy said.

He looked away. For a moment, Ivy thought his eyes teared up. Then one of those breath clouds rose over his face, obscuring it. When he turned back, his eyes were dry.

"What are you doing, Ivy?" he said.

"I just explained."

"You told me a crazy story," Danny said. "You didn't explain anything."

"Like what?"

"Like for starters, what makes you so sure he's even any good?"

"Any good?"

"At writing."

"Well," said Ivy, "that's . . ." Her strength; a strength that Danny believed in, maybe more than anyone else she knew. Didn't he?

"Did you show this work of his to anyone else?" Danny said.

"No."

"Whit, for example?"

"I didn't think I could do that," Ivy said.

"Why not?" Danny said.

She had no good reason; in fact, hadn't even considered showing Whit.

Danny didn't let it go. "Isn't there less vulnerability in pushing someone else's work than your own?" he said.

"Probably."

"So why not get Whit's opinion?"

"It's hard to say."

"Maybe for you," Danny said.

"What do you mean, Danny? You're acting weird."

"*I* am?" Danny said. "Here's a possible reason you didn't tell Whit—you didn't really think the writing was any good, not down deep."

"Then why would I be doing this?"

"Maybe that's what you didn't want Whit asking," Danny said.

"What are you saying?"

"Do you remember what I told you the very first time you mentioned this gig?" Danny said.

"You said Dannemora was an evil place."

He nodded. "And I asked why you were doing it. You never really answered."

"It's a good thing to do."

"For whom?"

"For them."

"And what about for you?"

"Yes," said Ivy. "Good for me, too."

Danny shook his head. "For God's sake, Ivy, it's a cliché—those women on the outside who get romantically involved with inmates."

Her voice rose. "I'm the writing teacher," she said. "I'm not romantically involved with anyone."

Danny stepped back. "Really."

She reached out, put a hand on his arm. "I didn't mean that," she said.

Danny pulled away. "I know the truth when I hear it," he said. He took something from his pocket, gave it to her.

What was this? A plastic rectangle, baffling for a moment, then understood: the key to their hotel room in the

Old Town. She looked up. He was already walking away, fast.

"Danny," she called after him. "Don't."

But he did, just kept walking till he disappeared in the night, one last breath cloud hovering behind. Ivy didn't run after him, saying she loved him, asking for another chance, more time, more talk. None of that. When you came to a turning point you had to be honest. She held on tight to the room key.

"Les Girls," said the taxi driver, pulling over. His eyes found her in the rearview mirror. *"Ça va?"* he said.

"Sorry," Ivy said. "I don't speak French."

"This is what you want?" the driver said. "The place here?" He pointed to it with his chin.

Ivy looked out, saw a big neon woman looking back through her spread neon legs. "Yes," she said.

Twenty-three

The Canadian ten-dollar bill was a beautiful purple thing with a portrait of an unfamiliar thin-lipped man on the front. Ivy handed one over at the door of Les Girls and went inside.

First time in a strip club. She took a seat at a table near the back. The place was about three-quarters full—lots of men up front by the stage, a few couples behind them. Up onstage, two naked dancers— one black, one white—wrapped themselves around brass poles and left nothing to the imagination, not even the possibility that they were enjoying themselves. The men didn't seem to mind or even notice: their eyes were filled with satisfaction, maybe of the grim kind.

A waitress in a G-string came over. "Hey, there," she said. "Something to drink?"

"Water," said Ivy.

"Still or sparkling?"

Ivy ordered sparkling. The waitress returned with a small bottle. "Seven-fifty," she said. Ivy pulled out another purple bill. The waitress's breasts swung closer as she reached for the money—heavy breasts, with hard cores and a thin pink scar tucked behind each. In that moment, with those breasts in motion by themselves, Ivy caught a glimpse of rib cage, the ribs sticking out the way they did in skinny little girls.

"Keep the change," she said.

"Thanks," said the waitress. She gave Ivy a quick glance. "You looking for work?"

"Work?"

"Most times when single girls come in here they're looking for work."

Looking for work: that was one way to go, but Ivy foresaw scenarios that might end in disrobing, auditions, something else out of the question. "I'm actually researching a book," she said.

"You're a writer?"

Ivy nodded, a vague little affirmative movement.

"Awesome," said the waitress, her breasts bouncing once or twice. "I'm a big reader. Have I read any of your books?"

"Probably not," Ivy said. "But maybe you could help me."

"Yeah?"

"The main character—the hero—of the story is a guy who owns a place like this," Ivy said.

The waitress frowned. "He's the hero?"

"Flawed," said Ivy. "In order to get the details right, I'd like to talk to the owner."

"The owner of Les Girls?"

"If he's around."

"I'll check," said the waitress, walking off. She had a snake tattooed on her ass, its mouth opened wide, fangs exposed; Ivy hoped the image wouldn't pop up in her dreams. She watched a man throw balled-up bills onto the stage, one of the dancers picking them up in a way she wouldn't have thought possible. Then, beside her, a man said, "You wanted to see me?"

Ivy looked up: a round little man, fleshy features, gray hair in a Nero cut. Nothing could have turned Frank Mandrell into this. "Yes," she said. "Thanks. Are you the owner?"

"Manager," he said. "You some kind of reporter?"

"Oh no," said Ivy. "Not at all. I write fiction."

"Fiction?"

"Made-up stories."

He squinted at her, uncomprehending.

"Like . . ."—she tried to think of a good example—*"Jaws."* The first thing that came to mind.

"You wrote that?"

"No," said Ivy. "It's just an example." She held out her hand. "Ivy." *You now entering a last-name zone.*

They shook hands. His was damp and bejeweled. "Vic," he said.

"Nice to meet you, Vic," Ivy said. "In this story I'm developing, the hero owns a strip club."

"A gentleman's club, you mean?" said Vic.

"I do," said Ivy. "That's why I really need to talk to the owner. The details have to be right."

"And this owner guy's the hero?" Vic said.

"Very much so," said Ivy. "And the hero's the most important character in the book."

Vic thought for a moment or two. "Like the star of it?" he said.

"Exactly."

"Follow me," said Vic.

Ivy got up, followed Vic past the bar and a little alcove where a muscular woman was performing a lap dance for a glassy-eyed man in a hockey sweater—seen from behind it looked like very hard work—and down a dim staircase. The bass line of some R&B tune—"Hold On! I'm Comin'" by Sam & Dave, Ivy recognized it from the jukebox at Verlaine's—thumped through the walls.

"What's your boss's name?" Ivy said.

There was a little hitch in Vic's stride, as though his sole had caught on something sticky. "Mr. McCord," said Vic. "Jake McCord."

"Good name for a hero," Ivy said. "How long have you known him?"

"We go back," Vic said.

They went down a long corridor, came to a door that said PRIVATE/PRIVÉ. Vic knocked.

"C'mon in, Vic," a voice called from the other side. Vic turned to Ivy with a conspiratorial smile, pointed out a video camera on the wall.

Ivy entered a small office lit only by a desk lamp. The man behind the desk was counting brightly colored money and stacking it in a steel box. All she really saw of him was his hair—long and platinum blond. Blond? Frank Mandrell's hair had been dark brown in Claudette's photograph. She'd gotten everything wrong.

"This here's the writer," said Vic, behind her.

The man looked up and Ivy's heart started beating faster. Blond, yes, but not naturally, not with those dark eyebrows. A very good-looking man, deeply tanned, with a few lines on his forehead that hadn't been there when Claudette's photo was taken, but: Frank Mandrell, no question. He was real. This was all real.

"Forgot your name," said Vic.

"Ivy."

"The writer Ivy," said Vic. "My boss, Mr. McCord."

"Nice to meet you," Ivy said, going forward, extending her hand across the desk.

Frank Mandrell shook it; he had a big hard hand and held on a little too long. *Anything that moved.* "Ivy what?" he said.

She tried and failed to come up with a quick alias. "Seidel," she said.

Maybe he caught her hesitation. "Got some ID, Ivy Seidel?" he said.

"ID?"

"Can't be too careful in this business," Vic said.

Ivy gave Frank Mandrell her driver's license. He glanced at it. "New York City," he said. "Course I knew you were American the moment you opened your mouth."

"Yeah?" Ivy said.

"Say 'about,'" Vic said.

Ivy said it.

"Hear that?" said Vic.

Mandrell nodded.

"How do you say it?" Ivy said.

"About," said Vic.

"And you, Mr. McCord?"

"Call me Jake," said Mandrell. "About."

Ivy listened carefully. The second syllable of Vic's *about* was close to *boot,* almost the sound of the Beatles talking. Mandrell's wasn't so pronounced.

"See?" said Vic. "You've got an accent."

The waitress with the snake tattoo stuck her head in the doorway. "Vic?" she said. "Sorry to interrupt—little trouble with a check."

"On my way," said Vic. He went out, closed the door.

Frank Mandrell dropped the last stack of bills into the steel box and closed it. "Take a seat," he said.

The only place to sit was the white leather couch that stood beside the desk. Ivy sat at one end. Mandrell swiveled around to face her. On the wall behind him hung video monitors, showing different views from inside the club: a bunch of college boys coming in the door; Vic pointing his finger at an unsteady Chinese man; a dancer on her hands and knees.

"No shortage of strip clubs in New York City," Mandrell said. "Why come all this way?"

"I wanted a fresh angle," Ivy said.

He nodded as though that made sense. That gave her an idea, maybe a little reckless.

"Did that ever happen to you?" she said.

"Did what ever happen to me?" he said.

"Going somewhere new," said Ivy. "To get a fresh start."

Mandrell's eyes hooded slightly. Very handsome, yes, and much younger-looking than the forty-four or -five which he had to be, according to Claudette, but there was something reptilian about him. "Why would I want a fresh start?" he said.

"I don't know," Ivy said. "I'm just trying to get a handle on your story."

Mandrell leaned back in his chair, looked down his nose at her. A fine, strong nose: Who was the actor Claudette said he resembled? Claudette hadn't been able to remember, but Ivy had a candidate: Victor Mature.

"Why me?" Mandrell said.

"Good question," Ivy said; and one she should have been prepared for. "It's kind of random, really. I asked around for the best strip club in Montreal and kept hearing Les Girls."

"We say gentleman's club," Mandrell said.

"So Vic was telling me," Ivy said. "But I can't believe that's what you call it when it's just the two of you behind closed doors."

A little pause. Then Mandrell smiled, a big white smile just like the one he'd flashed at the camera in Claudette's picture. "Got me," he said. He glanced down at her driver's license, still in his hand. "Ivy," he said. "We had an Ivy here not long ago. Or was it Ivory?" He looked her up and down. "We always need fresh"—*meat* was the next word, but he stopped himself—". . . new dancers. Done any dancing?"

"I've got no rhythm at all."

"Too bad," Mandrell said. He flicked the driver's license to her. Ivy caught it, put it in her pocket. "Couple of questions about this story of yours," he said.

"Shoot."

"First, no real names, right?"

"Right," said Ivy. "I deal in fiction."

"Second," he said. "Why strip clubs?"

"They carry a lot of weight," Ivy said, "metaphoric and thematic."

Mandrell looked blank.

"And I'd like to sell the stupid thing," she added.

Mandrell flashed that smile.

"Plus I thought it's the kind of business that attracts a self-made man," Ivy said. "The main character of the story—the hero—is a self-made man." She paused, actually found herelf looking him up and down right back. "Unless you grew up rich."

Mandrell laughed; a harsh, barking laugh. "That's a good one," he said. "I came from fuckin' nothing, honey."

"Good," Ivy said.

"Huh?"

"For the story," she said. "Tell me about your growing up. Maybe start with where."

"Right here," Mandrell said. "East End. My mom raised me. She's French-Canadian."

"McCord doesn't sound French to me," Ivy said.

"That was my father. Took off early."

"What's your mother's last name?"

"French name," said Mandrell. "You'd never pronounce it."

"I'd like to talk to her."

"Why?"

"To get her perspective on your rise in life."

"My rise in life," said Mandrell; the phrase pleased him. "Good idea, but she passed away."

"Sorry," Ivy said; although to that point, he'd been talking about her in the present tense, no problem. "When did that happen?"

"Long time ago," said Mandrell. He checked his watch. "What else do you want to know?"

"How you got started," Ivy said.

He shrugged. "Worked my way up—tended bar, saved my pennies, made some good deals."

"Where was this?"

"Here," said Mandrell.

"You stayed in Montreal the whole time?"

"Yeah," said Mandrell. "It's a great city."

"But aren't there more opportunities south of the border?" Ivy said.

"That's a real American thing to say," said Mandrell.

"So it's not true?"

"Check us out." He waved in the direction of the video monitors; one showed Vic walking down a shadowy corridor. "Country's booming."

"Never even tempted to try your luck down south?" Ivy said.

"Nope," he said. "Let's move on."

"Sure," said Ivy. She felt the need for a prop, took out her notepad. "A place like this must cost a lot. How did you raise your stake?"

"Told you," said Mandrell. "Worked my ass off. Denied myself luxuries. Denied myself fucking necessities."

"Mind if I write that down?" Ivy said.

"Be my guest," he said, and repeated the phrase at dictation speed: "Denied myself fucking necessities."

Ivy wrote it down. "So there were no windfalls along the way," she said.

"Windfalls?"

"Winning the lottery, for example," she said. "Or hitting it big at a casino."

A long pause. "Casino?" Mandrell said. He straightened in his chair; it squeaked beneath him. "What about a casino?"

Ivy shrugged. "Windfalls sometimes happen in casinos," she said. "A friend of mine won a big jackpot at one of those Indian places."

Mandrell's hands—hairy hands, dark hair that contrasted with the hair on his head in a way that made her a little queasy—were suddenly squeezing the arms of his chair. "Indian places?" he said.

Enough, Ivy. What was left to establish? But she couldn't stop. "Don't you have them up here?" she said.

His eyes did that hooding thing. "What are you talking about?"

"Indian casinos," Ivy said. "There's one just across the border, maybe an hour from here."

The skin around his nostrils went pale. He started to say something, swallowed, tried again. At that moment, there was a knock on the door. He and Ivy both checked the monitor: Vic, standing outside, fist raised to knock again.

"Yeah?" Frank called.

Vic came in, glanced at Ivy, turned to Mandrell. "Sorry, Jake," he said. "But Gina's upstairs. She wants to talk to you."

"Huh?"

"Gina."

"I heard you the first time," said Mandrell. "What about?"

Vic lowered his voice, oddly confidential with Ivy right there. "I think you should hear from her direct."

Mandrell rose. He looked down at Ivy, eyes thoughtful. "Be right back."

"I'll keep her company," Vic said.

"Yeah," said Mandrell. "Do that."

He walked out of the room. Ivy, busy with the implications of Gina Mandrell's appearance, almost missed it: that walk, that gait. She felt dizzy. Frank Mandrell had a clumsy walk, feet turned out, duck style. The facts of the Gold Dust robbery rescrambled themselves, the bloody little story changing shape again.

"Sorry," Ivy said. "I missed that."

"I said 'get you something to drink,'" Vic said.

Gina Mandrell picks up her phone. A caller asks for Frank Mandrell. Now Gina was at the club, interrupting this little conversation about Indian casinos. The thinking that came after that was pretty simple, and Mandrell had been the brainy one.

"Thanks," Ivy said, hoping Vic would leave the room. "Water, please."

Vic didn't go anywhere. He opened a wall cabinet instead. "Still or sparkling?"

"It doesn't matter." Ivy glanced at the monitors, spotted Mandrell's blond head by the bar upstairs. He was listening to a middle-aged woman with big hoop earrings. Ivy moved toward the door. "I'll just use the bathroom," she said.

Vic pointed to another door, this one behind the desk. "For you," he said, "the executive john."

One of the monitors now showed Frank Mandrell hurrying down a staircase.

Ivy went into the executive john. It had a Jacuzzi, a bowl of condoms, a high little window over the toilet, very small. Ivy climbed up. Her eyes were at ground level. Outside she saw a trash can, a cobblestone alley, a light in a building on the other side. Out in the office, the front door would bang open any second. Ivy glanced around, a little wildly, saw a filthy plunger standing by the toilet.

Out in the office, the front door banged open.

Ivy grabbed the plunger, smashed it through the glass. Then she pulled herself up, kicking with her feet against the wall, and writhed out the window and into the alley.

Voices rose behind her. Ivy picked herself up and ran—down the alley, around a corner, then another. She came out on a well-lit sidewalk, crowded with Saturday-night people. A cab appeared. She raised her hand. It pulled over.

Back at the hotel in the Old Town, a fruit basket sat on the table and chocolates lay on the pillows, but Danny and his things were gone. He'd left an unaddressed and unsigned note advising her that a Montreal—JFK ticket in her name waited at the airport. She went into the bathroom, washed the blood off her hands and held a towel to the cuts that were still bleeding.

Twenty-four

Ivy awoke in the night, something hard against her face. She jerked her head away, snapped on the light. The hard object: a foil-wrapped Belgian chocolate that must have slid off Danny's pillow.

After that, Ivy couldn't get back to sleep. She rose, went to the desk and began writing on the thick hotel stationery.

Gold Dust

The official story: Three masked robbers—Lusk, Carter, Harrow. Lusk and Carter killed. Harrow takes $. Leaves Mandrell hanging by the dock. Mandrell implicates Harrow. Harrow arrested at his house. Betty Ann gets away with $.

The real story: Three masked robbers—Lusk, Carter, Mandrell. Lusk and Carter killed. Mandrell takes $. He's arrested by the dock. Fingers Harrow.

*Harrow arrested at his house. Betty Ann and $
gone.*
   Therefore: ?

Therefore what? Ivy had no idea. So many questions, but
they all derived from the collision of two irreconcilable
facts: Harrow was innocent; he'd pleaded guilty.

Ivy showered, packed and checked out of the hotel at
dawn, the bill all taken care of. But she didn't go to the airport and catch her flight to JFK. Instead she rented a car
and drove back across the border, entering Raquette before
the sun—a pale, late-autumn disk that seemed smaller than
usual—had risen above the trees.

Casino, boat ramp, Harrow's house. They probably
formed some sort of triangle. Was the problem mathemati-
cal? Ivy knew that wasn't good. Her mind didn't work that
way. It wanted a story, and despite her MFA and all those
workshops, still preferred a story of the traditional kind,
with beginning, middle, end. She started at the casino.

Early morning, but the parking lot was already one-quarter full, or perhaps still one-quarter full from the night before. A crane stood in front of the entrance, removing the
Gold Dust Casino sign; a new sign—twice as big, with showers of gold coins and a miner clicking his heels—lay on a
flatbed truck.

She sat in the parking lot. *Official story: Frank Mandrell
waits by the boat ramp for Harrow, who never arrives.
Real story: Mandrell comes out of the casino with the duffel bag full of cash.* Supposing this was an outline: What
came next? Mandrell gets in a car. Is someone waiting in it,
at the wheel, or does he drive himself? Had Ferdie Gagnon
said anything about a car being found at the ramp? Not that
Ivy remembered.

Next question: How fast to drive the getaway car? On this, Ivy had no data at all. What would she herself do? Drive fast, yes, but not fast enough to attract attention from some random patrol car. Settling on ten miles an hour over the speed limit, Ivy clicked the odometer to zero and checked her watch: 7:58. She drove out of the Gold Dust parking lot.

Ivy followed the highway to a stoplight, turned down a street that led toward the river, then onto another one paralleling it, finally onto the bumpy dirt road where Leon Redfeather had taken her. A mile and a half later, the road dead-ended by the huge willow tree. A dirty froth, the color of roasted marshmallows, lapped at the foot of the boat ramp. Time: 8:14. Sixteen minutes.

Official story: Harrow, double-crossing Mandrell, is on his way home with the money while Mandrell waits at the boat ramp, about to be picked up by the Border Patrol.

Real story: Mandrell arrives at the boat ramp with the money.

A fact that Ivy believed totally, but it raised new questions. For example, there'd been no money when the Border Patrol arrested Mandrell. Where was the money? Missing, with Betty Ann. Did that mean Betty Ann had driven Mandrell from the casino, dropped him at the boat ramp, kept going to the house she shared with Harrow?

Ivy backed up, turned around, drove to the highway and into West Raquette. She passed the Main Street Diner—saw a patrol car outside, Ferdie Gagnon drinking coffee in the front seat—climbed the long hill that went by the high school, passed the Ransom Road sign. Exactly two-point-four miles later came that nameless track into the woods. Ivy followed it, around a bend and up a slope, stopping in front of the empty, numberless house with the faded For Sale sign.

Time: 8:38. Time from the boat ramp: twenty-four minutes. Total elapsed time: forty minutes.

Ivy gazed at the house. Trees stood close around it, branches hanging over the roof. Moss grew on the shingles; paint was peeling off the door and the window frames. Harrow had been inside, vacuuming the living room, Betty Ann already gone. How long after the robbery had Ferdie driven up? Had he told her? Ivy thought so but she couldn't remember.

She called the West Raquette police station, got transferred to Ferdie Gagnon.

"Sure I remember you," he said. "How's the mystery coming along?"

"Still in the planning stages," Ivy said. "I've got a few—"

"Do you start with an outline, that kind of thing?" said Gagnon.

"That comes next," Ivy said. "Right now I'm still trying to get the facts down."

"Facts? But—"

"Facts like how much time went by between the robbery and Mandrell's arrest," Ivy said.

"Twenty, twenty-five minutes," Gagnon said.

"And from then to when you picked up Harrow?"

She heard him take a deep thoughtful breath through his nose. "Call it another twenty-five minutes, half an hour, tops." *Warp speed.* "If you're ever back this way, I can check through the logs, give you something more precise."

"Thanks."

"But what I don't get," Gagnon said, "is how come it matters."

"Why wouldn't it?"

"Because you can make up whatever you want, right?"

"Right," said Ivy.

"Not telling you how to do your job, of course," said Gagnon. A phone rang in the background.

"One more thing," Ivy said. "Did Mandrell have a car down at the boat ramp?"

"Yeah," said Gagnon. "A Beemer—still on the road." He laughed. "Although not right now, come to think of it."

"I don't understand," Ivy said.

"That Beemer belongs to Claudette Price," Gagnon said, "and she's under DUI suspension."

"Claudette drives Mandrell's old car?"

"Can't remember the details of that," Gagnon said. "He and Claudette had an off-again, on-again thing of some nature."

"Where was Claudette the night of the robbery?" Ivy said.

"Don't recall—her name never came up in the investigation." Gagnon paused. When he spoke again, his tone wasn't quite so friendly. "But you can make it however you want. Long as you change the names."

Ivy got out of the car. She walked around Harrow and Betty Ann's old house. A gust of wind stirred up some leaves, hard, dead leaves that clattered against the aluminum siding. Ivy peered through a grimy window into the kitchen. A rat squeezed out of a crack in the wall, ran across the floor and through the doorway that led down to the basement.

Real story: Mandrell arrives at the boat ramp with the money. Within a few minutes, the Border Patrol picks him up. No money.

Ivy stared into the kitchen, bare now, no table, chairs, appliances, but once the setting for little domestic scenes—Harrow, perhaps, coffee in hand, coming up behind Betty

Ann at the stove and touching her hair. At that moment, Ivy remembered something Gagnon had told her: *After the robbery, they were all supposed to meet at the boat ramp, Betty Ann included. The fact that she didn't show is how Mandrell knew Harrow was double-crossing him.*

But Harrow hadn't double-crossed Mandrell: in fact, was serving real time on account of Mandrell's made-up story. Yes, he'd pleaded guilty, but because he was protecting Betty Ann: Betty Ann, gone with the money. Therefore: Was it possible that Mandrell had lied about her, too, and she'd been at the boat ramp after all? Just for a minute or two, of course, before the Border Patrol, but enough time to get the money. And after that? Ivy had no clue. She thought of Professor Smallian. He didn't like traditional stories, but to those who clung to beginnings, middles, and ends, he always had the same advice: *Start with the ending.*

Ivy got in the car. She took the dirt track out of the woods, bumped onto pavement, followed it back to Ransom Road. Then a left and down the long steep hill where it would be so easy to spin out in an ice storm. Ivy parked in front of Claudette's house.

By day, she saw what she'd missed at night: a carport beside the house, sheltering an old, rusted-out Beemer of the smallest kind. Ivy went up on the porch, knocked on the front door. No answer. She knocked again, harder. The house was still. Was Claudette back on the day shift? Ivy really wanted another look at that photograph: Harrow, Betty Ann, Claudette, Mandrell. She tried the door. Locked. Was there a difference between entering an unlocked house without permission and breaking in? Yes. But how big when stacked up against the difference between an innocent man—maybe a great artist—being a prisoner or being free? Not so big.

Ivy walked to the carport, tried the side door. Also locked. Next to it was a small window. She glanced around: she was practically invisible from the street, and there were no other houses at the bottom of Ransom Road anyway. Ivy pressed her palms against the window, pushed up. It pushed up. She paused for a moment: this was so much like what had happened at Les Girls, except she was going the opposite way. From prey to predator overnight: had to be a move in the right direction. Ivy boosted herself up and climbed into Claudette's house.

She was in a little hallway. Claudette's Wal-Mart smock hung on a hook. Would Wal-Mart issue more than one? Ivy didn't know. She walked through the kitchen and into the living room. Dark, the shades drawn. She took the photo off the mantel. In the gloomy light, they almost seemed like they could start moving—Harrow, Betty Ann, Claudette, Mandrell. That inward look in Betty Ann's eyes: Had she been worried about something? Photo in hand, Ivy moved toward the window. She was raising the shade to let in more light when a faint groan came from close by.

Ivy let go of the cord. The shade fell with a sharp *thwack,* the sound like thunder in the house.

Then came a voice. "What the hell?"

A woman's voice —thick with sleep, maybe hungover. On the couch, a heavy form changed shape.

"Claudette?" Ivy said.

"Yeah? Who's here?"

"It's me," Ivy said, raising the shade. A beam of light poked in. "Ivy."

"Huh?"

Claudette sat up, shielding her eyes from the light. One of her breasts flopped out of her tattered robe. On the table beside her lay a bottle of Bailey's Irish Cream and an ashtray with cigarette butts and a half-smoked joint. Ivy went closer.

"Remember?" she said. "We had dinner at the Tiki Boat."

Claudette squinted at her. "Do me a favor?" she said.

"Sure."

"Water."

Ivy went into the kitchen, returned with a glass of water. Claudette tilted her head back and drank it down; her neck was lined and puffy, looked much older than the rest of her. Ivy slid the Bailey's aside and sat on the table.

Claudette glanced at her and blinked. "Bit messy," she said. "Party last night."

"Big crowd?" said Ivy.

"Just yours truly," Claudette said. "Very private." She noticed her robe was open, pulled it together. "What are you doing here?" she said. "Hey! How the hell did you get in, anyway?"

"The door was open," Ivy said.

"Yeah?" said Claudette.

Ivy nodded.

"Shit," said Claudette, sinking back on the couch.

Ivy held up the photo. "I'd like to make a copy of this," she said.

"How?" said Claudette.

"How?" Ivy said. "Take it to Kinko's or someplace like that."

"Oh," said Claudette. "I was like—maybe you were going to draw it, you know?"

"Just make a photocopy," Ivy said. "I'll bring the original right back."

"I guess so," Claudette said, sitting up again. "How come you want it?"

"Remember the book I was telling you about?"

"Not really." Claudette's gaze went to the half joint in the ashtray.

Ivy started into her story about a book based on the Gold Dust case. She was only a minute or so in when Claudette held up her hand like a traffic cop and said, "Yeah, yeah, it's coming back to me. Thing is, I've got this splitting headache. Maybe some other—"

"Aspirin?"

"Allergic," Claudette said. "I'm allergic to all pain remedies." Her eyes went again to the ashtray, as though drawn by a magnet. "Alls that actually does any good is—"

Ivy passed her the ashtray.

Claudette picked up the joint. "Matches around somewheres."

Ivy found them on the floor. She struck one and held the flame for Claudette.

Claudette sucked on the joint till her cheeks went hollow. Then, eyes bugging out a little from breath holding, she passed the joint to Ivy. Ivy didn't like pot, but she needed things from Claudette, and how would she get them without some sort of trust between them? She inhaled.

"Ah," said Claudette. "I feel better already." Her eyes met Ivy's. "How do you feel?"

Ivy took another hit. "What a question!" she said.

"Like, um, how?" said Claudette.

Inside Ivy things were so complicated right now. She felt worried, anxious, scared, lonely—and maybe more than all those put together—she felt excited, big excitement, but tamped down, the way it would have to be if you were working on a long-term project with a potential jackpot at the end.

"Like an explorer," Ivy said.

"You feel like an explorer?" Claudette said, taking the joint from Ivy's hand, smoking a little more. "Cool."

"Yeah," said Ivy.

"Columbus," Claudette said.

"What about him?"

"That kind of explorer?"

"More like Lewis and Clark," Ivy said.

"What's the difference?" said Claudette.

What remained of the joint was back in Ivy's hand. She finished it and forgot the question. Then she gazed at the photo for a while and forgot that there'd been a question. "This picture is amazing," she said.

"Yeah?" said Claudette. "I'm looking at it upside down."

Ivy turned the frame so Claudette could see right-side up. "You've got a BMW," she said.

"Piece of shit," said Claudette. "Even if I could drive it, which I can't for three more fuckin' months."

Ivy put her finger on the photo, right above Frank Mandrell's head. "It used to be his."

Claudette nodded. "Brand-new, back then," she said. She gazed at Mandrell's image. "Tell you a secret if you promise to keep it to yourself."

"I promise," Ivy said.

She turned to Ivy. "Got a boyfriend?" she said.

"No," said Ivy.

"But you must be beating them off with a stick," Claudette said. "Someone like you—educated, pretty."

"Nope," said Ivy. "What's your secret?"

"Frank and I had sex in that car," Claudette said. "The seat goes way back. Ever done that?"

"No," said Ivy. A lie, but there was only so much she was willing to give.

"You should try it sometime," Claudette said.

"I'll let you know how it goes," Ivy said.

Claudette started laughing, couldn't stop. It went on and on—tears, mucus, breast falling out again. "You're hilarious," Claudette said, collecting herself at last.

"How did you end up with the car?" Ivy said.

"Asked for it," Claudette said. "It was just sitting down at the station after Frank went into witness protection. I said could I have it and they got back to me a week or so later with the okay."

"Meaning they talked to Frank."

"Must of."

"Didn't the BMW get left by the boat ramp?" Ivy said.

"Yeah," said Claudette. "Harrow double-crossed him."

"Did that surprise you?" Ivy said.

"Nothing men do surprises me," said Claudette. She took the picture from Ivy, held it close, a foot from her face, her eyes locked on the image of her sister. "Or women either, for that matter," she said. The look in her eyes suddenly turned hard. So hard and sudden it stunned Ivy for a moment. She double-checked to make sure.

"Was there some problem between you and Betty Ann?" Ivy said. At that moment, she remembered what Claudette had said to her the last time: *Just write that I forgive her.* Ivy lowered her voice. "What did Betty Ann do to you?"

The hard look began to fade from Claudette's eyes. She said nothing. Neither did Ivy. The look faded, faded, finally went soft. "It's just human nature," Claudette said. "We're animals, everything said and done. There's nothing to forgive."

"I don't understand," Ivy said. But she was getting the first glimmer: *anything that moves.* She rose from the table, sat on the couch. Claudette shifted slightly so they were sitting side by side, arms touching, the photo in front of them.

"He was very good-looking," Ivy said.

"Like a Hollywood star—didn't I tell you?" said Claudette. "Plus being ambitious—he was headed for big things, you could just see it. And of course she was ambitious, too, wanted to get out of here like she could taste it."

Ivy took in Mandrell's flashing smile, Betty Ann's inward look, Harrow's happiness. "And so?" she said.

"So?" said Claudette, all at once tossing the picture onto the table; it slid off and fell to the floor. "What do you think?"

"Frank and Betty Ann had an affair?" Ivy said.

"Known only to me." Claudette pointed down the hallway that led to her bedroom. "I caught them at it right here."

"How long was this before the robbery?" Ivy said.

"She was always the pretty one, you know?" Claudette said. "Why couldn't that be enough? Why did she have to take him away from me?"

"He's not worth bothering about," Ivy said.

Claudette faced her. "What do you know about him?" she said.

"Just what I've heard," Ivy said. "An ex-con and a thief, plus that big ambition of his was to own strip clubs." She got up, moved a few steps away.

"What are you—a snob?" Claudette said. "There's money in strip clubs."

"Jerry Redfeather died," Ivy said.

"Frank had nothing to do with that," said Claudette. "He wasn't even there. Harrow and the others fucked it up." She noticed that her robe was open, this time did nothing about it.

Ivy knew she'd asked Claudette an important question, still unanswered, but couldn't remember what it was.

"Clean out of dope," Claudette said. "Wish to God I had more."

"That was more than enough for me," Ivy said.

Claudette started laughing again. "Are all writers funny like you?"

"No," Ivy said. "I'm the funniest writer that ever hit a delete key."

More laughter. "You're wearing me out," Claudette said. "My middle part of my lungs."

"I'll tone it down," Ivy said.

Claudette giggled. The important question popped back up in Ivy's mind. She grabbed it while it was still available.

"Between, um, when you caught Frank and Betty Ann and the robbery," she said.

"Huh?"

"How much time went by?"

"Two or three days," Claudette said.

"That's all?"

"Or maybe one."

"One?" said Ivy. "You don't mean the same day?"

Claudette shrugged.

"Who else knows?" Ivy said.

"Knows what?"

"About Frank and Betty Ann."

"Nobody I know," said Claudette. "Didn't I say that? Or was it you?"

"You didn't tell anyone?" Ivy said.

"Like who?"

"Harrow."

"Why would I do that?" She closed her robe.

"He had a right to know."

"Not from me," Claudette said. "Betty Ann was my sister." Her voice broke. She took a deep breath. "Is. Not saying I wasn't upset—in fact I left town for a couple weeks, stayed with a girlfriend in Massena."

"Meaning you weren't even here the night of the robbery?" Ivy said.

"Heard about it on the news," Claudette said. "But you know what kept coming into my mind?"

"What?"

"That the whole time Frank and Harrow must of been planning the robbery together, all this, you know, sneaking around was going on. Isn't that weird?"

"Yeah," said Ivy. Details were missing all over the place, but she was starting to see the core of it, how Betty Ann got away with the money and Frank Mandrell got away with Betty Ann. And Harrow: still in the dark, still protecting her. "Frank was the brainy one," she said, "like everyone says."

"Tell me about it," said Claudette.

Ivy picked up the photograph, tried to read something in Betty Ann's eyes, got blocked by that inward look. "What else did you say about forgiveness?" she said.

"Huh?" said Claudette.

"The night we went to the Tiki Boat."

"Search me," Claudette said. She glanced at the photo. "And forget about making a copy. You can keep the fucking thing."

Twenty-five

Agreat yarn— *my agent kept hearing that,* Tony B had told her. *But no ending, not without finding Betty Ann Price and/or the money. How am I supposed to find Betty Ann when the cops couldn't?*

A question that had seemed unassailably rhetorical at the time. Now Ivy thought it had an answer.

She drove north, across the border, was back in Montreal in the early afternoon. A cold wind blew; people on the street wore winter clothing. She found St. Catherine, parked across the street from Les Girls.

Time passed. Ivy's strategy, cribbed from the movies, was to wait until Mandrell appeared and then follow him to wherever he lived. It had worked for Nick Nolte, Steve Mc-Queen, Humphrey Bogart, Batman, countless others; it didn't work for her. Lots of men came out of Les Girls, but not Mandrell. Maybe he wouldn't leave for hours; maybe he went out the back; maybe he wasn't there at all.

After way too long the obvious suddenly occurred to her. She called information. No McCords listed at all. Why would she expect that he'd have a listed number in the first place? But he had to live somewhere. Any cop— or even a reporter—would already be taking the next step. Did she know any cops? Only one, really, Ferdie Gagnon, and asking his advice was out of the question. Reporters? No. Except . . . except for Tony B.

"Sure I remember you," said Tony B. "Writing teacher from Dannemora. Gold Dust case. Nice lunch."

"I enjoyed it, too."

"And now"—he burped, but softly—"you've got a follow-up question?"

"Yeah," Ivy said. "Let's say you . . . you have a character that needs to find the address of this other character and all you—she—has is his name and the city. For the other character, if you see what I mean."

There was a pause. Then Tony B said, "Are you telling me you tracked down Frank Mandrell?"

"Frank Mandrell?" Ivy said, hitting—to her ear—nothing but false notes.

"Brains behind the robbery," Tony B said. "Disappeared into witness protection."

And then disappeared from that, too. But all Ivy said was, "Oh, him. Of course not. How would I do a thing like that?"

Another silence. "Maybe you got some in with the feds."

"The head of the FBI's my best buddy," said Ivy. "But I decided to call you about this address thing instead."

Tony B laughed. "Touché," he said. "But you can't be too careful in cases like this."

"Cases like what?"

"Where there's a scramble for pub rights," Tony B said.

"I don't understand."

"Something wrong with your memory?" said Tony B. "Maybe you should start taking notes."

"What do you mean?"

"There's already a manuscript, like I told you," Tony B said. "Three hundred and nineteen fucking pages, even if there is no ending. This story is mine."

"Absolutely," Ivy said. "I'll never write a word about it. My interest is in Harrow's fiction."

"Say again?" said Tony B. "You faded out there."

"I'll never write a word about it."

"We're clear on that?"

"One hundred percent," Ivy said.

"Deal," said Tony B. "As for this request of yours, there are several ways to go about it."

Ivy chose the one that involved posing as a buyer in a real-estate office, sitting in a conference room with a well-dressed woman and lots of literature, including municipal tax rolls. Not long after, she was driving through a fancy suburb in the western part of the city. She parked in front of the big stone house at 458 Rue Rançon, registered to Jake and Marie McCord.

And now? Ivy wasn't sure. She could walk up and knock on the door—but what if Frank Mandrell opened up? Or she could just sit and wait. Ivy sat and waited. A gust of wind raised some dead leaves from a lawn and blew them in the gutter. They settled in a little heap; then another gust

sprang up and they were on the move again. Ivy's mind
wandered over to *The Surveyor*. The surveyor's world didn't
add up. The surveyor would have to find out—and find out
painfully—that she didn't add up either. Maybe the survey-
or's whole history wasn't what she'd thought or been told.

Where to begin? Professor Smallian believed that more
stories failed from beginning in the wrong place than for
any other reason. Ivy mulled it over for a while, began to
wonder about the actual instruments of surveying. Learn-
ing all that was going to be important, the nuts and bolts
needed to be—

Ivy had sunk so deeply into all this that she almost didn't
notice the garage door at 458 opening up. A big black Mercedes glided out, Frank Mandrell at the wheel, his long
blond hair so strange with that dark face. Ivy shrank back
in her seat, a useless tactic. Mandrell drove right by her,
five feet away. All he had to do was glance over; but he was
on his cell phone and saw nothing. The Mercedes turned a
corner, flashed briefly between two houses on the cross
street, and vanished.

Ivy took one last look at Betty Ann's image on that deck
in Claudette's photo and got out of the car. She walked up
the flagstone path and banged the knocker—a brass replica
of the *Venus de Milo*—hard against the door.

Footsteps on the other side. Ivy's heart started beating,
fast and light, like a tiny drum. Betty Ann Price had met
Mandrell at the boat ramp, taken the money, money they'd
used to finance Les Girls and make Frank's dream come
true. Once he was lost to witness protection, what was there
to keep them from being together? Nothing: therefore probably part of the reason he'd gone missing. Some details
were still fuzzy, but the core story made sense. Betty Ann

was going to open that door. And then what? Ivy wasn't exactly sure, but it ended with Harrow as a free man.

The door opened.

Not Betty Ann.

Betty Ann would be thirty by now. This woman was about fifteen years older than that, had sharp features, a headful of graying curls, and a cigarette dangling from her mouth.

"Oui?" she said.

"Marie McCord?" said Ivy.

"Yes?" Marie McCord squinted at Ivy through drifting smoke. The tone of her voice, the look in her eyes, the tilt of her head: Ivy read suspicion in every detail. "If you're selling something I'm not interested."

Ivy shook her head. "I'm looking for Betty Ann."

"Betty Ann?" said Marie; Ivy was watching very closely: the name meant nothing to her.

"Betty Ann Price," Ivy said, still unwilling to let the idea go.

Marie shrugged. "You have the wrong house."

"I—"

Marie closed the door.

Ivy backed away.

No Betty Ann.

For a moment or two, Ivy felt light-headed. Had Betty Ann and Mandrell parted somewhere along the way, maybe splitting the money? Ivy didn't know: the Gold Dust story refused to add up. But some big things were still certain: Mandrell had an affair with Betty Ann; he set Harrow up; he made his strip-club dream come true; Harrow was innocent. Ivy drove to the airport, turned in the car, flew back to New York.

The city had changed. Ivy couldn't say exactly how. The quality of the light, the density of the shadows, the expressions on faces, even faces she knew: all just a little bit different, as though some supernatural being had tried to replicate New York and come very close. Unsettlingly close; and she'd always felt settled in New York. Falling asleep took a long time, and the sleep that finally came was troubled.

Ivy awoke, made coffee, cleaned her apartment, showered, and took a long walk that ended at Verlaine's. Pretty busy for a Monday: Bruce was working the bar, along with a slim black woman, very good-looking, whom Ivy had never seen. Ivy put her hair in a ponytail and stepped behind the bar, next to Bruce.

He was pouring a glass of red, that Chilean Pinot he insisted was wrongly unheralded, didn't look at her.

"Ivy?" he said. "What's up?"

"Here to work my shift," Ivy said.

"Shift?" he said, sliding the Pinot to a customer who gave it a cautious sniff.

"Monday, eleven till seven," Ivy said. Now he turned to her. She didn't like the look in his eye. "Sorry I'm a few minutes late," she said.

The other bartender was watching her, too.

"A few minutes late?" Bruce said.

Ivy checked her watch. "It's three minutes after."

"I'll try some of that," said another customer.

Bruce ignored him. "Are you stoned on something?" he said.

"Stoned?" said Ivy. "Of course not."

"It's a joke, then?" Bruce said. "An attempt at humor?"

"I don't understand."

"The Pinot," said the customer. "From Chile."

"It's Tuesday," Bruce said. "Don't pretend this is news."

"Tuesday?" Ivy said. Had she slept round the clock?

"It's not even original," Bruce said. "Another girl tried the same ploy on me a few years back."

Now everyone at the bar was watching, eyes going back and forth like tennis fans. Ivy lowered her voice. "This isn't a ploy, Bruce. I really must have—"

Bruce took a corkscrew to another bottle of the Chilean Pinot. "Crossed the line," he said. "I bent over backward. You know it and I know it." His hands were shaking. "Your check's in the office."

Ivy backed away. She caught a glimpse of herself in the mirror, red-faced, distorted, almost a stranger. Pinot slopped over the side of the glass Bruce was filling.

Bruce's office, originally a closet, stood next to the kitchen. The new cook was yelling in a language Ivy didn't recognize. She went into the office. Dragan was there.

"For real?" he said. "The boss is firing you?"

"For real," Ivy said, taking her check out of the mail slot. Her name tape was already gone.

"My heart is sick," said Dragan.

"Don't worry," Ivy said. "Everything's going to be all right."

Dragan gazed at her. "Cool," he said. "This is the famous way American woman handles setback—I have seen on Oprah." Ivy noticed a thick, brown-paper-wrapped package under one of Dragan's arms. "In this event," he went on, "maybe it would be possible you are still perusing my novel."

Ivy gazed back at him, saw he was growing a fuzzy little

mustache. She remembered a lesson on the feudal system, maybe from third grade. The illustration showed the king at the top, commanding the nobles, and ended with the peasant at the bottom, and the caption: *The peasant has no one to kick but his dog.*

"Happy to," Ivy said.

"You will peruse?"

"Just write your number on the package."

Dragan wrote down his number, ended with an exclamation point. "Good luck in all your endeavoring," he said. "Past, present, and future."

She took the package. Like Bruce's, her hands were a little shaky, too.

Ivy went home. She opened a file called *Surveyor Notes* and started trying to bend all the ideas she'd had so far into the shape of a story. It went well for a while; then she remembered Danny's offer to fund *The Surveyor* so she could quit Verlaine's. She'd ended up with neither, Danny and her job both now gone. Her mind went useless. It wasn't so much that the flow dried up, more like it became intractable, as though water had turned to wood.

"Jesus Christ," she said, putting her head in her hands. At that moment, she saw that her message light was blinking.

Danny? Ivy kind of hoped it was: an unforgivable moment of weakness.

But it wasn't Danny.

"Sergeant Tocco here. Good to go on that hospital visit. Get back to me if you're still interested."

Ivy called him before the playback ended.

"Hey," said Sergeant Tocco. "How's it going?"

"Good," said Ivy. "And you?"

"No complaints," said Sergeant Tocco. "Had a few snow-flakes this morning."

"Already?"

"It's coming," he said. "Still interested in the hospital thing?"

"Yes," said Ivy. "When would be a good time?"

"Whenever you like, just about. Give me a heads-up, that's all."

"How long's he going to be there?" Ivy said.

"No telling," said Sergeant Tocco. "He's picked up some sort of infection, maybe on account of how it was a tooth-brush that did it."

Ivy found she was squeezing the phone very tight. "Is it serious?"

"No idea," said Sergeant Tocco. "But the doc said he was okay for visiting."

"Is today all right?" Ivy said.

"Today?" said Sergeant Tocco. Pause: Ivy could picture his heavy features growing a little heavier while he thought. "Don't see why not," he said.

She gathered her folder and packed an overnight bag, just in case. Just in case what? Ivy wasn't sure. She hurried down the five flights, out onto the street, headed for the ga-rage where Bruce had that little deal for parking the Saab—something else that would have to change. And soon, as soon as she got back. Ivy had walked only half a block, was wondering how she could even afford to keep the Saab now, when she noticed a car going by. What attracted her eye wasn't the car so much as the driver. He was possibly the biggest man she'd ever seen, certainly the thickest, seemed to fill most of the car; the window was open and his huge bare arm hung outside like a prizewinning ham.

The car pulled over, right in front of her place. The big

man got out, slow and deliberate. A second man who'd been blocked from view emerged on the other side. A round little man with gray hair in a Nero cut: Vic Mandrell. They glanced up at Ivy's building and moved toward the door.

She hurried away.

Twenty-six

Ivy drove out of the city, headed north. The wind was against her. It blew stronger and stronger, like a heavy hand pressing on the hood. The car got very cold; Ivy had to turn the heat all the way up, as though this was midwinter, just to stop the shivering. Frank Mandrell hadn't taken more than a brief glance at her driver's license, surely not long enough to notice, let alone memorize, her address. But he'd memorized it, all right. Mandrell—despite his third-rate Hollywood looks and his ridiculous hair—was the brains. Ivy became very conscious of the back of her neck, couldn't get rid of the feeling. She didn't stop checking the rearview mirror until she parked in the visitors' lot at Plattsburgh Regional Hospital.

A nurse rode Ivy up in an elevator to the third floor, led her to a locked door. "The old psych ward," she said. "Now we get the inmate overflow." She knocked on the door. "Which presently amounts to one."

Keys rattled on the other side. The door—heavy, steel, from another era—swung open. Taneesha, in uniform, gun on her hip, smiled out.

"Hey, Ivy," she said. "Heard you was coming."

"Hi," Ivy said, entering. "Everything all right?"

"Going out of my mind from boredom," Taneesha said, locking the door behind her. They were in a wide hall with a yellow linoleum floor and green walls, the paint pocked and peeling. "Folder," Taneesha said.

Ivy handed over her folder. Taneesha went through it, laid it on a table. "No X-ray here," she said. "Gonna have to pat you down."

"You are?"

"Be done in a jiffy," Taneesha said. "Raise up your arms."

Ivy raised her arms. Taneesha started patting her down.

"Now your legs."

"My legs?"

"Gotta spread 'em."

Ivy spread her legs. Taneesha ran her hands up and down both of them; slow, careful, thorough, tracing the seams of Ivy's panties.

"All done," said Taneesha, straightening.

She'd only been doing her job, and she'd done it well, but Ivy could no longer look at her the same way. Taneesha saw that, and the expression in her eyes changed, too.

"Got him down here at the end," Taneesha said. She led Ivy past five or six empty rooms, the beds inside all stripped to bare mattresses. A card-table chair stood outside the last room, magazines scattered on the floor around it.

"Yo," she called. "Visitor."

Ivy paused outside the door.

"Go on in," Taneesha said.

Ivy went in. Small room, dusty window, strange smells. Only one bed: Harrow lay on it, hooked to an IV, his chest bare, the rest of him covered by a sheet. He looked too thin, the muscles of his face too apparent, sunken purple smudges under his eyes. The eyes themselves were closed, one lid twitching a little. Ivy was so busy taking in all those images that she almost missed the obvious: Harrow was shackled to the bed.

For a second or two, she hated Taneesha.

Ivy moved toward the bed.

Harrow moaned in his sleep. He moved his head from side to side, agitated, like someone denying something, or trying to make it go away. There were two little bloodstains on the pillow.

Ivy stood beside the bed. She wanted to touch his forehead, feel his temperature. She raised her hand.

Harrow's lips—cracked and dry—opened. He spoke, his voice weak and whispery, mostly just air. "How can I?" he said. His lips kept moving, but for a few moments he was silent. Then the sound came back. "How can I let you?" He fell silent again. From outside the door came the creaking sound of Taneesha shifting in her chair. Harrow took a deep breath, let it out with a long sigh.

"Felix," he said.

His eyes opened. They shifted toward Ivy. His eyes: still so surprisingly dark, but now dull, like a third- or fourth-generation reprint.

"Hi," she said.

"Teacher," he said, his voice a little stronger now, but low and grainy. His wrists were cuffed separately, attached to the right- and left-hand bed rails by chain links a foot long. The cuffs on the rail ends could slide about the same distance between two vertical supports. Harrow was free to move a bit, although probably not enough to turn on his side.

"How are you feeling?" Ivy said.

He licked his lips: so cracked and dry, the tip of his tongue white as bone. "I don't have anything for you," he said.

"What do you mean?"

"No pages, teacher," he said. "Haven't had any writing ideas lately."

"That's all right," Ivy said. She looked around for water, spotted a plastic cup on one of those tall rolling steel tables, way out of his reach. And empty. "Want some water?"

Harrow nodded, a slight movement of his head; a tendon stood out on the side of his neck. Ivy took the cup out to the hall. Taneesha sat on her chair, tilted back against the wall, eyelids heavy. They fluttered open.

"He needs water," Ivy said.

Taneesha pointed to a fountain. Ivy filled the cup, returned to Harrow's room.

"Here."

He got his elbows into his sides—every move accompanied by metallic sounds—and pushed himself up, his face paling a little more. Ivy held the cup close to his mouth, but he didn't want that. Instead he got one hand on the rail to support himself and raised his other. Ivy placed the cup in it.

Harrow leaned toward the water, the chains stretching tight, his body bent and twisted. He was just able to get the cup to his mouth. Harrow drank, his Adam's apple bobbing up and down. The cup emptied. Ivy took it.

"Good?"

"Yeah."

"More?"

"No."

He sank back on the pillow, but not before she noticed the bandages on his back, thick bandages spotted pink here and there.

"Aren't they taking proper care of you?" she said.

"No complaints."

"What does the doctor say?"

Harrow closed his eyes. "He's going to try deep-frying the turkey this Thanksgiving."

"I meant about how you're doing," Ivy said.

Harrow licked his lips. The tip of his tongue wasn't as white now, but still didn't look normal.

"I'm getting more water," Ivy said. She moved toward the door.

Harrow spoke behind her. "Beer would be nice."

She turned to him. Eyes open now, and he had a little smile on his face.

"Is it allowed?" she said.

His eyes closed and the smile faded, as though controlled by the same switch. Ivy went out to ask Taneesha about the possibility of one little can of beer. Taneesha, still in her chair, still tilted against the wall, was fast asleep now, her lips parted. Ivy filled the cup at the fountain, went back to the bedside. This time he let her hold the cup for him.

He drank it all down then sighed a deep sigh that shook his torso. "I was thirsty and didn't even know it," he said. He gazed at her.

"Want more?"

"More," he said. "Yes."

She went for more. Taneesha was snoring softly.

Harrow drank. He started looking better before he'd even finished the cup. Normal flesh tones spread across his face, driving out the pallor, as though some tide were turning inside him.

"What kind of care are you getting?" Ivy said.

"This minute?" he said, his voice still low, but not as grainy. "State-of-the-art."

"I meant the doctors."

"No complaints."

"What about this infection?"

He glanced up at the IV bag.

"What does the doctor say?" Ivy said.

"Not much."

"What kind of infection is it?"

"In the blood, maybe," Harrow said. "I've been a little out of it." He looked at her, his eyes not quite so dull now. "Pull up a chair."

Ivy pulled up a chair, sat by the bed.

"Hungry?" she said.

"Yeah," he said, sounding a little surprised.

"I've got a banana," Ivy said. She took it out of her folder, a lustrous, richly yellow banana; it almost seemed to glow. Ivy half peeled it, held it to his mouth. He took a bite.

"Ah," he said.

Ivy fed him the rest of the banana. He ate, slow and careful, as though savoring a delicacy.

"Thanks," he said.

"You're welcome."

He gazed at her. Faint snoring sounds drifted through the doorway.

Harrow's eyes moved toward the folder in Ivy's lap. "I never got to hear what you wrote in that last class."

Ivy reached back in the folder, found the page. She read silently.

Where was that photograph taken—you, Betty Ann, Claudette, Frank Mandrell? Claudette showed it to me. Did you know she lives on Ransom Road?

Ivy looked up. His eyes were on her; almost back to normal, that dark brown so intense. The piece itself seemed dated—she knew so much more now. Not only that: she had the actual picture. Ivy fished it out of the folder, held it so Harrow could see.

"I wrote about this," she said.

Harrow stared at the photograph, his eyes slowly tracking across the faces. Ivy found she'd leaned close to him, her mouth not far from his ear.

"I know you're innocent," she said, her voice very low. "Nothing you say can change my mind. Nothing."

Their eyes met. She saw something new in his—maybe not new, but now unconcealed—something that made, or induced, or compelled her to scan his body, past his bare chest, to where the sheet covered him up. The sheet now rose in a tent shape over his groin.

Ivy reached down, pulled the sheet away, freeing him. Some force took over, a completely righteous force, impossible to stop, as though the immediate future had already happened. Ivy was wearing a skirt that day, not quite knee length, not tight. It hiked up easily. She hiked it up, climbed onto the bed and straddled him. He pressed against her. She reached down, tugged the crotch of her panties aside. A sound rose from her throat, a sound she'd never made before, almost a growl. Then she thrust herself down on him, not gentle, but hard and all the way at once, so she felt his hipbones against the insides of her thighs.

Ivy started coming right away, no buildup, not her at all. Then another, and another, followed by a tiny little wait, as though some inner cells were gasping for breath—and why wouldn't they, because of course there'd been buildup, weeks and weeks—and then more, like a symphony that was all climaxes. His chains clinked as he tried to get his arms around her but couldn't. Right then, the metallic sound still in her ears, Ivy had her last orgasm, the biggest of all, very close to pain. His whole body went rigid and he made a little growl, too.

She fell on top of him, their faces pressing together, the IV tube twisted around her leg. They breathed. Ivy felt dampness on her skin. She opened an eye. It was right next to his. His was overflowing. She started crying, too.

Ivy pressed her mouth right against his ear. "It's going to be all right, baby."

What was that? A creaking sound from the hall.

Taneesha poked her head in the door.

"Everything all right in here?" she said.

Ivy sat in the chair, the folder in her lap hiding the fact that she had her skirt on backward. Harrow lay on the bed, all covered up.

"Fine," said Ivy.

Taneesha looked over at Harrow; her focus not on Harrow so much as the shackles.

"Does he have to be chained like that?" Ivy said.

"Procedure," said Taneesha, "when there's no bars on the windows."

Ivy glanced at the windows: grimy, thick, reinforced with metal filaments, but no bars. "We're three stories up," she said.

"That's nothin'," said Taneesha. "Supper's comin' up soon—you want some?"

"I'm all right," Ivy said.

"It's free," said Taneesha. She backed out of the room. Her chair creaked.

Ivy rose, took Harrow's hand. It was warm and dry, the steel cuff cold against her wrist. Her heart was beating like crazy. She wanted to just look at him, compose herself, understand what had just happened from all possible angles. But they didn't have time for that. Maybe Harrow realized it, too.

"Why do you say I'm innocent?" he said. His tone was different now in a hard-to-define way, almost as though they'd known each other for years.

"I told you," Ivy said. "I've seen the casino tape."

"So? What does that prove?"

Silence. A vein throbbed in the back of his hand, under Ivy's finger. How about climbing back on top of him, right now, and for once not giving a damn for anything but the moment? Ivy took a deep breath.

"You really want to talk about the tape?" she said. "Okay. Explain to me why you had to push that old black guy so hard."

Harrow gazed at her.

"The one with the shopping bags," Ivy added.

"He was in the way," Harrow said.

"There is no old black guy on the tape," Ivy said. "With or without shopping bags. You weren't there."

Harrow smiled, just a little smile, gone in an instant.

"So just admit it," Ivy said.

"And then what?"

"We can try to reopen the case," Ivy said. "But it has to start with you."

"Never happen."

"You're just going to give up?" Ivy said. "Don't you realize the kind of future you could have?"

"What future?"

"With your talent," Ivy said.

He pulled his hand away. "Haven't had any writing ideas lately, as I said."

"They'll come," Ivy said. "Especially when you're free."

A slight change in his eyes; not a weakening of their power—a combination of animal and intellectual, unique in her experience—more like it was being directed somewhere else.

"You know that's true," Ivy said.

His eyes changed: back on her. "It'll be even truer in eighteen years," he said.

Her voice rose, taking her by surprise. "What's wrong with you?" she said. "Why are you protecting her?"

Harrow glanced at the door. "Who?"

Ivy lowered her voice. "Don't treat me like an idiot," she said. "Betty Ann."

Harrow didn't answer. His silence infuriated her.

"Why don't you get it?" she said. "All you have to do is say where she is."

Keys rattled in the steel door. Harrow remained silent.

"You don't owe her a thing," Ivy said. "She was having an affair with Frank Mandrell."

No reaction.

Footsteps sounded on the linoleum outside.

"Who I tracked down, by the way," Ivy said.

Harrow sat up, very fast, his chains snapping taut, almost scaring her.

Taneesha entered, followed by an unshaven man with a stethoscope around his neck.

"Doc's here," she said.

Twenty-seven

Ivy sat beside Taneesha in the hall of the old psych ward while the doctor made his call.

Taneesha yawned, checked her watch. "Three more hours?" She shook her head as though trying to clear it. "Know what's crazy about this job?"

"What?"

"When you're on shift," Taneesha said, "time slows right down to almost nothin', just like you're an inmate. Then when you're off, it revs up to fast-forward, makes you jittery."

"What about when the inmates get out?" Ivy said. "Do they end up jittery, too?"

"Who knows?" Taneesha said. "They're never on the outside for long." She reached down into the magazine pile, took one for herself, passed one to Ivy.

An entertainment magazine, all about Hollywood. Ivy leafed through, not reading, not even really looking, just letting the images pass before her eyes. She almost missed Joel.

But there he was, bottom of page twenty-seven, standing by a plastic flamingo with Adam Sandler. The caption read: *Birds of a Feather: Adam Sandler and hot new screenwriter Joel Cutler team up on the set of* Ass Backwards.

Ass Backwards? That was the title of Joel's screenplay?

Adam Sandler had a big smile on his face. So did Joel. The flamingo's yellow teeth were arranged in a big smile, too. In the background, a waitress with a drink tray leaned over a table. She had a tattoo on her shoulder, something red, maybe a flower.

Ivy turned to Taneesha. Her eyelids were heavy again.

"Taneesha?"

Taneesha's eyelids slowly rose. "Yeah?"

"Have they moved Morales yet?"

"Back on the tiers, you mean?" Taneesha said. "He's still in the infirmary, far as I know."

"But Sergeant Tocco said Morales would be sent to another prison," Ivy said.

"First I heard of it," said Taneesha.

"Are you saying it might not happen?"

Taneesha shrugged. She opened a magazine, took out a pencil. "Thirteen down," she said. " 'Rear Window director.' Nine letters."

"Hitchcock," said Ivy.

"Oh, yeah." Taneesha penciled it in. "I knew that."

"Have they found who killed Felix yet?" Ivy said.

"Nope," said Taneesha. "How about 'Bergman and Boyer scarefest,' eight letters."

"Gaslight," Ivy said.

"Don't know that one," Taneesha said. "Any good?"

"Yes," Ivy said.

Taneesha wrote *Gaslight*. "You ever meet the warden?" she said.

"No."

"He was pretty pissed about Felix."

"Did it get him in trouble?"

"Huh?"

"The warden," said Ivy. "For having a fairly prominent inmate killed on his watch."

"Felix was prominent?" Taneesha said.

"In some circles."

"Not up here," said Taneesha. "Only way an inmate can hurt the warden is if he escapes. That was the thing with Felix."

"I don't understand."

"Most of the inmates are pretty dumb, right?" Taneesha said. "Part of how come they are what they are. Felix wasn't like that. Word was he'd put his mind to work on our security, come up with some sort of weakness."

"Felix was planning an escape?" Ivy said.

"Uh-uh," Taneesha said. "He wanted to make a deal."

"What kind of deal?"

"Trade this weakness he'd figured out for probation," Taneesha said.

"But the warden turned him down? Is that what you're saying?"

"Never got the chance," Taneesha said. "On account of Felix endin' up how he did."

"Does that mean the Latin Kings—" Ivy began.

The doctor came out, checking his watch.

Ivy rose and introduced herself. "I teach—taught—the writing program at Dannemora. Harrow was in the class. I—"

"Harrow?" the doctor said.

"The patient," said Ivy, her tone hardening on its own. "I was wondering how he's doing."

"Amazingly well, considering," said the doctor. "Some

of these guys are like another species, physiologically speaking—might be a research paper in there somewhere. I'm recommending he goes back tomorrow."

"Back?" Ivy said.

"To the prison infirmary," the doctor said. "At this rate, he'll be up and around in a day or two."

"Thank God," said Taneesha. "I'm goin' stir-crazy, Doc."

The doctor glanced around. "I hear you," he said.

Taneesha took out her key, turned to Ivy. "Might as well let the both of you out together," she said.

"But—" Ivy said.

Taneesha tapped her watch.

"Can I just say good-bye?" Ivy said.

"You already got extra."

"Two minutes," said Ivy.

Taneesha's gaze lingered on her. Then she nodded and led the doctor to the steel door.

Ivy went back into Harrow's room, barely able to keep herself from running. He was sitting up now, propped against the pillows.

"Where's Mandrell?" he said.

"We don't have time for that," Ivy said. "They're moving you back tomorrow."

"Montreal? Is that where you found him?"

"Are you listening?" Ivy said. "You're going back inside tomorrow. And Morales is still there."

"Good."

"Good? What are you talking about? Don't you see? You've got to tell me where Betty Ann is, and now."

"Forget it," he said.

"But she can prove you were innocent," Ivy said. "You can be free." *And alive.*

Harrow gazed at her. "You're very pretty," he said.

Ivy stepped forward, took his face in her hands, not gentle. "Where is she?"

"You'll never find her."

"Why not?"

"Did Frank end up owning those strip clubs?"

"It doesn't matter," Ivy said. "She's not with him." Keys jingled out in the hall. Why didn't he get it? He was going back inside. The Latin Kings would finish him off. Would she ever see him again? "Why aren't you telling me?" she said, shaking him a little. Then it hit her. "You don't know where she is? Is that it?"

Harrow had a faraway look in his eyes. "I know," he said.

"So if you tell me, why couldn't I find her?" Ivy said. She heard Taneesha's footsteps, on the way. "You're the only one who can do it?"

Harrow nodded, a slight movement, almost imperceptible. Ivy let him go.

Her mind was racing, pulling her ahead so fast she could hardly keep up. Harrow was the only one who could find Betty Ann. Why? Ivy didn't know, but finding Betty Ann was the only way to prove his innocence. At that moment, she understood what went on in the hearts of a human type that had always eluded her: the woman who drops everything to work with AIDS victims in Africa or the man who stands in front of a tank. "In that case," she said, "I'm coming to get you." And it would have to be tonight.

Ivy didn't linger to see his reaction. She darted to the window. A double-hung: she unfastened the catch, raised the window half an inch, just enough room for sliding fingers underneath.

Behind her, Harrow, very quiet, spoke two words: "Bolt cutters."

Ivy already knew that, although she'd never used bolt cutters, or even the term, couldn't picture them. She turned, crossed her arms, looked innocent.

Taneesha entered, glanced at Harrow, then at her. "Time," she said.

The coldest night of the year, so far. The wind had died down, but it must have been blowing high above because a solid line of cloud was sliding slowly across the starry sky, like the closing of a giant eyelid. Ivy had found a Home Depot over on the Vermont side of Lake Champlain, now drove back to Plattsburgh, credit card maxed out, with an extendable aluminum ladder tied to her roof and covered with a tarp. The bolt cutters, their two-foot-long steel handles coated in plastic, lay on the seat beside her. She felt nervous, but no more so than if she had to make a speech, say, or pass some entrance exam. Her mind, more logical and organized than it had ever been, was still racing along ahead of her. It had already divided the future into two possible paths.

Path one, and her instincts told her the more likely: Betty Ann was close by, and this would all be over by morning, almost before Harrow could even be missed, certainly before her role could be suspected.

Path two: Betty Ann was farther away, and they would need time. Ivy had a plan for that; it felt preordained. Her whole relationship to life had shifted, as though she were meeting it from a different angle, an angle that had to do with changing things—maybe just one thing—but for the better.

Ivy turned into the visitors' lot at the hospital, drove all the way to the back, past the last light stand into a shadowy corner. The hospital, three stories high, was T-shaped, the psych ward on the third floor at the end of the right-hand arm. That wing stood beyond a grassy rectangle about twenty or thirty yards from the end of the parking lot. Lights shone from many windows, but only faintly from the psych ward, and not at all from the last window. Ivy reached for the door handle. Her cell phone rang.

Ivy almost didn't answer. Then she remembered those late-night calls from inside Dannemora, and the cell phone better left unmentioned. Did he still have it?

"Hello?" she said.

"Ivy?" A man, vaguely familiar, not Harrow.

"Yes?"

"It's Whit," he said.

For a moment, the name didn't click. "Whit?"

"From *The New Yorker*."

"Sorry," Ivy said. "I just wasn't expecting—"

"Is this a bad time?" Whit said. "If you want, I could call ba—"

"No, no," said Ivy. A whole bank of lights on the second floor dimmed. "It's fine."

"You're sure?"

"Yes."

"Good," said Whit. "First of all, I apologize for making you wait on this."

"Oh, that's all right." A side door in the main wing of the hospital opened, framing a uniformed man in an oblong of light: security guard. He stepped out, closed the door, took the shape of a shadow in the darkness, hard to spot.

"I'm calling about 'Caveman,' of course," Whit said. "What happened is just extraordinary."

"Did something happen?" Ivy said.

"To 'Caveman,'" Whit said. "Sure this is an okay time to talk? You sound a little—"

"Yes," said Ivy. "Talk. I mean—it's fine."

Whit cleared his throat, the way people do when they're starting over. "In my experience," he said, "after a story gels in a given configuration, no amount of revision ever takes it to another level. But that change you made—I'm referring to the possible cannibalism sequence—is just magical. And then, when he tries to call his mother—chilling."

"Oh," said Ivy. "Um." The security guard stepped suddenly out of the darkness, just a few feet away. Ivy froze. The guard didn't look inside the car, didn't appear to even see it. He lit a cigarette, rested his back against the driver-side door—rocking the Saab on its springs—and tossed away the match.

"Mind if I ask you a question?" Whit said. Maybe he took her silence for a yes. "How did it come about?"

The guard sang under his breath: "Dooby dooby doo."

Ivy didn't breathe. She pressed the phone tight to her ear to keep sound from leaking out.

"I'm referring to the revision," Whit said. "Was it just one of those out-of-the-blue things, or did you start with a feeling that the story needed an element like that?"

Ivy said nothing.

"You don't have to answer, of course," Whit said. "I'm curious, that's all. I seem to remember you referring to a suggestion someone made."

Ivy didn't answer.

"I don't mean to be intrusive," Whit said. "The fact is I'm doing a short piece for the *Atlantic* on the writing process from a historical perspective. Melville's journals are really surprising."

The guard pushed himself off the car, ambled back toward the hospital.

Whit cleared his throat again. "Anyway," he said. "All this is beside the point, which is that we're accepting 'Caveman.'"

The guard flicked his cigarette away, a red pinwheel in the night, and opened the side door.

"You are?" Ivy said, very quiet.

"It'll be in our debut edition," Whit said, "featuring two other young writers you'll meet at a little party we're giving. Don't have the exact pub date yet, but the check is in the mail. Literally, as it were."

"Thanks," Ivy said. The guard disappeared inside.

"You're welcome," said Whit. "I love making calls like this."

"Thanks," she said again, this time adding, "very much."

They said good-bye.

This was great news, maybe the best news Ivy had ever received in her life, even a triumph. She recognized that intellectually. As for her feelings, she felt good about it, but more like the way she'd feel if it had happened to someone else, someone she was pulling for, not her in the here and now. She knew that would change; and Harrow would be with her at the little party, and get the credit he deserved.

Ivy stepped out of the car, hooked the bolt cutters on her belt, stripped off the tarp, and unfastened the ladder.

A trisectional ladder, heavy but not unmanageable. Ivy carried it under her arm, across the grassy rectangle to the end of the right-hand wing. The ladder rattled but there was nothing she could do. This would only work by pressing on as though it were daylight and she was just doing her job;

any other approach would paralyze her. Ivy calmed down inside, felt bigger and stronger than normal.

Almost all the windows in the right-hand wing were dark now, and those that weren't had drawn shades. Starlight gleamed on the ladder, but weakly; above, that line of clouds was moving faster.

Ivy laid the ladder down, the base about ten feet from the wall, directly under that last window on the third floor, and extended it the way the Home Depot clerk had demonstrated. Next step: lifting from the other end, walking the ladder upright rung by rung. It must have been heavy, especially approaching the vertical, but Ivy hardly felt the weight. The ladder swung toward the hospital wall, Ivy tugging on a chest-level rung to slow it down. Way up there, two or three feet from the base of the window, the rubberized tips struck the bricks with a thump—not loud, she thought, although there was more rattling, and maybe even an echo. She took a last look around. Nothing moved.

Ivy climbed the ladder, her sneakers soundless on the rungs. She passed the first-floor window—dark—and the second, where a blue light glowed through the shade. She heard TV voices, kept going.

Ivy stopped two rungs from the top. From there she could reach the sill of the third-floor window. The window: open just enough for her fingers to slide through. This was working. Ivy climbed one more step, got her hands under the window, palms up, and pushed. The window rose about a foot, maybe a little more, then got stuck. Enough.

Ivy peered inside. Dark, except for weak yellow light coming through the doorway to the hall. It gleamed on the bed rails, the shackles, Harrow's eyes, his gold incisor. Those eyes, like gold now, too, were turned toward her. Ivy climbed through.

She twisted around, got her feet on the floor. The sole of her right sneaker squeaked on a sticky spot. She went still, her gaze on the doorway. Nothing moved out there. From where she stood, she could see a blue-uniformed leg from the knee down, the heel of a big black shoe—a man's shoe—on the floor, toe raised, the pose relaxed, maybe even a sleeping pose. Stepping with the lightness of a little girl, Ivy approached the bed.

Harrow lay there, completely still, his eyes reflecting that yellow light. No time to talk and nothing to say in any case. Ivy took the bolt cutters off her belt. Would it have been smart to have practiced with them a little first? Probably. She lowered the bolt cutters.

"Hey!" A man's voice from the hall. Ivy jumped. Heart-stopping, thrill of fear, blood running cold: all those clichés, all true. She came close to diving for the window. Then the man said, "Didn't wake you, did I?" Pause. "Not much. Pulling the overnight." Pause. "Yeah? Not with coaching like that they won't."

No time, no time at all. Ivy leaned forward, got the edge of the nearest handcuff inside the blades of the cutter, and pressed the handles together hard. The blades made a snicking sound, sliced right through.

"You seen that kid in goal? Stoned Massena Monday night."

Ivy stepped around the bed, cut through the other cuff.

"Must of faced fifty shots."

Harrow slid his hands free and sat up. His bare shoulder brushed against her breast. Her temperature warmed up in an instant. Surely not possible.

"Way too much politics."

Harrow took hold of the end of the IV tube and drew the

needle out of his arm. Blood leaked out, like a line of india ink on ivory.

"Been the trouble with this league since day one, politics." Pause. "That asshole. When was this?"

Harrow got his legs free of the sheet; he wore pajama bottoms, nothing else. He swung his legs over the side and rose, standing beside Ivy. She mouthed the word *okay?* Harrow nodded. Then, as though all his bones had dissolved inside him, he started to sag toward the floor. Ivy caught hold of him, barely, redirected the fall onto the bed. They landed together, tangled up. A loose chain clanked against the bed rail.

"Hold on a sec."

Ivy grabbed the sheet, yanked it over them, leaving nothing but Harrow's face exposed. A footstep: it advanced; paused; withdrew. The card-table chair creaked.

"Nothin'. These fuckin' nights never end." Pause. "Overtime? Who are you kiddin'?"

Ivy put her mouth to Harrow's ear. "Okay?"

He squeezed her arm.

"Yeah? The one with the tits?"

They got off the bed. Ivy heard Harrow take a deep breath. She reached for his arm. They crossed the room to the window, Harrow a little unsteady. She tapped him on the shoulder, pointed outside. He got his bare foot on the ledge—a strong, well-shaped foot, even at that moment she couldn't help noticing—twisted around with a grunt, soft but full of pain, and climbed out backward.

Ivy stuck her head out, watched him make his slow way down the ladder, a pause on every rung except for the last few. Tendons and veins stood out like wires in his neck and shoulders.

"Wouldn't mind getting laid myself, comes to that."

She tucked the bolt cutters back in her belt, climbed out and went down fast, her hands and feet hardly touching the ladder. Up above the window was dark, nothing moving on the other side.

Harrow touched her back. "The grass feels good," he said.

"Let's go," said Ivy.

"The ladder," Harrow said.

"We're taking the ladder?"

"Everyone likes a little mystery."

They walked the ladder onto the ground, slid the extensions back down. Ivy carried it back to the car, Harrow at her side, gazing up at the sky. The line of clouds closed over what was left of the stars.

In the visitors' lot: no cars left but the Saab. They tied the ladder to the roof, covered it with the tarp, got inside. Ivy stuck the key in the ignition, turned to Harrow. He was smiling, looked like a happy kid on field-trip day.

"Where to?" she said.

Twenty-eight

Morocco," Harrow said.

"Betty Ann's in Morocco?" Ivy said.

Harrow laughed. Had she heard him laugh before? If so, not like this. It was a lovely laugh—soft, surprised, unself-conscious. "Morocco's just a place I always wanted to see," he said.

"Me, too," Ivy said.

"There you go," said Harrow.

They faced each other. Then they were kissing; a complete immersion in a tiny world of its own. Ivy would have torn her clothes off then and there.

Harrow leaned away. "No lights till we're out of the lot," he said.

Yeah, Ivy thought, *here we go.* This was right, this was what it felt like. She backed the car, performed the quickest, tightest three-point turn of her life, and headed across the parking lot, slowing down as they came to the road.

"Left or right?" she said.

"Depends where Frankie is," said Harrow. A car went by, its headlights shining on his bare chest, muscles taut, skin covered in goose bumps.

Ivy stopped the car, looked at him, saw a light sheen of sweat on his forehead. "But I told you—they're not together. I even went to his house. The woman he's married to isn't Betty Ann."

"I know," Harrow said.

"Then—then he knows where Betty Ann is?" Ivy said. "Is that it?"

"No doubt about that."

"I know where he lives and where he works," Ivy said. "But as for where he is right now, the fact is . . ."

"The fact is what?" Harrow said.

"He might be in New York." Ivy told him about her driver's license, and how Vic Mandrell and that huge guy had appeared outside her apartment not too many hours before.

"Did they connect you and me?" Harrow said.

"No," Ivy said.

Harrow raised his right hand, pointed north.

Ivy turned onto the highway. "Montreal?" she said.

"Not that far," Harrow said. "We'll have Frankie make the trip."

"How are we arranging that?" Ivy said. "And what makes you think he'll tell us where Betty Ann is?"

"Piece of cake," Harrow said, "unless he's changed an awful lot. Got his number?"

"No," Ivy said. "But Vic's in the book."

"Slow down."

Ivy saw she was doing ninety-five. She slowed down to normal speed, checked the rearview mirror. Nothing. Her inside self slowed a little, too. They drove in silence for a while. That term *companionable silence* was familiar to her, but not the feeling itself. A very good feeling; almost impossible to believe it could happen at a time like this, and therefore even better.

"There's some clothes for you in the back," Ivy said.

"Yeah?" He twisted around, found the bag from the Marshalls she'd spotted near Home Depot. He took out the clothes—a navy-blue flannel shirt, white boxers, navy-blue cotton socks, khakis, New Balance sneakers—and examined them by the panel lights. "Hey," he said, his voice soft.

"You like?"

"Oh, yeah."

Harrow started getting dressed. That meant taking off his pajama bottoms. As soon as she realized that, a hot, clogging desire built in her, and the moment those pajama bottoms came off, Ivy reached over and grabbed his cock, could not have stopped herself for anything. It hardened in her hand, real fast. He laughed, a low little laugh in which she read delight. Two separate reactions: she loved them both.

"Better call Vic," he said.

She let go of him, took her cell phone, got Vic's number from information.

"And tell him what?"

Harrow was all dressed, buttoning up his shirt. It was much too big. "Say you want to meet Frank," he said, "settle things."

"Settle things?"

"A hundred grand sounds right."

"Blackmail?" Ivy said. "We're trying to get money from Frank Mandrell?"

"That's the story," Harrow said. "The one he'll buy." He ran the back of his hand along her cheek: electric. "You're the one who's supposed to be teaching me."

"About story?"

"Yeah."

"You know way more about that than I ever will," Ivy said.

He nodded, said nothing.

"Where's the meeting place?" Ivy said.

"Where do you think?"

She thought for a moment. If it were a story, a story designed to sucker Frank in so they could find Betty Ann, the meeting place would be . . . "The boat ramp?"

"Sounds good to me," Harrow said. "Make it soon."

Soon: maybe before the escape was discovered, certainly before Mandrell could find out.

Ivy called Vic Mandrell's number.

"Hello?" A little slow, a little vague: Gina Mandrell.

"Is Vic there?" Ivy said.

"No."

"Still in New York?" A line that just popped out, but felt good. That sighting of Vic and the huge guy: she didn't like being followed around.

"Huh?" said Gina.

"Or maybe Vic doesn't tell you where he's going."

"Who is this?"

"Ivy Seidel."

Gina took a quick breath.

"Got a pencil?" Ivy said. "Here's my number. Frank's got an hour to get back to me."

"Frank?" said Gina.

Ivy clicked off.

Harrow put his arm around her shoulder. "Couldn't be better, how you did," he said.

Ivy put the pedal to the floor, if only for a second.

"Vroom," said Harrow. "Like Bonnie and Clyde."

"Except for the ending," Ivy said.

"Don't worry about that." He squeezed her shoulder.

"You know something?" Ivy said.

"What?"

"We can be in Morocco soon," Ivy said. "Like maybe next week."

That laugh came again, soft and delighted.

"Had you already thought about that?" she said.

"I will now," Harrow said. "All I'm going to think about—Fez, Meknès, Marrakech, Tangier."

No traffic at all: the road unreeled dark and empty, like they were the only ones around.

"Don't forget Casablanca," Ivy said.

"Casablanca's not like those other cities."

"No?"

"They all go way back, ancient," Harrow said. "Casablanca's new. We can skip it, no problem."

"Casablanca's new?"

Harrow nodded. "You know that word *cachet*?"

"Yes."

"French, right?"

"I think so."

"Gets its cachet from the movie. Casablanca the city, I mean."

"Yeah?" said Ivy. This was fascinating. "You must have done a lot of reading about Morocco, and all sorts of other things to—"

The phone rang.

Ivy answered it.

"Got your message," said the man on the other end.

"Hello, Frank," Ivy said.

"The name's Jake," Mandrell said.

"Sure," said Ivy. Somehow, with Harrow next to her, she knew how to play this role, slipped into it naturally, as though it were very close to her real self. "A hundred grand guarantees I remember the right name."

Harrow grinned, his teeth tinged green from the panel lights.

"That's a lot of money," Mandrell said.

"Not worth it to you?" Ivy said. No reply. "See you at the boat ramp."

"Boat ramp?"

"Couldn't have forgotten the boat ramp, Frank," Ivy said. She held up two fingers. Harrow nodded. "Be there at two A.M."

"No way I can make it by then," Mandrell said. "Not if you want the dough."

"Then make it three," Ivy said.

"What's your hurry?" said Mandrell. Ivy said nothing. "Five's the earliest."

"I'll hold you to that, Frank," Ivy said. Harrow, his arm still around her, pressed the tip of his finger into her shoulder, quick, gentle. She got the message. "And you'll be alone," she added. "No need to even mention that."

"Yeah," he said. *Click.*

Ivy put down the phone.

"Couldn't have done better," Harrow said.

Ivy felt herself flushing with pride. This was getting crazy. All those Shakespeare sonnets she'd never quite understood: she understood them now.

"Think he'll actually bring money?" Ivy said.

"Some," Harrow said. "What else is he going to do?"

"I don't know," said Ivy. "Threaten me?"

"Looking forward to that," Harrow said. He glanced at the dashboard clock. "Leaves us some free time."

Almost six hours. Ivy took a deep breath. It seemed like a long, long time. "I know just the place," she said.

"Yeah?" said Harrow.

"It's kind of a shortcut," Ivy said.

"To where?" said Harrow.

Ivy hadn't tried the shortcut at night, but somehow it turned out to be easy: narrow blacktop to rutted lane, rutted lane up to the clearing.

"This is where I saw the bear," she said.

The clearing was empty now, shadows on the perimeter, all of them still. Harrow nodded; he'd been silent the whole way, his eyes barely blinking, his eyelashes—long and finely shaped- -tipped with silvery light. She could feel him absorbing everything. She thought of saying, *They took my story, thanks to you,* decided it could wait. Rutted lane down to the dirt road. The flat, blank-face rock went by.

"I keep wanting to write something on it," Ivy said.

"Like what?"

"Don't know."

She drove on. Harrow slid down his window.

"I smell water," he said.

A minute or two later, Ivy pulled up in front of the Wilderness Lake Cabins. The cabins were dark, the lake beyond them even darker, but with a slight gleam, like polished coal. The headlights shone on the door to cabin one. A sign read: CLOSED FOR THE SEASON. SEE U NEXT SPRING.

Ivy drove a little farther, stopped in front of the last cabin, number four. She took the flashlight from the glove box; and the key.

"How come you've got the key?" Harrow said.

She'd forgotten to put it back under the mat; a simple mistake, she'd thought at the time. "An accident," Ivy told him; but maybe, as some people said, there were no accidents.

They got out, walked to the cabin. No stars, no wind, no sound but their footsteps. Ivy switched on the light. Harrow passed through its circle and she spotted that sheen of sweat on his forehead.

"You all right?" she said.

"Yeah." He shielded his face. She pointed the light away from him, but not before noticing that it wasn't just his shirt: the pants she'd bought him, probably even the sneakers—too big.

She unlocked the door. They went inside. Ivy panned the beam around the room: knotty-pine floors, brass bed still made up, with those clean white pillowcases and the rose-colored duvet, the wooden desk and chair at the window, and the stone fireplace, logs in the grate.

"I'll light a fire," Ivy said.

"I'd like to do that," Harrow said.

He went to the fireplace, opened the flue, struck a match. The tiny flame glowed in his eyes. Lighting a fire, and all that could mean: How long since he'd done that, been free to make fire? Ivy took off her clothes and got in bed. A minute or two later, a fire was crackling away and he was lying beside her, red-gold light from the flames ebbing and flowing in the cabin.

"Hungry?" she said. "I've got sandwiches in the car."

"Later," Harrow said.

He rolled on top of her, penetrated her without foreplay, or kissing, or a word, omissions so obviously intolerable to someone like her that no man had ever dared try anything close.

But it was perfect.

And this was just the start. How long before they found Betty Ann, she told her story to the authorities, and the hard part was all over? Twenty-four hours? Less? Morocco could really happen, although staying right here for a week or so seemed pretty good, too.

"Maybe I should apologize," Ivy said.

"For what?" He looked over, the firelight flickering in his eyes. "I would have bet you were thinking about Morocco," he said.

"How much?"

"The works."

"You'd have won," Ivy said. "But I was thinking about Betty Ann, too. My apology is about her."

"Oh?" he said.

"It was such a horrible way to find out," Ivy said, "me telling you like that."

"Find out what?" said Harrow.

"That she was having an affair with Frank," Ivy said. "But I had to get you to stop protecting her."

Silence. Was he in some kind of emotional pain, all mixed up inside about Betty Ann? Ivy thought so.

"Who's your source?" he said at last.

"Claudette."

They lay without talking, their sides just touching. Was

he trembling? Maybe the littlest bit. The fire hissed, flames finding moisture under the bark.

"You're angry," Ivy said.

"Who could be angry at you?" He took her hand. "You're my savior," he said.

"Don't be silly," Ivy said. All at once, she felt very sleepy, fatigue closing in like huge rolling clouds in her mind. She tried to fight them off; there were loose ends to tie up, and she wanted them tied up now, here in this cabin before their first night together, before they really got started.

"Did you even know about the robbery?" she said. "Or did Betty Ann keep you in the dark about that, too?"

He let go of her hand. "None of that matters anymore."

"Sure it does," said Ivy. "Betty Ann was the inside person, must have been planning to leave you all along. She met Frank at the boat ramp and took off with the money. Then he turned you in, made his deal. They were probably together within days."

"You're good at figuring things out," Harrow said.

"I'm really not." Ivy turned, kissed him on the cheek, gazed into his eyes. Enough thinking, enough figuring things out. It was time just to feel. Her own eyes started closing; there was nothing she could do. Enough thinking.

Sometime later, Ivy awoke. The fire was out, now just a faint red glow from the embers. Harrow was way down under the covers, his face between her legs, active, desperate, like a starving man. Ivy thought at once of the bear and the deer, a confusing thought, and then she was just launched. Her legs clamped closed around him, pressing against the bandages on his back. She was far above, maybe miles, didn't come down for an eternity.

* * *

Ivy slept. During the night, her mind busied itself with *The Surveyor*. It figured out the very first line, which turned out to be dialogue: *"An inch is as good as a mile."* It worked out all the major incidents in the story, culminating in the collapse of an enormous dam in some far-off and pitiful country. And even the very last line came, without the slightest effort on her part, for free: *The sun touched the horizon, flattened out, wobbled and lost its shape.*

Twenty-nine

Ivy awoke, cabin number four completely dark, the embers in the fireplace dead. She felt around beside her: he wasn't there. She'd known that already, the feeling-around part unnecessary.

She sat up. The door opened: Harrow. Ivy knew it was him, just from the shape of his silhouette against the night.

"You're up," she said.

He came in, his steps silent, and closed the door. Then a quick, rasping sound from over by the desk, and a candle was burning.

"Morning, sleepyhead," he said.

"Are we okay for time?" Ivy said.

"Ahead of schedule," said Harrow.

"Did you sleep at all?"

"Like a baby."

She noticed he no longer wore that too-big clothing she'd

bought at Marshalls, now had on a sweatshirt and jeans that fit him better.

"I snooped around a little," he said.

"I'll know your size next time," Ivy said. Harrow smiled, the candlelight gleaming on his teeth. Ivy patted the mattress beside her.

"Not that far ahead of schedule," Harrow said.

Ivy rose, got dressed. She felt his eyes on her and did everything a little slower than normal.

"All set?" he said.

She noticed his bandages, lying in a clump on the floor.

"You all right?" she said.

"Never better," he said. "And that's the whole truth." Ivy believed him. He looked great, forehead free of that sweaty sheen, his face fuller than it had been in the hospital or even at Dannemora, as though he'd managed to put on weight overnight. *Some of these guys are like another species, physiologically speaking.* A disgusting remark, and false in more ways than one: Why couldn't some of the innocent be as strong, too, or in Harrow's case, considering what he'd been through, even stronger?

Harrow picked up the bandages, straightened the bed. They went outside, the sky starless, the air cold and still. "You like swimming?" he said.

"Yes."

"Me, too." He walked down to the lake, tossed the bandages in the water. "The Lusks couldn't swim a stroke. Scared of the water, every goddamn one."

They moved around the cabin. Ivy could make out the shape of the Saab parked out front where she'd left it—deformed now, with the tarp-covered ladder still on the roof, and beside it, another, bigger shadow. She switched on the flashlight and recognized the old pickup that Jean Savard kept beside cabin one.

"Switching rides," Harrow said.

"Are they looking for us already?" Ivy said.

"Probably not," said Harrow. "Shift doesn't change till eight. And even then they'll just be looking for me at first. But why take chances?"

"Right," she said. The question didn't seem ludicrous at all. "You think Betty Ann's close by?"

He nodded and got in the driver's side. Ivy went around, climbed up on the seat. One of those bench seats: she slid over next to him.

"That means it'll all be over soon," Ivy said.

He nodded again, turned the key. The pickup started with a sharp explosive sound.

"Was the key in it?" Ivy said.

"Found it in cabin one, where I got the clothes," said Harrow. He glanced at her, maybe saw her gazing closely at his profile. "The door wasn't locked," he said.

"Really?" But then Ivy remembered Jean and her bottle of gin: could have happened, easily.

Harrow drove down the dirt road, into the woods. One of the headlights out, the other off center: but he was at ease, hands light on the wheel.

"This must feel good," Ivy said.

"Everything," he said. "Everything feels good."

The beam of the lone headlight passed across the flat, blank-faced rock at the entrance to the rutted lane. Harrow slowed down, as though to make the turn, then came to a complete stop. He got out, reaching into his pocket, and walked over to the rock, now out of the light. He leaned forward, paused for a moment, then returned.

"What?" she said.

"Nothing." He turned up the rutted lane. Ivy twisted around, shone her flashlight through the pickup's narrow back window, just in time to catch a glimpse of the rock. No longer blank. Instead, she saw a chalked heart and inside the words *you and me*. No names. Just you and me. Ivy draped her arm over his shoulders, a position she was coming to love.

He drove through the clearing at the top, down the other side to the narrow blacktop. Not long after, they were on the road to Raquette. One or two cars passed them going the other way, just ordinary cars without banks of lights on top. Ivy noticed that the hands of the clock weren't moving.

"What time is it?" she said.

"We'll be early," said Harrow.

"But what time is it?"

His wrists were bare. The inmates didn't have watches, and Ivy no longer used one, relying on her cell phone. She patted her pockets: not there, probably in the Saab.

"Relax," he said.

She relaxed.

"I brought those sandwiches," he said, tilting his head toward the long storage shelf behind the seats.

Ivy reached around, found the sandwich bag lying on a rolled-up blanket with something that felt hard, like tools, underneath.

"Roast beef or chicken?" she said.

"Roast beef?" he said. "You really got roast beef?"

They ate the sandwiches. Ivy could see him trying to eat slowly, not to wolf it down, but he couldn't help himself. After, they shared a Coke.

"God damn," he said. He looked over at her and grinned.

Another mile or two went by. Was it her imagination, or was the eastern sky lightening just a bit, as though skim milk were leaking in?

"Tell me about the Lusks," she said.

His hands tightened on the wheel.

"Sorry," Ivy said. "But they sound awful. It must have been so bad."

"I guess I opened the door to this," Harrow said.

"How?"

"Giving you the ice-storm story."

"What's that supposed to mean?" Ivy said.

"Only good things," he said. He patted her knee. The feeling went zinging through her body, like every cell wanted in on the action. "What do you want to know?"

Everything about your life from the day you were born to the day we die, including how many children we're going to have plus their names, was the answer, so far over-the-top it might have come from the mind of someone else; but true. Ivy just said, "Start with the ice storm."

A half mile more of empty road went by. Ivy was beginning to think he hadn't heard, when Harrow said, "Glass on glass."

"I love that line," said Ivy. "So scary. But what actually happened?"

"What actually happened?" Harrow said. "I didn't think we talked like that in the writing game."

She took her arm off his shoulder. "This isn't the writing game."

His eyes shifted toward her. "We're on the same page about that?"

She laughed. He laughed, too. "Not much to tell about

the ice storm," he said, his laughter fading. "My parents got killed in a car wreck up in Canada, which I'm sure you found out already. Then I went to live with the Lusks. Mrs. Lusk and my mom were some kind of cousins."

"This is when you were seven or eight?" Ivy said, trying to remember what the West Raquette High football coach told her.

"Five," said Harrow.

"What was Mrs. Lusk like?" Ivy said.

"A whore," Harrow said. "Although I didn't really get what that meant till a couple years later. She took her tricks to the basement bedroom I shared with Marv, on account of her scruples about using the marital bed. Lusk himself couldn't have cared less. Irony—right, teacher? He was a trucker until he lost his license for good—an alcoholic, of course, the raging kind. Want me to describe this belt he had?"

"No." Ivy couldn't have said one more word without crying. So easy to see how a little orphan boy might hide out in a world of make-believe. She remembered those lines he'd written out loud, if that was how to put it, in the Dannemora library: *They say life is all about connecting, like that's a good thing. But when brain and eyes are lining up you know different.* An insight she'd admired for its pizzazz at the time and now actually understood. At the same time, she thought: *But what's the alternative?* And barged ahead: "I've done some thinking about the curly-haired girl. The daughter in your story. At first I assumed she was the daughter of you and Betty Ann. But everyone says you didn't have a daughter. True?"

"True in actuality," Harrow said.

"And therefore I've been wondering whether the curly-haired girl was in fact your sister, and maybe she died in the car wreck, too."

Up ahead the landscape opened up. Dark fields sloped
down to an even darker horizontal: the river. Lights flickered on the other side.

"You're so good," Harrow said.

"What does that mean?"

"You can even figure things out that can't be figured out,"
Harrow said. "There's no sister." A sign went by: RAQUETTE:
YOU ARE NOW ENTERING TRIBAL LAND. He'd come by some
route she didn't know. "Unless you count Marv's sister," he
added, slowing down. "She was much older. Also a whore."

Harrow turned onto a lane that curved through scrubby
woods and ended by a broken-down shed. He parked behind it. "A little early," he said, although Ivy had no idea
how he knew that. "But better to arrive first, this kind of
adventure. Got the flashlight?"

"Yes."

He held out his hand.

"I've been thinking," said Ivy, giving it to him. "He's going to ask me questions, like how did I track him down and
who else knows."

"Don't worry about any of that," Harrow said, getting
out of the pickup.

"But what do I say?"

" 'Let's see the money,' " Harrow said. "He's comfortable
with talk like that."

She followed him along a narrow path through the trees.
He carried the flashlight but didn't use it. "Another thing,"
she began.

He grabbed her arm, hard.

Ivy went silent.

They'd walked only thirty yards or so before they stepped
out of the woods and onto the bumpy dirt road that ran by
the river. On the other side of the road stood the willow

tree, like a huge, low mushroom cloud in the night; and at its foot the boat ramp, slanting into the water.

Harrow switched on the flashlight, his hand hooded over the lens. Very quickly, he went from place to place, poking the beam into the darkness: along the sides of the ramp, at spaces between rocks on the riverbank, in bushes by the side of the road. He even waded into the river, shone the light down on the water at the end of the ramp. Then he paused for a moment, his head tilted—that bearlike tilt, at the willow tree.

Harrow walked up the ramp to the base of the tree. He aimed the light here and there, up the trunk, into the branches, back down. The beam steadied. He laughed, very low. Was Mandrell hiding up there? Ivy stepped closer. All she could see was an oblong hole in the trunk, about ten feet up, big, but not big enough to hide a man.

Ivy raised her hands, palms up, in a silent question. Harrow switched off the light, tousled her hair, whispered, "That Frankie."

"What?" she said, as softly as she could.

"Tell you later." He handed her the flashlight. "Keep this on Frankie, that's all you have to do."

"Where are you going?"

He leaned close, his lips brushing her ear, causing so much static in her brain she hardly heard the words. "Don't want to scare him off. I'll be close by. Everything's cool."

He moved away, silent, and vanished.

Ivy stood beneath the willow tree, the flashlight off. This was where it had happened, also at night—Betty Ann meeting Frank, driving off with the duffel bag of stolen money. She could picture it. The river had probably made these

same sounds: sucking, near the bank; gurgling, out in mid-
stream.

Ivy listened for other sounds—a car, footsteps, the rustle
of clothing—heard nothing but the river. She rehearsed her
line. *Let's see the money.* Easy to remember. And after
that? Harrow would appear. Mandrell would reveal the
whereabouts of Betty Ann. He would reveal it one way or
another, probably take a beating in any case. Ivy was prepared for that, but Harrow turning up like this was bound
to shock Mandrell, probably shock him into giving up his
information pretty quickly. All he'd want would be to get
away, back to Les Girls and the life of Jake McCord.

And that would be that. Would they actually end up with
the money? Ivy didn't want it, but would Harrow? Maybe
some equation was at work, trying to find a balance for those
seven lost years. A hundred grand seemed a little puny when
you put it that way, but how much money could possibly—

What was that? Had she heard something, a car, maybe?
Ivy peered down the road, saw nothing. She faced the
woods, waiting for a glimpse of headlights through the
trees, but none came. As for the sound: she didn't hear it
anymore. Just the river, sucking at its bank, gurgling farther out . . . and now making another sound as well, soft
and rippling. Ivy, turned, gazed out at the water.

A boat took shape in the darkness, came gliding in,
barely moving as it touched the boat ramp, swinging sideways, rocking to a stop. A big, open powerboat twenty feet
long or more, with no one aboard but a single man at the
control console. He grabbed a line, climbed over the side,
tied up to a cleat at the side of the ramp. Then he looked
up and went still; he had good eyes, seeing her like that.
What light there was reflected off his platinum hair: Frank
Mandrell.

"You're early," he said.

An easy line to remember: *Let's see the money*. Ivy opened her mouth to say it, but that wasn't what came out. Instead she said, "Where's Betty Ann?"

"Huh?" he said.

Ivy had forgotten all about the flashlight, even though she had it in her hand. She switched it on.

"Hey," said Mandrell, shielding his face. He wore a full set of foul-weather gear, as though expecting a gale.

"Where is she?" said Ivy. "That's all I want to know."

He came up the boat ramp. "Why?" he said.

Ivy backed up a step or two.

"And get that fucking thing out of my face," he said.

Ivy lowered the beam a little, centering it on his chest. "She met you right here and took off with the money. Now you've got that stupid strip club. So there's no way you don't know where she is."

He came closer. "You're getting me confused, little lady," he said. "First I took you for a simple blackmailer. Now this strange line of talk. Makes me wonder who else is in on our little secret." Somehow he was now standing right in front of her.

Ivy didn't remember him being this big. Now, maybe a bit late, she spoke her line. "Let's see the money."

He gazed over her shoulder, across the dirt road and into the woods. "How you found out in the first place would be another question."

"A hundred grand," Ivy said. "Have you got it?"

Mandrell's gaze moved down to her face. She didn't like the look in his eyes at all. He reached inside his foul-weather jacket, withdrew a banded stack of bills, not very thick.

"Doesn't look like a hundred grand to me," Ivy said.

He smiled. "That writer story was pretty convincing," he

said. "A convincer like that might have a few other ideas going on."

"Not me," said Ivy. "I just want the money."

He waved the stack of bills. "Ten grand here," he said. "Down payment. To be on the safe side, I got the rest close by."

"Where?" said Ivy.

"A short boat ride away," said Mandrell. "Fun. How about we get going while it's still nice and quiet?"

Ivy pointed her beam down at the boat. From this angle, higher up the ramp, she could see the deck. Some nautical-type stuff lay in the bow, like coiled rope and a big anchor; and some not-so-nautical stuff, like four or five heavy dumbbells and rolls of duct tape.

"I'll wait here," she said.

Mandrell laughed. "Not an option," he said.

Ivy backed away. Then, from behind, she heard footsteps. Harrow, thank God. She turned, shone the flash across the road. Two men came out of the woods, side by side, caught in the circle of light: Vic Mandrell and that huge pal of his.

Ivy thought: *They found him. I'm alone.* She took one running step toward the road. The huge guy turned out to be very quick, blocking her way before she could take another.

"Who's up for a little boat ride?" Mandrell said.

"Sounds good," said Vic.

The men formed a circle around Ivy, closed in.

At that moment, a voice spoke. It came from above, like in some biblical tale.

"No boating tonight."

They all looked up. Vic had a flashlight, too. He shone it at the willow tree. Harrow sat on a thick, low branch, that rolled-up blanket from the pickup in his lap.

Mandrell recognized him at once and rocked backward, as if dodging something hard thrown his way. Harrow laughed that soft, delighted laugh.

Vic said, "What the hell? Is that—?"

"Step aside, teacher," Harrow said. "And keep that light on Frankie, if you don't mind."

Ivy darted past the huge guy, into the road.

"Grab the bitch," said Frank Mandrell.

The huge guy lunged for her. Blinding light flashed from inside the blanket—blue for the tiniest instant, then hot red—plus a boom, and the huge guy pitched sideways as though knocked over by a killer wave.

"The light," Harrow said.

Ivy stabbed the beam around, tried to find Mandrell, but it landed first on Vic. He had a gun in his hand, was starting to raise it. That was as far as he got: another blast came from the willow tree and Vic's face disintegrated in bloody airborne bits.

Mandrell crouched at the shadowy edge of the light, wobbly now from Ivy's shaking hand, and pulled out his own gun, bigger than Vic's. He pointed it at the willow, but in the darkness there was nothing to see except its mushroom-cloud form. Mandrell turned and aimed the gun at Ivy, an expression on his face of pleasure in the offing.

An idea came to her, simple but maybe the best of her life: she switched off the light. Mandrell's gun flashed. She stood where she was, untouched. Then, from the base of the tree came a thump, followed by running footsteps.

Ivy's eyes adjusted to the darkness, only it wasn't so dark now. The subtle predawn milkiness that they'd all been blinded to by the intensity of the flashlights was now spreading across the sky, and in that light Ivy saw Mandrell running toward the boat, Harrow close behind. Harrow had a shotgun—the shotgun from cabin one?—in his hands, had it by the barrel with the butt raised high. Mandrell was making a whimpering noise in his throat, like some frightened animal. Harrow swung the butt down so hard on the back of Mandrell's head that it whistled in the air. Mandrell slumped face-first into the water. Harrow dropped the gun, went in after him.

Ivy went in, too. Harrow was on top of Mandrell, pressing him under.

"Stop. Stop." He had to stop. This all had to stop.

But Harrow wouldn't stop. He was growling, cords of muscle standing out all over his body.

"Stop." Ivy tugged, pulled, yanked at him. Finally she got a handful of his hair and jerked it with all her might. He went slack, turned to her, no recognition in his eyes.

Mandrell came up to the surface. Ivy cupped the back of his head—all slimy, and soft where it should have been hard—in her hands, held it above the surface. His eyes were open. He coughed up some water. Harrow leaned toward him, teeth bared.

"For God's sake, stop," Ivy said. "He's got to tell us about Betty Ann."

Mandrell stared right at her. His mouth opened. "Is something wrong with you?" he said. Then blood came pouring out, unstoppable.

Thirty

After that, they were on the move. Ivy didn't see much for a while, couldn't get past a dark blur that was unspooling just behind her eyeballs. Her memory recorded a few things only: Harrow tossing Mandrell's body lightly, like it was filled with straw, into the boat; Harrow untying the line, and the boat drifting away downriver; Harrow picking up the shotgun. They crossed the road, not running, although Ivy formed the impression of tremendous speed. At that point, with her in the middle of the road and Harrow already starting up the path that led to the pickup parked by the broken-down shed, Ivy glimpsed a little movement just to her right. She turned in time to see the huge guy, a bloody mess, raise his head an inch or two off the road. His eyes shifted slightly, found hers, sent some sort of message. Ivy didn't know what that message was; but it had nothing to do with hatred, revenge, greed, crime, any of that.

She kept going.

Because—because what was the alternative? Telling Harrow? What would happen after that? Ivy didn't want to see it. And she could think of no other plan: which was why she left the man on the road, still alive. A few steps later came an unpleasant sound her mind refused to identify at first, and then did: sirens, on the way.

They got in the pickup. This time Ivy stayed at her end of the bench seat. Harrow drove away from the broken-down shed. Her body was still in the grip of the sensation of way too much velocity, like a roller coaster taking the last big drop, although the speedometer needle never exceeded the limit. They passed through the scrubby woods, onto blacktop, then back on dirt roads; Ivy totally lost.

"Where are we going?" she said.

"We've got options," said Harrow.

"Like?"

He made a little sound, half laugh, half snort. "We're starting to sound like an old married couple," he said.

The remark stunned her on many levels, but three were apparent at once. First, how did he know things like that, the sound of old married couples? Second, what was going on in his mind, that he could have such a thought so soon after what had just happened? And third, he was right.

Ivy stared straight ahead, through a windshield dirty with dead bugs and bird shit. "Did you use me back there?" she said.

"Use you?"

"As a lure."

"Come on," Harrow said. "You found Frankie all by yourself. And didn't you tell me they were outside your place?"

"Yes."

"Think Frankie was going to leave it like that?" She didn't answer. "Happen to glance inside that boat?" he said.

"Yes," Ivy said. If not for Harrow, she would now be at the bottom of the St. Lawrence, weighted down, most likely forever untraceable.

"So what are we talking about?" Harrow said.

They drove on in silence, crossing a highway, back onto a dirt road. Dawn broke around them, but not very bright, the clouds low and heavy.

"What about Betty Ann?" Ivy said. "I thought she was the point of the exercise."

Harrow looked over. "That's where it went wrong," he said.

"One way of putting it," Ivy said.

"Things happened in the wrong order," Harrow said. "Like in your story, the scene where Vladek goes to the job interview."

"I don't want to talk about my story."

"What do you want to talk about?"

"What happens now," Ivy said. Was there anything else?

"In what sense?" Harrow said.

"For God's sake," said Ivy. "How are we going to find her? Find her and prove your innocence—what's left of it, before—before . . ." She couldn't bring herself to voice the chaos waiting at the end of that sentence, or more likely that was already happening.

"We'll have to think a bit, that's all," Harrow said. "Which is why it's good we've got these options."

"Maybe I'm stupid," Ivy said. "Go over them for me."

"Nothing stupid about you, teacher," he said.

"And stop calling me that," Ivy said, her voice rising. "I don't want to hear it again."

"I mean it with respect," Harrow said. "But whatever you say."

They were on a two-lane highway now, winding up through steep hills, snowflakes drifting down, way too early in the year. A few cars came toward them around the bend. Harrow switched off the headlights—just the one, Ivy remembered. The cars went by, the last a state trooper. He had a coffee cup in one hand, didn't even glance at them.

Harrow laughed that low laugh. "No reason they know I'm gone, not quite yet," he said. "They've still got work to do. Nothing to tie you to me, or us to Mandrell. Maybe they'll think the three of them went down in some drug thing gone bad."

As long as the huge guy dies soon, before the police get to him: that was Ivy's immediate thought. And yes: *Die soon.* Because otherwise she was just like everyone else in Harrow's life so far, no help. He was capable of violence, yes, but only in self-defense, or in her defense. He'd killed three killers. Horrible, and she knew her mind wasn't going to let go of what she'd seen, but she had to hold on to fact one: he was innocent of the crime that had started all this. What had happened at the boat ramp could be explained, as long as they found Betty Ann.

"Anything left to eat?" Harrow said.

That stunned her, too, but only for a moment. She had to toughen up, and fast. "Just an apple," Ivy said, feeling inside the bag.

Harrow bit into it. "Never seen this kind before," he said. "What is it?"

"Pink Lady."

"Best I ever tasted." He tossed the core out the window. There was blood on his hand.

His body relaxed a little, a hungry man who'd just taken

the edge off his appetite. "First they put things together," he said. "Then comes the search."

"I know," Ivy said. She was starting to shake. Had she been in shock? If so, she was coming out of it; and fear was taking over. She hugged herself.

"A search like this is an inflating balloon," Harrow said. He didn't seem scared at all. "The center is where whoever it was went missing. Then it expands and keeps expanding. Trying to get away now, that's what they'll expect. So the best option is lying low, letting the skin of the balloon pass by."

The image made sense to Ivy. "And Betty Ann?"

Harrow sighed. "Which will give us time to put our heads together on that," he said. "While we're lying low."

"Lying low where?" Ivy said.

"You know where," said Harrow. "It'll be like one of those retreats."

She laughed. One of those laughs with bitterness in it; she heard that distinctly.

He reached across, touched her knee, very lightly, but the electric feeling went through her just the same. "Let's not fight," he said.

A childish remark, or possibly teenage: Ivy knew that, but couldn't help responding to it anyway. "Did you bring the money at least?" she said, thinking somewhere along the way they might need it.

"What money?" Harrow said.

"The ten grand," said Ivy.

"I'm not a thief," Harrow said.

That was the whole point. Ivy slid over next to him.

Back in cabin four at Wilderness Lake, under the rose-colored duvet, in that little world of its own: at first a world in motion and then still, except for the snowflakes outside the window.

"Claudette showed me the Valentine's Day card you gave Betty Ann," Ivy said. "The one about the longest fall and the softest landing."

"Yeah?"

"You must have really loved her."

"Must have."

So quiet in cabin four on Wilderness Lake that Ivy actually heard a snowflake make the tiniest thump against the window. "And now?" she said.

He faced her, his eyes looking tired for the first time since the escape. "Far from it," he said. Then came a little smile. The rest—*You're the one* or *I'm in love with you* or something like that, he left unspoken, but Ivy heard it anyway, in her mind.

His eyes closed. So did hers.

Ivy slept a deep sleep, dreamless until the end, when her mother started whipping up some icing in the electric mixer, and Ivy sat up on the counter, waiting to lick the mixing blades.

Then came a sudden, violent motion next to her, like an eruption. Ivy awoke, startled. Harrow was halfway across the room, headed for the window. From not far away, and getting louder, came the *whap-whap* drone of a helicopter. Harrow peered up through the glass. The wound on his back looked red and sore.

"State police," he said, stepping away from the window.

The sound grew louder, for a moment or two loud enough

to vibrate the cabin roof, then quieted and finally faded to nothing.

"Thank God we didn't have a fire going," Ivy said.

Harrow turned to her, uncomprehending.

"Or they'd have spotted us," Ivy said. "From the smoke. This way, it's just a vacant camp off-season."

"And that red car of yours?" Harrow said. Parked right outside the cabin.

Ivy jumped out of bed, threw on her clothes.

"What are you doing?" he said.

"We're leaving, right?" Ivy said. "In the pickup."

"Won't work," Harrow said. "They'll have roadblocks up in an hour, even less if he's radioing in."

"But maybe we can get out first." She could hardly keep from running out the door.

"Maybe," said Harrow. "But we wouldn't get far."

Ivy paced back and forth, one flawed idea after another spinning through her mind. Then she thought of the expanding balloon, and the strategy of lying low. "What if we do it again?" she said.

"Do what again?"

"Lie low."

"How?" said Harrow.

It turned out to be a three-step process.

Step one: Ivy drove the Saab to the end of the dock, opened the windows, shifted to neutral, got out. Harrow gave the car a push. It splashed down in the water, floated for a few moments, more and more sluggish, then with a heavy wobble sank out of sight. Bubbles burst on the surface, big and small, then just small. A paperback book floated up. Ivy recognized it, the novel Ferdie Gagnon had lent her. It got waterlogged, sank back down. Too late, she remembered her cell phone; but who would she call and what would she say?

Step two: they carried the rowboat, *Caprice,* from its winter storage place under cabin two down to the water. All their things went inside, plus the shotgun and a bottle of gin Harrow found in cabin one. They left everything the way they'd found it and got in the boat. Looking back, Ivy noticed a broken pane in the side window of cabin one. Had it always been like that?

Step three: they rowed out to the craggy island, the one that could have been lifted from a medieval painting. Harrow rowed the first few hundred yards, but Ivy saw it hurt him; she took over the rest of the way. They hid the boat under branches on the far side of the island and climbed to the top, four or five hundred feet above the water. Ivy showed Harrow the cave, with its little entrance, just big enough for a crouching person.

"How did you find this place?" he said.

"By accident." *If she believed in them anymore.*

"It's perfect." Harrow put his arm around her, kissed her on the lips. "We're in the driver's seat."

The snowflakes kept falling, still not many, and far apart, no snow sticking to the ground. A strange snowfall: it reminded Ivy of confetti. They entered the cave.

Not long after that, maybe only ten minutes, the droning *whap-whap* returned. Ivy and Harrow sat side by side on the cave floor, just out of the light from the mouth. The sound intensified, grinded overhead, lessened, and then went silent. Harrow crept out of the cave. Ivy followed.

They crawled across the ledge, peered through the rocks.

The helicopter—dark blue, blades still—stood on the little sandy beach in front of the cabins. Half a dozen squad cars, maybe more, were parked here and there. Lots of tiny people, all in uniform, were moving around—in and out of the cabins, along the dirt road, by the pickup, into the woods; one little figure spent a few seconds on the dock. From time to time they bunched together for a minute or two, then separated and tried the different places again. Later a canine unit arrived, and a dog led its master around the camp.

The woods darkened, then the sky, and last the lake. Lights flickered around the camp. Then headlights started flashing on. The helicopter took off, soared in a long rising curve and disappeared in the night. Ivy and Harrow stayed on the ledge, invisible. The squad cars drove away, one by one, taillights blinking through the trees and then gone; all of them in search of a red Saab.

"Wish I'd met you long ago," Harrow said.

Thirty-one

"This is nice," Harrow said.

They were in the cave, darkness complete, the wind rising outside, snow starting to pile up at the entrance—Ivy knew that only from the soft accumulating sounds. Nothing at all to eat; nothing to drink but Jean Savard's gin. On the plus side, the dirt floor was surprisingly warm.

"How about a drink?" Harrow said.

"Not for me," Ivy said.

"You mind?"

"Of course not."

A metallic *snick:* the seal on the cap, broken. Then came a little gurgle.

"Ah," Harrow said. "This is nice."

"You like gin?"

"Never had it before," Harrow said. "I wasn't much of a drinker—a few beers now and then, that kind of thing." Another gurgle.

"What about Betty Ann?"

"What about her?"

"Was she much of a drinker?"

He was silent for a few moments. The sound of falling snow, already hard to hear, faded away.

"What's the point of your question?" Harrow said.

"The point?" said Ivy. "Curiosity." She laughed.

"What's funny?"

"Plus I've seen Claudette drink," Ivy said, expecting him to laugh, too, but he didn't.

"Is that when she told you about this—what did you call it, affair?" Harrow said.

The knowledge had actually come from the pot-smoking episode, but Ivy didn't want to get into that. "Are you telling me you don't believe it, about her and Mandrell?"

Silence.

"Because I only wish she'd told you," Ivy said. "Told you at the time."

Gurgle.

"Are you listening?"

"Yup."

"Because then none of this would have happened."

"Why is that?"

She didn't get it. What could be more obvious? "You wouldn't have cared about protecting her," Ivy said. "She's your alibi. You'd have pleaded not guilty and gone free, or more likely not even been charged at all."

"How come you're so good at figuring things out?" Harrow said.

"I'm not," Ivy said.

He moved in the darkness. The bottle touched her hand. She changed her mind and took a little sip, registering liquid but no taste; and gave it back.

The night didn't seem so dark. Ivy went through the opening, stood on the ridge. The air was still, but up above the wind must have been blowing hard, to be tearing up the clouds like that and driving them away. The moon appeared, at first veiled, then fully exposed. It shone on the lake, the forest, the mountains, a black-and-silver landscape. Nothing human showed. Had she ever seen anything more beautiful? Ivy felt like she was inside some great painting, a nocturnal masterpiece.

Harrow came up behind, put his arms around her waist, the bottle dangling by her leg.

"What worries me," Ivy said, "is the thought that maybe you're still protecting her."

"Then you can stop worrying," Harrow said, his lips just brushing her cheek.

She had to force herself not to say, *Promise?*, like a high-school girl.

Harrow gave her a little squeeze. "I promise."

A big bird, an owl, maybe, with moonlit wings, glided across the sky.

"I believe you," Ivy said. "It wouldn't even make sense otherwise."

"What wouldn't?"

"Escaping now," Ivy said.

"I'd have got out sooner or later," Harrow said.

Ivy laughed. "Eighteen years is hardly sooner or later," she said.

Harrow backed away, took another drink, the gin like mercury in the moonlight. The level in the bottle was down to half.

"I'll have a little more," Ivy said.

They stood side by side on the ridge outside the cave, cold beauty all around, sharing the bottle.

"We don't have any food," Ivy said, "or even water."

"Lake's full of water," said Harrow. "I can hunt and fish."

What a thought: to live forever in this masterpiece, just the two of them, safe and sound. "But realistically," Ivy said.

He made that little half snort, half laugh. "Realistically," he said, "we can go without food for a day or two."

"Meaning after that we'll be gone?" Ivy said.

"Have to be."

"To find Betty Ann, right?"

He gazed up at the moon. "Know what I like about this planet?" he said.

"What?"

"That when you're on it the sun and the moon are the same size. What's that all about?"

"Does it have to be about something?" Ivy said.

"Funny question, coming from a writer," said Harrow. "Think of the odds against something like that happening. Got to be sending us a message."

"Who is us?"

"Everybody who ever lived," Harrow said. "You and me."

"And what's the message?"

"I don't know exactly," Harrow said. "But it's about death."

Ivy drank some more. Something made a silver splash in the lake, twenty or thirty yards from the shore of the island, the sound clear in the still air. She shivered.

"And who's sending it?" she said. "Are you saying there's a God?"

"No way," said Harrow.

They stood in silence, just touching. The immensity of space, the insignificance of people, the need to live now:

the real meaning of those concepts hit her deep, deep down
for the first time, all of them so obviously beyond dispute.
An unsettling and scary realization; but the touch of this
man gave comfort.

Harrow took the bottle, drank.

"How about you?" he said. "Think there's a God?"

"My heart says yes," Ivy said. "My mind says no."

"Got to be one or the other," Harrow said.

At that moment, Ivy remembered the cross on the top-
most crag of the island. She looked up and saw it, but barely
visible, for some reason failing to pick up any moonlight at
all.

Harrow finished off the bottle. He caught her glance and
smiled, his teeth, small and perfect, the color of the moon;
except for that gold incisor. "This is a free night," he said,
and drew the empty bottle back, preparing to throw it into
the lake.

Ivy caught his arm. "We'll need it," she said. "For water."

"Always thinking ahead," Harrow said. He gave her an
elbow in the side of her arm, very soft, then went into the
cave, taking the empty bottle with him. Ivy stayed outside,
trying to absorb every little visual bit, but after a while it
got too cold.

Much warmer in the cave, but warm enough to lie there
naked? Ivy wouldn't have thought so, but soon they were.
The moon sank a little, then hovered right outside the cave
mouth, and things got even warmer: a strange moon-heat
that bleached their skin, damp now, the color of bone.

Later, they lay on their sides, Ivy behind him, holding on
to what was now in its resting state. That brought to mind

the image of Felix in Sergeant Tocco's surveillance photo, pale and defenseless under the showerhead, a few minutes before he died. And after that came what Harrow had told her: *Oh, Morales did Felix, all right.* Which was what Sergeant Tocco had thought, too, until he put that taped evidence together.

"Awake?" she said.

"Barely."

"I keep thinking about Felix."

"Nice little guy."

"They found out Morales didn't kill him."

"Who told you that?"

"Sergeant Tocco."

"And you believed him?"

"Yes. He—"

"Tocco's a goon," Harrow said. "And goons are liars." He didn't sound at all drunk, not in the conventional way, but there was an edge in his tone she hadn't heard before.

Ivy thought of Sergeant Tocco's house with the white picket fence, a neat little house missing only wife and kids. She liked Sergeant Tocco. "He never lied to me," she said.

"Why would he?"

"What do you mean?"

"You're a civilian."

"But—"

"Do me a favor," Harrow said. "Go to sleep."

"You don't understand," Ivy said. "He—"

Harrow sat up, very quick, twisted around, leaned over her "No more about Tocco," he said. "He's feeding you lies."

"Why would he?"

"A million reasons, not even worth discussing," Harrow said. "But I know the truth, Ivy. I saw the whole thing."

Ivy: Had he actually called her by her name before? "What whole thing?" she said.

"When Felix got shanked," Harrow said. "It happened in the gym, in this little corner where they keep the equipment." His eyes gleamed in the moonlight. "Nothing I could do, if that's what you're thinking," he said. "These things go by fast."

Those photos, with their time codes: it couldn't have happened like that, in the gym. There was no doubt at all about the where or when. "In the gym?" Ivy said.

"Yup."

"You're sure?"

"About what?"

"How Felix died."

"I saw it with my own eyes."

"In the gym."

"That's what I said." His eyes gleamed down at her. He reached out. His hand touched her neck, gentle. He lowered his voice, although the edgy part didn't go away, sharpened if anything. "Any reason to doubt me?" he said.

The moon sank lower, dimming the cave. "No," Ivy said.

"You're shaking."

"Just from the cold."

"Poor Ivy," he said. "How about if I warm you up?"

He rolled on top of her. His body felt warm, even hot, but it didn't rub off. Not long after, he was doing all the things he'd done before, maybe better: she realized how much he'd learned already about her sexuality. But to no effect this time; a development he didn't seem to notice.

They lay side by side, on their backs.

"Tell me the story," Ivy said.

"What story?"

"How Felix died."

"You really want to hear that?"

"I do."

A long silence. Then: "The Death of Felix Balaban," Harrow said. He took a deep breath. "It was my fault, in a way, what happened to Felix. I suggested he hit the gym, try to get stronger, even though I knew he was one of those types who can't really get strong, no matter what they do. All mental, guys like Felix." He paused. Ivy got the strange feeling that he was starting a new paragraph in his mind.

"They've pretty much stripped the weight room down to nothing at Dannemora—the warden got tired of breeding monsters. Now there's just this one little corner with a bench, a leg press, a rusted-out old Universal machine, no free weights. I drop by—I used to—to shoot some hoops. I could just see Felix, lying on the bench, straining under the bar. Then Morales stepped into the picture. You know how you can tell a lot just from how people are standing? Morales was standing in a way that said, *My turn.* And Felix was lying in a way that said, *Two more,* or *One more,* or some other rational and completely wrong answer, given how things were between him and the Latin Kings. I turned away, put up a shot, looked back. Morales was bent over Felix. Out came the shank. And then the slice, real deep, Felix's neck so exposed, the way he was lying on the bench. But the sound that went with it was a little *swish.* That was my ball, falling through the net, which only shows how fast things can go bad."

Silence.

"And then?"

"The end."

"But what happened after that?"

"Nothing," Harrow said.

Nothing happens after the end of a story. "Something must have happened," Ivy said.

"Nothing important," Harrow said. "Whoever was around just melted away. Standard procedure."

They lay in the cave. Harrow's breathing was shallow at first, then got deep and slow. "The Death of Felix Balaban": a little gem, the characters true to themselves and completely believable, the resolution inevitable, the details just right. A little gem, but false from first word to last.

Things that had been fixed in Ivy's mind—clues, if you wanted to call them that—became unstuck, began moving around on their own, searching for a new pattern. Felix had an escape plan, but hadn't been planning to escape, just trade the idea for probation or a lighter sentence. He'd run into trouble with the Latin Kings and been moved in with Harrow for his own protection. Someone—not Morales—had killed him in the B-block showers, not the gym. And: *I'd have got out sooner or later.* A remark of Harrow's that had struck her as funny, stoical, even gallant; but: suppose he had known the escape plan. Then it might have been a simple statement of fact. And if Harrow had discovered how Felix was going to use his plan, making a trade that would render it useless? Ivy's mind writhed away from what came next. But why? Her body was already there.

She got colder, started shivering again. His skin had cooled a little, but still felt warm. "Did you kill Felix?" she said.

No answer.

He was capable—immensely capable—of killing in self-defense or in her defense, but little Felix? "You couldn't have."

He just breathed, long, slow, deep. She smelled gin.

And if he had? Horrible, all the more so since he'd gone in an innocent man. Ivy went over everything—all those clues—reassured herself that that was the case, that the innocent-man pattern still held true. Three masked robbers: Mandrell, Lusk, Carter. Mandrell alone survives, takes the cash in a duffel bag to the boat ramp. He's picked up within minutes, but the money is gone, and so is Betty Ann. Mandrell fingers Harrow as the third man, goes into witness protection, somewhere along the way rejoins Betty Ann, and recovers the money, or enough of it to set himself up. Had she discovered anything to undermine that story, to disturb the pattern? No.

But for some reason, her mind kept tugging her back to that willow tree, specifically the way Harrow had examined it so closely with the flashlight, stopping only when he found that oblong hole in the trunk. At first, she'd thought he'd been looking for Mandrell, but the hole was too small for a person. Something about that hole amused Harrow: he'd laughed and said, *That Frankie.* As though . . .

As though he'd figured something out. But what? A hole in a tree, too small for a person—what possible significance could that have? Was he afraid Mandrell had planted a gun there? What sense would that make? Mandrell had been carrying a gun, and so had Vic. And then it hit her, something as simple as Tab A and Slot B: the duffel bag. What was the ending of that little piece he'd written "The Cop Who Busted Me"? *Ferdie asks the big question, the one about where the money is. I can only laugh.*

Ivy sat up. Without even following all the links, she knew that Mandrell could have handled the money part all by

himself. The combination of that duffel bag full of cash and
the hole in the willow tree knocked Betty Ann right out of
the story—or into another part of it.

And where would that other part be?

Ivy gazed down at Harrow, lying in a diffused moonlight
beam, the empty gin bottle on the ground nearby. She covered him up with his sweatshirt. He made a grateful little
sound in his sleep. He looked peaceful in that pool of light,
and years younger. The jeans he'd found in cabin one lay
bunched beside him. Ivy felt around in his pockets, found
the key to the pickup. She put on her own clothes and left
the cave.

Thirty-two

The moon hung low in the sky, almost full, missing only a thin slice at the bottom of its left side. Ivy lowered herself over the ledge, got a foothold on the rocky path, started down, the sound of her steps muted by the inch or two of snow that had fallen. She corkscrewed down the island, half the time in moonlight, half in darkness. A few times she stopped to listen, heard nothing but her own breathing and once, the beating wings of a heavy bird, passing close by, invisible.

Down on the pebbly shore, Ivy pushed the branches off the boat, flipped it over into the water, set the oars. Then she got in and rowed. A little breeze sprang up, rippling the lake, tiny reflected moons bobbing all around. The silhouette of the island shrank in front of her. She could make out the moonlit horizontal plane of the ledge. Nothing moved up there. Now, maybe because of the snowfall, the cross was visible, silver and sharply edged. Ivy rowed harder, rising off the seat with every stroke. Sweat was dripping off her chin when the bow grinded into the sandy beach in front of the cabins.

Ivy jumped out of the boat, took one last look at the island, spiky, dark, distant. She ran to the pickup. It started with that explosive sound. She drove off, dirt road to the flat-faced rock, *you and me* caught for a moment in the single headlight, then up to the clearing and down the other side. She was on blacktop, five or six miles from the lake before she saw another car, coming the other way. It drew closer, very fast, then zipped by. A minivan with a white-haired woman hunched over the wheel and an alert dog poised beside her: Jean Savard and Rocky.

The moon sank out of sight. As Ivy entered West Raquette, the night was at its darkest. She drove down the steep hill to the bottom of Ransom Road, parked in the carport behind Claudette's rusted-out Beemer. Ivy switched off, listened. She heard a few pings from the hot engine, then nothing.

Ivy got out of the pickup, walked to the side door. She raised her fist to knock. An alarm buzzed in the house, startling her. But it wasn't a burglar alarm, only a wake-up from a clock radio. Then came a groan, and a minute or two after that the sound of a flushing toilet. A light went on in a side window. Ivy stayed where she was, in the shadows under the carport roof.

A sneaker squeaked in the house, close by. The door opened, and Claudette came out, backlit from the light in the hall, wearing her Wal-Mart smock. She saw Ivy and her eyes opened wide. Ivy put a hand on Claudette's chest, pushed her back in, swung the door closed with her foot.

"Oh my God," Claudette said, covering her mouth with

both hands. "You were on TV." She glanced back into the kitchen, where a phone hung on the wall. That maddened Ivy; up to this point in her life she hadn't done much hating, but now she felt it. She pushed Claudette again, the other way, down the hall. Ivy felt absurdly strong, and completely free from physical fear. Claudette retreated, backing into a tiny bathroom at the end of the hall, the kind with only toilet and sink. Ivy kept pushing until Claudette had nowhere to go.

"What are you going to do to me?" Claudette said.

"If you tell me the truth, nothing," Ivy said.

"Truth?" said Claudette.

From the corner of her eye, Ivy saw something on the wall. It broke her concentration for a moment.

"About what?" Claudette said, close to wailing. "Don't look at me like that."

But Ivy had no control over the expression on her face. "Why did you want Betty Ann's forgiveness?"

"I didn't say that. I said I forgive *her*."

"You also said, 'Maybe she'll forgive me, too.' "

"I never—"

"The night you were drunk, when you said my book wouldn't work."

"Drunk? Then I don't—"

"I don't care whether you remember," Ivy said. "Why did you want her forgiveness? What did you do?"

"Nothing. I didn't do—"

Ivy smacked Claudette across the face with the back of her hand, hard. "Stop lying."

Claudette started crying, sank down on the toilet. The seat was up and she went right into it. "I'm not lying."

Ivy raised her hand again.

Claudette flinched. "What do you want me to say? That I told him?"

Ivy stood over her.

"Okay, so I did," Claudette said; and Ivy knew, way too late, that nothing would ever be the same. "Vance had a right to know," Claudette went on. "Just like you said before."

"This was the day of the robbery," Ivy said.

"The day of the robbery?" Claudette said.

Ivy raised her voice; Claudette shrank away. "When you told Harrow."

"It turned out to be," Claudette said. "That stupid fuckin' day." Her eyes shifted. "And I called Frank, too, right after, if you want the whole truth."

Ivy didn't get that. Claudette had walked in on her sister and Frank: Frank knew she knew. "To tell him what?" she said.

Claudette bit her lip. "That I'd given Harrow a heads-up about him and Betty Ann." She avoided Ivy's gaze. "Why should everyone else get off scot-free? I was lashing out, like anybody else. I was young. I still had hopes."

Ivy lowered her fist. It took an act of will. She stepped back, glanced at the wall again. A photo in an oval frame hung there, stained and old: two little girls in party dresses, one plain-faced and lank-haired, the other pretty and curly-haired. "Betty Ann had curly hair?"

"She straightened it when she got older," Claudette said, sniffling.

Claudette's house was old and unrenovated, the bathroom locking with a key. Ivy locked Claudette in and, once outside, threw the key as far as she could.

Night was fading when Ivy drove up Ransom Road, turned right, kept going that two-point-four miles she'd measured before, found the dirt track into the woods. Around a bend, up a slope, and there was the small house with trees closing in, the fading For Sale sign out front: the house Harrow had shared with Betty Ann. He'd been busy vacuuming when Ferdie Gagnon came to get him.

Ivy walked around to the back, tried the door. Locked, but with windowpanes in the top half. She picked up a rock and broke one of them: a broken window, just like the one that had appeared in cabin one, before Jean Savard's shotgun entered the picture. Ivy reached inside and opened up.

She went in, walked around the house, all the rooms empty and bare. She ended up in the kitchen. A spider was spinning a big web over the sink; the filaments caught the early-morning light. Ivy opened the door to the basement, gazed down the dust-covered plywood stairs. She flicked the switch, remembered it didn't work; also remembered what she'd glimpsed down there before.

Ivy went down the stairs, through pools of gloom. Weak light shone through a dusty window high on the wall, falling on that stack of cement blocks on the dirt floor: a stack four blocks high covering an area about seven feet by three. Ivy picked them up and threw them aside, one by one. Dust rose and swirled in the light. She got down to the bare dirt.

Ivy looked around: no shovels, no tools of any kind, nothing to dig with. She knelt on the floor and dug with her hands, clawing away at the earth, *warp speed*. But after a while, her mind, so jumbled, in such a frenzy to prove herself wrong, to find a pattern she could live with, began to clear. Digging took over; she thought only of digging, became a machine for it, aware of nothing but this hole in the ground, its contours, moisture content, textures, colors, propensity for cave-ins. The hole widened and deepened, reaching a diameter of about five feet and a depth of about

three, with Ivy down inside it. She crouched, bent over
awkwardly, scooped out a double handful, then clawed
down for more. Her fingers touched something unearthlike,
something hard.

Ivy got onto her knees, brushed away dirt down there in
the deepest part of the hole. A human hand appeared—a
left hand, nothing remaining of skin and flesh but putrefy-
ing lumps of grayish stuff. But the nails were still painted,
dull red, and a gold ring was caught in a cleft between the
knuckles on the fourth finger.

There was nothing more to see, nothing more to know.
Ivy rose, slow and unsteady. Harrow was innocent of the
Gold Dust robbery, just as she believed. Here was his alibi,
oh, so unusable. Everything locked into place, the pattern
final. She climbed out of the hole and vomited. Tears
streamed from her eyes, but vomiting sometimes made that
happen. She'd gone wrong, completely. And now? How
could this be fixed?

Ivy took a deep breath, turned to the stairs. Harrow was
sitting on them, halfway down, the shotgun in his lap. For
just a second, she took him for an apparition. But there
were too many little details, like how pale he looked, and
the bones in his face sticking out, and his clothes still damp.
He was good enough to make this stuff up out of nothing,
but not her. His feet were bare, completing the story of a
long swim—heroic in another context—in cold water.

"It doesn't change how much I loved her," Harrow said.
"Proves it, in a way."

"I don't want to hear it," Ivy said. "Did you kill Jean,
too?"

"Who's she?" said Harrow.

"The old lady from the camp."

"Of course not," Harrow said. "I borrowed her car, that's all. And tied her up in a gentle way. She's fine."

"And the dog?"

"Not as fine."

Ivy was almost sick again. He watched her.

"Me finding Mandrell," she said. "That's when you had to get out."

"I couldn't resist," Harrow said.

"You should have done your goddamn time and counted yourself lucky," Ivy said.

"Exactly what I was doing, till you came along," Harrow said.

She vomited again. His eyes didn't leave her.

"So," he said. "What's next?"

Ivy wiped her mouth. "I'm leaving."

"I can see us leaving together," Harrow said. "But not you alone."

"Leaving together is out of the question," Ivy said.

He looked her up and down. "I thought we had a relationship," he said.

"It was false."

"You're just telling yourself that now," Harrow said.

"No," Ivy said. "It was false. You made yourself up. I fell in love with that."

"Now you're getting too complicated," Harrow said. "You know what we're like together, the two of us. Think of how we could be in the future."

"The future?" Ivy said.

"Sure," he said. "Nothing bad has happened yet. We have to move fast, that's all."

Nothing bad has happened yet? Ivy shook her head. "There's nothing left between us."

"Don't you believe in me?" he said.

"Believe in you?" She almost laughed in his face.

"My talent," he said.

His talent? What did it matter? "I was wrong about that, too," Ivy said.

Harrow's face flushed. He rose, came down the stairs.

"Say that again?"

"I was wrong about your talent," Ivy said. "It's nothing special."

"I hope you don't mean that," he said.

Ivy said nothing. He stepped off the last stair, stood on the dirt floor, the dust still swirling around a little.

"Do you mean that?" he said. "That there's nothing special about my talent?"

Ivy remained silent.

He came closer. "Do you mean it? Yes or no."

A strange situation, where the brave choice was to tell a lie. Ivy did the brave thing; a small, partial compensation for all she'd done wrong. "Yes," she said. "I mean it. There's nothing special about your talent."

His face changed, went pale and ugly, the teeth exposed. Had that been Betty Ann's last sight of him? "Maybe you're right after all," he said, his voice not loud, but suddenly in a deeper register than she'd ever heard it. "About this being the end for us." The barrel of the gun rose an inch or two.

"Don't," Ivy said. "It's enough."

He nodded. "But I can't come up with a better scenario on the spur of the moment," he said. "Can you?" For a second or two it looked like he might smile or even laugh.

"What's funny?"

"Just that you could save your life with a timely plot twist," he said. "A real test of the writer's skill."

Was he toying with her? Was he capable of that? How

could she have been so wrong? That feeling of hatred: it came again, pulling at her face. Ivy tried to master it. "I'm leaving," she said. "I never harmed you. Get out of the way."

But he didn't move. The barrel rose an inch or two more. She glanced around. No exit but the stairs.

"Shift to the side," he said. "A titch."

Meaning closer to the hole. Instead, Ivy backed away, toward the furnace in the corner. Of course she didn't want to die, but even more, she didn't want to die down in that hole with Betty Ann. Harrow started toward her.

"This is pointless," he said.

"That's right," Ivy said. "I'm not your problem."

"A loose end," said Harrow, "is a problem." His finger shifted on the trigger.

"Don't," Ivy said.

"I have very strong feelings for you," Harrow said. "What's about to happen doesn't change that."

"It does," Ivy said. "Completely."

"Maybe for you," Harrow said. The barrel came up a little more, now pointed at her heart.

"It will change you, too," Ivy said.

He looked interested. "Oh? How so?"

Was there a right answer, one that would keep her alive? Ivy's mind went blank. And she didn't find out, because at that moment a tremendous crash came from above, as though something big had struck the house. Then a cop in riot gear burst through the doorway at the top of the stairs, followed by another, both of them with guns drawn.

"Drop it," shouted the first one.

But Harrow didn't. He was already turning toward them, swinging the barrel, so quick.

Don't, don't. Ivy thought she was screaming at the top of

her lungs, but no sound came. The cops fired, three, four, five, six times, more. Harrow fell, rolled to the edge of the hole, lay still, one hand dangling down.

More cops came down the stairs, some in uniform, some not. One of the latter approached Ivy: Ferdie Gagnon. He took her by the arm.

"You're under arrest," he said.

Dragan tried and failed to persuade Danny to pay for Ivy's defense. He organized fund-raisers at Verlaine's. By the time that got going, *The New Yorker* had printed "Caveman" in its fiction debut edition. Partly as a result, the fund-raisers were a big success. Herman Landau found a good defense attorney, gifted in the science of jury selection. He also made an excellent summation that brought tears to the eyes of juror number ten, in the back row. Ivy got seven years, meaning out in four with good behavior.

Corrections sent her to the women's prison, downstate. She'd been there for a few weeks when a rising young editor at the one of the big publishing houses came to visit. Ivy told her about *The Surveyor*. She signed a contract not long after.

Out in Hollywood, Joel teamed up with a producer and offered her fifty thousand dollars for her story. Ivy refused. They came back a few times, finally doubling the offer. Ivy stopped taking their calls. She read Dragan's manuscript and didn't know how to tell him.

No laptop in prison, of course, but plenty of time to write. She used legal pads, wrote in longhand, soon preferred it to keyboarding. *The Surveyor* came together very fast. Once she'd sketched in an outline, Ivy wrote one hundred and nine pages in the first ten days; although she was hardly aware of time, completely lost in the story. And it was good, the best work she'd done by far, on another level from before.

Then, one day at lunch, a new inmate took the seat beside her in the cafeteria. She was a big Hispanic woman with muscular arms like a man and tattoos all over.

"Yo," she said.

"Hi," said Ivy.

"You the teacher?"

"I don't do any teaching."

"But you that Ivy girl, no?"

"My name's Ivy."

The woman smiled, pulled her chair a little closer. Her front teeth were missing but the incisors were sharp.

"Hector says hello," she said.

"Hector?"

"Hector Luis Morales," the woman said. "Who wrote about that Camaro? He be hurt, if he thought you forgot him."

Ivy got stuck on page 109.

If you loved OBLIVION and
END OF STORY,
don't miss NERVE DAMAGE,
the next thriller from Peter Abrahams
to be published in March 2007

Roy Valois meant to keep the news to himself, had no intention of telling Turk anything. Turk McKenny was the goalie for the Thongs, and also Roy's lawyer. He had an office on the top floor of a white house overlooking the green. Roy could see part of Neanderthal Number Nineteen through the window.

"Hell of a game, Roy," Turk said.

"Thanks."

"Shoulda seen the look on Normie's face when you stole the puck."

"A fluke."

"I don't know," Turk said. "Raised your game a notch or two lately. What's up with that?"

"That will you've been bugging me about," Roy said.

"Huh?"

"I'd like to get it drawn up."

Turk took his feet—he wore shetland-lined suede slippers—off the desk.

"Now," said Roy, "if possible."

Turk slid a notepad closer, put on half-glasses. "We can certainly get started," he said. His head tilted, eyes peering over the rims. "Anything special get you motivated?"

"The usual," Roy said. Which was pretty funny—so funny, in fact, that Roy started laughing. For a moment or two he wondered if he'd be able to stop. Then out of nowhere the cough erupted, swallowing the laughter, taking over completely. Roy lurched from the room, hand over his mouth, and hurried down the hall to the bathroom. He coughed over the sink. No blood this time, only a little yellowish liquid, the consistency of raw egg white. Egg white instead of blood: good sign or bad? How could it be bad? Was there hope? *Always.*

Roy went back to Turk's office. Turk was hovering by the door.

"What is it, Roy? What's going on?"

"Nothing."

"Come on."

Roy shook his head.

"It's me," Turk said.

Roy was silent.

"And if that's not enough," Turk said, "at least let me do my job."

"What does that mean?" Roy said, the sound of his voice rough and ragged.

"I'm your lawyer," Turk said. "Don't keep me in the dark."

They were friends, went back a long way: had played against each other in college—Turk a four-year starter in net for Dartmouth—and even before that in a high school tournament final in the old Boston Garden. Delia had liked him, too: Turk had been a pallbearer at her funeral. And Turk *was* his lawyer, the only lawyer he'd ever had, looking over everything—taxes, investments, contracts, including the one with Krishna. Roy took a deep breath, aware at the same time that it wasn't as deep as his normal deep breaths, not nearly.

"Totally confidential?" he said.

"Goes without saying," Turk said. "But I'll say it anyway."

Someone had to know. Otherwise: potential chaos. So, standing right there by the door—both of them on their feet—Roy told Turk everything. That turned out to be hard, speaking it aloud, somehow making it more real. Roy couldn't imagine doing it again.

Turk didn't interrupt, didn't make a sound, just went a little pale around his lips. When Roy was done, he said, "God help us." Turk put his hand on Roy's shoulder. Roy didn't really want that, certainly didn't want hugging or anything of the kind, and none happened.

"What's this Hopkins thing?" Turk said.

"Waiting to hear," said Roy.

"Meaning there's some hope."

Always.

They sat down. Out on the green, a little kid was throwing snowballs at Neanderthal Number Nineteen.

"Anything in the bottom drawer?" Roy said.

"Read my mind," said Turk. He opened the bottom drawer, took out a bottle of single malt and two glasses, poured an inch or so in each one. That was gone right away. He poured more. An expensive single malt, but for some reason it had no taste, not to Roy.

"What I want is pretty simple," he said. "Jen gets one half, the rest goes to my mom."

Turk wrote on the pad; he had neat, small writing, kind of strange given those fingers, twisted and thick. "The house?" he said, not looking up.

"Sell it."

"And your inventory?"

"Sell that too."

"What about the effect on prices?"

Roy didn't care. But why not maximize what Jen and his mother ended up with? "Krishna will know what to do."

"Have you talked to him?"

"No."

"Jen?"

"No."

Turk opened his mouth to say something, closed it. Roy slid his glass across the desk. Turk poured more, paused, and poured more for himself. He put down his pen, drank, leaned back in his chair. Silence fell over the room, thick, as though it had a physical dimension, seeming to block the passage of time.

"Remember that goal you scored against Harvard?" Turk said. "I was thinking of it the other night at Waldo's."

Roy hadn't scored enough in college to forget any of them, but that had been the biggest, maybe the only big one, an overtime game-winner in the national semifinal; they'd lost to Minnesota in the championship game. He had a crazy thought: *I wonder if it'll be in my obituary?* Not so crazy—he understood at once where it must have come from: Krishna's remark about Delia. *This one will be in the first paragraph of your obituary, my friend.* The cold feeling came again.

"What was that thought?" Turk said.

"Nothing."

"Totally confidential."

Roy laughed, a normal laugh this time. "It's stupid," he said. But with all the blurting he'd been doing in this office, why stop now? "I was just wondering whether that goal would make it into my obituary."

"They'll probably just stick to the art, don't you think?" Turk said.

That struck Roy as funny, too. He drank more, made himself really taste it this time and found he could; it tasted great. His head buzzed a little. Why the hell not?

"Maybe we could find out," Turk said.

"Find out what?" Roy said.

"What's in your obituary. Aren't they written way ahead of time, all set to go except for the last little . . . ?" Turk abandoned the rest of the sentence.

Roy hadn't known that, hadn't thought much about obituaries, didn't spend any time on that page of the paper. But some reporter, or maybe more than one, had already gone over his life, got all the plusses and minuses in black and white. How did it add up?

"Didn't Mark Twain get to see his own obituary?" Turk said.

"How did that happen?"

"His death was falsely reported," Turk said. "He wrote something funny about it. But in this case I was thinking along the lines of one of those kids."

"What kids?" Roy said, struggling all of a sudden with a complex thought based on the notion that only the living read obituaries and therefore reading your own was somehow cheating death.

"The kind that knows how to get past all that internet security," Turk said. "Root around behind the scenes at some big newspaper. Aren't kids like that a dime a dozen these days?"

Roy knew of one. Cheating death: that sounded pretty good.

"Some weird stuff turned up in the yard the other day," Skippy said. "Mr. . . . um, Roy?"

Roy glanced up. He was working on a pencil sketch of the new idea, this attenuated silent thing, and getting nowhere. "Sorry," he said. "Missed that."

"Weird stuff," said Skippy, hooking up a new tank of acetylene. "In the yard. Uncle Murph says it's from a nuclear power plant."

"What does it look like?"

"Hard to describe," said Skippy. "All bent up. Shiny. Wanna see it?"

"Yes," said Roy. "But later. Right now, I'm hoping you can help me with something on the computer."

"The free phone service?"

Roy shook his head. How to make this sound sensible? "It's one of those places where you're not supposed to go."

Skippy perked up. "Oh, yeah?"

"But I'm not planning to do any harm," Roy said. "Just looking for a piece of information, to . . . to settle a bet."

"What kind of information?" said Skippy, already moving toward the computer.

"It's a little complicated," Roy said, launching into a long and disorganized story about college hockey, the satisfaction of beating—and beating up on—the Harvard boys, the preparation of obituaries, the eminence of The New York Times. Skippy had all sorts of questions—why the teams in the Kegger league had the names they did, how much the bet was for, whether college was fun—but none about the legality or difficulty of hacking into *The New York Times*. It took him ten minutes.

"Here you go, Mr. . . . uh." The printer made its chugging sound. Skippy handed Roy his obituary.

Roy Valois, Sculptor, Dies at [INSERT]
by Richard Gold

Roy Valois, a sculptor whose large works are displayed in many public spaces around the United States and at several prominent museums, died yesterday at [INSERT]. He was [INSERT].

The cause was [INSERT], according to [INSERT].

The self-taught Mr. Valois worked almost exclusively with recovered materials, usually scrap metal, but he was "no primitive," according to Kurt Palmateer, former head of the Mass MoCA Museum in North Adams, Mass., where the first sculpture in what became Mr. Valois's Neanderthal series is part of the permanent collection. "There is a sense of refinement and a deep formal concern that, if anything, connects him to Henry Moore and even to neoclassicists of the nineteenth century," said Mr. Palmateer.

Roy Valois was born in the western Maine town of North Grafton on [TO COME]. He went to local schools where he excelled at sports, eventually entering the University of Maine on a hockey scholarship. But it was while working at a summer job that involved welding and other metal work that Mr. Valois found his true calling. His first piece, now standing in front of the public library in North Grafton, was built in his off-hours during the summer of his junior year in college. Made from brass fixtures salvaged from a sunken freighter and titled "Fin-

*back," the piece attracted the attention of Professor
Anna Cohen of the University of Maine art depart-
ment and led eventually to a two-year fellowship at
Georgetown University.*

*It was there that Mr. Valois began to attract the
attention of collectors. Prices for several works in
the Neanderthal series—"a tragic epic in scrap
steel," in the words of the critic Hilton Kramer—have
topped $100,000. It was also at Georgetown that Mr.
Valois met his wife, Delia Stern, an economist later
employed by the United Nations. She died in an airplane crash off Venezuela in [TO COME]. They had
no children and Mr. Valois never remarried [VER-
IFY]. He is survived by his mother [VERIFY], Edna
Valois, of Sarasota, Florida.*

Roy read his obituary twice, his hands a little shaky the
first time, steady the second. A tragic epic in scrap steel—
he could live with that. That crazy juxtaposition made Roy
laughed out loud; looking up, he saw Skippy staring at
him.

"They have humor in obituaries?" Skippy said.

"Maybe not intentionally," said Roy.

Skippy nodded as though that made sense. "Win your
bet?" he said.

Roy didn't answer. His attention was suddenly drawn
back to the last part of that last paragraph: his wife, Delia
Stern, an economist later employed by the United Nations.
That was a mistake. Delia had worked for the Hobbes Insti-
tute, not the United Nations. Not a big mistake, in no way
central to the story, but Roy didn't like the idea of a mistake
appearing in his obituary. Plus he remembered that Delia
had written a very negative analysis of U. N. budgetary

practices, an analysis that had provoked a condescending letter from some bureaucrat in New York. Letting the mistake go seemed disloyal.

He grew aware of Skippy, still watching him, a funny look on his face. "Something wrong, Skippy?"

"Your nose is, like, bleeding, Roy."

A drop of red fell and blotted the obituary. "It's nothing," Roy said. He went over to the kitchen area, held a paper towel to his face.

"You okay?" said Skippy from the other side of the counter.

Roy nodded. He removed the paper towel. Another red drop fell, this one landing on the pine floor.

"That'll do it for today, Skippy," he said. "Thanks for the help."

"Hey, you're welcome," said Skippy. "But what about the nuclear thing I was telling you about?"

"I'll come over tomorrow," Roy said. "And let's keep this little computer adventure to ourselves."

"Adventure, yeah, sure," said Skippy. "I already forgot."